The Return

by

David Hatton

Front cover by Warren Designs

For the People of New York

September 11, 2001: Citizens of the U.S., besieged by terror's sting, rose up, weeping glory, as if on eagles' wings.

Aberjhani (from The River of Winged Dreams)

Prologue

Amelia Hahn sat in her bedroom completing her maths homework. A knock at the door interrupted her.

‘Thank God for that!’ She sighed with relief and pushed the geometry assignment, set by Miss Hubbard, across her desk. She had squinted at the questions for over an hour like a magic-eye portrait, but all she had achieved was a headache.

She prompted her visitor to enter, stretching and yawning as the door opened. It was her older brother, Benjamin, who held equally droopy bags beneath his eyes. He hadn’t changed out of his white shirt and charcoal trousers since he arrived home from school, but his stripy tie and blue blazer were quickly abandoned on his bedroom floor.

'Are you OK, Kid?' He approached her desk and rubbed her shoulders. 'They’re not distracting you too much, are they?'

'I can't decide which is worse; their shouting or this dumb assignment.’ Of course she knew which was truly worse; the homework would at least be over soon.

'Do you want some help?'

Benjamin picked up a pen and pulled up a seat next to her. The wooden desk sat beneath her bunk bed. A cotton candy machine appeared to have erupted in Amelia's sleeping quarters as every inch of the walls, floors and bed covers were coated pink. Even her grey onesie had sneaked in the occasional pink love-heart, stitched into the breast pocket and hood.

Pulling the textbook towards him, he read the questions which she was struggling with, before gazing through her exercise book to assess her answers. A smile scarred his face as he filled in the blanks.

‘I wish I could be more like you.’ Amelia groaned. ‘You manage to answer the most complex of puzzles, while I struggle to add up the simplest of figures.’

‘Hey, don't be silly. Don't tell anyone... but I'm jealous of you too. Life ain’t exactly an easy ride for me either, you know?’

‘What do you mean?’

‘I might be able to answer a few sums, but you're good with the people stuff. I'm hopeless at all that.’

Three years his junior, Amelia was shorter and plumper than her sibling. Her curly blonde (almost white) locks, tied up in pigtails, contrasted with Benjamin's dark short hair. Amelia looked more like her mother with her petite nose and unusually pale skin, while her brother took after their father with his strong jaw line, olive complexion and Roman snout.

'Well you'll be off to Cornell in a few years. That's something I'll never get a chance to do. You'll make Mom and Dad proud.' Benjamin had visited the Ivy League college twice already with his parents to ensure his personal development plans captured all of their entry requirements.

'Have you ever considered that I don't wanna go to Cornell?'

'You don't? But Dad will be devastated! You need to keep up the family tradition.' Amelia pleaded, crushed that her own academic record failed to continue the Hahns' long line of Cornell graduates.

'No. I wanna go Harvard and study American History. I wanna get far away from here. I doubt they'd notice if I was here anyway,' a bitter Benjamin grouched, nodding his head towards the corridor.

'What about me? You can't leave me here with them! You're the only person to keep me sane in this house. I can't cope with their arguing alone.'

'Hey, don't worry. Why do you think I picked Harvard? Boston is near enough so you can come and stay. Anyway it's all a dream. I doubt Dad will ever be able to afford the sixty-grand fees anyway. My only hope is a scholarship with the mess we're in.'

'Do you think they'll ever get on again?' asked Amelia. Their parents' arguments had continued for almost two years and she'd grown accustomed to the noise, but this evening's row had dragged on for longer than usual. 'I know they love us, but I can't remember one day when there wasn't a row in this house. We couldn't even escape an argument on Christmas Day for God's sakes.'

'It depends if Dad ever manages to sort out our money problems.' Benjamin explained.

They had been up to their eyes in debt since their father stepped down as Regional Director for a national communications firm. Marty was a good man but management was not his gift and he made some terrible errors of judgement, which led to profit losses and redundancies. Since his downfall, he worked as an office administrative assistant for a rival organisation for just ten dollars per hour.

For many people it was a liveable wage, but they wanted to live the high life during the peak of their financial success. Bank loans and credit cards paid for their lifestyles, including their two Lexus four-wheel drives and the mortgage on their four-storey town house on the Upper-East Side of Manhattan. The banks gave out loans like Seattle gave out rain and everybody wanted a lush lifestyle even if it meant living beyond their means.

'Is it my fault they argue?' Amelia asked, wiping a tear from her cheek. 'I'll go to a state school if that's what it takes.'

'Don't be silly,' Benjamin intervened, aggravated by his sister's self-deprecation. 'You didn't do anything wrong.'

'But it could save them so much money if I went somewhere else. There are some awesome state schools. You'll be fine because they don't pay for your education as you have the scholarship, besides I don't think I can keep up with my class. They're all so bright and I'm just hopeless!'

'There was a great thinker who said '*If you judge a fish by its ability to climb a tree, then it will live its whole life believing it's stupid'*. There are lots of different types of genius, Kid, you just need to find what you're good at.'

'See, you always manage to do that!'

'Manage to do what?' Benjamin appeared perplexed.

'Pull out some quote from *a great thinker*, I wish I could do that. I wouldn't know where to begin!' Amelia's voice ached with despair.

'I can regurgitate what I read in a book, big deal. It's those people who can apply their knowledge who're really intelligent. That ain't me.'

'Sorry Benji, but I struggle to believe that.'

The siblings enjoyed each other's company today, but that hadn't always been the case. During their younger years, Amelia despised her brother as he was older, cleverer and was allowed to do the things which her parents considered her too young to do. Benjamin stayed out late and attended parties without their mother calling their friends' parents ahead of the celebrations. Now that she was older, she had the same privileges that he had and her brother's genius became vital, ensuring she passed her exams, even if it was a mere pass that she achieved.

'They've really dropped the ball this time.'

'They're not bad people, Benji.' Amelia said. She stroked the pane glass of a frame holding a photograph of the family at the Cape.

'No, I know. They're just caught up in their money problems and trying everything they can to overcome them... just like we are. I just wish they could do more to meet your needs.'

'I have you.'

It was to him whom she had first come to when Amelia received her first period. She brought her stained underwear to him and cried on his lap. He researched sexual health information on the Internet and took out a book on family planning from the school library to advise his younger sibling.

Their lives contrasted from outside to in. On the outside they posed as rich upper class some-bodies, who despite their setbacks still lived the high life. The reality was they lived hand-to-mouth and were no different to the poor white trash that filled the streets of Bronx.

'We better finish up, Kid, I gotta go.' He clipped the cap on her pen and placed it in her pencil case.

'Where are you going tonight?' Amelia always asked, knowing the answer would always be the same.

'Never you mind. You really wouldn't wanna know. Anyway, I think the civil war is over.'

Slamming the hardback text book closed, he looked up at the clock for the time; it was almost midnight. He listened out for any noise below, but for the first time that evening, the house was blissfully silent.

Amelia collected her books and placed them into her bag, which sported a picture of the Backstreet Boys on the back of it. She threw the backpack onto a white plastic chair in the corner of the room and embraced her brother.

'Tell me we'll get out of this.' Amelia sobbed into his chest,

'We will, one day. We just need to win the lottery,' he joked, but neither of them laughed. Kissing his sister's forehead, Benjamin said goodnight and returned to his room. The teenager chilled out in his room, smoking from his pipe, which he retrieved from a shoe-box under his bed. The box stored his cigarettes, a collection of porn, a clump of marijuana and a stash of rolled-up dirty cash.

Secure with the knowledge that his family were all in bed, he retrieved his black hooded top from the closet, sneaked out of the window and climbed down the drainpipe.

The tube to Christopher Street took minutes. He approached the bustling street, ignoring the drag queens coercing passers-by into their bars. He hung out by a corner beneath a street lamp until a black Jaguar pulled up and the window slid down. After several minutes of whispered negotiation, Benjamin slipped into the vehicle and left the bright lights of The Village behind.

*

On the fourth floor of the town house, Marty and Beverly Hahn lay in bed watching their favourite movie, *Meet Me In St. Louis*. They heard the creak of their son's window opening below, but it was a warm September evening, therefore it was understandable that their first-born might be a little uncomfortable in an unventilated home.

The exhausted couple recovered from the row and the post argument make-up session. They refused to retire to bed on an argument; unfortunately they always picked up where they left off the next evening. However, these late night moments in bed, as they snuggled up and looked out at the stars through their rooftop window, reinforced their devotion to each other.

Marty stroked his wife’s red hair and kissed her forehead, coated with her unusually pale skin. Her scrawny physique hid any evidence that she had given birth to two children. The gel, mixed into Marty's spiky black hair, had hardened and flattened from the pressure of his pillow as he lay with his wife. Fragments of hair, detaching from his head, floated down onto his toned stomach.

'One day, Hunny, we’re going to be right on top again,' Marty insisted. He smiled as he kissed his wife's neck. A light tickle caused Beverly to shiver as her husband stroked her arm.

'How do you manage to remain so optimistic?' Beverly asked. As she lay on his chest, she breathed in his fragrance: *Old Spice*, a familiar scent he had worn since the day they met.

'I just know it. One day we’re gonna be rich again and when that happens I'm going to marry you all over again! We’ll renew our vows in Las Vegas!'

Marty stared up into the roof window in wonder, gazing into their future. The September evening sky remained light and he used a remote control to shut the mechanical blinds, blocking out the summer glare through the glass ceiling pane.

'Las Vegas? *Classy.'* Sarcasm reeked in Beverley's tone.

'It'll be awesome just to elope and marry all over again, somewhere away from everyone. Just us two this time, rather than those hundreds of guests, half of which we couldn't have picked out of a line-up.'

'It was all image to my dad. He wanted to impress his friends, rather than securing a special day for me. We could ask him for money.' Beverly suggested.

'Not this again.' Marty sighed viciously. 'I've told you time and time again, we're not asking that man for money.'

'You and your pride.'

'Yeah, exactly, I have pride and I'm not going begging. I promised him I'd look after you and as God as my witness, I will, without his help. I got us into this mess and I'll get us out of it.'

Silence filled the room for several minutes while they cooled off. Nobody wanted round two of their earlier fight. They were already on thin ice with their neighbours.

'So how about that Las Vegas trip?' Marty changed the subject.

'Well, maybe that sounds OK.' Beverly cautiously accepted. 'It'll never happen though... we'll never get out of this mess, no matter how hard we work.'

'We will.' Marty assured. 'I promise you.'

The movie ended and Beverly yawned.

'I better go to sleep, Hunny, I have an early start. Another long day ahead. I just wish we could see the difference our hard work makes. Our salaries barely pay off the interest on our loans, while the repayments never reduce.'

'Our house hasn't been repossessed. That's surely a good thing to focus on. Our hard work is paying off right there.'

'I suppose.' Beverly's pessimism echoed in her voice. 'Anyway, goodnight Marty.'

'Goodnight Hunny, I love you so much,' he whispered as she closed her eyes. The guilt of their earlier argument festered within him as they ended the night in each other's arms. He kissed her cheek and she smiled.

'I love you too.' Dreaming of the movie they had just watched together, Beverly had only one wish. ‘Take me to St. Louis one day.’

‘I will.’ Watching her eyes flicker as she dreamed, he thought about everything they had come through together. Marty knew his wife would soon face the same nightmare, which he shared every night. The ugly visions of their beloved home and children being snatched away haunted him too. Distressed by his wife's financial concerns, he needed a solution.

*

The blaring ring of an alarm bell woke Beverly up. Making her way to the en-suite shower, she rinsed away the smell of sweat and sex from the evening before off her bony body. Her red hair grew grey roots as she ceased to rectify her decay. Detaching the shower head, she forced the water into her eyes to wash away the strain in her heavy eyelids. The feeling of nausea hung over her, but she reassured herself she only had two more days to get through before her next day off.

Beverly dressed and made her way down the two flights of stairs to the kitchen. Behind the central breakfast island stood her son, Benjamin, still in his uniform, helping himself to some toast, which he prepared on the grill. Above the island, sunburnt crockery hung from the ceiling and dirty dishes spread across the worktop from the previous evening.

'Wow, you’re up rather early today, Pumpkin.' a surprised Beverly said. It was unusual for her to see anyone when she woke up as early as she did for work. 'Couldn't you sleep?'

'I woke up early and thought I’d catch up on some homework, I didn’t get much sleep.’

'You were probably too warm, we heard you open the window.' Benjamin looked up, startled, wondering how much she heard. His fears were soon put to rest as her attention drew to the refrigerator where she burrowed around for a pot of frozen yoghurt for breakfast, blissfully unaware of her son's late night escapades.

'I'm going to carry on with my homework, Mom.' With his distracted mother giving as little as a wave in response, Benjamin made his way back to his room.

He entered his haven and punched a wall, piercing his knuckles upon impact. He shook away the pain like a rapper and quivered at his failure to discreetly sneak out. It had been a long night; his customer the night before had insisted on receiving a little extra. The money was just too tempting. Now he was back, sweaty and tired, and was due in school in just a couple of hours. He rushed to bed for some shut-eye before his alarm screamed.

Downstairs, Beverly rushed out of the door and rode the subway to Times Square. In the early hours of the morning, she shared the carriage with fellow hoteliers, rushing for their early morning shifts, and young adults making their walk of shame home, still dressed in last night's disco dresses. Across the carriage, she spotted a teacher from Amelia's school in a beige overcoat and grey flat-cap. *Mr Cross? Mr Caruthers?* They all blended into one. He smiled and returned to his broadsheet newspaper, providing a wall against any awkward small-talk.

The glass doors automatically slid open to the Times Square hotel. Black and white tiles, suitable for a human-size chess board, escorted guests to a mahogany reception desk. Behind, a young twenty-something girl manned the desk.

'Morning Bev!' she said with a tone which was far too optimistic for the early hours. Beverly grabbed the pen off the desk and noted the time to clock in the register.

'Have you been on your own all night again, Sandra?' Beverly tutted and shook her head. The receptionist's short light-brown hair, dark skin complexion and petite frame, both in height and width, made Sandra a desirable and indefensible target. 'I've complained to the management several times. It's just not safe for you to be here at night alone.'

'Don't worry about me, Beverly. I can look after myself. Anyway, I'm just grateful for a job. I need to fund my studies.'

'Will you ever finish that degree? What is it you study again?'

'Business at New York College,' Sandra laughed and rolled her eyes. 'And I'm studying part time so it does take a little longer.'

'Business ey? You'll be running this place in no time.'

Turning on the televisions in the lobby, Beverly switched over to CNN to allow morning business travellers to catch the headlines before they set off for work.

In the kitchen, she found Jose frying up the breakfast. The Hispanic chef spoke little English and their exchanges were no more than a fanatic cheer as she entered the kitchen and he embraced her with a friendly cuddle. With his chubby frame, José's embraces were particularly tight.

'Not today, Jose! We're opening soon. Get those eggs ready.'

She glanced at the clock, it was almost seven and her husband was due to set off to work for a day like no other.

*

Marty woke with less optimism than the night before; his inability to cope with early mornings was crippling. He showered and walked downstairs to have breakfast, where he found his daughter, Amelia, making her own eggs.

'Where is your brother?' Marty asked. *When did she suddenly grow up so quickly?*

'He's in bed,' she replied with an abrupt tone.

'Well go and get him out of bed, you'll be going to school soon, won't you?'

The flashing red digits on the oven clock alerted him to the time; he couldn't lose another job. The embarrassment of his career failures would appear minuscule compared to the shame of a firing from an administration job which barely paid the bills. Grabbing his wallet, keys and pass, he ran to the underground station to board his commute to work.

Marty arrived at the office at nine on the dot. His manager met him with raised eyebrows as he ran through the door.

'Marty, what time do you call this? You're supposed to be starting work now and you haven't even turned your computer on.'

'Sorry, Boss,' Marty searched for an excuse while tightening the red tie wrapped around his throat, causing the white collar to gently choke him. 'The elevator was playing up again.'

'I'll be checking that up with the building security staff,' his manager responded sharply. Marty gulped. 'I appreciate it's a hassle to get up here sometimes, Marty, but that's why we expect you to arrive earlier to give time for any delays.'

Marty sat down at his desk and texted his daughter's phone. '*Are you at school yet?'*

'Y *do u care? But yes,'* Amelia replied.

'Is Benjamin with you?'

He hated texting; he wished he could just pick up the phone and call her. However, on a day like today where he was already walking on thin ice, the ability to sneakily send a cheeky text under the table away from his manager's prying eyes was a blessing. Amelia's dwindling use of her vocal chords made the text messages one of the only methods of communication Marty could have with her anyway.

'Yeah, omg dad ur like big brother lol,'

Her abbreviations baffled Marty, who required a translator to interpret her messages. Despairing of teenage fads, he hoped her reference to Big Brother was in reference to the George Orwell novel, Nineteen Eighty-Four, rather than the tacky reality television show, which had recently become a popular phenomenon in the United States. He grudgingly suspected it was the latter. He also assumed that her sign-off stood for something other than *lots of love.*

With the comfort that his children were safe at school, he began his work. Anticipating a long day, Marty hoped a fire alarm would ring so he could have an excuse to leave the office, a wish which would soon come to haunt him.

*

Benjamin woke up tired and hung-over. The hands of a wall clock created from a Red Hot Chili Peppers Vinyl alerted him that he was late for school again. He rolled over and felt around for his phone before sending Amelia a text.

'Hey, did you call in for me?'

'Yeh I saved your ass again. I'm getting quite good at pulling off Mom's voice. If anyone asks, you have a stomach bug.'

'Thanks Kid.'

Nausea overcame him as he relived the repulsive acts he had undertaken the previous evening with the obese old man. The dirty drunk was so inebriated, he struggled to hold his bladder, wafting his urine stained cash at the youngster to encourage him to go further into unfamiliar territories. Now alone in his room, he continued to breath in the malodorous odour and winced at the tender tingle of his bruised arms.

The abrasions tempted him to give up the outlawed occupation, but a photograph, affixed to the sky-blue wall with an adhesive tack, reinforced his determination to provide for his younger sister. The photograph, hanging amongst his gig tickets and posters from his favourite rock band's tours, was of Amelia and himself in the Bahamas with cocktails in their hands, mine-swept from another couple's table. Little did the teenagers know at the time that the bank had paid for the holiday, rather than their father’s income. Reminiscing of a happier time, Benjamin would do anything to reclaim her glowing smile.

He crawled out of bed and climbed down the spiral stairs. After regurgitating in the downstairs toilet, he retired to the lounge and switched on the television. The sixteen-year-old lay on the maroon leather couch with vomit-stained pyjama pants but his torso remained bare. The scent of rotting eggs, rising from the extinguished coal fire behind him, maintained his nausea.

CNN aired the morning headlines, but he had little interest in current affairs and turned over to MTV instead. As Black Sabbath blasted out of the speakers, he pulled out his roller and began to roll himself a joint, content that his truancy had remained undiscovered once again.

*

The glare from the overhead projector blinded Amelia's tired eyes. Her tutor, Miss Hubbard, projected the answers to the home-work, which she had set the previous day. With the help of her brother's assistance, Amelia scored a high A+, but she took little joy in her unmerited achievement. If she was lucky, her parents would place the test results, stamped with the circled high grade in red biro, onto the fridge when she got home.

A knock on the classroom door disrupted the class. Her science teacher, Mr Cross, entered the room and the pupils stood up in respect. Raising his eyes over the class, he glanced at Amelia as he approached her form tutor. As the teachers mumbled and stared at the school girl, a lump of guilt lodged in Amelia's throat. A nod of the head indicated Miss Hubbard's approval of the visitor's intentions and the science teacher approached Amelia.

'Miss Hahn, please could I have a word?'

She nodded, closed her exercise book and followed the silver haired teacher out of the classroom and into the corridor. His black cape flowed along the floor, catching on the door as he closed it. The teacher towered over her like a Tyrannosaurus-Rex hunting for its pray. Mr Cross's contrasting white hair and thick black eyebrows were scary enough to the children of Kings Brook Grammar, without his height of six-foot-four brought into the equation.

'How's your brother today?' he asked.

Shit, they know it was me.

'He was feeling unwell when I left the house this morning.'

'I spoke to your mother on the telephone at half-past eight this morning, she *claimed* to be at home with your brother.'

'She was,' Amelia stared down at the floor and rubbed the sole of her shoe along the floor.

'Funny, I saw her in the early hours of the morning on the subway to work, I catch her most mornings.'

Amelia's mind raced for an excuse, anything, which could stop him from discovering her lies. She could already hear the lecture from her father towards Benjamin.

How could you waste your education?

While they didn't pay for Benjamin's classes, institutions like Cornell checked academic attendance within their applicant entry reviews, therefore Marty would be far from lenient.

And for Amelia? The lies? Potential expulsion?

After everything we've put ourselves through for you?

Not that she'd asked them to.

'Yeah, I called her when I realised how ill he was, so she went home to look after him.' Amelia wrestled between the feelings of shame and pride as her natural ability to lie became apparent.

'Well I'll be checking up on that, Miss Hahn. I hope you're not lying to me, otherwise you'll be in big trouble. It's the Lincoln Hotel on Times Square that your mother works at, is it not?'

'Yeah.' Amelia gulped. *Confess now! The repercussions will be lighter! No wait... he'd have called her already if he was suspicious. Call his bluff.*

The chimes of a bell disrupted the argument in her head.

Hundreds of children left their classrooms, rushing through to the school hall to attend the morning assembly. Amelia joined her best friend, Amy, a petite girl with blonde plaited hair, glasses and bright multi-coloured braces, which shone out of her mouth.

'Did they find out?' Amy asked. Amelia told Amy everything.

'They're investigating it. I just hope something happens to distract him.'

*

The call to attend a group huddle disrupted Marty's phone call with a client. His manager insisted all colleagues attended every morning, even if it meant losing a potential sale.

'I have good news and bad news.' his manager, Girvin, commenced the meeting. 'The good news is that you've all met your weekly targets. The bad news is that we're downsizing.'

The group groaned as the impending threat of redundancies loomed. Marty's own position was particularly fragile. He was the last to join and his boss despised him; it was the perfect cocktail for a firing.

'We'll have more information for you in the next week. In other news, we've had more updates from head office. They're pleased with our results but they want us to do a little better, therefore higher targets will be implemented for bonus pay-outs and they'll be revealing some new processes to ensure we're much leaner during our daily tasks.'

'Cost effective you mean...' Carl Simpson heckled. '... so you need even less of us!'

'Erm…' Girvin stuttered. 'Well that's all for this meeting. Great week guys.' The group dispersed apart from Girvin, who approached Marty. 'Before you walk off, Marty, can I have a word with you in my office?'

Following Girvin into his office, he shut the door behind him with a slight slam. The room was poky, fitting just a desk and a chair on either side. To the right of his desk lay a glass cabinet, filled with awards and business text books, written by some of the country's most famous billionaires. Behind Girvin, the green glimmer of the Statue of Liberty rose out of New York Harbour.

Dandruff drifted down onto Girvin's steel-blue pinstripe suit from his fine orban hair. Apart from the flakes of dry skin, his tailored attire was far more polished than Marty's machine-washable black suit, purchased off the rack at his local supermarket.

'I spoke to security, they said there was nothing wrong with any of the elevators this morning. They were working perfectly.'

Marty bowed his head. Why didn't he say the subway was delayed or his kids were ill? Something his boss couldn't check up on?

'I'm going to write up a disciplinary. It's a verbal warning; three strikes and you're out. Do you understand?' Marty nodded. 'If there's nothing else, you're free to leave.' His manager lifted his hand and wafted towards the door.

Marty stood up and made his way to the exit. A loud shriek from his colleague caused a sharp chill to shiver down his spine. He opened the door to discover the nose of a Boeing 767 flying towards him.

*

The smell of coffee beans had lost its' indulgent impact on an exhausted Beverly. Having served guests in the restaurant for over four hours, she welcomed a distraction from Sandra.

'Phone call for you, Bev.'

She handed the pot of fresh filter coffee over to Sandra, before heading to the telephone on reception and answered.

'Hello? Beverly Hahn speaking.'

'Oh hello, Mrs Hahn.' a recognisable man's voice responded on the other end of the phone. 'This is Mr Cross, from Kings Brook Grammar.'

The hairs on the back of her neck rose as the caller confirmed his identity. The school only called in emergencies. An anxious Beverly hoped his call referred to his intolerance of her children's behaviour, rather than an emergency trip to the hospital; they could *fix* behaviour.

'One second, Mr Cross, I'm just going to put this call through to the back.' She transferred the call to the office behind reception and chased the ringing to a private space away from the curious ears of her guests and colleagues.

'I'm sorry to disturb you. I did try you at home but nobody answered so I called your work number.' Mr Cross's assumption baffled Beverly, who had bumped into the teacher earlier in the morning during her commute to work.

'No, I'm at work, so whatever it is, please can you hurry up as I need to get back to serving guest. It's a busy morning and I'm the only person scheduled in the restaurant today.'

She opened the door a peak and saw Sandra picking up her duties, running between reception and the restaurant to satisfy their guests' every need.

'I wanted to talk to you about your son, Benjamin,' the teacher said. 'How is he, because I heard he wasn't well?'

'Benjamin?' Concern crept into Beverly's voice. 'As far as I know, he is fine. You tell me, he's your problem during the hours of nine and three.'

'Did you not call the school this morning, Mrs Hahn?'

A knock on the door disrupted their call. Behind it, a flustered Sandra frantically waved the waitress to return to the lobby. Beverly raised her finger and mouthed *one minute.*

'Did I call the school? No, why would I call?'

Sandra's waving become more hysterical, her pale face shook towards the lobby and with her free hand she pulled on Beverly's apron. The mumblings on the phone deteriorated as Beverly brushed the distraction off her apron and pushed the door to close, but Sandra's black heeled shoe prevented it from shutting.

'Beverly, you must come into the lobby!'

'One second, Mr Cross.' Beverly held the phone to her chest while she acknowledged her colleague. 'Sandra, can't you see I'm on the phone, what is it?'

'You need to come out now…' A shaken Sandra appeared white as snow. '…it's Marty!'

*

MTV played the best of eighties rock. The phone rang several times, but Benjamin knew better than to answer a phone in a supposedly empty house, even if it was a simple sales call. Yes, we all wanted a time share in the Cayman's but *Hunny,* we can't afford ourselves new shoes right now.

He laid on the couch with an ash tray on his bare chest. Smoke filled the room, but it was nothing a scented candle couldn't fix. Sweet

Child of O' Mine was number three on the arbitrary list, sparking a head-banging motion to overtake the truant teenager. But as Slash poured into his solo, an announcement disrupted the music video.

'We now interrupt the scheduled program to present a special news broadcast.'

Benjamin sighed. His favourite shows had been regularly interrupted since the new President's inauguration earlier in the year. Government reforms and new bills meant regular broadcasts could barely go a day without a cut to a news program.

Anticipating tedious information regarding new senators, Benjamin switched the television off before the program began. Walking over to the Hi-Fi, which sat within a black entertainment unit, he turned the volume right up to ten as Pearl Jam rolled into Jeremy, blissfully unaware of the horrors unfolding in his father's office.

*

The hardwood flooring caused her buttocks to become numb. A wriggly Amelia, shaken by Mr Cross's threats, sat restlessly in the school hall with three hundred other students.

She feared the punishment she'd face with both the school and her parents should they discover her lies, she anticipated a suspension followed by a grounding. Marty and Beverly hadn't just paid for her education in dollars, her schooling had cost them blood, sweat, tears and their marriage. How could she throw away the pearls of wisdom?

The pupils repeated the Lord's Prayer, engraved onto a wooden tablet at the front of the school hall. Beside it, the Ten Commandments were listed. On the stage, a table held a large wooden cross. Kings Brook was not listed as a religious school, but her surroundings said otherwise.

The head teacher, Mr Noble, dressed in a black gown and a mortarboard cap, walked onto the stage to tell his weekly fable. Noble, every week, inspired the teenagers through short stories, influenced by notable characters in history, who had overcome barriers and achieved their dreams.

This week's story was inspired by Anne Frank, who managed to love and forgive despite the atrocities she faced during the holocaust camps at Auschwitz. After describing the horrors of the Nazi death camps and Anne's ultimate fate, the principal read out a quote from the young writer herself: '*In spite of everything, I still believe people are good at heart.*'

After the lecture, Mr Noble asked the pupils to stand and sing the national anthem. The music began and the pupils broke into the first verse, besides one of the students, who rebelled.

'Why aren't you singing?' Amy whispered, nudging her incoherent classmate.

'I can't stand it.' Amelia replied. 'Does it mean that I love my country any less if I choose to not sing it? It's just weird.'

'You'll get into trouble!' Amy peered around her, checking that no one had spotted her unruly friend.

'Let's see what happens.'

As the children approached the third verse of the Star Spangled Banner, Mr Cross entered the room from the back of the hall and walked up to the stage. He approached the principal and bent over to whisper in the ear of the much shorter and balder teacher. A surprised Noble pulled his ear away from Mr Cross's mouth and looked at him face-on.

Mr Cross whispered again into Mr Noble's ear and the headmaster nodded his head, but continued to stare forward while the science teacher removed himself from the stage. When the song ended, the principal stood silently before the pupils. Looking down at his sheets, he tried to assemble his words, but found himself stuttering.

'Boys and girls, I have something to inform you of…' he took a deep breath as he explained. 'Something horrible has happened…'

*

A cloud of smoke blocked his windpipe. Marty coughed and spluttered, clearing his airway. As his eyes regained focus, he witnessed pockets of fire and rubble surrounding motionless bodies. The raw heat from the roaring fire stung his open wounds and blood trickled down his cheek from a gash, breaking the skin over his temple.

'Help! Where am I?' Sally-Ann McDermott yelled. The accountant panicked and reached around for some familiarity. Her question puzzled the groaning bodies surrounding her. It was a war zone. The blaring siren, penetrating their ears, registered their location, the familiar galling echo of their office fire alarm, warning colleagues to leave the compromised building. The bodies shuffled; those who could, stood up, staggering across the room to aid others. Marty acquired enough strength to pick himself up, but a sharp blow to his head brought on a concussion.

'Is everybody OK?' Marty shouted. Mumbling echoed around the room as his colleagues shuffled. He hobbled over to his colleague, June, who lay beneath a toppled desk.

'What happened?' June asked with a frail voice. 'I heard a bang and all went black.' She placed a hand over her head and felt the warm damp of blood soaked into her curly grey hair. 'Oh God, I need to go to hospital!'

'I think a plane crashed into the building. It was flying far too low. There must be an issue with their on-board navigation or something.' Marty knew little about aircraft technology, but this just *had* to be an accident.

Girvin walked out of his office in a high-vis vest.

'Guys, we need to make our way downstairs now. No Pamela, you can't take your shopping. Leave it where it is. We need to go now. No handbags either!'

The group began the slow decent. Above them, a scorching wind blew down from the fiery hole where the aircraft had ripped through the building. Smoke hovered above and the panicked escapees crouched down to avoid the fumes. Debris flew past the employees, building up speed as it dropped down the gap beside the escape-route.

'We need to walk down as quickly as possible, OK?' Girvin shouted. Behind them, the distressed calls of their co-workers echoed. They peeped back, against their manager's wishes, and witnessed the shadows of terrified workers flickering within the firelight, reflecting onto the cracked walls.

'We need to go back and help those people,' June cried hysterically. 'My Billy is up there!' Bill was a recruiter in the Human Resources department. Nobody from HR had been seen since the impact. Determined to get to his side, she pulled away from the group and marched up towards the burning hovel.

'We can't do that, June, we need to get out of here. We need to leave him for the emergency services. They are trained to face these situations. Don’t be a hero, June!' Girvin yelled as he marched the group further down the stairs. Wiping a tear away and staring into the unknown, June accepted her limits and returned to her team and continued her descent.

An explosion rattled the escapees, who fell to their knees, while those who could, clung onto the bannister. The building vibrated for several minutes and a waterfall of dust poured from the ceiling. Marty and his peers picked themselves up and ran to the nearest floor. Unlike their own office, this working environment had remained intact, with their tables and chairs remaining in place. Its inhabitants had escaped already.

The windows on each floor stretched from floor to the ceiling. Before them was the south tower, a tall replica of the building they worked within. Smoke radiated out of the top of the building and a fire-filled hole ripped through the centre, mirroring the desecrated structure they were trapped within. Placing their hands on the glass, they peered over to the scared inhabitants of the office parallel to them, staring back in as much fear and confusion.

‘This was no accident.’ Tommy King, an analyst from IT, said what everyone else was thinking.

'This is the work of Almighty God himself, it is the end of days,' declared Willy, in a Texan brogue. His southern roots were visible within his cowboy hat, bolo-tie and white handle-bar moustache. 'I've been saying all this time that those damn homosexuals would anger God, and here he is, mad as hell.'

'Now is not the time, Willy, we need to get out!' Marty called.

'Only God will save you now, Son.’

An object fell from the window of their neighbouring tower, pausing their debate. A closer look allowed them to observe that the object was a suited black businessman, picking up speed with every floor he passed. The terrified team gawped in horror as he passed, turning their heads away as he plummeted towards the concrete below.

'Come on guys, we need to go!' Girvin called; his motivational techniques remaining lost on his horrified subordinates, who softly nodded their heads and began to shuffle towards the exit like racing tortoises. Another glimpse up towards the trapped office above forced June to pause and stare, eager to see her husband.

'Come on, June, he’ll be OK!' Marty linked arms with her and pulled her towards him.

'I can't do it. I can't leave without him.' June turned around and began to make her way back up the stairs which they had just descended from. Marty chased after her, but a vibration on his chest distracted him. He lifted into his in-side pocket and took out his cell phone; it was Beverly.

'Hi Hunny, are you OK?'

'Oh my, thank God you're alright!' Beverly's voice echoed relief. 'Where are you?'

'I'm still at work. We're just making our way down the fire escape. Have you seen what's happened?'

'Yeah, two planes have hit both towers. They're saying it's a terrorist attack!' Marty's heart pounded as his wife delivered the devastating news.

'Please get out soon, Marty. I can't bear to be without you!' Looking up the stairs, he witnessed June stumbling over as she rushed to get to the top of the tower to find her better half.

'I'll get out soon, Hunny, but first I need to help a colleague. She's running back up.' As soon as the words came out of his mouth, he regretted informing his distressed wife of his risky plans.

'Please just get out of there, Marty!'

'I have to go, Angel, I love you.'

'Don't you dare say that, Martin Hahn! If you want to say that to me, you'll have to come and say it to my face!'

'I will, Hunny, bye!'

'Marty… you better…' but he hung up, silencing her requests.

Against Girvin's protests, Marty ran up the stairs. His manager had given up protecting his co-workers and made a run for it himself, leaving his confused and frightened colleagues behind.

Panting and sweaty, Marty found June, screaming for her husband four floors above. He pulled her away from the fire-filled hole. A yellow stripe of hope marched up the stairs as a fireman approached; an axe and extinguisher in hand and his identity sprouted across his helmet.

'We can take it from here. Get yourselves outa here!'

June relaxed and embraced Marty, who gave her a minute to compose herself before edging her down the stairs. They had walked these steps a dozen times as they experienced numerous drills, but nothing had prepared them for the real event. Their hearts raced, blood pouring across their faces bubbled from the heat, scarring the skin it drizzled upon. A saving grace arrived from the cooling allure of a fire exit beneath them.

As they reached the fifth floor, a relief that the end was in sight allowed them to take a moment to catch their breaths. A water fountain brought a welcome refreshment for their dry throats. Their momentary bliss ended quickly as June felt a tremor beneath her.

'What's that?' she nervously called, gripping onto the bannister for support.

'I think we need to get out of here.'

Marty grabbed June's hand and ran. The walls shook and a loud rumbling vibrated every bone in their bodies. Dust showered down on them as the ceilings began to crumble and the pair disappeared into the dark.

*

The scent of freshly cooked bacon couldn't tempt the guests away from the television screens at The Lincoln Hotel. Amongst those glued to the news broadcasts, Beverly Hahn's heart pounded, hoping to see sight of her husband. News anchors held interviews with escapees from the tower, but Marty had yet to be seen.

Sandra, Jose and a number of guests surrounded her, waiting in suspense for updates. Their mobile phones constantly rang, their colleagues and friends getting in touch to check they were safe. A gentleman in a business suit passed the screen and dropped his briefcase as he witnessed the images on the headline news.

'Holy Moly, I was supposed to be there today, I thankfully slept in!' The observers diverted their eyes away from the screen and glared at the gloating man.

'Well lucky for you. Unfortunately for us, some of our husbands are in there right now.' said Sandra, nodding her head towards Beverly, who wiped her nose as she sobbed. The gentleman held his head down in shame. Hundreds of businesses filled the World Trade Centre; anyone who had lived in the city long enough knew somebody who worked there.

Sandra held onto a traumatised Beverly, both with tears

streaming down their faces, as they watched the north tower crumble to the ground.

*

The school hall had never seemed so quiet. Three hundred children shut together in a cramped room for hours would usually make them restless; but not today.

In the third row, Amelia sat in a state of shock as she heard the news that the World Trade Centre, where her dear daddy worked, was under attack. She asked many questions but none of the teachers could answer them. The children remained in the school hall until they received further announcements.

After consultation with the police, the head-teacher decided to abort their afternoon classes and encouraged parents to collect their children. Those minors whose parents were unaccountable remained in the school hall while they waited for their guardians to collect them.

The secretary made several attempts at calling Amelia's mother. The Lincoln Hotel claimed she had gone home, but her calls to the family home remained unanswered. Amelia tried herself to call her mother's cell phone, but the reception in the city had cut off.

Amelia did not know what to do with herself, so she waited in the hall with several other school children whom she had struggled to find common ground with before, but all had moms and dads working in the World Trade Centre that day. They tried not to think about that.

*

Bon Jovi's hit, *Livin' on a Prayer* blasted out of the speakers. Benjamin turned the dial up to the maximum volume so he could feel the base vibrate throughout his body. As he danced around the living room playing on his air guitar, the music suddenly stopped and he turned around to see his mother, Beverly, standing beside the stereo, her eyes red raw.

'Why the hell aren't you at school?' she snapped. 'Your teacher called me today. Apparently I phoned them this morning to tell them you wouldn't be attending class?'

'I wasn't feeling well,' he jittered, ‘so I stayed at home.’

Beverly opened her mouth to continue her lecture, but acknowledged the more pressing matters.

'Oh what does it matter...' She sat down and stared at the wall, shaking in distress. The sleeve of her white shirt, coated in tomato juice and coffee stains, was now a tissue to capture her tears. Benjamin sat next to her and rubbed her back. He looked at the clock on the stereo; it was only lunchtime, she should still be at work.

'What's up, Mom? Have you been fired again?'

Beverly's ability to retain a job had proved difficult over the previous two years. She had gone from one temporary role to the next as employers could no longer afford to keep her on. Where she had secured a permanent role, her loose hands on the kitchen supplies, which she brought home to feed her hungry family, forced her managers to let her go.

'You're not usually this upset.' Benjamin pressed. 'They're just dead end jobs, you'll find another. It's New York for God's sakes. It's inundated with hotels.'

He placed his arm around her and placed his cheek on her shoulder. It had been years since they touched like this. They had grown apart as they found their own ways to make money, but this momentary affection made Benjamin realise that something was truly wrong.

'What's happened, Mom?'

'I don't know, Pumpkin…' she whimpered. '…but I think your father is dead.'

*

For the following two weeks, the three of them remained at home. Together they waited for Marty to return. Amelia and Benjamin made occasional visits to Ground Zero, asking anyone if they had seen their father. They added his photograph to the many thousands that lined the walls surrounding the site where the towers once stood, searching the rubble for any evidence of his whereabouts.

Desperate loved ones pleaded for help in finding their families. They were all in the same boat with nobody to help. For weeks, the headlines released more names of people returned to their relieved families, whether they were dead or alive; the wait was over for them.

But for the Hahns, each day brought a devastating blow as no news grew further away from good news.

After two weeks, the mounting bills forced Beverly to return to work and Benjamin returned to his secret duties down in The Village. Amelia returned to school, where she became distant from the popular group she used to hang with, and became closer to those who had also lost parents in the tragedy.

Stories spread of missing victims returning home. Theories circulated of falling debris causing head injuries, leaving victims with amnesia, which led to unrealistic hopes to the families of the missing that they too would return home. For the Hahns, their initial hopes of their father being found alive turned to hopes of his body being found, just to end the misery of the unknown.

A lot changed for Amelia in the following weeks, but two major changes happened at school. She began to stick her nose up at the Anne Frank quote, read out by Mr Noble, that there was still good in people.

'What did she know?' Amelia bitterly barked. 'She was just a stupid little girl stuck inside a loft. She didn't know what the outside world was like until it was too late!'

Amelia couldn't see good in anyone anymore. How could anyone do this to her family? They were pure evil. The second change began in the school assembly, where she began to sing out loudly and proudly the words of the national anthem every single day.

Chapter 1

The mid-summer heat cooled as New York approached the end of August. Green leaves yellowed and the bright early mornings were losing their charm. An alarm woke Beverly up. It was five AM. Sluggishly, she hopped into the shower, wolfed down a frozen yoghurt in the kitchen before setting off for work. Her routine had remained the same for the past decade as she stumbled into The Lincoln Hotel on Times Square.

As she walked through reception, she took a glance at herself in the full length mirror. She was presentable enough; she straightened her name badge, still baring the Guest Service Representative title she'd had printed on the clip when she first joined. The years had been relatively kind to a woman who had battled as much as she had; her eyes sprouted a few more wrinkles and she spent a little longer in the hairdressers to ensure she maintained her distinctive red hair, but otherwise she was relatively happy with the person who stared back at her.

Behind reception, her daughter stood proudly in her new uniform; a black blazer with *Supervisor* stitched into the breast pocket. She'd achieved the promotion just a week earlier and she still maintained the glow of superiority. Her colleagues allowed her to have her moment in the sun and Beverly couldn't have been prouder. Amelia was no longer her little girl; she had overtaken Beverly in height, her once plump figure had moulded into shapely curves and the pigtails had gone. Her now chocolate brown hair was shorter, her fringe sweeping down to her cheek, covering her left eye, which hid the dark shadow brought on from her fifth nightshift in a week.

'Morning Hunny!' Beverly approached her daughter and kissed her on her cheek. 'How are you on this sunny morning?'

'Morning.' Amelia groggily replied, forcing a smile as a guest passed. 'I'm alright, looking forward to going to bed.'

'I'm going to speak to Sandra about this. It's not fair that you've been left on your own at night again. I worry about you.'

'Don't meddle, Mom. You did this last time and what happened?'

'She said *if she could do it for all those years, so could you.* I know.' Beverly put on a squeaky voice as she mimicked her manager.

'*And?*'

'*And* you're old enough to fight your own battles.'

'Correct.' Amelia gave her mother a thumbs-up. 'Besides I have this panic alarm.'

She tapped beneath the desk. They smirked, reliving Amelia's first night shift when she pressed it wondering what the device did. She soon found out; armed police swarmed the hotel.

'I just think today of all days she could have been a little supportive. She's really changed since she was made General Manager.'

'Mom, she's looked after us all over the years! She got me this job when I flunked college and helped me get this promotion. She even fought for you to get that accountancy role, it's not her fault you failed the credit check. Give the woman a break.'

'I still think we could've had the day off.'

'It's Dad's day, I know. It's not like he's here to celebrate it.'

It had been three years to the day since his funeral. The certificate declared Marty as *'presumed dead'*, although to the Hahns, there was no presumption about it. Martin Hahn evaporated within the crumbling towers of the World Trade Centre. Like most of the missing, there was nothing left to prove that he died within the terrorist attacks other than witness reports.

The Hahn family waited seven years so they could finally hold a funeral for their departed loved one and begin to arrange the necessary financial arrangements. Marty's name entered the remembrance list at Ground Zero, and the previous year, President Obama for the first time read out Marty's name, now that all evidence pointed towards his passing in the tragedy. Without a body, they filled a casket with photographs, clothing items and keep-sakes. They buried the goods in a local church in Brooklyn, near the apartment where they now lived.

It was almost seven and the guests were due to arrive for breakfast. Beverly walked into the kitchen to find Jose, dressed in his white chef's hat, white coat and stripy black and white pants, ready to fry up the breakfast. His hair grew greyer by the day but miraculously his moustache remained black. The leftovers he devoured after the restaurant closed now sat on his waistline, which steadily expanded as each year passed.

'Mrs Beverly, you look tired.' Jose's English had developed over the past decade but was far from fluent. 'Too much Tequila?'

'No, no.' She giggled and waved her hand away. 'It's just been a long week. It's my sixth day of working. Not long until my day off though.'

'Erm... hello?' The Mexican chef held up his hands and shrugged.

'Never mind.' She waved her finger. 'It won't be long until I'm out of here for good anyway. I just wish I knew when.'

The kitchen door swung open and Amelia walked in. She circulated the kitchen and inspected the metal surfaces and the trays of food ready to go out onto the buffet.

'Well done, Jose. Another fine job! The guests will be happy.' Amelia smiled and nodded, before helping herself to a crispy slice of bacon. Jose bowed in acceptance, while Beverly eagerly waited for her review.

'Mom, don't you think we need to have a big clean in here? We could have inspectors any day now. We have to make this place spotless.'

'Will do.' Beverly replied, sighing like the teenager Amelia once was. 'How the tables turn hey, Jose? It wasn't that long ago I was telling her to clean her room.'

'Come on, Mom. I know you've lost all motivation for this job, but do it for me. I'm working tirelessly to help make this place a success and you're crushing that hard work in one Trip Advisor review. Just yesterday someone put what a state the restaurant was in.'

'OK, OK, cut me a little slack, will you? Just remember how much I've done for you over the years, *Young Lady*!'

'I'm not even going to bother dignifying that with an answer. I always keep work and home life separate. I hoped you would do the same. Anyway I'm going home, I expect this clean by the time I get back here tonight.'

She stormed out of the kitchen, attempting to slam the door, but it held no catch and instead swung forwards and back, narrowly missing Beverly who attempted to run after her.

In the lobby, a young gentleman dressed in a charcoal suit with a hotel-branded badge on his chest stood beside reception waiting to relieve Amelia of her duties. He walked up to the night-supervisor and kissed her on the lips. Beverly spied on the exchange from a circular window on the kitchen door and smiled. He was blonde, toned and everything that any young lady would dream of. Hell, Beverly would have even had a go had she been twenty years younger. She waited for Amelia to depart and then sprung onto reception.

'Good morning, James.'

'Hey, Mrs Hahn.'

'Please, you can surely call me Beverly by now, it's been ten years for God's sakes. Besides Mrs Hahn is my mother.' She laughed and James awkwardly giggled, unsure as to why what she said was funny. 'Are you in all day?'

'No just the morning, I have college this afternoon.'

'How's the plumbing course coming along?'

'It's ok, I just wanna get out there and do it now.'

'Believe me you'll regret that. Before long you'll be dreaming of your eight week summers and resenting ever wishing it away.' Beverly looked out of the lobby windows to the sky in reminiscence of her Cornell days.

James Gates had been a rock of support for Amelia since Marty passed. They met at school on that fateful day back in 2001 and soon realised how much they had in common; tragedy. Like Amelia, he had lost a parent too. His mother was on board flight United 93, which went down in history as a botched attack on the White House. Julie Gates helped fight against the terrorists and brought the plane to the ground before they could attack the capital. Julie and her fellow passengers died as heroes.

When Amelia met James, he was a fourteen year old spotty kid with braces, thick brown glasses and gelled back hair. Known as a dork to his peers, James had few friends in school, but Amelia appreciated the empathetic chaotic being he was. Her investment paid off; he was the ugly duckling who turned into a swan as today he was a handsome mid-twenties lacrosse player, learning a valuable trade.

'I know today is a tough day for you, Beverly.'

'Oh…' She stumbled for words. 'Yeah well we all have to get through it. You know as well as anyone.'

'It never really gets any easier though does it? Like, I still don't believe my mom has really gone.'

'I get what you mean.' Beverly wiped a small tear from the

corner of her eye. 'When I'm home alone and I hear Amelia come in, I sometimes think it could be Marty, returning home.'

'That'd be magical.' James smiled and rubbed her shoulder.

'Wouldn't it?'

*

A pile of paper welcomed Amelia home. The doormat had enough envelopes to take out an entire rainforest. Page after page of junk mail, takeaway menus and invitations to reclaim PPI, most of which was placed in the recycling.

Three packages she held onto; the first was from Ticketmaster. BonJovi were playing later in the year at the Garden and she hung onto the hope that Benjamin would be home to join her, otherwise she'd have to drag a reluctant James with her; it wasn't really his scene.

The second envelope from AT&T had her monthly phone bill. She placed that one in a drawer; it was a week before payday and she didn't dare look at how much was going to come out of her account before then. The waste paper basket had endless tariff offers to reduce her monthly payments but that seemed like a lot of effort after working a twelve hour nightshift.

The final document was addressed to her mother. It was stamped with The United States Government logo. Intrigued, she turned the document over to open it, but paused. '*What am I doing? I'd kill her if she opened my mail'*. She threw down her handbag and walked through to the living area.

After Marty died, they moved to an apartment in Brooklyn. It was a modest space, open-plan, with a white breakfast bar separating the kitchen and lounge. She placed her mom's mail on the counter and slumped onto the brown leather couch, brought over from their home in Manhattan, and switched on the TV.

Abc aired a talk-show, where a politically mixed group of celebrity women aired their views on current affairs, whether it was a White House scandal or the best Oscar's dress. Today's topic was the Iraq War; should America have invaded?

'Urgh, not today, thanks.' She switched over to a music channel and closed her eyes for five minutes, but kept sneaking a peak at the counter-top towards the mysterious post, as if it could disappear at any moment.

The temptation was too much. She rushed over and picked up the envelope. Rummaging with the package, she spied through the plastic address window for any clues to its contents, but alas the government were smart enough to avoid any tampering. She quickly abandoned the plan.

Attempting to distract herself, Amelia made herself a grilled cheese sandwich and sat at the breakfast counter, staring furiously at the package. It taunted her.

She gave in. She wiped down the knife she had used to slice her sandwich onto her white shirt and slid it within the gap between the envelope seal. Sweat poured down her forehead, there was no going back now. If her mom came home, she'd have to admit what she had done.

She unravelled the letter and read through its contents. Her heart raced as she turned to its attachments. *After all this time!* She had to tell someone. She lifted out her phone and dialled.

*

The bristles of the brush detached. Despite an hour of scrubbing, the metallic surface of the kitchen bench still bore a sticky residue. Beverly was determined to remove it having been embarrassed earlier by her daughter. Yes she had lost a little interest in her work, but she was still proud and she'd sure as hell show her. '*My God, when did I become the teenager?'*

At the grand age of fifty-five, Beverly was over a decade older than when she began the role, and she certainly felt it. Dreaming of an easier life, she looked forward to the day when she could hang up her apron and relax a little more. Her daughter remained optimistic in the hospitality game as she rose through the ranks. But what did Beverly have?

Outside of work, her social life was as eventful as her career. Apart from her annual weekend away with her children, she had no hobbies and few friends. And apart from a couple of drunken one night stands with Jose, she hadn't held onto a man since Marty.

The grime continued to taunt her. She'd need a special cleaning product to remove it, one of those off the TV ad with a catchy jingle.

She abandoned the task and returned to the lobby.

'How's it going, James?' A bored Beverly approached her daughter's boyfriend, stood behind the desk appearing equally jaded.

'I'm alright, it's a quiet morning. Where is everyone?'

'It's summer. Everyone'll be up in the Hamptons. Are you coming for your dinner tonight?'

'I can't, I've got college.'

'Fair enough.' Beverly replied with a disappointed head-tilt. 'You must be sick of the sight of me.'

'Nah, you're not *all* bad.' He winked and they smiled.

When Amelia first introduced him to the family she was just sixteen. A concerned Beverly considered her too young to have a boyfriend and banned her from seeing him. Amelia's threats to move to Europe, where their relationship would be recognised, forced Beverly to meet this young man and give him a chance; at least if he was in her own home she could keep an eye on them. As soon as he walked through the door, his radiant smile won her over. But there was something more; it was his eyes. There was hurt in those eyes. She recognised that pain in her own daughter. And as soon as Amelia saw him, that radiant smile of his mirrored onto her. He somehow made her morose teenage daughter happy and that was good enough for her.

'I'm really glad Amelia has you, after all you two have been through, I'm glad you have each other to go through it all with.' Beverly said and paused and reflected on her own situation. 'I just wish I had someone myself.'

The phone rang, allowing a flustered James to escape Beverly's awkward pep-talk.

'I better leave you to it, Hunny.' Beverly excused herself and walked away from the desk towards the restaurant where there was a trail of dirty dishes leftover from breakfast. 'I better finish cleaning the restaurant before *Madam* returns.'

'Hi Beautiful!' Beverley's ears perked up as she heard James greet the caller. She hid behind a pillar, listening to the call. Why was Amelia calling so early? *'It better be Amelia,'* she considered as she wondered who else he'd dare call *beautiful.*

'Yeah, she's right here, I'll pass you over.' He pulled the phone away from his head and lifted it in Beverley's direction. 'Hey, Beverly, there's a phone call for you. It's Amelia.'

Her eyes widened. She grabbed a dirty cloth out of her pinafore and pretended to dust the pillar before making her way around into James's sight.

'Oh, I wonder what she wants. I hope it's not an emergency. I've had enough of those calls to last a lifetime.' Beverly rolled her eyes, grabbed the phone off James and spoke to her daughter. 'Hi Pumpkin, is everything OK?'

'It's here.'

'Thanks Hunny, we'll talk later.' Beverly passed the phone back to a suspicious James, who hung up on her behalf.

'That was a short call. Is she OK?'

'She's fine, she was just letting me know about a delivery I've been expecting.' Beverly stood still deep in thought for a moment, before smiling and walking towards the back office. 'I need to go see Sandra.'

The office had two large desks facing parallel walls. One for the General Manager and the other for others to use for general administrative tasks. Files filled each table, filled with receipts ready for the end-of-year tax returns. The weekly rota, health and safety notices, and thank you messages from guests filled the walls and a framed photograph of the team at a hospitality award ceremony the previous year sat beside the trophy they collected that night.

Behind the desk, Sandra sat writing up the rota. She appeared tired as she worked tirelessly following a tip-off that the hotel inspectors were in the area.

'Hi Sandra, I hope I'm not disturbing you.' Beverly whispered and gave a light knock onto a filing cabinet beside her.

'Good morning Bev, is everything OK in the restaurant?' Sandra smiled, glad of the distraction. 'Or is this a social visit?'

'No. I wanted to tell you that I'm handing in my notice.' Sandra's smile retracted as she took in the news. 'I'll work my notice of course, but a month from now, I won't be here, I'm sorry. I hope it doesn't leave you too understaffed.'

'Is it something I've done?' Sandra's voice broke. 'I know I'm... *we're* a little stretched at the moment but I hope things aren't that bad here. If there's something I can improve...'

'Oh no, it's nothing personal.' Beverly quickly intervened. 'I'm ever so grateful for everything you've done for me over the years. I just can't do this anymore. I'm exhausted and I need some time for me.'

'What will you do about money?' Sandra asked, sneaking a peek at Beverly's pay slip.

'I'll be fine, don't you worry about me.'

The two of them worked out her notice, giving Sandra enough time to replace her. Once complete, it was almost lunch time and Beverly finished her shift. Rejecting the overtime on offer, she could not wait to get home to see the arrival from the US government.

*

Amelia remained seated at the dining table, staring at the letter from the government. She hadn't moved since opening the envelope. Her right foot furiously tapped the table leg as she anxiously waited for her mother to get home.

The magnolia coated walls throughout the apartment bored the Hahns since they moved in but their rental contract prevented them from making it their own. The delivery before her would change that.

The door rattled and her mother rushed in. Beverly threw her handbag down on the chair, ran to the table and looked at the document which Amelia held in her shaking hands.

'Is this it?' Amelia handed her the papers. Beverly unravelled the pages and took in all the information. 'I can't believe we have a letter signed by The President himself! He's written to me! What an honour.'

But The President's signature was the least enticing piece of the package. Browsing over the attached documents accompanying the letter, Beverly retrieved a cheque out of the envelope.

'So there you go…one million dollars.'

Chapter 2

Amelia picked up her electronic tablet and logged into the instant messenger application. The device was originally purchased to play games but since her brother moved away, it became a valuable tool to ensure they remained in contact.

Amongst the long list of contacts were her brother's details: *Benjamin Hahn, Iraq*. Double clicking on his name opened a new window, she clicked a green phone symbol which dialled his account.

'Hello Kid,' her brother answered. Amelia switched on her web cam, and he, in turn, switched on his. The grainy image of a soldier appeared on the screen. He had beefed up since he departed months before. His shaved head displayed several scars; the carvings of playful youth and the near-misses of war.

'Hi Benji, are you well?' Embarrassed by her question, Amelia silently questioned how anyone could be *well* in Iraq; it was a dusty battle-ground where death was imminent. The Middle East was a far cry from the Ivy League college where her brother should have been teaching had he followed his academic dreams. The plan to teach the Civil War to college kids died the day his father did.

'Things are good, although we lost one of our men last night. Private Kerry.' His lip trembled. Amelia bowed her head, uncomfortable with the news of fatalities within her brother's unit. It hit home how close he was to the danger himself. 'How are you?'

'I'm ok thanks.'

'You've been eating properly haven't you?' He wiped the tear away and raised his eyebrows, staring down the camera.

'Yes of course!'

'And keeping it down?' One of his eyebrows lowered, while the other arched higher.

'I told you I'm behind that now.' Amelia wrapped her free hand around her stomach. 'Besides my problems are nothing compared to yours.'

'Don't you dare ever say that! Bulimia is a different kinda battle, but it's still a battle.'

The illness developed gradually after her father died, but she managed to keep it away from her family for over a year. The signs were all there; weight loss, hair loss and decaying teeth, but it wasn't until she fainted at school did they realise anything was wrong. They put her in front of a counsellor and while she had since managed to largely keep it under control, she still faced the discomfort whenever the anniversary of her father's death grew near.

'So what's new over there?' Benjamin changed the subject.

'Well, we had a package arrive. The money came from the government.' Amelia grabbed the cheque and waved it in front of the camera.

The September 11th Victims Fund was formed under an Act of Congress, offering families support following the loss of loved ones. Further support was delivered from the September 11th Fund, a charitable donation set up in the city of New York.

'Huh, that's great, just a shame about the circumstances.' Benjamin shrugged. 'When you see death on a daily basis, you soon realise how little money's worth in the bigger picture.'

'I guess with how you used to earn your money…'

'Hey, I thought we agreed not to talk about that.'

Amelia stared down at the floor in shame. She wished he could talk about it to her but it was a taboo topic. Guilt rumbled in her stomach as she relived the day she discovered how he had sourced the cash to keep her in school dinners and a tidy uniform.

'We've been invited to a dinner with the other survivors and their families. It's when you're back home next month, you will come won't you?' The whiney tone made its debut appearance since she was little girl. 'Mom never comes, it's too upsetting, and James… well he'll be there with his own family. Please don't let me go alone.'

'Of course, Kid.' The soldier smiled and she smiled back, nodding her head in gratitude.

Amelia attempted to catch a glimpse behind her brother to see the environment he inhabited; a dark tent hid any secrets regarding his location. She was disappointed with her limited access but at least she had the device, before the Internet she'd have had to cope with a letter home. Today they could have been in the same room.

'So what's Mom going to spend the money on?'

'She's already quit her job and the cheque hasn't even cleared yet.' Amelia rolled her eyes and threw her hands up. 'I'm just grateful she hasn't got a credit card.'

'Me too, you keep an eye on her.' Benjamin barked, before

closing the call. ‘Anyway I have to go, Private Ross is outside and he’s waiting to speak to his wife.’

They said their goodbyes and closed the call. The screen went black and Amelia’s eyes welled up. It was only a few weeks until he returned home, but their goodbyes continued to hurt.

As she packed the tablet away, her mother, Beverly, walked into the room with the New York Express. In her hand, she had the middle pages open with all the latest apartments which were up for sale. Since they had received the cheque, she spent her days circling the crème-de-la-crème of New York’s real-estate.

‘Look at this beautiful apartment. Separate living room and kitchen, a dining room, en-suite bathrooms and a view over central park! Isn’t that amazing?’ Amelia looked at the apartment details before glancing at the price.

‘It’s beautiful, but you won’t have any money left after.’

'So what? We have a million bucks to spend, why can't we go a little crazy?' Beverly sulked. 'I know we can't have the house we once had, but surely we can live somewhere a little luxurious?'

'But how do you expect to afford bills and food once you've bought the apartment? You don't have a job anymore!'

‘Well I can always pick up a few shifts here and there, but look, we would be so happy there. And it has three bedrooms so when Benjamin comes home we can all be a family again. The three musketeers! We could be so happy together. It’s worth the money just for that. What do you think?’

‘Mom, Benjamin only ever comes home for a few weeks at a time. The army is his life now.’

‘He’ll be discharged someday.’

‘And even then he won’t come back to New York. Let’s face it, this city is full of bad memories for him.’

‘Well we can always have a spare room for when he visits then, I feel terrible when he crashes on that couch.’

‘Well, you’ll still only need two bedrooms as I don’t think I’m gonna move in with you, Mom.’

Silence hovered.

Beverly began dusting the top of a chest of drawers with her hand, avoiding eye contact with the girl who had broken her heart.

‘So dusty in here. We really need a spring clean. What…what

do you mean you're not moving in with me?'

'I think I'm gonna move in with James, I'm sorry.'

Silence returned. They stared at each other, each refusing to break the lingering discomfort.

'Well that's *fine*,' Beverly broke, but a crack in her voice said otherwise. 'You don't wanna be stuck with me forever, do ya?'

Humming a familiar tune, she walked out of the room, avoiding any further discussion. Amelia knew it was far from fine, but it was time to move on. While most evenings they were able to cosy up with a glass of wine and watch a movie, at other times the pair clashed like titans.

'Oh, I must go out and buy a new dress!' Beverly walked back in, wiping an eye. Her mother glanced into the mirror, looking at the extra lines, which appeared below her teary eyes. 'Maybe I should get myself some Botox too.'

'What for? You never go out anywhere and, when you do, you wear sweat pants. Don't tell me you and Jose are fine-dining now you've got money. It's a far cry from the burrito bar anyway.'

'I didn't know you knew about Jose.' Beverly's jaw dropped.

'Mom, you two are hardly subtle. We all know!' She laughed and rubbed her arm. 'We don't mind.'

'Well it's nothing serious. I just get lonely.'

'No one's judging. Seriously, what are you dressing up for?'

'The memorial dinner, of course!'

*

Benjamin closed the lid on his lap top and walked out of the room. Behind the door, Private Ross eagerly waited for some Face-Time with his wife. He smiled and nodded at his colleague before walking out, shutting the door firmly behind him, placing a *Do Not Disturb* sign on the door, made just for Private Ross.

It was an unspoken rule to avoid Ross when he was on his web cam. Benjamin had made that mistake once before. The hero was nearly hit by a 5.56 when he stepped in to find his colleague's wife in her knickers providing a cheeky show for her lonely husband on the computer screen.

It was hardly a new sight for Private Hahn. The entire Sixty-Ninth Regiment of New York had caught a glimpse of her naughty photograph stored in Ross's wallet, but her exposure was the least of her problems. Benjamin turned away to avoid eye contact with the screen to find Ross himself with his trousers around his ankles. It was unwise to surprise a man who had a MK19-3 on him.

'Why the face, Hahn?' his colleague, Charlie asked. He sat on his bunk bed, polishing his boots. The pair had matching camouflage cargo pants and white vests, showing off their moist muscles.

'Just thinking about Kerry.' Benjamin said.

'We can't get too attached, Dude, otherwise we'll never go out there and do what we do. He was a great soldier, but that's the game.'

'Not much of a game with those barbarians.'

Ross walked out of the room, he appeared as glum as Benjamin.

'What's up, Ross? You thinking about Kerry too?'

'No, the Internet's died again.'

Benjamin and Charlie glanced at each other and grinned. The messages for the sleazy soldier were a little different to the *love yous* and *miss yous* which the rest of the boys in the regiment received.

It was a dark room with no natural light and the heat was unbearable in the desert heat. A small fan in the corner provided some relief and a lemon air-freshener improved the aroma of the stuffy room. Photographs of loved-ones back home brightened up the walls and beside each bed, a small white chest of drawers kept the few keep-sakes soldiers were allowed to bring with them on tour.

Private Ross walked over to his bed and retrieved a bottle of vodka out of his bag, which he had sneaked into the compound a few days earlier. He opened it and took a straight swig. Benjamin winced imagining the sharp sting of his colleague's throat as he downed the spirit without a fruity accompaniment. Lifting the bottle in their direction, Ross offered his fellow troopers a sip, but the sensible soldiers shook their heads.

'Pussies,' he sniggered. 'Right come on, lads, let's go out.'

Ross downed the rest of the contents of the bottle and bolted towards the door, but found his colleagues blocking it.

'What gives, guys? Move out my way.'

'No, you're drunk. We're not letting you get into trouble

again.'

'I'll be *fine!'* He slurred his words.

'You cause mayhem every time you go out. I'm not risking it.'

'Are you coming with me or staying here, Hahn?' Ross raised his chin above Benjamin's and looked down at his fellow comrade. Benjamin, in turn, broadened his shoulders refusing to submit.

'We're all staying here, come on, don't be stupid. Don't you remember what happened last time? You nearly died.'

'Oh come on!' Ross whined. 'That wasn't my fault, it's not my fault that gal's husband came home. She shoulda said she was married.'

'Like that would've changed anything.'

'You might not be so fortunate this time.' Charlie intervened. 'Come on, just stay in and calm down. What if we get a call out and we're not here?'

'Are you coming with me or staying here?' Ross repeated, stroking his gun as he glared at his fellow trooper. Benjamin registered the threat and gulped. 'Just remember, you owe me, Hahn.'

'Fine.' Benjamin rolled his eyes. 'Come on, Charlie, you're coming too.' They grabbed their weapons and shirts and walked out onto the streets of Bagdad.

The two boys walked through the city centre following the drunken soldier. For some, the trip through the Middle-Eastern city would be a terrifying experience, but this was now an everyday normality for those who lived and worked there. Baghdad remained surprisingly calm, just like any city, until the perils of war made its grand entrance.

Most Americans struggled to comprehend the peaceful scene, which Benjamin painted to his friends and family back home. They only saw the war-zone that CNN represented as the city only made the news when tension rose. Most of the time, he could walk through Baghdad like he could in New York.

'Do you want some of this?' Ross yelled at a young woman in a burka as she passed, grabbing his crotch to display the package which was on offer.

The Islamic woman glared and waved him along. This was not some down-town bar in Detroit, this was a predominantly Muslim country and the girls were a little different here. Benjamin gave her an apologetic smile as she shook her head at the men whose job involved protecting the locals' welfare.

Having found that his moves were redundant, Ross attempted a different approach. He walked over to a market where three women eyed up shoes.

'Hey ladies, I'm Private Ross,' he smoothly stepped in. 'Just checking everything is OK here tonight, no suspicious packages or anything.'

The three Middle-Eastern ladies turned around and giggled, fanning themselves as they were introduced to the soldiers. The three men before them were buff, tanned and in camouflage; perfect choices for an annual charity calendar.

'Wanna come see a movie?' Ross asked, lowering his sunglasses to eye the girls up and down. The pack leader looked to her accompanying followers and nodded. She linked arms with Ross, while the other girls latched onto the nervous cadets behind.

They followed Ross and his new friend to the Anjuman Movie Theatre on Al Rashad Street. They paid their entrance fees, feeling the burn of the glare from the elderly cinema owner, who served them their tickets behind a glass box, barely passing a smile as they walked in.

'You know this show is in Arabic, right?'

'And?' Ross raised his eyebrows above his sunglasses.

'I don't want any trouble.' He threw the tickets down on the counter and looked the three women accompanying the soldiers up and down, spitting on the floor as they passed.

Inside the cinema, there was only one screen. The seats were old and worn. Sponge leaked out where the material had torn. Cigarette smoke filled the room and loose butts scattered across the floor.

Charlie and Benjamin sat in the front row with two of the girls, while Ross took a seat on the back row with his new mistress. The girls could have been triplets; they all had long flowing black hair, olive skin and only the colours of their vibrant saris allowed the boys to tell them apart.

Benjamin caught a nervous Charlie move the hand of the young girl next to him off his leg and back onto her arm rest. The girl to Benjamin's right appeared as anxious as a virgin on her wedding night, wishing she could be anywhere than beside these Americans. Sensing her wishes to be alone, he shifted his attention towards the screen and allowed her to have full use of the arm-rest between them.

Giggling echoed from the back row but the soldiers stared forward avoiding any sight of the activities behind them. They slumped down into their seats avoiding the glares of the surrounding spectators, who would easily connect them to the shameless soldier.

'What do you think's happening?' Charlie whispered.

'On the screen or at the back?' The pair sniggered.

'In the movie.' Their understanding of Arabic was slim. The audience giggled, suggesting it was comedy. A shushing behind them halted their chatter.

The swing of the back door and a bright white light beaming onto the screen drew the attention of the audience away from the movie. Behind, the cinema owner shone a torch on the raunchy couple in the back row. Surprised and shrieking, they retrieved their loose clothing from the floor as the owner yelled at them in Arabic.

Ross's companion sobbed, pleading with the manager, while the soldier looked over towards Benjamin and shrugged his shoulders, a smirk still stitched to his face. His smile broke as the manager pulled at the soldier's arm.

'Hey, get off me, man, what the hell do you think you're doing? Do you know who I am?' The two men yelled at each other, but the differences in their languages meant that their points remained lost on each other.

The grievance became physical between the soldier and the cinema manager, it was time for them to intervene. Benjamin and Charlie ran towards the back row but a flash of light and deafening bang blocked their paths. Debris flew across the room and the soldiers fell over. A ringing stung their ear drums. Fire roared through the aisle and smoke tunnelled its way into Benjamin's lungs.

The cloud cleared. Charlie's face appeared before him. He shouted but the commotion made him inaudible. He could feel blood and a sharp pain to his side. A second blast caused a tremor to rock the cinema and Charlie disappeared. The heat rose and the room grew darker. Benjamin lay motionless until all went black.

Chapter 3

The CV-22 Osprey Cargo Aircraft landed at the Dover Air Force Base in Delaware. Soldiers surrounded the plane as it came to a complete halt. Inside the base, Beverly and Amelia stood in anticipation for Benjamin's arrival. They both wore black, veils covering their distraught faces.

'I had nightmares of this moment for so long, I never expected it to actually arrive.' Beverly said. Amelia put her arm around her mother; she too had the nightmares.

'We have to be strong for him, Mom.'

'I thought that once we had the million dollars, all our problems would go away. How wrong we were.'

They completed months of administration work, attended hearings and proved what their husband would have earned across a lifetime. Countless numbers of witnesses were called upon to state that they had seen Marty inside the twin towers, but hadn't seen him since.

But after all the meetings and paperwork, they held onto the hope that once that money was in the bank, all their problems would go away. A wake up call from the United States Army regarding the fate of their son brought a realisation that money could not solve everything.

'He was supposed to be coming to the gala dinner to meet the other 9/11 victims.' Amelia said. 'At least you're coming now. I won't be completely alone.'

'Well, we'll just have to see, we don't have to go.'

The door on the side of the aircraft opened and a grounded soldier walked up the steps towards the aircraft with a folded US flag and disappeared inside.

A coffin poked out of the doors, covered in the country's stars and stripes, and slowly descended onto the air field, carried by six uniformed officers. Beverly clutched her chest and fell backwards onto her daughter.

'Hey Mom, it could have been worse…' Amelia said as she gripped onto her mother. '…at least he's still alive.'

Behind the coffin marched out Benjamin, who followed his comrade, Private Michael Ross, who died suddenly in the suicide bomb attack in the Baghdad cinema. He hobbled down the steps, reaching out to grip the bannister, but his injuries prevented him. Like his colleagues, he honoured the hero in his uniform, however his right sleeve was rolled up and pinned to his shoulder. A fellow soldier, walked up the stairs and linked arms with his remaining limb and supported him with his descent.

At the bottom of the stairs he saluted with his remaining hand. His surrounding soldiers shot their guns three times in respect to the fallen soldier. They carried the coffin away and Benjamin hobbled over to his family. Beverly removed the black netted vale away from her face, grabbed her son and held him tight.

'Thank God you're alright.' She cried into his chest. 'I don't think I can ever let go of you again.'

'Careful, I'm still in quite a bit of pain,' he winced as he held onto the stump where his right arm once rested. Amelia rubbed his left arm, kissed him on the cheek and broke into tears.

'Hey, I'm the lucky one, don't do this.' He shook her. 'I'm alive, be glad I'm here. Anyway I have someone to see.' He turned away from them and walked over to Katherine Ross, the wife of his deceased friend.

'Mrs Ross, please accept my condolences. I'm so sorry for your loss. He was a good man and a good soldier. He saved my life once and I'll never forget that. I feel honoured to have known him.' Katherine nodded her head in gratitude. He didn't expect much of an exchange with the widow, so he simply saluted and walked away.

'Private Hahn,' she whimpered. Benjamin turned back towards his colleague's wife.

'Can I be of assistance, Mam?'

'Yes, you see, no one will tell me what happened to him. The papers haven't reported anything and his sergeant couldn't give me any information. I understand in some cases these things have to be kept private for security purposes, but you have to give me something. I need closure.'

Benjamin witnessed the despair in this widow's eyes. She was only a young woman. A small boy stood beside her, who he registered as Ross's son, Bradley, who was ten years old. Ross often talked about his young son on their travels through the Middle East and kept a photograph of him in his wallet. The boy had his father's freckled skin and snub nose, but his white-blonde hair was as radiant as his mother's.

Upon their discharge from hospital, both he and Charlie faced interrogation from their superiors for leaving the grounds and causing distress to the local people. Charlie pleaded his innocence, blaming his actions on protecting Private Ross, but his excuses fell flat on their bosses. However, he faced a light punishment due to his previous good behaviour.

The same couldn't have been said for Private Hahn. The investigation board warned him that he was lucky that his injuries allowed him to leave on medical grounds with his pension rather than dismissal for conduct. This wasn't his first adventure with Private Ross and had warnings already on his file. The hospital visit from his sergeant made him almost grateful that he had lost a limb. Regardless, he was honoured to follow Ross, he'd saved his life before and wouldn't be around to face the repercussions without him.

'You're quite right, for security purposes we can't disclose the full details,' Benjamin lied, saving Mrs Ross from the pain of knowing what her husband was really up to when he died. 'However, what I can tell you is that he was protecting local civilians at the time and he was a hero.'

It wasn't a complete lie. Ross had saved the life of the young woman he was advancing on in the cinema. She survived with just a severed leg, rather than facing the same fate as he had. While the media praised Ross as a brave man, his heroic deeds were not all that they seemed. The lady's life hung in the balance of Ross, saved only by the Private's large physique, which collapsed on top of her as the blast penetrated the structure of the cinema, crumbling on the couple. The US Army wasn't ready to have their hard work spoiled by an individual soldier, so they spun an alternative headline to the media.

Katherine nodded in gratitude and a look of pride blossomed over her as she acknowledged the illusive explanation for her husband's death. Benjamin looked down at Bradley, who appeared lost without his father. Heartbroken by the orphan's grief, he bent down to speak to the young boy.

'I lost my dad when I was a couple of years older than you, Kid. It hurts but I promise you it gets better. You should be proud of your daddy. He helped a lot of people and tried to stop the bad people who killed my dad. Like you, I'm proud of my dad. He was in the attack on the twin towers in New York before you were born. He went back to help people escape but the building collapsed on him. That's why I'm in the army now... to stop the bad guys. And that's what your dad was doing. You can tell all your friends that your dad was a hero.'

Benjamin tapped the young boy on the shoulder, stood up and walked back to his family. Placing the one arm he had left around his mother's shoulder, Benjamin walked out of the airbase with the two most important women in his life beside him. They remained the three musketeers.

Chapter 4

The crackles from an old black and white movie and the clink of a bottle of brandy meeting a crystal glass were the only dissonance in an almost silent room. Beverly sat alone with her legs up resting on the couch, sipping the spirit she had just poured herself.

It was the first time she had managed to sit in her new apartment alone. It was spacious, modern and in the heart of Manhattan, with a view over Central Park.

The gala dinner for the 9/11 victims and their families was due to commence the following day. Beverly looked at the speech she had recited earlier, requested by the organisers. Doubt overcame her as she considered whether it was appropriate for her to be there after all that had happened. It had been just three weeks since her son returned home and he was still healing. She'd have cancelled had he not insisted that they attended. This was a special year. Not only had she received a benefit from the victims fund, it was also the tenth anniversary of the terrorist attacks.

The movie finished and she turned off the television. The apartment was as silent as a graveyard at night. Amelia had since moved in with James and he was hosting a house warming party for her. Benjamin was out celebrating with her, but Beverly thought it was kinder to stay away; who wants their middle-aged mother damaging their street cred? Instead, she took advantage of having the place to herself.

The eerie silence caused a slight chill down Beverly's spine. Scared to be on her own in an unusual space for the first time, goose-bumps spread across her skin.

There was nothing to be scared of. The front door was bolted shut, the tower block entrance required a key fob to enter and a security officer guarded the apartment block on the ground floor. What could possibly happen? She shook herself back to reality and slipped on her woolly red dressing gown, covering her satin blue pyjamas.

To break the silence, she walked over to her record player and picked out one of her Louis Armstrong LPs'. She filled up her brandy glass and sat back with the drink as she sang along to *Wonderful World.* The song took her back to her first dance with Marty at the Cornell student ball. She swayed, reliving the movements which they later performed at their wedding.

A knock at the door disturbed her tranquillity. She glanced at the time; it was almost midnight. '

That'll be Benjamin, she sighed, 'always forgetting his keys.'

Beverly stood up to answer the door. A slight dizziness caused her to stumble down the hallway, which fed from the living room to the front door and provided access to all the bedrooms and bathrooms in the apartment. *How much have I had to drink?*

As she approached the entrance, she could hear a man singing in the corridor the words to Louis' song. *My God, he's beginning to sound like his father.* She enjoyed the familiar sound, if only for a moment. The knocking grew louder, drowning her husband from her memories.

'OK, OK, Benjamin. I'm coming. Let me just get my keys.' Ruthlessly rummaging through her purse, deep enough to put Mary Poppins' bag to shame, she pushed around the loose change, receipts and lipsticks which scattered across the bottom. The sharp tip of her keys nipped at her fingertips. She grabbed them and inserted the largest silver one into the lock. Pausing for a moment of evocative pleasure, she closed her eyes and imagined her husband singing those lyrics. *Just to see him one more time.*

The continuous knocking brought Beverly back to reality. Twisting the key anti-clockwise, she listened for the click and opened the door. Catching a glimpse of the visitor, she dropped her keys onto the floor in shock. The man in the corridor was not her son. The colour drained from her face as if she had seen a ghost. Staring at the man for the first time in ten years, she called out his name.

'Marty'

Chapter 5

'Hello Beautiful.' Marty was as calm as a Saint in Paradise. He epitomised a man who had nipped to the shops and back, rather than resurrecting from the dead.

A petrified Beverly clung onto the door. The colour had drained from her silent face and her jaw hung as she searched for the right words. Her heart thumped at a rapid pace and her temperature rose to levels she had not experienced since she ran the New York Marathon in 2007.

'Are you going to let me in?' Marty smiled; he still had that glowing grin. The hair had become greyer and thinner, and he had more lines around his face, but he was just as dashing as the day he left the family. His sparkling blue eyes contained a slight twinkle as he looked at the love of his life for the first time in a decade. A black overcoat covered a dowdy blue hoody and brown cords.

'What... what...' Beverly stuttered. 'What are you doing here?'

'I've come home to see you, Hunny, it's been a long time.'

'How... how...' The colour returned to her face rapidly and her skin turned a lighter shade of red as shock evolved into fury. 'How in the hell are you here? You're supposed to be dead!'

'Well I'm obviously not dead, otherwise I wouldn't be stood in front of you, would I? I'm not a ghost. Go on... touch me.' He held out his hand. Beverly touched him and jumped back as soon as her fingertips made contact, as if he was electrically charged.

Struggling to catch her breath, Beverly grabbed her chest as her rib cage violently pushed outwards. A sharp pain radiated from her diaphragm, tightening as she hyperventilated. Marty grabbed her hand and pulled her into the living room before sitting her down on the armchair. He retrieved a paper bag from the kitchen and emptied the prescription sack onto the dining table. He handed the bag to his wife to breathe into and restored her usual rhythm. As her chest relaxed, Beverly threw the bag on the floor before lying back, wiping the sweat off her forehead.

'Are you OK?' Marty knelt down, holding onto her hand throughout her attack. 'I feel terrible that I've done this to you. You're my entire world, do you know that?'

'How are you here?' She ran her fingers through her hair to wipe the damp locks away from her face. Her perspiration flowed like Victoria Falls. 'I thought you were dead.'

'I survived the terrorist attack. I got out of the building just as it was collapsing.' Marty explained. 'The debris was crumbling just as I got out. How I survived the collapse was nothing short of a miracle.'

'So then why didn't you come home?' Tears flowed from her eyes. A shaking hand covered her mouth. 'We waited for weeks, watching the phone, hoping it would ring. Every time our front door knocked, the children ran to it, hoping for it to be you! Now you're here and I don't know whether I should kiss you or slap you!'

'I couldn't.' He looked down at the floor, looking for the right words to explain his absence. He had run this conversation in his head for years, practising what he would say. Now he had the opportunity, his throat closed up.

'What do you mean you couldn't? We are your family, you had to come home. We were losing our minds here! Where have you been for all this time?'

'Indiana.' Marty shrugged.

'Indiana?' Beverly tried to piece together why he had chosen the Hoosier State. They had no family, nor friends, to her recollection, there. Besides visiting the place on a business trip, Marty had few ties to the Mid-Western state.

'Gary, Indiana, to be specific.'

'You were a short drive away from my dad and you couldn't drop in and say *hello* and let us know you were alright?'

'I had to hide, I'm sorry.'

'Well where did you stay?'

'I have a friend out there, Gordon. He hooked me up with a room to sleep in and got me a job in a kitchen at the steel factory where he works.'

'But why? Why wouldn't you just come home and end our pain and misery? Why the hell would you go to Indiana?'

'I did it for you. I did it for the family. You see about a year before the attacks happened, I took out life insurance. I had been planning for some time to fake my death. But when the attacks happened, it was a perfect moment. I just ran.'

Marty ran away from the building as it crumbled behind him, but failed to stop once he arrived in a safe place far away from the inferno. Nobody noticed as the panic-stricken New Yorkers ran alongside him. They ran *for* their lives, while he ran away *from* his. He tried to jump on a train but all public transport had shut down while the most terrifying events overtook The Big Apple. He hailed a cab and escaped the city.

Arriving in Westchester, he ran into a Wal-Mart and purchased a hoody and jeans; the suit he was wearing had ruined as the rubble tore through the polyester. The white dusting on the black material mirrored a chalk-filled blackboard. Nobody questioned the dusty stranger as they had seen similar sites all day as the public rushed to get home to their families.

Local residents of the suburb approached him, offering assistance and cash. He accepted offers of lifts to other suburbs until he eventually got out of the state. From there, he took Greyhound bus after Greyhound bus to Indianapolis, where his friend, Gordon, picked him up and took him home to Gary.

'So you faked your own death and didn't think to let us know? We were horrified! We couldn't sleep, we couldn't eat. And you were out there building yourself a new life!' Beverly hit his chest with both of her fists and sobbed. 'For years, I prayed to God every night, asking him to bring you home. But now you're here, I wish he'd take you back! Why didn't you call? I feel so betrayed!'

'I was going to tell you when I initially planned it, but when the opportunity came up, I just had to go. I had to get away and telling you would only have led to suspicion. You were never a good liar. That's why I love you.' He stroked her hair but she pushed his hand away.

'And this Gordon guy? What was he getting out of this? Why would he help you?'

'I promised him a cut of the insurance money when it came through, I'm assuming it has done by now?'

Browsing around the living room, Marty knew an apartment like Beverly's didn't come cheap. Gold fibreglass-weaved wallpaper covered the walls, a white marble fireplace formed the focal point of the room and a crystal chandelier hung from the ceiling. Even the red leather couch had a designer name, far above the IKEA models he had slouched on for the past decade.

'Your insurance money never came through.' Beverly smugly replied. 'You forgot to check the small print on the contract. It seems they were used to little scams like yours. They refused to pay out without a body. You never were good with details though, were you?'

'But what about this apartment? Where has this come from?'

Views of Central Park were the most desirable assets in New York. Few could afford it. They were a short walk from the some of the best shops and restaurants in the city and Marty had already spotted a Hollywood movie-star on his morning jog past the tower-block earlier in the day.

'Yeah, thankfully your death did give us access to some money, quite a blessing really, otherwise you'd have wasted ten years of your life.' Beverly's eyebrow arched. 'No, the money you see around you is from the 9/11 Victims Fund. You see you didn't scam some huge evil capitalist corporation. Instead you fooled a fund set up to help genuine victims of the terrorist attacks. Peoples' lives were destroyed that day and you took advantage of that.'

'I'm sorry.' Marty said. 'It seems I can't even arrange a simple insurance plan. I wish I *had* died in there... at least if I had, you would've had a body to claim the insurance with and you wouldn't hate me. '

'Oh… and if Gordon's looking for his cut he can forget it...' Beverly snapped. 'It was all spent on this apartment and I don't plan to give up my home. So I suggest if that's what you've come home for, you should leave.'

'I didn't come back for the money!'

'No? Well what did you come home for? A spare pair of pants?'

If he had, it was pointless; she gave his clothes to a homeless charity months after his death. Her mother pushed her to move on, insisting the best way to get over his death was to clear her husband out of the home. Even if Beverly had wished to hold onto a keepsake, there was little room for Marty's belongings in their tiny apartment in Brooklyn, where they were forced to move after their home was repossessed.

'I came home for you.'

They sat in silence and stared at each other. Conflicted, she didn't know what to do. One side of her head urged her to kiss the man she had longed to be with again. However, the other half wanted to punish him for deserting his family.

'You're a lucky man, Martin Hahn. If it wasn't for the fact that I could lose my home, I would pick up the phone this second and call the police. I'd have no difficulty having you arrested.' The sudden realisation of what she could lose made her nauseous. ‘Excuse me.’

Beverly stood up and ran to the bathroom. Hovering over the toilet, she retched. Her abs hurt as she tried to force the bile out of her stomach. Marty rushed over and rubbed her back but she brushed him off her.

‘Get off me!’ she yelled. Spitting the last of the rancid saliva into the white porcelain bowl, she stood up and dabbed her mouth with a towel. Wiping away the sweat off her forehead, she made her way back into the living room.

‘I hope you’re proud of yourself.’ She threw the towel onto the couch and sat back down. ‘You’ve made a middle aged woman ill.’

‘Can’t you see I did this for you and the kids?’ he said with a broken voice. ‘We were heavily in debt. I didn’t know how long we could go on. Every night I lay awake in fear of the debt collectors coming to repossess the house. We worked every hour God sent just to repay the interest. We were never going to rid ourselves of that debt. I had to do something. I had to secure our future.’

‘And so you just left me to deal with the stress and the repossession myself?’ Beverly asked with folded arms. 'I was lying next to you for all of those nights remember? Wide awake, wondering when the banks were going to throw us out of our home. It was absolute torture when they finally turned up to collect our belongings. You weren't there and I felt utterly powerless! But I didn't run away. I didn't do anything this stupid! Christ, Marty, you're supposed to be the smart one.'

‘It was never meant to be like that.’

‘For the past ten years, I’ve been sat here, night after night, whether I had enough money to eat that day or not, believing that money wasn't everything... that I would give up everything to be with you again. I could live with the debt, the red letter threats and the debt collectors, but I couldn’t live without you. Apparently you saw things differently.’

'I don't know what to say...' Marty held his head in his hands, crushed by the pain he had unintentionally caused. 'It was so hard, knowing that I could just drive home. It nearly killed me. I just wanted to be near you... to just pick up the phone.'

Marty called the landline many times over the years to hear her voice again. As soon as he heard her say '*hello',* he hung up.

'I did it all for you. I did it for the family.'

'You say that, but you haven't asked about any of us so far. Do you even remember your children's names?' Beverly stood up and placed her hands on her hips.

His eyes watered as he considered the children he left behind. He had far from forgotten them. He regularly sneaked a peak at their social networking profiles. However, their locked down privacy settings only allowed him a glimpse of their profile pictures but little else.

'How are Benjamin and Amelia?'

'A little messed up. It's surprising how much the lack of a father in their lives has had an effect on them.'

Marty held his head in his hands and sobbed. Beverly saw how much her description of their broken children hurt her husband and felt the need to assure him that they were OK. Having played the part of bate in her own parents' divorce, she struggled to allow her own children to suffer such a fate.

'Amelia is a supervisor at The Lincoln Hotel where I used to work. She impresses everyone. We think she might be made manager some day.'

A smile of pride overtook his face as he absorbed the news of his daughter's success. Amelia didn't have the academic abilities that her brother had, which had always caused some concern for the family.

'Did she finish high school?'

'We had to take her out of Kings Brook. I couldn't afford the tuition fees with one salary coming in.'

Beverly nervously informed her daughter that she could no longer afford her prestigious education. To her surprise, Amelia was relieved to return to a school where she could be on a level playing field. Furious with his departure however, Beverly held back on Amelia's delight to a disappointed Marty.

'She finished at a state school but she only just passed her exams. The move made it difficult for her to adjust. Not that it had any effect on her later in life. She's done well for herself, considering what she had to go through. I think her biggest problem was that she had to take care of me.'

'Don't say that.' Marty said, frustrated by her self-deprecation.

'She doesn't have that problem anymore. She lives with her boyfriend now. He's a sweet guy. You'd like him. They had a lot in common. They got together after they both lost parents in the terrorist attacks. I don't want to be there when she has to tell him that it's all been a lie.'

'And what about Benjamin?' Marty asked, changing the subject. 'Did he manage to go to Cornell?'

'No, he never made it to college.' Beverly explained. Marty's jaw dropped faster than the Tower of Terror. Following his high school successes, Marty held high expectations for his son to follow his academic aspirations.

'Did he not receive the scholarship?' Marty asked. 'I'll be heartbroken if I failed to get him into university. I'll work every hour God sends to ensure he can attend if he's still able to! Even if he has to go to a state college, I'll help, any way I can!'

'He never applied.' Beverly said. 'You see he was so devastated by what happened to you, he wanted to ensure it didn't happen to others. So he joined the army.'

'Oh wow, so is he like a sergeant or something now?'

'No, he *was* a Private. He's actually just been discharged. He's back in New York after a trip to Iraq.' Beverly looked over at the time, suddenly aware of her son's absence. 'He's currently at a party. He'll be home soon. You can see him if you like.'

'That would be amazing, I don't know whether it would be a good time though, maybe he should settle with the idea before he meets me.'

A mixture of alcohol and psychological traumas, lingering from the army, could make a dissatisfying cocktail if mixed with a resurrected father.

'Oh, so I'll be telling him, will I? Picking up your mess like I have done for the last decade?' Beverly sighed. 'I don't know how I'll break this to them. This is an unbelievable situation. Your absence has damaged our children for years, now your presence is going to do the same.'

'I didn't mean that, I just didn't want to scare them.'

A noise in the corridor outside of the apartment caused them to sit up in fright. A man singing *Moves like Jagger* walked out of the elevators. The volume rose as it grew closer to Beverly's front door.

'It's Benjamin!' Beverly whispered. 'You need to hide.' Marty jumped up. 'Quickly go into my bedroom.' Marty ran into the hallway but became lost in the unfamiliar territory. 'The one on the left!' She attempted to shout in a whispered voice. Marty disappeared into Beverly's room just as Benjamin stumbled through the door.

'Hi Mom!' he slurred. 'You're the best mom ever, do you know that?' He walked over to his mother and hugged her. 'I love you!'

Marty glanced through the gap in the door to see his inebriated son, but could just make out the top of his forehead.

'I love you too, Benjamin, now come on. Grab a glass of water and go to bed. We've got a big day tomorrow, you don't want a hangover for it.'

Benjamin stared at the door, which Marty stood behind. Marty stayed idle, petrified of being caught. Beverly turned around to see what Benjamin was looking at.

'Are you OK, Pumpkin?' Beverly asked, attempting to block his view of the doorway. The drunken veteran stumbled. Helping him up, Beverly took him over to the kitchen. She grabbed a tumbler and filled it with tap water, before edging her son over to his room. 'You have a rest, Son, and I'll see you in the morning.'

As she closed the door, Marty watched her hold her hand over her forehead and sigh in relief. She looked over at the door, which Marty stood behind. He pushed the door back and walked out of her bedroom.

'Is it safe to come out?' he whispered.

'Yes, but you need to go. It's not safe for you to be here. I need to talk to him properly another time and let him get his head around this whole idea first.'

An exhausted Beverly sat down on the couch and laid her head back. Her right hand lifted and she placed the back of it on her forehead and closed her eyes. Marty sat beside her and held her other hand. She turned to him and stared in awe of his presence before rubbing her thumb over his hand.

'My God, Marty I'm so tired.'

'You understand why I did it, don't you? I never meant to upset any of you. I thought I was doing the best I could,' he said. She nodded her head. 'I love you so much, Beverly, I've missed you.'

'I've missed you too.' She looked up and found herself kissing the man she fought with moments before. It was just like the old days. Suddenly everything became so familiar again as he held her. 'Don't leave me alone again.'

Grabbing his hand, she took him to her bedroom and closed the door.

*

An hour later, they lay cuddling in bed. It had been a long time since they had seen each other's bodies and they took great joy in pointing out the parts of each other which had drooped or protruded since they last met. She rested her head on his chest and listened to his heartbeat.

'That was amazing…' she said, struggling to regain her breath. But it wasn't long before guilt etched its way in. 'Nothing's changed though has it?

'What do you mean?'

'Ten years ago, we'd row all evening, make love and pretend it'd never happened. We're doing it all over again. We've learned nothing.'

They rested together, considering the reality of where they had been and where they were now. A million dollars richer and yet no better off. He kissed her forehead, but suddenly he became interested in something she said earlier to their son.

'So what's happening tomorrow?'

'What do you mean?' Beverly asked, pondering over her schedule.

'You said to Benjamin earlier that tomorrow was a *big day*.'

'Oh yeah.' She closed her eyes and rolled off him as she realised which event she would have to endure the following day. 'We've got a memorial dinner tomorrow.'

'A memorial dinner? Who for?'

‘You haven’t realised what date it is, have you?’

'One second...' Marty reached out of bed and grabbed his trousers from the floor. Pulling a ticket from the Greyhound bus he had taken earlier in the day, he glanced at the date. 'September the tenth. What's so special about that?'

‘It’s a memorial gala for the victims of 9/11.’

‘Oh, well that’s ok.’

‘No it’s not, Marty.’ Beverly banged her head repetitively against the headboard. ‘I’m going to have to face the people who supported me through the grief which I never had any right to feel.’

Chapter 6

It had been a wild night. Her head pounded and her eyes stung. Amelia rolled over to her right and found her other half beside her, dribble pouring down from his lips and the stench of beer hit her nostrils as he breathed towards her.

The guilt oozed in. How could she pay her respects to her late father when she felt so nauseous? But it was the task itself which led her to drink to excess. Ten years of attending the functions did not make the experience any easier and she became just as worked up today as she did when she was a teenager.

She slipped out of bed and tiptoed into the spare room, dialling her brother en-route to ensure he arrived home safely the previous evening. Obliterated after downing far too many Jaeger Bombs, Benjamin left Amelia's new home singing loudly the lyrics of Adele's *Someone like You,* as he stumbled down the street towards their mom's apartment.

'Hey Kid,' he groggily answered.

'Oh thank God you got home OK!' Amelia replied in relief. 'Why didn't you take the subway?'

'What? After Mom's experience. No thanks.'

The subway provided a cheaper alternative mode of transportation. Commuters paid the same rate no matter how far they travelled upon it. However his mother's experience would frighten any visitor to New York. Returning home from a late shift at work, a gang of masked thugs mugged Beverly at knife point.

Benjamin decided to walk home instead. It was hard to get lost in New York. The numbered-grid system of the streets allowed anyone walking through the city to be able to establish their location as soon as they reached any cross-roads.

'So how are you today? Still celebrating the good news?'

'Apart from the hangover, I'm still celebrating. It came as quite a surprise, but a good one.'

'When do you plan to tell everyone?'

'I don't know. Seeing both of our families will be at the memorial today, I thought we could bring it up then.'

'You're all grown up, Kid.'

'I wish I could say the same about you!' she cackled. 'How are you today, anyway?'

'I'm a little hungover, but I'll live.' Benjamin explained. 'I was wasted when I got home. Mom had to come and pick me up off the floor.'

'She was still up? That's not like her.'

'Yeah, she'd been up listening to her records and drinking brandy. She was probably nervous. It's a big day today.'

'It is indeed...'

After closing the call with her brother, Amelia walked into the kitchen and found her partner, James, now awake and cooking sausages. He placed the square flat meat onto a muffin and served. Amelia gagged as she breathed in the smell of cooking oil.

'I don't want anything.'

'You need to eat.' James said, pushing the plate towards her. 'We're not going to get another chance until later this afternoon. Eat up, you'll feel better and you need your strength.'

The couple met at school shortly after the attacks. The school offered group counselling for the children affected by the 9/11 events, allowing them to build a network of people who they could count on for support. Amelia and James were in the same school year but had different friendship groups and had little contact before the tragedy. It took James six months to pluck up the courage to ask her out.

James Gates lost his mom on the failed attack in the White House. The passengers of United 93 brought the plane down, preventing the terrorists from crashing into the White House, but the have-a-go heroes died during their attempts. James was on recess in the school playground when his cell phone rang. When he answered, it was his mom. Julie Gates sobbed down the phone as she said her heart-breaking goodbye to her only son. She knew, like everyone else on board that aircraft, that this was her last phone call.

Initially James was dubious about group counselling but his father encouraged him to attend. Agreeing to one session, he reluctantly attended, but took a sudden interest after meeting fellow griever, Amelia Hahn.

Their social status in the playground prevented him from asking her out; she was part of the cool crowd and he… well…. wasn't.

However, with time, as they grew and drew strength from each other, he finally developed enough momentum to ask her out to the movie theatre.

They went to see *Signs,* a film which neither thought was particularly thrilling, but they had it on DVD and occasionally stuck it on to reminisce of their first date.

It hadn't all been plain sailing, especially when Amelia moved from Kings Brook Grammar to a local state school. The distance for them had been tough, but both Beverly and James's father, Ray, knew how strong their friendship had been post 9/11 and did everything they could to ensure they spent time together.

It was almost eleven AM and Amelia had less than an hour to prepare herself for the memorial dinner. She shoved the sausage sandwich down her gullet as fast as she could before running to her bathroom to get ready. On her way to the shower, she checked her handbag to ensure she had the speech, which her mom was due to deliver at the memorial service later that day.

*

Beverly too had awoken with a headache. The midnight glasses of brandy were a bad idea. It wasn't the hangover that was the problem though, it was her husband.

She was supposed to pay respects to the dead man who now lay beside her. Apprehension bubbled inside of her as she braced herself to face the people who had genuinely lost their loved ones.

The smell of *Old Spice* filled the room. When he first disappeared, she took the last of his bottle and sprayed the perfume on his clothes and dressed in his jumpers. Eventually the bottle ran out and since only caught a whiff of her husband's memory when she strolled through Bloomingdales' fragrance department.

Today she took in that sweet scent and knew hc was near. She could feel his soft skin and taste his moist lips. He might appear older, but he was the same man as he was ten years before. His big blue eyes remained so invitingly deep that she could have drowned in them. The tight grip of his hands around her waist was as reassuring as the comforting warmth he provided during the days they spent riddled with debt.

'I'm still angry.' she said. 'I can't believe you've done this to the children. You could have called and let us know you were OK. But what hurts the most, Marty, is that you believed we considered money more important than you, as if our problems would have just vanished if you did.'

The problems remained visible on Benjamin's wrist, where scars still bore. His sister's teeth had repaired, but food continued to torment her. Beverly was hardly a shining beacon of hope herself; she spent her evenings in the company of a bottle of Merlot, occasionally inviting Jose, a man who could barely speak English, back for a late night booty call.

Beverly called for an intervention on their family crisis after hearing her son leave their home in the late evening. Following him out of the house, Beverly found him catching the attention of curb crawlers on Christopher Street. The following evening, she borrowed José's car and drove up the road. Benjamin waved the car over and nearly jumped out of his skin when the window rolled down to reveal his mother.

Upon their return home, Benjamin revealed his attempt to save the family from poverty. With no one to turn to, Beverly spoke to her manager for support. Sandra's brother was a former drug addict but found an outlet in the US Army. She gave Beverly some reading materials to take home for Benjamin, who didn't need much persuasion; it was the perfect way to honour his father and gain some discipline in his life.

The Army also provided college funding for those who served, however Benjamin soon forgot about his academic prospects and became obsessed with stopping the Taliban, who were responsible for his father's death.

Beverly now lay beside the man her son had risked his life for. Morning-after regret swept in. It was nearly time for her to get ready and a rustling from next door suggested Benjamin would soon appear.

'You need to leave!' she said. Marty sat up and rubbed his eyes. 'Benjamin will be awake soon and I don't want you around when he gets up!'

'Do I have time for a shower first?'

Her furious eyes gave him the answer. She climbed out of bed and hid her nakedness with her dressing gown. She held out her hand and pointed towards the front door, nodding her head in the same direction. Marty pulled on his clothes and walked towards the door, which Beverly held open. As he passed, he leaned in to kiss her, but she turned her ahead away. Instead, he reached for her cheek and planted the peck on her pale skin.

'Don't.' she said. 'Just go, quickly. I have to get ready for your memorial service.'

Marty smirked.

'Why are you smiling?'

'Can I come? It's not every day you get an opportunity to see people mourn over you. It would be like attending my own funeral!'

'This is no laughing matter, Marty.' She pushed him out of her bedroom and whispered. 'You have no idea how much hurt and pain we've had to endure these last ten years. Now I'm going to have to face these people and pretend I'm still grieving. Now get out, you're making it harder for me to believe that you're dead.'

Marty walked towards the front door and Beverly followed behind to let him out. As he opened the door, he turned around to face his wife.

'Can I come back tonight?' He reached over and ran his fingers through her fringe, moving the hair away from her moist green eyes.

'I don't know. I think it's best if you just leave us alone. I think you should go away, go back to your life in Indiana. There's no place for you here. I'd love you to stay, but it's not feasible.'

'I can't go back, not now I've seen you. I love you. Please, we have so much to talk about, please see me tonight.'

'OK, OK' she relented. 'But not here, I'll meet you down at Champs at eight. It's a small sports bar, a block away. Now goodbye!'

She pushed the door to shove him out. As the door closed, she heard a familiar voice behind her. It was Benjamin.

'Is that who I think it is?'

Chapter 7

Beverly stared at her son. She stumbled for words, wondering how to answer him, unsure of what he had actually seen. Benjamin stood in his blue and white striped dressing gown and his hair, ruffled with flat patches where it had rested on a pillow as he slept, had grown long since his return home from the army.

'Well then…? Was that who I thought it was?'

'Who do you think it was?'

Her heart pounded and her lip trembled.

'Jose?'

Her shoulders dropped and the colour returned to her face.

'It *was* Jose.' she said. 'He just…' But her son, accustomed to her late night escapades, lifted up his hand and shook it.

'Don't... it's fine. Like… whatever you do with him makes me feel physically sick, but you're a single woman now and you can do what you want in your own pad.'

'I see.' She opened her mouth to say more, but figured the less she said the better.

'Are you ready for your speech?'

The speech, prepared with the help of Amelia, now held a compromised page of lies. Together, they spent two weeks trying to find the right words to give an insight into their lives since their loss, as well as providing the victims a symbol of hope for their own futures.

In the hallway, she opened the cabinet drawer and lifted out the A4 sheet of paper with her prepared words. She was tempted to leave it behind. *Oops forgot it, sorry can't go ahead with it now!* But there was no point; Amelia had a second copy in her own handbag, knowing her mother's habits.

'Please don't remind me. How's your head this morning?' she asked. He was pale and shaking. 'You don't look too perky this morning, Pumpkin. Maybe we should stay home?'

'Don't even think about abandoning this. I feel rough, but I'm ready for today.'

'You need to remember that you've lost a significant mass of your body and you can't drink like you used to.'

'Yeah I know. Anyway, I'm sorry about being so obscene last night when I came home. I feel so embarrassed now I know you weren't alone.'

'What do you mean?' Beverly panicked. Had her cover been blown?

'Jose? I'm guessing he was here when I came back. I bet that was fun for him to hear me singing as I stumbled in. Talk about a mood killer.'

Beverly grabbed her chest in relief and breathed. Her son's surprise entrance the previous evening was comparable to a poor American Idol contestant. She could feel his embarrassment.

'I didn't do the dance, did I?' He put his remaining hand in front of his squinting eyes.

'You were barely able to stand, never mind dance.'

Beverly giggled, but it was false. She contemplated how she could get out of the speech she was due to deliver later in the day. The other dilemma was deciding what to say to her supposedly-late husband when she met up with him later that evening.

*

The memorial took place at The Plaza Hotel. The three musketeers arrived by a chauffeur driven black Jaguar, which had blacked out windows in the passenger seats. While the Hahns lived within walking distance of the grand hotel, the invitation came with luxury travel and Amelia insisted they arrive at The Plaza in style.

As they arrived, the paparazzi greeted them at the entrance. Flash photography blinded Beverly as she stepped out of the car. This year's memorial was a prestigious event, acknowledging the ten year anniversary. The newspapers were filled with stories which still pulled at America's heart strings.

They walked amongst Hollywood's elite, all attempting to gain the right pose; a mixture of respectful sadness with a glimmer of hope. A champagne reception welcomed them at the black-tie event in the grand hallway, before they were taken to the conference suite.

Chandeliers hung down from the high ceilings and gold brocade salon chairs surrounded round tables, covered with white cloths and silverware.

The dinner included a five course meal, with fine wine, canapés and beef so tender that it fell apart at the slightest touch. The Hahns hadn't enjoyed such luxury since Marty's director days when they joined him for board dinners and award evenings.

After the third course, The State Senator, Mick Washington, stood up and walked over to a glass plinth, which sat on the stage before them.

'Ladies and Gentlemen, it's an honour to be here today to meet with the people who have managed to hold so much strength after everything they've been through. Each and every one of you has been impacted by the brutal events of 9/11. Some of you survived the collapse of the towers, while the rest of you have suffered loss. I congratulate you for pulling through during this painful period and putting on a brave face to join us today. You are great ambassadors to the American spirit. As Senator, I can only say how proud I am to have you as citizens of New York.'

The audience applauded as the Senator prepared to introduce his next guest. 'And now we get to speak to one of those inspiring people. Please put your hands together for a woman who raised her two children alone with thousands of dollars of debt after her husband was tragically killed in the towers. She has strived through and we are very fortunate to have her here today. Please welcome to the stage, Ms. Beverly Hahn.'

Beverly rose from her seat with her speech in hand and walked up the steps onto the stage. Her black Gucci dress flowed down to the floor but left her arms exposed. A pearl necklace hung down on her chest, an anniversary present from her late husband. She placed her sheets of paper down on the plinth and looked up at the people before her.

'Lifc has been very hard. When my husband…' she paused, hovering over the next word. '*...died*, we were in thousands of dollars of debt. He was a director but he lost his job. After he was fired, we went from one dead end job to another to try to pay off the interest which we owed to the bank.'

Beverly discussed the day the terrorist attacks occurred, how she watched the towers collapse on television and her last words to her husband. Onlookers reached for tissues as they absorbed her harrowing story.

'The worst part was the waiting. We waited and waited for him to come home or for the police to find a body, but nothing. We never have found his body and so we never really got the closure we needed.'

'But we won't be brought down. We have suffered pain but we have also had joy.' Beverly stopped and stared at her speech. All she saw before her was a page of lies.

The audience applauded to encourage her to continue. She held her head in her hands and wept.

'I have something to tell you...' Beverly broke away from her speech. 'My... my...husband...' she stuttered. The words lingering on the edge of her tongue but failing to make their way down the microphone before her.

In the second line of tables, Benjamin and Amelia clasped hands as they witnessed their mother fall apart on stage. Benjamin dressed in his camouflage uniform, with an arm of his jacket tied up where his limb used to fill. Amelia's navy empire waist dress held a high neck-line but exposed her bronze legs, spray-tanned by a local beauty parlour. A supportive hand stroked her back; James, fitted in a black tuxedo, provided comfort as his girlfriend dabbed her eye with a handkerchief. Amelia placed the tissue down and gripped onto her boyfriend's hand. The three held onto each other tighter than the clench of their stomachs as the awkward atmosphere spilled out over the audience.

Unable to watch her mother fall apart, Amelia stood up and made her way up to the stage. She embraced her, before browsing over the speech to establish whether she could carry on where her mom had paused. Lost in her mother's words, she decided to turn the event around by introducing her own news.

'Like my mom said, we've had a lot of pain but we also have a lot of joy. Since my dad died, I went to a group counselling session where I met my boyfriend. He too felt the pain of loss from 9/11 as his mom was killed that day. Together we got through it. We were just thirteen then. Ten years later we're still together. Yesterday he proposed to me and I said *yes*!'

Amelia turned to her mother, whose tears turned to joy. A standing ovation greeted the pair as they embraced. A member of the audience encouraged James to join his fiancé on stage. The overwhelmed couple, caught up in the moment, locked lips, producing an ecstatic roar from the onlookers. A cluster of cameramen rushed towards the stage, catching the image of hope for America.

Behind, a lost Beverly gripped onto her pearls, more sure than ever that her dirty secret could not be exposed.

*

The five course dinner had merely lined their stomachs. Three hours later, the two families met at Morton's Steakhouse to celebrate the surprise news of Amelia and James's engagement. The Hahn's were joined by James and his father, Ray.

An eccentric artist, Ray's multi-coloured suit and curly red hair led his friends to give him the nickname, *Sideshow Bob.* The Victims Fund pay-out and the sale of his art had made the widower a wealthy man following his wife's death. Ray used his fortune to treat his son and his fiancé's family to the meal and filled the table with wine.

'I believe we need a toast!' Ray said. He stood up and held onto the table for support as the alcohol massaged his head. 'While we remember those whom we have lost, we can today celebrate new beginnings and new friendships.' The tipsy painter gripped onto Beverly's shoulder and smiled.

'I'm so proud of my son. He's been a rock of support over the past ten years. And now I'm lucky enough to gain a daughter too... our dear Amelia, who will soon join the Gates family. We only have to look at her dashing mother to measure whether she'll retain her looks.'

A blushing Beverly hid her face. As she glanced back at the table, she found Ray shooting a wink in her direction. Their spark erupted jeering whoos from their fellow diners.

'Hey, are you guys trying to steal my thunder?' Amelia barked.

'No, no! Hey, this is your night!' Beverly said.

As the wine flowed, her concerns for her husband disappeared. She had plans to be with him in Champs but she decided that it was not a day for the past, it was for the future. The family who joined her now were her future and she did not see Marty Hahn as part of it.

*

Having waited for his wife for over an hour, Marty left Champs. Baffled by her absence, he stopped by her apartment to check on her following their emotional reunion.

The Dakota apartments surrounded a courtyard, used to park up horse drawn carriages by its first residents in 1884. The sandstone exterior raised no more than nine storeys high, yet the building still managed to compete with the skyscrapers for architectural elegance and touristic attention.

Marty approached the arched coach gate. Security guarded the entrance, stepped up since Mark David Chapman murdered the building's most famous former resident, John Lennon. The guard on duty called the Hahns' apartment, but no one answered.

Trying his luck, Marty asked if he could go up to the apartment, but his charming ways failed to impress the guard. Hal was not as easily manipulated as his colleague, Jim, who Marty had charmed the previous evening and had allowed him to enter despite having no identity to prove his residence.

Acknowledging his attempts to infiltrate the building were redundant, Marty stepped away. A familiar laugh penetrated his ears. It was his own, but it had not derived from his own body.

Intrigued, he walked across the road and hid behind a bush in Central Park, peaking out to see who the late night visitor to the apartment was. Walking towards the building he had just exited was Beverly. To her right he could see Benjamin, who had a long coat drooped over his shoulders. Behind his wife, a young woman followed, who he assumed was his daughter, Amelia.

The ladies linked arms with two men, whom he did not recognise. He enviously watched the man holding his wife's arm. They walked into the apartment, passing Hal, who lifted his top hat as he welcomed them into the apartment block.

Once the coast was clear, Marty stepped out of the bushes and looked up to the apartment where his wife lived. The lights came on and a silhouette filled the window, before the closing of her curtains blocked out the action inside.

'Well she might be able to go on pretending everything is normal...' Marty muttered to himself. 'But I'm not going to let go of everything so easily.'

Chapter 8

A hangover struck the soldier for the second consecutive day. Sobriety seemed like a long lost friend to Benjamin, who'd had little time without the comfort of Jack Daniels since his return to New York.

The soldier stared down at the stump where his arm used to attach. Grief overtook him every morning as he woke up and accepted the reality of his fate. This morning was no different; aroused, he reached down with his right side before realising he had nothing to grab himself with. He could still feel the weight of his missing arm like it remained attached to the rest of his body. An itch festered on his elbow, but he found himself scratching the sheets beneath him. It was an optical illusion as he continued to feel the arm, which was no longer visible.

The alcohol put him to sleep, but it was hardly peaceful. Visions of war made it an uneasy rest. Dreams teased him, reuniting him with his lost arm. Anxiety brought him round to a harsh reality in the early hours where he lay until sunrise.

The lack of sleep was the least of his problems. The loss of his friend hurt him much more than the loss of his arm. As a cheating husband and a lousy drunk, Private Michael Ross was far from an honourable soldier, but he saved Benjamin's life and that alone took him to the top of his friendship rank.

The boys raided an abandoned building where they believed members of al-Qaeda were hiding, plotting a threat on the American embassy. Upon entering the shack, grenades exploded and bullets flew across the room. The soldiers dodged the copper missiles for over twenty minutes. With each explosion, the light faded out as the bulbs blew. The gunfire halted as the soldiers disappeared into complete darkncss.

Benjamin walked across the building alone, using a small torch to guide his way. Missing floorboards made it a tough mission, the soldier carefully eased his way past the gaps in the flooring. The only sound he could hear was his own breath. Following his training, he kept his back to the wall at all times, keeping an eye on all angles of the room. He reached a large, visibly empty room and walked into it, keeping his back to the door. Secure with the knowledge that the room was empty, he walked in. The sharp cold of a metal barrel met his temple. A gun, aimed at his head, caused Hahn to drop his own weapon and place his hands in the air.

‘Get down on your knees and pray to your god,’ the enemy demanded. Benjamin obliged and closed his eyes, sure that his time was up. He heard the gun explode, but remarkably he remained conscious. The terrorist beside him fell to the floor and behind him stood his comrade, Private Ross.

'What the hell did you think you were doing, Hahn?' Ross yelled. 'Didn't you learn anything in basic training? First rule: check behind a door to see if anyone's there! You could have been killed, you moron!'

Benjamin remained grateful to his fellow soldier for saving his life. Allowing Ross to step out of the compound drunk became Hahn's biggest regret, however he did not regret following him. He owed Ross his life; an arm was a small price to pay.

He wrapped his robe around himself and walked out into the living room, where he found James's father, Ray, on the couch wrapped up in a sleeping bag. In the kitchen, James filled the coffee machine with beans.

'Fancy a cup of joe?' he asked as he switched on the machine.

'I'd love one.' Benjamin replied. 'I see your dad slept on the couch. That's a relief!'

'They certainly seemed close last night, I was sure something was going to happen.'

'I'm just grateful I haven't seen my mom with two different men in under twenty-four hours!'

'Two men?' James giggled. 'Wow kinky Mrs Hahn!'

'Careful! That's my mother you're talking about. Your future mother-in-law!'

'Sorry, Dude,' he said. 'Last night was fun though and although there were some tears, I definitely had a good time.'

'Yeah that's true, I can't help but thank you and Amelia for that. Your news certainly perked everyone up on what could have been a depressing day.'

While the evening was a joyous occasion, something bugged Benjamin about his mother. She seemed distant for most of the day. Something wasn’t quite right with her. Beverly avoided discussing their father, despite the dedicated day belonging to him.

At times, Beverly appeared to forget her husband had passed. On two occasions she said '*Your father is'* rather than *'was'*. She corrected herself and a look of sadness overcame her face as she realised the mistake.

The front door opened and in walked his sister, wrapped up in her coat and scarf. In her hand she held the *Manhattan Express,* which had a photograph of the loved up couple spread across the front page with the headline '*HOPE*'**.** The papers compared their story to a poppy sprung from a battlefield. They had become the nation's favourite love story. For at least one day, they were as big as Brad and Angelina.

Behind the kissing couple, their mother's teeth shone through the photograph from her glowing smile as she absorbed the news of her daughter's engagement.

'Wow, when are they making the movie?' Benjamin teased. Amelia rolled up the newspaper and hit him on the head with it.

'Cheek, you're just jealous.'

'I'm glad they haven't got any pictures of me. The last thing I need is my ex-girlfriends or school buddies seeing me with this thing.' He lifted his stump, before pointing to a small scarring on his left cheek. 'This ain't too pretty either.'

'Oh like anyone's going to notice that!' Amelia winced, trying to focus on the small disfigurement on his face.

'I notice it.'

'I've offered you my foundation. It'll cover it up in no time.' She reached into her bag, grabbed the pot of make-up and placed it on the bench. Benjamin picked it up and glanced over the application instructions.

'If only I could cover my stump so easily.' He awkwardly laughed.

Beverly walked out of her bedroom. Her entrance woke up Ray, who rubbed his eyes and smiled at the widow.

'Good morning, Beverly.' A red glow covered his cheeks.

'Hi.' Beverly awkwardly replied. 'I didn't know you were still here.' A rustling from the kitchen interrupted their prickly exchange. 'The kids are in the kitchen, let's go and see them.'

They surrounded the island, covered with the front page of the newspaper, which their photograph filled. Ray placed his hand around

Beverly's waist, but she shuffled away. Together as a family, they read the details surrounding the events of the previous day.

True love has come out of America's worst tragedy. Amelia Hahn and James Gates met during a counselling session shortly after the 9/11 attacks on the twin towers. The sweethearts met at high school and today they announced their engagement, ten years after they got together. Gates lost his mother in the United 93 plane crash. While Hahn's father lost his life in the twin towers, his body was never found. The two have since gone onto find true love and they have never been happier. 'While I would never wish anything like this to happen to either of our parents, I'm glad some good has come out of it,' commented 23 year old Amelia. The two announced their engagement at the 9/11 victims gala dinner yesterday where they were joined by the State Senator, Mick Washington. The Senator joined a whole host of survivors and families of the victims who died that day. Washington said he had never been so proud to have so many remarkable people in his city. Answering a question about the young love birds, he wished them a lifetime of happiness.

'Look at that, the State Senator knows you! You're like royalty now!' Ray said and laughed. 'What do you think of that, Beverly?'

'It's great.'

Browsing through the story in the newspaper, the supposed-widow witnessed the blown up photograph of her daughter on the front page and gasped in surprise. In the background she could see herself.

'Thank God I'm smiling,' she thought.

Ray turned over the page where the paper provided a detailed biography of Marty and the family. To the right of the page was Marty's photograph. Glancing at the younger picture, Beverly realised how much he had aged.

'I'm going to go for a walk.' she announced and abruptly picked up her coat.

'I'll come with you!' Ray said.

'No!' Beverly snapped; everyone glanced at her in surprise. 'I mean, no thank you. I'd love some time alone, a stroll through the park to clear my head.'

Ray appeared disheartened, but Beverly did not stick around long enough to view his thwarted face. Grabbing her purse, she ran out of the apartment leaving her baffled children behind.

'Is she OK?' Benjamin broke the silence.

'It's probably all the 9/11 stuff and constantly being reminded about Dad. Keep an eye on her over the next few days.'

*

The golden change of fall did little to uplift Beverly's spirits. The roar of leaf-blowers, clearing the scatterings of autumn, drowned out the birds whistling their calling tune. Skateboarders rolled past, narrowly avoiding the dazed woman, who walked alone through the world's most famous park. It was a quiet escape from the hustle and bustle of the city, allowing New Yorkers to quietly reflect.

She ran to a trash can and vomited. The raw burn rushed down her throat and the putrid stench of bile tickled her nostrils. Exhausted, she rested on a nearby bench and ran her fingers through her damp hair and tightened her coat around her to prevent the chilly shakes from overtaking her fragile body.

'There you are.' Marty crept up behind her from a nearby bush. 'Who was that man you were with last night? Is he your new boyfriend?'

'What? Have you been spying on me? What the hell do you think you're doing?'

A snooping Marty appeared scruffy and smelled like a dumpster. Screwed up newspaper pages filled his coat, mirroring the tramps she avoided on Times Square. 'What happened to you?'

'I had nowhere to go. I had to sleep in the park last night.' Marty explained. 'Why didn't you turn up to Champs last night?'

'I'm sorry, things got a bit carried away yesterday. Amelia announced her engagement and we ended up having drinks with her fiancé and his family. He and his dad were with us last night, and no I don't have a boyfriend.'

'I saw they were engaged. It's in every newspaper this morning. Somebody left one on the bench near to where I slept. She's a beautiful girl.' Marty said. 'I was gutted not to be there last night. I'd do anything to celebrate with you guys. I might as well be dead for all my presence is worth. I can only watch from a distance now, I can't even congratulate my daughter on one of the happiest days of her life.'

'Well that's hardly our fault.' Beverly reminded him.

'No I know. What's he like?'

'Who, James?' she asked and Marty nodded. 'He's a wonderful boy. They've been together a long time.'

'And it was my death that brought them together. You see it wasn't all bad what I did. They'd never have met otherwise!'

'I think a lot more went wrong than right.'

'Oh yeah? Like what?'

Beverly considered what they had all battled in the ten years and didn't know where to even start. It was easier for him to see for himself.

'I think it's time you met your children.'

*

Billie Jean blasted out of the living room speakers. The soles of Benjamin and Amelia's shoes pounded against the oak flooring, spurring their neighbour in the apartment below to bang the ceiling in despair of their disruption.

Beverly entered the living room to find her children recreating Michael Jackson's famous dance moves on their Wii console. With her two arms as an advantage over her brother, Amelia won the dance off.

'Where are James and Ray?' Beverly enquired. They looked up at their mom but they were quickly drawn back to their game.

'They went home.' Benjamin panted as he spoke. 'James has work and Ray had little to stay for after you gave him the cold shoulder this morning.'

'I'm glad I have you two alone, I need to tell you something.' The two stopped dancing and muted the television.

'What is it, Mom?' Amelia asked. Lifting out her hand, she tapped the seat to signal to Beverly that she should sit down next to her, but she remained standing.

'I need to tell you... I...' Beverly grasped for words as she stuttered. 'I can't tell you.'

'Of course you can, Mom, you can tell us anything.'

Beverly looked at her two children who stared back at her with glowing smiles. Her heart raced, aware her news could wipe the optimism off their faces. Her eyes watered and the nausea returned as she took a deep breath, ready to reveal the big secret.

'I think I'd prefer to show you. I had a visitor the other night…' She walked towards the door. The siblings stood up and followed her. 'There's somebody you need to meet.'

'Mom, what is this?' Amelia asked, eager to know who stood behind the door. 'Is this an episode of This Is Your Life?'

Beverly, ignoring her daughter's wit, opened the door to reveal their resurrected father. Benjamin remained silent, clenching his fist, while his sister screamed.

Chapter 9

Marty was a lucky man. If his son had two arms during the moment they reunited, Benjamin would have sent his father to the grave where they believed him to be. Petrified, Amelia hid behind her brother. Unsure if this figure was real, she closed her eyes and gripped onto her mother's hand as she faced the ghost from her past.

'Mom, what's going on?' She wept on her mother's shoulder. 'What's he doing here?'

'I'm sorry, Amelia.' Marty uttered his first words to his children for the first time in a decade. 'Don't be scared. It's me.' He turned to her mother. 'I said you should have spoken to them first before reintroducing me to them. It's not fair to spring this on them.'

'Don't you dare talk to me about fair, Marty.'

A scarred stump poked out of Benjamin's t-shirt, bringing home to Marty the reality of the damage he caused by disappearing from his son's life. 'Oh, Benjamin.'

'You better explain.' Beverly barked.

Attempting to embrace his children, Marty stepped forward, but they jumped back in terror like rabbits approached by a blood-thirsty wolf pack. They used to go to this man for support, but today they ran away from him in fright. A visit from Charles Manson would have been more welcome than this escape artist.

'I'm sorry. There's really no need to be scared,' he said. 'You see, ten years ago we were in so much debt. It was causing so much anguish for the family and I needed to save us. I took out life insurance and when the attacks happened, I saw it as a great opportunity to get away.'

He left a gap of silence to allow his children to respond but they merely remained mute, abhorred by their father's return.

'I wanted to tell you but I figured it would be so much harder for you guys if you knew I was alive. You could have all got into a lot of trouble if you had known. I did it all for you.'

Acknowledging who the real coward was, Amelia stopped crying and walked forward, no longer afraid of the man who escaped his problems.

'You were doing this for us? Yes we needed money but we needed a father more! Where were you when I graduated high school?

Where were you when Mom was forced to sell our home? Where were you when I battled bulimia? Where were you when your own son was renting himself out to perverts so I could go to school with an appropriate uniform?'

Gasps echoed around the hallway as Amelia revealed the grimy secrets behind the aesthetically pleasing front, which they displayed to the world for years. To their neighbours, they had everything, but if anybody dared scratch the surface, they would have a true insight into the dark world of the Hahn family.

Benjamin glared at his sister as she discussed the past, which he wanted to forget. Their mother may have known about his dirty past, but his father was the last person he wanted to inform of his sordid sexual history. A flabbergasted Marty stumbled for words.

'I'm so sorry.' Marty wept. His absence had caused so much pain for those he left behind, but now his presence triggered more damage. The revelations allowed Marty to see the emotional scars, as well as the physical scars, which his son had faced during the past decade.

As furious as a caged leopard, Benjamin stepped forward and raised what remained of his right arm towards his father.

'Look at this! I did this for you.' Marty stared at the gap where his son's arm should have been. 'I joined the army to stop the criminals who caused your death. I wanted to ensure that no child was left orphaned by terrorists again. This was all for you! You ruined my life! I should be teaching History at Harvard. Instead I'm unemployed, have one arm and enough nightmares to make a sequel to The Texas Chainsaw Massacre!'

'Let's go inside.' Beverly intervened. 'Let's not argue on the doorstep, it's rather ungainly.' She tried to usher her daughter away from the hallway and onto thc couch, but Amelia barricaded her access.

'I'm not going anywhere with him. And how long have you known about this? Where did he come from?' Amelia stared at her mother, flabbergasted by her silence. 'Did you know about this all this time?'

'He came round the other night. I didn't know when to bring it up, so I told him to give us a little space until we worked out how to tell you. I didn't know before then, I promise you!' The heat was rising as the tables turned towards Beverly's involvement in her husband's treachery. 'I've only known for a couple of days, I swear.'

'Wait, yesterday morning...' Benjamin said, scratching his stubbly chin. 'You were at the door waving off a guest. It wasn't Jose, was it? It was him! You spent the night with him, didn't you?'

Beverly hung her head in shame. In any other circumstances it wouldn't be so unusual for a woman to sleep with her own husband, but given the extraordinary situation, she could understand her children's horror.

'You deceitful bitch! I can't believe you stood there yesterday pouring your heart out to the victims of the terrorist attacks after making love to the man you claimed died in it! You sicken me! I need to get out. I need to go now!' Amelia grabbed her coat and purse and scowled at her parents. Benjamin followed shortly behind.

'Please don't go!' Beverly pleaded.

'I'll go. Don't leave on my account. It's me who's caused the trouble. I'll leave.' Marty intervened.

'No you stay here and continue your sordid relationship. We'd hate to be in the way. I don't wanna be near either of you right now. I wish you were dead, at least then I could still look back on my childhood and have fond memories of my father. Don't ever come near me again!'

The siblings stormed out of the apartment, slamming the door behind them. Beverly threw her hands in the air in frustration. She shook her head at her husband and returned to the living room before crashing onto the couch. Marty joined her and put his arms around her.

'What have we done?' She sobbed into her husband's arms. 'We've ruined their lives.'

'It was me that put them through this, not you. You've done nothing wrong.' He kissed her forehead.

Lost for words, Marty struggled to comprehend the destruction he had caused. While he imagined the army would have left behind an amount of emotional distress, he had failed to contemplate the life-changing injuries his son had faced. He had seen Benjamin twice since returning to New York; his distorted vision on both encounters caused him to miss the complications forced upon him from the army.

'They hate us.' Her shoulders shook as she wept. She placed her head on her husband's lap, suddenly finding his presence comforting.

‘They’ll come around. It’s me they hate, not you. They’re just angry with you. I’m the one who destroyed their lives.’

‘Every night for years, I prayed you’d come home, hoping you had lost your way. I hoped you would somehow find your way back. I prayed I would open the door and you would be there. I dreamt the children would be ecstatic that their father had returned. I knew it wouldn’t be easy, but I never envisioned it would ever be this painful.’

'It will get better, I promise you.' Marty assured, but his commitments fell flat on his wife, who had been let down far too often by Marty. She ignored his promises and invited him to lie with her. Together they cuddled until they fell asleep, allowing a temporary escape away from their problems.

*

Max Spielberg took the evening off work to have dinner with his wife. They'd had little time to catch up over the previous weeks as his exhausting schedule took over. The glamorous efforts she had made for her husband sparked a moment of guilt for his recent absence.

His role as senior reporter at the Manhattan Express had been tough over the previous weeks as they led up to the anniversary of the September 11th terrorist attacks. The annual date was already a big deal, but the tenth anniversary, as expected, caused a media storm.

Max had reported for the paper for eleven years. When he first entered the business, his reports went unnoticed by his manager. He failed to make an impression on any of his superiors and required a big story to ensure his reports were recognised within the organisation.

The newspaper was a small production and the readership reached a tiny population in The Big Apple. Pressure to reach a wider audience increased with every story written. Their competitors, The New York Times, had achieved success across the USA, rather than just the surrounding areas of newspaper's production office.

Max’s big break came along after the New York attacks. He ran a biographical edition focusing on the victims. His tribute was well received and his manager had since put him in charge of all September 11th news pieces. While the paper had done little to pull in more than the Manhattan and Brooklyn population, they continued to dream of the headline story, which would reach beyond New York State. Max

Spielberg was determined to get his hands on that story.

Light jazz played in the background and a candle-light shimmered on the table between them. Spielberg drooled over his wife's revealing red dress, which showed off her tanned legs and large chest. Her black hair was curled and drooped down to her shoulders. She was far too good for him.

While he still had a head of hair, a slim physique and few wrinkles for a man approaching forty-eight, Max remained a very average looking man, who sparked little attention from the opposite sex. Only his name and career choice had generated any interest in the mundane man, until he moved to New York. The city was a place where few people had what outsiders defined as a *normal* career and his exotic name blended in amongst the Kylies and Bensons who inhabited the island.

As their main course arrived, Max became distracted by a fellow diner. A woman entered the restaurant, dressed in a palatinate blue dress, which drooped down to the floor. Her arms were bare and she wore a dazzling pearl necklace.

Max recognised the diner from the gala dinner he attended just a day earlier. He witnessed her on stage in the same pearls, pouring her heart out over her late husband, but perked up following the news of her daughter's engagement.

The lady dined with a gentleman dressed in a blue tailored suit with silver pinstripes. The widow made no reference to a new romance as she discussed her own hope of future happiness in her speech the day before. Max watched the pair as they sat down, already developing in his head a new story of hope for the people of New York; *The Widow Who Found Love Again* would pull at his readers' heartstrings.

Feeling to the side of his pocket, he grabbed his cell phone; the device had a camera, which was as good as some of the modern digital ranges. His wife insisted that he left his professional equipment at home. The journalist fulfilled her wishes but kept his phone with him just in case. A story could crop up anywhere.

'Are you paying attention to me?' Moira asked. His eyes had wondered as she filled him in on her sister's illness. 'What did I just say? You weren't even listening, were you?'

'Sorry Hunny, I need the rest room.' He stood up and left his wife appalled.

Max walked away from Moira and made his way around the restaurant, keeping his eye on the table, which he hoped would make his next tribute a fulfilling one. The gentleman who joined the 9/11 widow had his back to Max throughout the meal, but he was now in full glimpse of him. Max recognised him.

He struggled for a moment to figure out where he knew this man from. Was he at the memorial too? No. But then he remembered...

He was a little older than the last image Max had seen of him, but it was definitely him. The Manhattan Express would make its' first exclusive story the following morning, which would hit the headlines all over the world, not just in Manhattan. Max took out his mobile phone and captured a photograph of Beverly and Marty Hahn.

Chapter 10

Amelia had little sleep. She tossed and turned all night, reliving the unwelcomed reunion with her father. It's what she had always dreamed of, but now he was here…

'Are you OK?' a disgruntled James asked, disturbed by her shuffling.

'I'm fine.'

'Are you sure? You seemed restless. Is something on your mind?'

'No.' Amelia sharply said. 'I'm fine.'

'You can tell me, you know? We're going to be married soon, we have to tell each other our problems.'

'I told you I'm fine.' Amelia snapped.

'Fine.' James rolled over in a huff, leaving Amelia to stare at the ceiling, now concentrating on how to remain still, as well as how to deal with her problem.

The previous day, she'd met with Benjamin in a bar downtown. They discussed their options as they came to terms with their predicament. Should they call the police? No, Mom would lose the money. Should she tell James? No, their entire relationship was founded on Marty's death; now he was alive, what did it mean for them? And how would he react? His mother died in the attacks. What would stop him seeking revenge and blowing their cover? It was a minefield.

As the sun rose, she escaped the apartment, avoiding a further grilling from her fiancé. A peaceful morning stroll did little to clear her head, if anything New York's unusual silence forced her to listen to the thousand voices in her head.

She walked down to 7-Eleven to purchase a bite to eat and the Manhattan Express. Folding the paper in half, Amelia engaged in friendly chit-chat with the shop assistant.

She waved goodbye to the shopkeeper and walked over to Christopher Park, a green area of the city, resurrected as a tribute to the LGBT community of Manhattan following the prejudice they received in the city. It was a quiet park and Amelia enjoyed the silent ambiance, although it remained tainted by her brother's part-time job during his teenage years. Benjamin had subjected himself to child prostitution just yards away from her favourite hotspot.

Passing a statue of a loved-up lesbian couple, she found a bench to perch on. She lifted the newspaper out of her plastic bag, which stored her breakfast donut and a can of cola. She unravelled the paper, wiping her hands as the ink rubbed off onto her flesh.

A recent photograph of her parents on the front page, feeding each other canapés, covered the front page. Above them sat the headline 'BACK FROM THE DEAD!'

*

Beverly and Marty cuddled up on the couch and drank coffee as they watched their favourite television presenter interview one of the most influential billionaires. Dressed in only their robes, they rested like it was 1998, when all their problems were far away.

Their bliss had been mildly marred by the arrival of their son, who walked in on them kissing the previous night after dinner. He sneered at his snuggly parents and stormed to his room.

'He's very quiet.' Beverly said. He hadn't left his room since their encounter the previous evening. 'Too quiet.'

'He's in shock.' Marty replied. 'I'm surprised you're not more concerned about Amelia. She yelled at us.'

'But at least she's vocal. We know what's going through her head. Benjamin's a fragile guy, I'm concerned.'

'He's ex-army. He's dealt with a lot worse in his short life and the army instils a calm nature in soldiers so they can remain composed in the face of adversity.'

'You think he's OK?' Beverly asked, desperate for re-assurance.

'I think he'll be just fine. He needs time and space away from us. He'll come around.'

The interview finished and abc news was due to follow. They switched the television off and moved to the kitchen to brew up a fresh pot of coffee. The couple sat on stools surrounding the island in the centre of their kitchen and smiled longingly at each other.

A banging on the front door distracted the couple. The forceful fists, hammering against the entrance, pounded harder with every minute that passed.

Fearing for his safety, Marty ran to his wife's bedroom and hid while she went to see who had caused the disturbance. Beverly peered through the spyhole and saw their daughter, Amelia, who appeared ready to overthrow a government.

A landscape A4 photograph of herself and her husband in a restaurant together greeted Beverly as she opened the door. She gasped as she witnessed the headline and grabbed the newspaper out of her daughter's hands.

'What were you thinking?' Amelia raged. 'Do you wanna get arrested, you stupid woman?' Beverly struggled to hear Amelia's rants as she absorbed the information below the photograph.

9/11 widow, Beverly Hahn, has been spotted in a fine dining restaurant with the man she claimed had died in the twin tower attacks. Hahn, 55, claimed her husband, Marty, had evaporated in the World Trade Centre in 2001, however these photographs of her in a New York bistro with her husband were taken just hours ago. Hahn, just weeks before, received a large pay out of one million dollars from the 9/11 Victims Fund, which, given her husband's sudden appearance, suggests the family were taking part in an insurance scam. Beverly, just twenty four hours before this photograph was taken, gave an emotional speech to the victims of 9/11, discussing the pain of her loss. Their daughter, Amelia, made yesterday's Manhattan Express headlines as she and her fiancé, James Gates, had found love after they both lost parents in the attacks. Whether Amelia and James were aware of Marty Hahn's schemes is another matter to be investigated.

'Thanks for getting me and James involved too by the way. I hope you two are happy with yourselves.'

'Hunny, we won't let anything happen to you. We'll explain.' Beverly said.

Marty re-entered the living room, convinced he was safe in Amelia's company, despite her hostility.

'You have some nerve coming here. Do you know what you've done?' Amelia drummed her finger into his sternum.

He joined his wife and read the contents of the newspaper, placed over the dining table in the kitchen. Witnessing the photograph on the front of the paper, he gasped.

'How the tables have turned.' Beverly sighed. 'Just twenty-four hours ago, we were heroes. Now we're crooks.'

'We need to leave.' Marty said. He looked up at his wife and awaited a response, but she remained silent. 'We need to leave now before the police arrive.'

'What do you mean '*we'?* I'm not going anywhere!' Beverly insisted. '*I* haven't done anything wrong. It was *you* who fooled the world and your own family. I was blissfully unaware you were alive for the past decade.'

'And do you think anyone will believe you when you've been photographed having dinner with me? They're going to take everything off you. We need to go before they arrest us.'

He ran to Beverly's bedroom and rammed essentials into a bag. With little time to shower before the police arrived, he pulled on the dirty clothes, which lay on the floor from the night before. Beverly turned to her daughter, hoping she'd have the answers.

'You're not considering going with him, are you?' Amelia asked.

'What should I do? You're the smart one in the family. Sure, Benjamin can pass any exam, but you're street-smart. Help me, Amelia. Tell me what to do.'

'You have to stay and explain to the police what you've done. If you run away, you'll be accused of knowing all along about his crimes. You have to stay, if for nothing else, to ensure Benjamin and I are not accused of being entangled in your web of lies.'

Marty ran around the apartment filling his bag with anything he could get his hands on. Despite having no confirmation from Beverly over her decision to stay or go, he packed a bag for her too.

A torn Beverly stood staring at her daughter while her estranged husband ran around her. She looked left to right as if she was at a tennis match, but now she was unsure of which player to back.

'Do you have any cash in the bank left, or is it all bricks and mortar now?'

'It's all about the money once again, isn't it, Dad?'

'I have just over one hundred grand in the bank.' Beverly said. Amelia threw her hands in the air and shook her head.

'Are you serious?' Amelia cried.

'Perfect.' Marty ignored Amelia and continued the planning

with his wife. 'That should be just enough. We need to empty your account and get the hell out of here. Now come on, you need to get dressed if we want to go before the police arrive.'

Beverly grabbed her daughter and kissed her on the cheek.

'I'm sorry, Hunny, I have to go. I have nothing to stay for.'

She rushed over to her bedroom, whipped off her dressing gown and grabbed her clothes. Unfazed by her mother's nudity, having lived together for years, Amelia followed her into the bedroom.

'Nothing to stay for? What about me? What about your son?' Amelia pulled at her own hair, stressing over her mother's decisions. What had this imposter done with her mom?

'I know you'll be OK, but what about me? I can't sit and watch them take everything away from me again. I've seen it happen before and I can't see it again. I'll be in touch when it's safe again.'

Beverly pulled a navy sweatshirt over her head, completing her outfit suitable to rob a bank, before supporting her husband with the bags.

'Do us both a favour and don't bother getting back in touch.' Tears streamed from Amelia's eyes. 'I don't want to see you ever again.'

Unable to look at the woman who betrayed her, Amelia stared out of the window. Below her, the flashing blue lights of a police car caught her attention.

'If you're leaving, you'd better go now. The cops are here.'

'You gotta be kidding me.' Marty ran over to the window to confirm Amelia's claim. A white car, stamped with the letters NYPD on the side, parked on the curb beside their apartment. 'She's right, we need to go.'

'I love you, Hunny.' He tried to touch her but she pulled away. 'I'm so sorry this is happening and I'm sorry I hurt you.'

Amelia shrugged her shoulders.

'There's no point in doing this. I said my goodbyes to my dad at his funeral three years ago. You're not my father. My dad's dead.'

Her words remained lost on a distracted Marty, who continued to glance around the apartment, ensuring they had everything they needed.

'You're really going then?' Amelia turned to her mom, who walked over and placed her palm on Amelia's arm.

‘Please let me go, Pumpkin. I love you so much. Forgive me.’ Her eyes flared up with bloody red blotches as she held back the tears. She wrapped her arms around her daughter but her embrace went unrequited.

'I can see you've already made up your mind. Thanks a lot, Mom.' She folded her arms and turned towards the window, shutting out her mother.

'Come on, Beverly.' Marty insisted.

'I need more time.' Beverly begged. 'I don't know if I should go. I can't leave her.'

'We need to go now.'

‘Just go.’ Amelia said. Beverly squeezed her daughter's shoulder, grabbed her bag and followed Marty out of the apartment.

‘Mom!’

Beverly turned around.

‘Good luck.’ They smiled at each other before Beverly turned around and walked out of the door. The door slammed shut and Amelia broke down in tears.

The apartment had never seemed so empty. As she sat on the floor grasping onto her stomach, aching over the loss of another parent, a knock at the door paused the emotional agony. Had they forgotten something? Had they changed their minds?

She stood up, wiped her eyes and opened the door. Two police officers greeted her.

‘Can we speak to Beverly Hahn please?’

Chapter 11

Out of the fire escape, Marty and Beverly ran for their freedom. Their infamy remained lost on those who rushed by, eager to get to work, ignoring the runaways with their life belongings in hand.

Two armed police officers perched on the corner of 73rd and Columbus Avenue. The Hahns inconspicuously walked up behind the officers.

'Hey! Isn't that the guy from the news?' A tourist, kitted out with a Statue of Liberty hat and a novelty map of the city, pointed at Marty. The officers turned around to see who the pedestrian was pointing towards. 'It is! It's that guy who faked his death!'

The officers turned to each other and nodded before approaching the suspect. The screeching of wheels diverted their attention. A yellow school bus, filled with minors, swerved off the road. The hood of the vehicle crunched upon impact with a fire hydrant. Water sprung into the air as the faucet burst, forcing the officers to rush over to the incident.

With the officers momentarily distracted, Marty hailed a cab and dragged his wife inside the car.

'That was fortunate.'

'What have we become, Marty? We're running away from the police!' Beverly panted, exhausted from the run. 'Where are we going anyway?'

'We need cash, so to the bank.' The driver took them to the nearest Chase branch where Beverly held an account. She got out of the car, and with her passport in tow, she walked in to empty her savings. Marty waited in the car; enough people had witnessed the return of the dead man over the last couple of days.

A marble arch formed the entrance of the bank, leading into the grand atrium, lit up a by glass dome rising high above the financial activities below. Rows of cubicles lined the room, providing a private space for consumers to sign away their assets in exchange for loans, and a steal door protected the millions of dollars, which the building had enclosed.

A long line of customers queued to seek financial support, allowing Beverly to find time to compose herself before approaching the cashier. She was drenched from the water, which rained down from the exploding fire hydrant. She impatiently tapped her foot with every minute that passed. The queue disintegrated and Beverly nervously handed her debit card and passport to the cashier.

'I'd like to withdraw all the money from my account please... in cash.'

Beverly looked around her nervously. A lump lodged in her throat as the cashier checked her identification and account details on the computer.

'One moment, Mam.' The cashier stepped away from her desk and spoke to her colleague, who glanced over at Beverly as they mumbled. The runaway turned a ghostly pale of white. After several interchanges, the cashier returned.

'Mam, we need seven days' notice to provide that amount in cash. We can write you a bankers draft if you would like?'

'I really need the cash now. How much can I withdraw?'

'May I ask why you need the money, Mam?'

'I need a deposit for a holiday home in the Hamptons. I'm buying it with a friend and we would prefer to pay in cash.'

'I'm afraid the most we can offer you today, Mam, is five thousand dollars. We just can't give you the amount you requested in cash at this time.'

Beverly wanted to argue, but she worried that causing a scene would lead to unwanted attention from the cashier, whose glasses hung off her nose, glaring at the dodgy customer. There would be little chance to take on any cashier, regardless of size, as they hid behind bullet proof glass with just a small gap to hand over cash and identity papers.

'I'll take it,' Beverly relented. The cashier began to tally up the cash. Minutes dragged on as the cashier counted each one hundred dollar bill separately. 'Is there no quicker way of doing it? I trust you can give me the correct amount.'

She anxiously looked at her watch.

'I have my husband outside in a cab and I'm concerned the metre's on. It's going to cost us a fortune.'

'I'm sorry, Mam, we have to do this correctly. We can get into big trouble if we don't provide the right amount.'

Beverly sighed and waited for the cashier to count the cash. A policeman walked in and Beverly's heart beat faster.

Fifteen minutes later, the cashier finished counting the money and handed it in a small sack to the customer.

'Here you go, Ms Hahn, all the money we can provide you today. Is there anything else we can help you with? We have some excellent mortgage rates if you're interested in buying property.'

Beverly shook her head, bewildered by the offer of the loan, before recollecting her lies. A mortgage would come in handy if she planned to buy a house in the Hamptons.

'I'm fine, thank you.' She signed for the money and poured the cash into her purse.

'You should really come in soon and update your details, now that you've remarried.' the cashier explained.

'What do you mean?' a baffled Beverly asked.

'You said earlier your husband was waiting outside. We have it on file that you're widowed. You should really allow us to update your details soon, for security purposes. Please bring in your marriage certificate.'

Beverly kicked herself. Of course the bank had her listed as *widowed.* She had to have her husband taken off when he supposedly died.

'Will do.' Beverly smiled and hurried out of the bank. She looked around for her husband. A honk to the right of her caught her attention and she found her husband waving to her on the side of the road in the yellow cab. Eager to escape, she jumped in the car.

'Did you get the cash?'

'I could only get five grand.' she explained. 'I figured it would hold us off for now. Where are we going?'

'I figured we'd go out-of-state. We'll catch a bus across to Indianapolis. There isn't a direct route so we'll have to get off and change somewhere but we'll work it out.'

Beverly followed the same footsteps her husband took when he made his original escape ten years before. He had become the expert and now Beverly was joining him as his accomplice. Together they ran from their problems, but this time neither of them expected a pot of gold at the end of the rainbow. With just the cash in Beverly's bag, they escaped New York City as fugitives.

*

The neighbours huddled outside the Dakota building, speculating over the building's unexpected visitors. The NYPD vehicle outside spurred gossip throughout the tower as the inhabitants questioned which apartment had rocked the peace of the respectable residence. Excitement turned to fear as they questioned if the visit would knock the value of their homes. Inside, two policemen questioned Amelia.

‘So where is your mom?’

'She's just out with a friend for lunch.' Amelia explained. 'She'll be back shortly.'

‘So you weren't aware that your father was alive?’

Amelia shook her head. ‘Astonished.’

She played up to the shocked daughter who knew little about her mother’s secret. It was an easy part for her to portray as it had been just twenty-four hours since she found out herself.

Avoiding intense questioning, she offered to make the policemen a pot of coffee. As she brewed the beans, she quickly hid the newspaper, which outlined her mother’s crimes.

‘When did she say she’d be home?’

‘She said she’d be back later this afternoon. I saw her earlier and she seemed her normal self. She was just happy to be meeting her friend.’

'Do you know who this friend is?'

'Just someone from college. I don't know her name.'

‘Did she have any bags or documents with her?’ The policemen looked around for any evidence that Beverly could have escaped. Amelia shook her head.

‘Listen, this is very out of character for my mom so I struggle to believe she knew anything. She’s also incredibly vain and wouldn’t go anywhere without her hair curlers, so if she is planning any form of escape with my father, she would definitely come back to the apartment first.’

‘Very well, Miss Hahn.’

Above the fireplace hung a clock, mimicking Salvador Dali's melting masterpiece. Amelia repeatedly glanced at the art-piece, calculating the distance of her parents.

‘Are we keeping you from something?’ the officer asked.

'I promised my fiancé I would be home soon.’ she lied, smiling at the officers. 'I live downtown. We've got a lunch date to attend.'

The clinking of keys and the rustle of the lock interrupted their line of questioning. The door opened, revealing Benjamin, who turned pale as he clasped his eyes upon the unexpected visitors.

'Officers!' He scanned the apartment for his parents. 'Is this to do with my parents?'

'It is indeed. I take it you're aware of your father's return?'

'Yeah but we only found out yesterday, didn't we, Amelia?'

'Oh that's funny, Mr Hahn, as your sister has just informed us that she didn't know he was back. Maybe you would like to make a visit down to the station with us, Miss Hahn?'

*

It was later in the afternoon when James woke up. It had been a long night; he finished work late and his fiancé shuffled all through the night. He finally managed to drift off when she left the apartment earlier in the morning.

'Amelia?' Silence met his calls. He smiled, feeling rather chuffed that he finally had control over the remote. No trashy reality TV for him today.

The top of the foot-board on his bed opened and out raised a plasma television. It slowly lifted out until the entire screen was visible. The television switched on, and before James could turn the channel over to watch his afternoon fix of Ellen, a news caption on CNN drew him into the headline story.

The article covered an incident in New York. He recognised the apartment as he had been there just twenty-four hours before.

The news anchor discussed the story of a 9/11 insurance scam, whereby a family had faked their father's death to scam money out of the victims fund. James watched on with interest.

Staring at the screen, he witnessed live coverage as the production crew waited for the con-artists to make an appearance. He gasped in horror as he caught a glimpse of armed police escorting Amelia and Benjamin out of their apartment.

'They must have it wrong!' he shouted at the screen. The news cut to the photograph, which the Manhattan Express published earlier that morning. Repulsion overtook him as he realised the family he had trusted for the past decade had deceived him.

Chapter 12

On 153rd, East 67th Street, the New York City Police Department Station opened its' doors to the public. The station sat suitably next to a nursery school, set up to educate children with learning difficulties. It was a blessing for the school to have a police department located nearby as gun crime remained uncontrollable in the state and an increase in classroom related incidents spurred citizens to question the laws on the sale of weapons.

Inside the station, Detective Lynwood Grisham and his colleague, Detective Jodie Green, questioned Amelia. The pair had spent the morning investigating her involvement in her father's insurance scam. The NYPD were searching all over the city and beyond for the convicts who were now on the run.

'Miss Hahn, please can you tell us when you first became aware that your father was alive?' Detective Grisham led the questioning.

'I only found out yesterday. My mom brought him home and said she had a surprise for us. It certainly was a surprise but it wasn't exactly a nice one.' Amelia held her head in her hands. 'I'm furious with her for leaving me to deal with this. I wish I hadn't let her run away.'

The room held no windows and just a small blue bulb hung over them, providing little light. The atmosphere was intense. Long periods of silence sprouted an eerie chill upon the suspect, with the movements of the rolling cassette player providing the only sound as it captured every word Amelia uttered.

'So when one of our law enforcement officers saw you this morning, why did you say you had no idea that your father was still alive?'

'I was scared, I could get into trouble. I knew about it for twenty-four hours but hadn't said anything. You have to understand I was still trying to get my head around the idea that my dad was alive after all these years. I was all over the place and couldn't decide what to do.'

'Where has your father been hiding?' Detective Green quizzed.

'I really have no idea. I was so angry, I didn't give him much time to tell me.'

'Do you have any idea where they planned to go?'

'I really don't.' Amelia assured. 'They left in such a hurry when the newspaper exposed them. We have family in California and Chicago, I guess they could be heading to either of those places.'

'Do you have any indication as to how long your mother knew about your father's scam?'

'She said she'd only known a couple of days.' Amelia sat quietly with her thoughts, considering everything her mother had said and done over the past decade. Had it all been a lie? Was her mother really that good of an actor?

'Listen, this is totally out of character for her. You have to believe me when I say that she was no wiser than we were. Her head is all over the place at the moment. She'll come around and come home. She's a desperate woman in love and I don't think anyone can blame her for running away with him.'

'That may be so, Miss Hahn…' Detective Grisham explained, '…but we'll be the least of her worries when she's found. The citizens of New York are going to be incredibly bitter that this so-called *victim* has taken advantage of one of the most horrific events in US history. I certainly wouldn't like to be the one to face the public after what she and your father did.'

*

The white walls appeared blue under the reflection of the dim glow. The grey glimmer of clay peaked through where a thin layer of paint had chipped. Trapped within the fading décor, Benjamin awaited interrogation.

He received a negative vibe off Detective Grisham, concerned that he hid a deeper interest in his father's scam. He wasn't far wrong; Grisham was on duty that day. Having lost colleagues and friends in the attacks, the detective was horrified by Marty's ability to take advantage of the tragedy for his own personal gain and would ensure he paid a hefty price for his crimes.

Grisham looked at the veteran before him, surprised that a man who had faced the front line of suffering for his country could end up involved in this exploitation of the very nation he risked his life to save. He stared at the stump, where Benjamin once held an arm, and saw that he had suffered.

'So you've been living in the same apartment as Beverly Hahn and had no idea she was seeing your father? That doesn't sit right with me.'

'I found out two days after my mom did, the same day as my sister. He had apparently been in the apartment when I was there, but I was too drunk or asleep to notice. I was out at a party on the night he returned.'

The veteran displayed little emotion as he defended his role in his father's deceit. He caught a glimpse into the passion behind the detective's role in protecting the city and decided to play on their shared calling.

'Officer, as you can see from my appearance, I'm a man who has served in the army. I gave up my dreams of going to college and spent four years in Iraq to stop those people, who I believed had killed my father, from destroying any more lives. Now believe me, I'm just as pissed as you probably are right now that his death was a lie. The last few years of my life have been a complete waste of my time and I'd be grateful if you didn't waste any more of it.'

Grisham could see the man before him was telling the truth; his story matched his sister's and empathised with his need to protect the city he grew up in. He could smell a criminal a mile away and Benjamin Hahn was not one of them.

'You're free to leave, Mr Hahn.' Benjamin thanked the officer, stood up and made his way to the exit of the interview room.

'Hey buddy!' the detective called and the suspect turned around. 'You may have joined for the wrong reasons but you have certainly not wasted your time in Iraq. You boys have done a tremendous job over there and I, for one, am grateful. So thank you.'

Benjamin nodded his head and raised a slight smile. Their jobs were very similar and it was an honour to hear a man, who spent every day defending his city, compliment him on a good job. With his faith restored in his duties in the Middle East, Benjamin raised his left arm, saluted the detective and left the station.

*

Max Spielberg celebrated throughout the night. While he was in the dog house with the wife after he abandoned her at the dinner table on her birthday, he was certainly in the good books with his boss. In the office, they celebrated his success with champagne and canapés, but his work was far from over.

They only had a small piece of the pie so far and Max wanted it all. If the police got to the escapees first, the newspaper could miss out on a potential exclusive. There could be enough material to write a book.

Max had little sleep the previous evening. By six AM, he was outside the apartment waiting for the couple to appear. The daughter approached the apartment in the early hours. The reporter snapped up the action, intrigued by her involvement in this theatre of treachery.

His excitement of an exclusive was compromised when the police turned up. Spielberg feared his dream of publishing his first book was over, but his optimism restored when he witnessed the fugitives sneaking out of the fire escape.

'Now we have a story...'

Three hours later, he travelled on a coach heading towards Harrisburg, Pennsylvania. Mid-Atlantic views of the Great Lakes spell-bounded the commuters on the coach as they travelled towards the state capital.

Max Spielberg's interests drew away from the picturesque postcard sites which the Quaker State had to offer. His attention focused on the couple sat two seats in front. He watched Beverly and Marty Hahn as they slept, blissfully unaware that they hadn't quite escaped all of their New York demons.

Chapter 13

After a tiring day at the police station, Amelia returned home. The exhaustion ploughed her down, both physically and emotionally. Just forty-eight hours before, they celebrated her engagement, but now her life had turned up-side-down.

'I wish I'd called the police.' Amelia told her brother of her regrets upon leaving the station. 'If I'd called them in the first place, I wouldn't be a suspect, Mom would be home and that bastard of a father would face the consequences for destroying our family.'

Amelia entered her apartment alone. She had only inhabited the place for a couple of weeks but it already felt like home. As she walked through the front door, the silence brought a pleasant surprise to a fatigued Amelia.

'James must be out' she thought. She sat down on the couch, rested her head back and closed her eyes, grateful for the opportunity to relax and gather her thoughts before facing the difficult task of breaking the news of her father's return to James, if he hadn't heard already.

They lived in a small apartment but it was enough for the engaged couple. While she had to reduce the feminine charms in her new home, James allowed her to keep the fluffy pink cushions and pot-pourri filled bowls in the living room, taken from her Brooklyn abode.

'They let you out then?'

Amelia jumped up and turned around in surprise. She found her fiancé stood in the doorway of their bedroom, leaning against the wall. 'You made quite the news story today.'

'James, I didn't realise you were home. It's been one hell of a day.' She patted the seat next to her on the couch, encouraging James to join her. He walked into the lounge but refused to sit next to her. Instead, he perched on a seat opposite, using a coffee table as a barrier.

'I think you have some explaining to do.' James sat back and folded his arms. She sighed; she'd already had one grilling today, she wasn't quite ready for another.

'Yesterday, shortly after you left my mom's, she came home with a surprise for Benjamin and I: my father.' She broke into tears as she told her side of the story. 'I... I don't know how to explain what's happened. But basically he's been pulling some insurance scam for the past ten years and he's come home to claim the money.'

‘I just can’t believe you’ve been lying to me for all these years.’

‘No, James, I haven’t. I promise! I knew nothing about it until yesterday.’ Amelia pleaded, bouncing onto her knees and lifting her hands up as if in prayer. He saw the despair in her eyes as she begged for his trust. Accepting her honesty, he walked over and embraced her.

‘I’m sorry, it’s just when I saw you being arrested on the news, it ripped me up inside. I saw our entire relationship, all those counselling sessions, every memorial and every moment we spent aching over the deaths of our parents and thought that suddenly it was all a lie.’ They held each other for several minutes while she sobbed into his chest. ‘Come on, you’ve had a long day, let’s watch some television.’

They lay on the couch, spooning as they watched an episode of their favourite sitcom, *How I Met Your Mother.* When it finished, Fox News came on the television airing the day’s headlines.

'Urgh, can we avoid the news. I've seen enough for one day.' Amelia asked. The doting boyfriend reached for the remote but it was out of reach.

'Meh, too far.'

'Oh well, I don't want you to have to move, I'm enjoying the cuddle far too much.'

Their content did not last long as the news anchor revealed some breaking news.

‘Fox News has just learned that the daughter of the man wanted for faking his own death in a 9/11 scam has been photographed helping the fugitive escape.’ The Fox News presenter introduced the hot topic of the day. *‘Amelia Hahn was arrested this afternoon for her involvement in the case but was later released when police felt satisfied that she had no involvement in the scam. The pictures purchased by Fox today may suggest otherwise, however...’*

The news cut to a series of photographs. Each image displayed the date and time of the snapshot. The first displayed Amelia entering the apartment. Approximately fifteen minutes later, the police arrive. Five minutes after the arrival of the authorities, the photographs show Beverly and Marty exiting the fire escape.

‘...I think the photographs are quite compelling and show Miss Hahn’s support for her law-breaking parents.’

Amelia slapped her forehead and sighed, tired of the

accusations. She turned to James for support, who glared back with an intense gaze. His neck turned red, matching the shade of his bloodshot eyes, and the nasal walls surrounding his nostrils vibrated as his breathing grew heavier.

'I promise you, it's not how it looks.'

'I don't want to hear about it, just get out of my apartment.'

*

Amelia had lived in New York her entire life and yet she had never been more lost. The landmarks of the city had become unfamiliar. She walked around for hours looking for somewhere to crash, but few doors were left open for her in the city, which supposedly never slept.

Unable to go to the apartment she shared with James, she attempted a visit to her mom's place, but Benjamin was out and her calls went unanswered.

The bright lights of Times Square called to her, a second home to tourists and residents alike. However, the most famous square in America was no longer the magical wonderland she grew up to believe. Passers-by shouted profanities at the infamous woman, furious by her family's ability to take advantage of a national tragedy for their own gain. The scolding burn of hot coffee sizzled on her flesh, thrown over her by a disgusted citizen as she passed the national Caribou chain.

Minutes away, the comfort of The Lincoln Hotel enticed a homeless Amelia to find refuge in her employer. Her manager, Sandra, played a positive role model in Amelia's life. Like the sister she never had, she had provided her a job when she finished school and a place to stay when life with her mother became all too much. Confident her saviour would support her in her hour of need, Amelia approached the hotel.

The usual friendly faces had disappeared and she was greeted by disgruntled guests.

'What is *she* doing here?' one guest asked the reception staff, before spitting on her shoe.

'Will you tell *her* to leave?' demanded another.

Answering the guests concerns was Anand, who waved Amelia over to provide her a safe sanctuary away from the angry mob. Originally from India, the guest service representative was half way through his one-year internship with the hotel. He greeted Amelia as she approached the desk.

'Miss Amelia, I'm very surprised to see you today. You were on the television. You are famous.'

'Infamous maybe. Work's sure going to be fun tomorrow when I come back to serve those guys.' Amelia gulped. 'Is Sandra in?'

'Ah, Miss Amelia. Yes, she is in the back. She said she wants to see you.' The intern's stern tone suggested Amelia faced more upheaval, but his foreign brogue brought doubt over her fears. Unsure of what to expect, she walked behind the front desk and into the back office where she found Sandra sat behind her desk. Her usually warm welcome appeared cooler.

'Sit down.' Sandra spoke with a firm tone. As requested, Amelia took a seat before her manager's desk. Pulling out Amelia's employee file from a drawer, Sandra placed the documentation on the desk. Amelia pulled the piece of paper towards herself and browsed over the details. A form titled '*Termination of Employment*' sat before her. Amelia's bottom lip trembled as she took in the details.

'Have I done something wrong? Sandra, I can't believe you're doing this to me!' Amelia reached for a tissue from the box on Sandra's desk and dabbed her eyes. 'Please, Sandra, this has been the worst day of my life. I've lost my mom, my boyfriend and now you're sacking me?'

'Amelia, if it was just down to the fact that you and your family have lied to me for the past decade, deceiving me and taking advantage of my kind nature, then I'd consider giving you another chance. I imagine sacking someone for simply upsetting a family friend is something I could be sued for anyway. But you have brought this business into disrepute. I can't have someone who has been nationally shamed checking in our guests on the front desk. It'll damage the company brand. Therefore I have no other option but to let you go.'

A thousand apologies could not change Sandra's determined mind and she had already drawn up the paperwork to end her employment contract. Amelia wanted to defend herself, but she thought twice. If her own fiancé didn't believe her, how could she convince her manager? She collected her belongings out of her locker, said her goodbyes to Anand and walked out of the hotel.

The city felt bitterly cold, much cooler than earlier in the day, but she suspected it had more to do with her loneliness than the impending arctic freeze reported earlier on the news. Fearing the backlash from the patriotic New Yorkers, Amelia hailed a cab and asked the driver to take her to her mom's apartment.

A glum Benjamin welcomed her. She sat down next to him and placed her head on his shoulder. The bags below her eyes stung as the dry salty tears soaked into the skin; she sobbed all the way home leaving her tear ducts empty. Nothing could possibly get any worse, or so she thought.

'Today has been the worst day of my life.' she explained. 'I've just been dumped, I'm homeless and I've lost my job. What has that bastard done to us?' Amelia sobbed. Benjamin gripped his sister tight and kissed her on the forehead. 'At least we have this place.'

'Every cloud and all that jazz...'

'I can't believe two days ago I was announcing my engagement. Now it's all over. I don't even want to think about taking the news of my proposal off Facebook. Oh the embarrassment.' Amelia cringed, anticipating changing her relationship status to *single* on the social networking site. 'I just can't believe it's over, or that he believed the media over me.'

Benjamin lifted off the couch and walked into the kitchen. He grabbed an envelope, resting on the side bench, and hid it in his back pocket. His sister had been through enough and did not need any more bad news. He would make it right, any way he could. He was her protector and wouldn't allow anything to happen to his little sister.

In the private sanctuary of his own bedroom, he took out the envelope and read over the contents inside. Prying eyes could no longer peer over his shoulder to read of their doomed fate.

The letter was from a lawyer, who dropped by the apartment earlier in the day to inform Benjamin that his family had been served. The lawyer represented the 9/11 Victims Fund, outlining their plans to sue the family for one million dollars. He screwed up the letter and hid it under his bed.

Chapter 14

Harrisburg, Pennsylvania played a notable part in the American Civil War and the Industrial Revolution. Today the history is embedded in the city's many museums and parks. Marty and Beverly Hahn had little time to visit these tourist hotspots, which made a significant influence on American history, as they hid in a roadside motel.

The standards were far above the infamous *Bates Motel* experience they had envisioned. However, while the upgraded room was better than they expected, it failed to live up to the five star service they experienced when they last travelled together. Their holidays used to include a luxury, personal service with Jacuzzi baths, soft robes and a mint on the pillow. Today they could afford little more than a room which was smaller than the walk-in-wardrobe she enjoyed in the four-storey house they once lived in but the accommodation did ensure their infamy remained overlooked. Roadside motels were the perfect environment for discretion as they joined prostitutes and cheating husbands, who also came to the property to remain inconspicuous.

They lay on the twin beds, pushed together to create a double. Nicotine stained walls surrounded the dimly lit room. Beverly switched on the news to see if their story remained a headline. The exterior of the heavy brown square box doubled the size of the small screen. Circular dials to the side made up the remote and a crooked aerial sat on top.

'Wow, this should be in a museum.' Marty laughed. His humour remained redundant on his wife who eagerly waited to catch the news.

The delay was in the hands of her husband, who spent fifteen minutes playing with the antennas to get a semi-decent image. The anchor-man on the screen bounced and his voice crackled as the box lost signal.

The anchor-man on NBC informed viewers of Amelia Hahn's arrest. The current affairs programme displayed the photographs of their escape as their daughter distracted the police inside. NBC sent correspondents around New York City, surveying citizens on their opinions of the family's plan to extort money from the victim's fund.

'They should give us our money back and they should all be put in jail!" yelled one citizen.

'How could they take advantage of that tragedy? They should face the death penalty!' ranted another.

The escapees cuddled up, petrified of the anger vented towards them. The Big Apple, which they called home, rotted as they feared the resentment their children would now face alone without their parents' support.

'They won't all feel like that.' Marty assured his wife. 'This is an entertainment programme and it's their job to show the most extreme of views.'

'Why are they focusing on us trying to extort money from the Victims Fund? It's not true! You were trying to scam a capitalist insurance corporation, not some government fund to help genuine victims.' Beverly stressed. 'How could you possibly plan to scam a fund which didn't even exist when you disappeared?'

They stared on and watched more opinions pour in, highlighting Twitter responses from high profile celebs and angry trolls.

'We need to go home.' Beverly snapped. 'We can't let our little Millie take the blame for this.'

'We can't go home. They'll put us in jail.'

'But our little girl… I can't let this happen to her. I don't care about being arrested, I've already resigned to that inevitability.'

As Beverly pleaded her husband to take her back to New York, the news anchor announced Amelia's release.

'Oh thank God!' Beverly exhaled with relief.

'You see, she's fine. We just need to focus. We're going to be in Indianapolis tomorrow. No one will know where we are.' He kissed his wife's forehead and wrapped his arms around her.

'You always manage to reassure me everything will be OK. That was the hardest thing when you were away, I didn't have your reassurance that everything would sort itself out.'

Ten years on, she began to doubt that everything would eventually be OK. She had waited for her life to *sort itself out* for over twelve years since her husband lost his job in 1999.

Her life finally had direction once the victims fund pay-out allowed her to retire and no longer worry about their money issues. Just as everything finally flowed in the right direction, her dead husband returned and screwed up any chance of living a normal life again.

'If you hadn't come home, I'd be attending Amelia's wedding and welcoming grandchildren. Now I won't be invited to any family parties. It's too dangerous and I wouldn't be welcome anyway.' She sobbed as she comprehended what she had left behind.

'Hey, Hunny, please don't cry. I promise you, we'll make this work. By the time we've stopped travelling, we'll have the most wonderful life. We'll want for nothing.'

'Except for our children…' Silenced hovered for several seconds as they considered the people they left behind in New York.

'It won't be forever. Eventually when we're safe enough and this tornado of a story has passed over, we'll be able to visit and they can come and stay with us. Or we can meet somewhere neutral.' Marty explained, although he failed to be truly convinced by his own words. The risk was too high but he needed to satisfy his wife until they arrived in a haven away from the aggravated New Yorkers.

'Like they'll ever forgive us.' Beverly sniffled. 'Why would they ever want to see us again after we abandoned them? I've made a mistake, Marty, I need to go home.'

Marty rubbed her shoulder and decided they both needed a strong drink. He left the room and walked down to reception, where they had a drinks counter to the side of the check-in desk. The white walls of the lobby, corridors and bedrooms were smudged with nicotine and the worn red carpets had questionable stains. Behind the reception desk, a plaque advertised the hotel's *Best Motel* award, however after a closer inspection, Marty found the honour was received in 1989 when the property first opened.

Picking out two miniature bottles of gin, he took the items to the counter to pay. The young gentleman behind reception barely moved his eyes as Marty approached. His focus drew to the television hung in the corner. The news story of the man who faked his death to commit insurance fraud filled the headlines. The customer service assistant did a double-take at thc man before him and compared the guest to the image he had on the screen.

'He's my cousin. We look very familiar.' Marty said and placed the money for the gin miniatures on the desk. The receptionist took the money, placed it into the cash-register and handed Marty his change.

'Nothing to do with me, Man, we have all sorts in here. As long as you're a paying guest, we don't care who you are or what you've done.' Marty smiled at the young man who served him and returned to his room, confident that he could trust the motel representative.

Opening the door to his room, Marty discovered his wife had left the bed where she lay before. He checked the bathroom. Mold filled the gaps between the white tiles, a lone hair stuck to the toilet basin and a spider crawled into the bath. However, Beverly was nowhere to be seen.

A cold breeze drifted in from the open window in the bedroom, which was closed before he left the room. Concerned that his wife had escaped, he hunted around for her purse, something she would never leave without.

It had disappeared.

*

Few cars filled the allocated spaces outside of the motel. A dim beam from a lone street lamp made up the only security for the guests' vehicles. A white Ford Transit slept peacefully at the far end of the car-park, away from suspicious guests, concerned by the stranger keeping watch on the building with binoculars.

Max Spielberg's heavy eyes closed, struggling to focus on the inactivity inside the budget accommodation. An audio book from his favourite crime writer had relieved his boredom, but the tape finished, leaving the restless reporter requiring entertainment. Few guests had arrived and as it approached midnight, the journalist expected little to unfold until morning.

A distressed woman ran out of the entrance of the motel, disturbing his nap. The woman he had followed with her husband throughout the day from New York was now alone. She ran down Jonestown Road towards Highway 39.

Holy shit! Has she lost her mind?

Seconds later, her husband ran out and followed behind, shouting her name as they made their way to one of the busiest highways in the state.

'*Are these people crazy?*' Max asked himself. They were America's most wanted right now, and yet they ran down the middle of the street shouting in the late night, catching attention from the local neighbourhood.

The reporter switched on his engine and drove slowly down

the street, following the felons. He drove in a low gear to keep within distance of the couple while sustaining the peaceful quiet of the Pennsylvania night.

The vehicle drew closer to the escapees. Max had to overtake them before he aroused suspicion. Taking the next right, he turned around and stopped the van, watching the couple pass. The quiet neighbourhood saw little action. The only disturbance rang from the water sprinklers, hydrating the lawns of the suburban residence. He took photographs with his phone as they ran across the cross-junction, dodging the sprinklers which rained down on the runaways.

Beverly slowed down; she was not as active as her husband and his long legs allowed him to easily overtake her smaller limbs. Out of breath, she hobbled over to a bar and leaned on the wall below an illuminated sign of the bar's name and the logo of the main beer they served.

'They ain't going inside are they?' Max considered, puzzled by their outlandish behaviour. The commuters, which they boarded the bus over with earlier in the day, may have been ignorant to their infamous status, but the punters inside the popular sports bar were familiar with current affairs. Little satisfied the punters more than to perch up at the bar, read the newspapers and call their bookmakers to place their bets on their local NFL team, while enjoying a pint of Miller Lite.

Beverly composed herself before approaching the entrance to the bar. However, as she opened the door, she paused. Something had caused the fugitive to stop and think again about entering. To her right, Marty stood to the side of the road, catching his breath, waiting for his wife's next move. She turned around and looked at her husband, and with all her energy, she ran over to him and embraced him.

Max snapped away with his camera, ensuring he captured every second of their interchange. He got out of his car and sneaked up a little closer to the bar. As he approached the venue, he heard a popular tune by Louis Armstrong. The clicks of his camera did little to distract the occupied couple, oblivious to the activities behind them. Marty and Beverly swayed, intensely staring into each other's eyes, and lip synced: *'And I think to myself, what a wonderful world.'*

*

They gleefully skipped back to the motel, no longer avoiding the sprinklers. They danced within the showers, singing the lyrics to *'Singing in the Rain'.* Their frolicking freed any animosity between the couple, who during their moment of madness could forget their troubles, which they left behind in New York.

Beverly had little else besides Marty. After years of independence, she suddenly found herself reliant on him. She couldn't return to New York, where she would soon be relieved of her assets. Her children refused to speak to her, and if she was lucky enough to escape jail, there wouldn't be a single employer in the country who would offer her a job.

It was the Louis Armstrong single which had brought her to see sense. That piece of music struck a chord with her every time she heard it. It brought fond memories of when they first met at the Cornell annual freshman's ball. They had initial interchanges in the debate society in college. They were on separate teams and spent weeks raising each other's blood temperatures as they aired their conflicting viewpoints.

Their difference in opinion caused them to scowl at each other when they passed in the corridors or the college canteen. She couldn't comprehend at first why Marty, out of all of the debate team, made her so infuriated, but he really made her blood boil.

All that changed at the freshman's ball, when he finally introduced himself formally. They had never indulged in a conversation outside of the debate society, nor had they learned each other's names. He asked if she would like a drink and she accepted.

They smoked during their college days, a habit they quit when Beverly fell pregnant. Marty shared a cigarette with the feisty student on the grassy acre outside of the entrance hall when the Louis Armstrong song came on.

'I love this song!' a young Marty declared.

'Me too!' Beverly replied. 'It was my Granddad's song. He used to roll his cigarettes, sit back and smoke with his eyes closed, singing along to the lyrics. They played it at his funeral. I guess it's a bit of depressing song for me these days.'

'Well we should change that.' Marty stood up. 'Wanna dance?' He took her hand and escorted her up the stone steps, stepping through the French windows and into the hall, where they slow danced to the optimistic tune. Attendees were obliged to dress to impress and the couple welcomed the dress code. Marty suited up in a tuxedo with a black bow tie. His dance partner struggled to remain composed as she tripped over her lilac ball gown, sprouting a dome from her waist down to her stiletto heals.

'I'm surprised that a man with such little integrity when it comes to debating, has such fantastic taste when it comes to music.'

'Well now you've seen a different side of me, why don't you try to get to know me a little better?' Marty said. 'Have dinner with me.'

'Maybe.' Beverly teased.

Since that day, she no longer associated the song with her grandfather. It was the first dance of her wedding, the song they played when they made love and the accompaniment to every road trip. For the past decade, the hairs on Beverly's neck stood on end and her stomach fluttered every time she heard the tribute to her late husband.

During those early days when they first dated, she struggled to understand how she had fallen in love with someone who rattled her cage in the debate society. They had spent weeks arguing before he plucked up the courage to ask her out. With age, she could believe it, as it was how they had continued to behave in their turbulent marriage throughout the years. They spent their days arguing and their nights engaged in passion.

Now in bed in the motel, they cuddled up once again after another steamy session. The heating had shut off and the cold bite of the Pennsylvania fall whistled through the cracks of the decaying walls. She hadn't noticed the cold earlier outside as the adrenalin took over. Now she shivered and cuddled up closer to her husband for warmth.

She reflected on the lyrics of the Louis Armstrong song, considering for the first time that Louis might have been wrong regarding his optimism for the planet, as the world that she had seen was far from wonderful. Beverly had witnessed twelve years of pain and the future didn't look any brighter.

Her pessimism extended to her marriage too. Thinking back to her debate-society days, she wondered whether she could put up with many more fights with the man she once knew as her husband.

Chapter 15

The ride across the Midwest was a tedious one. Mile upon mile of prairies made the states all roll into one. They could have been in Ohio or Indiana, the lack of change in the landscape made it difficult to determine. The transport did little to raise their spirits. The stale scent of nicotine radiated from metal ashtrays, built into the arm rest, and the worn upholstery emitted a cloud of dust every time a commuter sat down.

The plain scenery caused the time to drag, providing too much thinking time for Beverly. Reflection caused her pain. She had made too many rash decisions within the past twenty-four hours and wished she had paused the day before instead of recklessly escaping the city she called home.

The police should have been her first port of call when her husband returned. Her children would respect her and she wouldn't have entered America's most wanted list. While she wasn't on the official FBI list, she had made the list that pulled at the public's heartstrings, which was far more daunting. She had human rights in the eyes of the law, but the general public may not have as much mercy.

To her right, her husband slept. His nose squashed up against the window and moisture dribbled down from his open mouth. The dreary view disappeared within the condensation from Marty's breath. Leaning her head back on the rest, she sighed, wishing she could be a woman without regrets. However, she had to stick with her choices now, there was no going back.

America wanted her blood, the police wanted justice and the 9/11 Victims Fund would surely want their money back. How had she let her heart rule her head? That man had always had a hold on her. When they graduated, she had desires to move back to Chicago where her family lived, but his insistence to stay in New York made her remain in The Big Apple rather than returning to her Illinois roots. When she married him, she agreed to stand by her man no matter what they faced, but living a life of crime was far from what she had signed up to.

When they left New York the previous day, while they were upset to leave their children, they held onto the optimism for their futures together and excitement for the adventure they were embarking upon. They were like two teenagers escaping the clutches of authority.

Initially when they escaped New York, she dreamed their escape would be similar to the adventures of Thelma and Louise, without the messy ending. But twenty-four hours into their escape, she found herself on an uncomfortable coach, with little leg room, having spent the night in a dingy road-side motel. This was far from the glamorous adventure that she had hoped for. The same could be said for her marriage.

They arrived in Indianapolis at lunch time. While they waited for Gordon to arrive from Gary to collect them, they spent time in the city, buying items which would cover up their recognisable identities. They appeared on every news programme across America and while Indiana held the title of The Hospitality State, the infamous couple would face pure hostility should the locals discover who they were.

They stopped by the Circle Centre Mall and found a wig to cover her now infamous red hair. It was only a month away from Halloween and all the local stores sold fancy dress items. Amongst the scraggy green witch wigs, she settled for a medium length brown hairpiece.

Marty shaved his head and allowed his facial hair to grow out. While they endured strange glances along their journey, few recognised who they were. Those who double-took as they passed assumed they had already met the inconspicuous couple, or they placed the pair in one of the latest series of some glamorous housewife reality show.

Gordon met them at the Weber Grill restaurant, where they treated their saviour to lunch as a thank you for collecting them from the state capital. As he ate, a shifty Gordon looked around nervously.

'What are you so worried about?'

'Your image wasn't splattered across every media outlet in the country last time I collected you.'

Gordon was right, while Marty's face was printed in nearly every newspaper on his previous escape, his image merely blended in among the many victims who had disappeared in the towers.

'Well thank you anyway,' Beverly tried to break the tension. 'We're really grateful for putting us up.'

'You know it's only for a few days, right? I can't risk being seen with you guys.' Beverly's heart sank as she envisioned an uncomfortable few days ahead.

Three hours later, they arrived in the small town of Gary. Along the drive to Gordon's house, Marty pointed out some of the places which had made some significance within his life over the previous decade. He showed her the steel factory where he worked, the local bars where he socialised and Lake Michigan where he reflected and thought about her and the children.

'I would sit on that beach and look across towards Chicago, wondering if you were over there visiting your dad.'

Beverly was glad to hear her husband had considered the family during his absence. What upset her however was the normality he appeared to enjoy in Indiana, while they all suffered his loss at home. It had eaten her up for ten years, while he was in Gary, working in the factories and drinking in local bars.

Suspicious of his other-life, she wondered what else he had been up to, especially in those bars he drank in. Had he seen other women or had he remained celibate for ten years? Believing ignorance was bliss, she decided to focus on the future, rather than the past.

They arrived on Jackson Street and pulled up at a small white one-storey house, which looked more fitting as a shoe box than a place to live. They got out of the car and walked into the two-bedroomed home.

Beverly found out which was her room and rushed into it to escape the company of the increasingly distant Gordon. She lay down on the bed and sighed. The room smelled of damp, the grey curtains had torn, allowing light to pour in through the cracks, and the aubergine carpet had arrived direct from the seventies.

I left my life in New York for this?

'I can't wait to vacuum and wash the sheets. After the beautiful home you left in New York, how did you live in such squalor?'

'I was desperate. I had nowhere else to go. When you're desperate, you'll do anything, no matter what the consequences.' Marty explained. 'You can tell me in a few days how you left your home to live here, as it's exactly what you're doing now.'

She lay on the bed and cried. Marty joined his wife and gripped her tightly. Attempting to kiss her neck, she raised her shoulder to block his affection.

'What's up, Hunny?'

'I'm just wondering how we've ended up here.' A tear dribbled from her eye and ran down her face. 'How did you let us end up living like this?'

'It's only a pit stop, Baby. We'll be outa here before you know it.'

While she looked forward to escaping the shanty, the thought of moving on exhausted her. She had been travelling for only twenty-four hours and she was already fatigued. Marty kissed his wife before shuffling off the bed towards the cabinet, which sat across from where his wife lay.

'I have a surprise for you!'

He retrieved a DVD from the chest of drawers and chucked it onto the bed. She picked up the case and saw the surprise he had presented her was the movie, *Meet Me in St. Louis.*

Beverly smiled. 'You remembered!' She hugged the case, overwhelmed with nostalgia of the days before her husband disappeared. They watched the movie on their last night together, one of dozens of times they had enjoyed it together.

'Remembered? Do you know how many times I've watched this movie and thought of you.' He sat down on the bed next to her and she sat up to place her arms around his neck.

'Do you wanna watch it?'

She smiled and nodded.

For the following two hours, she forgot about her problems. She forgot her children were over seven hundred miles away, that she was one of America's most despised individuals, and that she lived in a dump with no idea of how long she would have to endure it, or where she would end up next.

As they watched the movie, she looked longingly at the large Victorian home, which thc film centred around. She dreamed of living in a similar house when she was a little girl. The building shaped their vision for their eventual house in New York. Their lives would be as perfect as the Smith family's.

'I still can't believe you've never been to St. Louis. It's only a four hour drive from your dad's house.'

'It just never happened. Life flies by and then thirty years later you're wondering where the time has gone, regretting the things you never did… and the things you *did* do.'

'You don't regret me, do you?' Marty asked, sadness breaking his voice.

'How could I ever regret being with you? We have two amazing children.' Beverly explained, before stuttering on her poorly chosen words. 'I didn't mean that's the *only* reason I love you. I just...'

'I know what you mean.'

'And I'm here with you, aren't I? I think that's enough proof of my lack of regrets when it comes to you.'

'But seriously, we need to go to St. Louis. We can't have any more regrets. Let's go someday.' Placing his head on hers, they snuggled up for warmth and watched the movie.

'I hate, loathe, despise and abominate money,' claimed Rose Smith. Beverly empathised with her favourite character. Money had ruined their lives. Money had brought two years of arguments before Marty disappeared, and money had left them in a shack, running away from the police and the angry New Yorkers.

'*You also spend it,'* replied Alonso.

Beverly agreed with that too.

*

Over the following weeks, Beverly worked on the hovel they now called home. While Marty looked for work, she spruced the house up, scrubbing the bathrooms, shampooing the carpets and vacuuming every last inch of the building.

She took regular trips to the beach and looked across Lake Michigan towards Chicago, longing to speak to her dad. Her mom died of cancer the year before and she now only had her father in The Windy City.

Anticipating disappointment, she wondered what her father thought of his little girl these days. Francis Goldberg was a proud man and her stint in the news would have caused him great embarrassment. While he was now retired, he still played golf with his former colleagues who once joined him as The Kings of Wall Street. There was no doubt that his daughter's recent affairs would have fuelled gossip on the Back Nine.

It was a Tuesday morning when her husband left for his first day at his new job. He found work at one of the local steel factories.

Petrified of his former colleagues recognising him, he refused to return to his previous employer in case somebody connected his *Marty Reece* identity he had once created to the now infamous Marty Hahn.

The new job would bring in an income. They could stop sponging off their landlord and save for a deposit for a place of their own. Beverly planned to find work herself but allowed herself to settle into Gary first. She struggled to get her head around their current situation. Her husband had ten years to get used to the lifestyle they now lived, but it was all very new to her.

While she was emotionally unprepared, she did have the documentation to allow her to work without arousing suspicion. Her husband sought her identification from the black market. He used the market on his previous visit after a referral to the underground store by an illegal alien. They both required new identities as his former made up name may have become compromised as the media investigated his absence. Today, their passports, driving licences and social security numbers displayed the names *Martin and Beverly Singer.*

A knock at the door distracted Beverly away from her chores. She ran to her bedroom and grabbed her wig. Looking into a mirror, she adjusted the hairpiece, ensuring she appeared unrecognisable to anybody who had seen the news.

The knocking continued. Beverly shouted *'I'm coming'* as she made her way to the door. Behind it stood a petite blonde slender woman who appeared surprised that a lady was in the house.

'Oh hi, I'm Caitlin, is Marty there?' Beverly turned around but remembered her husband was out. She turned back to Caitlin, wondering why this attractive woman asked after her husband.

'He's at work. Can I help you with something?' The young woman appeared disappointed.

'Can you just tell him I called?' Beverly nodded; she would certainly ask him about young Caitlin when he arrived home from work. 'So are you Gordon's new girlfriend?'

Beverly cringed just considering the idea of dating Gordon. He was an old, overweight sweaty man with dandruff-filled matted hair. While his odour suggested he spent hours at the gym, his physique said otherwise.

'No, I'm Marty's wife. How do you know Marty?'

'I'm his fiancé.'

Chapter 16

'Excuse me?' Beverly asked the visitor to reiterate her relationship with Marty, horrified by Caitlin's announcement. *What did she mean she was his fiancée?*

'We got engaged last year on holiday in Mexico.' Caitlin took out a photograph of herself with Marty. Beverly took the photograph and examined it; it was definitely her husband. The man in the photograph sported a beard and had long hair, but it was clearly him. She placed her shaken hand over her mouth. 'I don't understand. How can you be his wife?'

Caitlin had a southern Hick accent, a brogue which Beverly's father would associate with '*poor white trash'*. The Marty that Beverly knew could not stand the southern twang. While he loved her music, he had to mute the television if Dolly Parton spoke. Now, here he was, willing to marry her.

'We've been married for twenty-seven years.' Beverly looked Caitlin up and down; she wasn't a violent woman, but she summed up that she could easily take on this feeble girl.

'So you're Mrs Reece?'

'No?' For a moment Beverly sighed with relief, hoping this young woman had the wrong address, but then she remembered her husband's other identity. She scrambled for words as she nearly exposed their true identities.

'I mean, yes, I'm Mrs Reece, although I kept my maiden name, so I get confused when people call me that.'

With Marty publicly shamed in the national media, Beverly questioned Caitlin's intelligence if she failed to connect him to America's most wanted man. But Caitlin seemed vulnerable, delicate and easily fooled. It was easy for Beverly to judge but that cheat had fooled *her* too.

Caitlin broke into tears. Despite her desires to teach this woman a lesson for stealing her husband, Beverly couldn't help but feel sorry for her. She wasn't to know he was married; it was her husband's fault. He took advantage of this girl and lied to them both. They were in the same boat, unaware of the *other woman* for all of this time. Stepping off the door step, she wrapped her arms around the inconsolable girl and brought her into the house.

Beverly brewed a pot of coffee while they talked. The young hick's make-up had run where she had been crying. Her yellow skirt barely cover her thighs and her white crop-top showed off her tight pierced belly and her bulging bust. A gold chain with her name in italics hung down her chest.

'So where did you meet Marty?'

'I was a receptionist at the steel factory where he worked. We met for a drink after work on his first day and we fell in love.'

'If you're engaged, why don't you live together?' Beverly asked; she and Marty moved in together upon graduating college, long before he proposed.

'I'm a traditional girl from an Irish Catholic family. And... no offence... I didn't wanna live here.'

'I don't blame you.' Beverly scrunched up her nose as she took in her surroundings. 'Why haven't you got married then? I thought you Catholics got married fast so you could get on with your lives without breaking one of *Leviticus's rules...*'

'He was always putting it off. He's a difficult man to pin down. He only proposed when I threatened to leave him because our relationship wasn't going anywhere. Every time I asked him to meet my folks, he'd have some excuse to avoid it, I haven't even mentioned our relationship to them.'

She paused before considering the other woman in Marty's life.

'But how have I never seen *you* before? I've spent a lot of time here and we've never once crossed paths. I know Marty was visiting his cousins for a while, but how could we have never met if you've been married for nearly thirty years?'

Like a burglar passing through infra-red security detectors, Beverly had to remain cautious. While she was heartbroken, angry and wanted revenge, if she stitched up her husband, she would cut off her nose to spite her face.

'My mother was ill for a long time, she had cancer. I used to go and stay with her in Chicago and was absent from home for long periods of time.' Beverly wasn't lying; she had spent endless time away from home visiting her sick mom in Chicago, she just failed to mention that *home* was in New York and not Indiana.

'I don't know what to do, I'm heartbroken. He was my life and now I'm left with nothing!' Caitlin sobbed onto Beverly's shoulder.

She looked down at this fragile being and wondered whether this girl realised that she'd suffered less than the woman who consoled her. Caitlin would move on and find love again. Trapped with no home and just five grand in her pocket, Beverly had no hope of a normal life again.

She was upset but she didn't cry. Hoping to restore her life, she wanted out of this mess of a marriage and to return home. It had only been a few weeks since she was living blissfully in New York, in her new apartment, with her son home in the safety of the United States. She was without a care in the world, but in just one day, her husband had managed to ruin her life.

'Well you're welcome to him now, Caitlin. I'm done.'

*

Marty finished his first day at the steel factory. Nerves overtook him on the first day of any job, wondering if the HR department would accept his fake ID and stolen social security number.

When he first moved to Indiana, he worked besides illegal immigrants in cash-in-hand jobs, who managed to secure work with fake documentation. Marty asked for their supplier details and visited the recommended market. Pirated movies filled the stall, but once customers spoke to the tradesman and asked him for what they really required, he could get whatever they desired; identity, drugs, illegal firearms… he had it all. It had been the scariest experience in Marty's life and it wasn't any easier returning for a second time with his wife in tow.

Without a car, the walk home from work was long. The factory was a little further than where he used to work and no buses travelled along this particular route.

He quit his old job without any notice as he had no plans to return to Indiana once he was reunited with his wife. With the life insurance, he planned to return to New York and live a quiet life in retirement in the suburbs away from everyone they knew.

While he accepted it as a possibility, he had not expected the police to catch up with him so soon. He now acknowledged that the eve of the 9/11 anniversary wasn't the best time to return to New York. If the press hadn't surrounded his wife, exploiting her grief to sell newspapers, then friends and family would have rallied around her to provide support. It would have been impossible to remain in the city without a neighbour or friend spotting him.

Winter was setting in therefore his walk home had become compromised. Snow fell and the side-walk became icy. It was bitterly cold, and despite wearing two pairs of gloves on his hands, he lost the feeling in his fingertips. While he looked for other employment closer to home, he would soon require a car if he continued with his current job, which he could purchase with the savings they had run away from New York with.

They only had a limited amount of cash and planned to keep this aside for emergencies. They could potentially have to dash at any moment should their identities become exposed. Money was also a sore subject with their landlord, Gordon, who Marty owed one-hundred grand to, so he avoided appearing too flash around him. Neither of them had discussed the money he owed, Gordon quietly allowed them to settle in before he questioned where the money Marty promised him would arrive in his account.

Arriving home, he found his wife sitting on the couch. She had her arms folded, her legs crossed and a face like thunder. Furiously biting her bottom lip like a dehydrated pill-popper, Beverly was irate.

'Hi Hunny, are you OK?' He leaned over to kiss her, but she turned away. 'What's up? Has something happened?' Her glare created a burning sensation on the back of his head as if she had lasers streaming from her pupils through to the back of his.

'I had a visitor today from a friend of yours: Caitlin.' Beverly raised an eyebrow as she waited for her husband's explanation. Stumbling for a response, Marty gulped with guilt.

'That woman is crazy! We used to work together and she became obsessed! She's been stalking me ever since, convinced we were in a relationship!'

Beverly reached into her purse and pulled out the photograph that Caitlin had provided her from their holiday in Mexico, which proved his infidelity.

'And I suppose she kidnapped you, dragged you to Mexico and forced you to propose too, did she?' Marty sat down and held his head in his hands, accepting the game was up.

'It was never meant to happen.' Marty said. 'I'd been faithful for so long. Then about two years ago, I met Caitlin. I thought she was stunning, and what made it worse was she was a wonderful person too. I couldn't help myself, and before I knew it, I was in love.'

Beverly's stomach flipped as she heard her husband's adoration for the young hick. Everyone had needs and ten years was a long time, but this was more than just sex; this was love.

'Seeing you claim to have run away to save the family, you don't seem to have spent much time considering us.'

'You must have slept with other people.' Marty snapped. 'It's been ten years, for Christ's sake, you must have had other relationships.'

'The difference is, Marty, I thought you were dead. In my mind I was a single woman, while you were supposed to be counting down the days until you came home, not sleeping with some southern whore.'

'That's not how it was, I promise. I never expected to fall in love. It was an accident.'

'Do you know what hurts the most? It's that since your little resurrection, you claim that you've been sat by the beach, thinking about me, while you were shacking up with Jodie fucking Foster!'

'Jodie Foster?' Marty asked, confused by the reference to the actress.

'The accent…' Beverly shook her head, exasperated by her need to explain her metaphorical insults. 'You dragged me half way across the country, you've made me the most hated woman in America, and I've done nothing wrong. It's like the Louise Woodward case all over again!'

'I don't think things are quite *that* bad.' The British nanny was wrongly accused of killing a child whom she cared for. Marty failed to see how America could possibly hate his wife more than they hated the nineteen year old au-pair back in 1997, before a jury finally declared her innocent.

'Are they not, Martin?' Beverly used his full title when she was angry. 'Those terrorist attacks killed thousands of people. The entire country was in mourning, and *you* took advantage of that!' She jammed her finger into his chest as she yelled. 'What's worse is my children now hate me. I'll never see them again! But I was willing to take on all that anger and hate. And now I find out that you've not only had a secret life out here, but you've also had another woman. I can't deal with this anymore.'

'Can't you see that I came back for *you*? I might have been with Caitlin, but I came back for *you*! I could have easily stayed here, set myself up a nice little life with her. But I wanted you and I risked everything to come and get you back.'

'Well I really wish you hadn't.' In the bedroom, packed suitcases awaited Beverly's collection. She didn't have much since running away from New York, but the emotional baggage which she carried had nearly doubled. Grabbing her belongings from the cold damp bedroom, she looked around one last time, relieved to leave the hovel.

'I'm leaving you. And I'm not coming back. You can keep the money, but that's all you're getting. You got what you came for now. Did you really expect me to believe you came back for me? One million dollars is what you came home for.'

'Please don't go.' he begged, his eyes filled with tears but she didn't respond. She had lost everything but she wouldn't let him take the remainder of her dignity.

With her life belongings in her hand, she walked out of the door. As she walked to the bus stop in the state known as The Crossroads of America, she wondered which road she should take.

Chapter 17

Writing a curriculum-vitae was a difficult task when you had few qualifications and only one previous job. Amelia spent hours on a word processor rewording and re-arranging her experience and education. She'd never needed a CV before as Sandra provided Amelia the opportunity to work in the hotel without prior assessment when she left school. Now she had no job, no résumé and had never faced an interview. She couldn't even rely on a reference from her former employer to guarantee her a job.

After working all night on the résumé, she resigned and printed the document. Winter was imminent and the city rushed with shoppers preparing for the Thanksgiving holiday the following day. Amelia walked the streets of Manhattan, handing out her CV. Thanksgiving generated a rush of tourists to cram into the many hotels in the city, hoping to capture a glimpse of the Macy's parade the following morning.

Employers required as much support as possible over the holidays and Amelia would happily step in. She spent years working the holidays and missing her family. This year she had no scheduled responsibilities, but for the first time, she hoped to keep busy away from their joyless apartment. There would be no turkey on the table this year with just the two of them wallowing in the misery of their abandonment.

Thanksgiving would never be the same again. As a child, her father would wake them up at the crack of dawn. Tired but excited, they would walk down to Dunkin Donuts for breakfast, before finding a good spot along 6th Ave, ready for the parade. It didn't matter whether it rained or shined, they would stand together, huddled up with their take-out coffee, waiting for the floats to arrive.

Following Marty's disappearance, they left all that behind. Their move to Brooklyn meant travelling into New York early enough to obtain a decent spot became difficult, and their apathy towards the holiday season forced them to avoid the celebrations.

Amelia walked into the Blue Lodge Hotel on 5th Avenue and made her way up to the front desk. The guest service representative finished up serving the guest she was dealing with and approached Amelia, asking how she could be of service.

'I was wondering if you had any jobs available at the moment? I'm willing to work any hours and ready to start right away if you need.'

The long queue over-whelmed the pretty young customer service assistant and she desperately required support. Amelia hoped to take advantage of her struggle.

'I don't think so, Mam. While we do have openings here, you are not welcome in this hotel.'

For a girl who worked in the hospitality industry, she was less than hospitable. Amelia's mouth dropped open and her face reddened.

'Why? I haven't done anything wrong! I never knew my father was alive! Please give me a chance.'

'That may very well be the case, Mam, but if I'm thinking it, our customers are thinking it too, and I can't risk the reputation of this hotel being scarred by your recent escapades.' The receptionist folded her arms and raised an eyebrow before the job seeker. 'Now if you don't mind, as you can see we're busy, so if you could move aside...'

A security guard approached her and placed his hand on Amelia's arm. She shrugged him off her, insisting she would leave voluntarily. Without any prospects, Amelia walked past the angry guests queuing behind her, feeling the heat of their glares as she passed.

Hoping for a little more luck, Amelia tried the hotel next door. The Sleep Tight Hotel formed the bottom floors of one of the largest skyscrapers in the city. Above the hotel, America's most influential billionaires rented lush apartments. The hotel lobby was much grander than that of The Lincoln Hotel where she once worked. Marble floors led up to the check-in desk where guests checked in on electronic tablets, light rained down into the grand hallway from crystal chandeliers and a champagne reception welcomed guests.

With her confidence knocked, shc timidly shuffled to the concierge and asked if she could speak to the manager. The young British receptionist made a call and a large African-American woman walked out in a navy business suit, introducing herself as Sharon, the hotel general manager. Her long black curly hair had so much volume, Sharon would have fit easily into a shampoo commercial.

'Hi, I'm Amelia. I was wondering whether you had any jobs available at the moment? I'll do anything, whatever you have!'

Sharon looked the young woman up and down. Amelia's white

shirt and black trousers had not met the warm face of an iron for some time. Coffee stained her collar, where she had spilled serving a guest, and the faint scent of toast remained embedded into the cotton. Desperate to find work following weeks of lethargy, she had little time or energy to wash the only attire she owned suitable for an interview.

'Come this way.' She escorted Amelia into the back office. Sharon's office was much larger than Sandra's back at The Lincoln and her desk peered over The Rockefeller Centre. She invited Amelia to sit on the opposite side of the room where two chairs were separated by a glass coffee table. Sharon placed two mugs down on the table and poured them both a fresh cup of coffee, before sitting down adjacent to the interviewee. Amelia had little experience of interviews, but she had expected something a little more formal.

'So you're looking for a job. I suppose you must've faced quite a bit of rejection being the infamous girl that you are.'

'It's been horrible, but I assure you I really didn't know. I can't understand why my brother and I are receiving such a backlash when we've done nothing wrong.' Amelia said. The manager picked up her coffee mug, took a sip and exhaled in satisfaction of the refreshing brew.

'*I* can understand the anger. You may not have had anything to do with your father's actions yourself, but you've received and are still living the benefits of those actions.' She glanced down at the applicant's CV towards her address. 'The Dakota Building, that can't be cheap.'

Embarrassed, Amelia hung her head in shame of her financial fortunes. She had urged her mom to choose somewhere a little more modest. The tower was one of the most prestigious apartment blocks in the city, known to celebrities and politicians alike, taking up entire floors and duplexes. While the Hahns' apartment was much smaller than their famous neighbours', there was no doubt they had money.

'You see you got your pay-out and yet no one died, while there are people out there, like *me*, who did lose someone in those attacks and received nothing.'

'Why didn't you receive anything from the Victim's Fund?' Amelia asked, her eyes widened. 'We managed to claim ours without a body.'

'My husband was there that day. He'd just lost his job and like you was wondering around New York City looking for somebody to give him a chance. He was rejected and rejected, and so he looked up at those two tall towers in the distance and thought '*There has to be something there.''*

'I can understand why. I was only young when they collapsed, but I remember vividly the impact they made on the city's skyline.'

'He was walking up to the reception desk when the plane hit. He could have easily got out but he was the kind of man who would help anyone. He walked up thirty-five floors to get people out of that building. He called me to say that he loved me just seconds before the building collapsed in on him.'

Sharon's voice broke as she relived the story. Amelia leaned in to place a hand on the manager's arm, but she raised her hand, rejecting her sympathy.

'I waited around for weeks to hear they had found a body, but it never came. There was no evidence of him ever being in those towers as only I knew that he was in there. He was a stranger to the people working there. He hadn't signed in or contacted anybody and there wasn't a single soul who knew he was in those towers. He saved quite a few lives that day, but not one person could describe the lone stranger who helped them or remember his name.'

Amelia dabbed her moist cheek as she took in Sharon's heart-breaking story. There were thousands of stories like Sharon's, but they never became any easier to hear.

'Your family got their fund because your father worked in the building. He had countless forms of identity there as well as eye-witnesses who could confirm he was there that day. My Billy had nothing and I was left with nothing. Don't get me wrong, if I had the choice between having my Billy back or a million dollars, I'd take Billy in a heartbeat. But I've struggled, girl, oh I have struggled. I've worked and worked and got myself to where I am now, and that has taken ten years to do.'

The door opened and the British guest representative poked his head around the corner. He saw the applicant sobbing and mouthed to his manager, *'Is everything OK?'*

Sharon waved her hand and shot him a smile. He nodded and closed the door, leaving the pair to continue their intense conversation.

'I was pregnant when those towers collapsed. I was left as a single mom with no prospects and no job. I was left without. But then there were people like your father, who took advantage of that day, got away scot free and was handed a million dollars. That's why America is angry. You may not have been personally involved, but you're living in a million dollar home while the rest of us struggle through.'

'I'm sorry to hear about your husband, Sharon. And I'm sorry for wasting your time here today, but thanks for giving it to me anyway.' Amelia picked up her purse, stood up and made her way to the exit.

'Where are you going?' Sharon stood up, stopping Amelia in her tracks. 'I ain't done with you yet.'

'Listen Sharon, I'm sorry you're hurting, I feel terrible, but I'm having the worst few weeks of my entire life and that includes when I was told my father was dead. I can't face any more hostility and I really need a job, so I have to go.' Amelia opened the door.

'So when are we going to do this interview?' Sharon asked.

Amelia, surprised by Sharon's proposal, turned around and closed the door. 'What interview?'

'You came in for an interview, didn't you? Are we going to do this now or later?'

'I thought you wouldn't want me, especially after what happened to your husband. How could anyone work with me after what my father did?'

'Girl, didn't you listen to my story? My Billy walked from door to door and ended up dead because no one would give him a god-damn chance. What kind of person would I be if I couldn't learn from that?'

Amelia sat back down before Sharon. She smiled, as for the first time since her engagement dinner, she began to feel a tiny speck of hope for the future.

*

With a job secured, Amelia pranced home. The urge to skip overcame her as a shimmer of excitement tickled her arms. She inhaled the sweet aroma of optimism and pumpkin spice lattes as the magic of Thanksgiving returned to New York City.

The stern glares from pedestrians, aware of her infamy, failed to dampen her excitement for the opportunities which lay ahead. She joyfully kicked the crisp orange leaves in the park, dancing in autumn's offerings.

A meatloaf welcomed her home, prepared by her brother. He hadn't seen daylight in days, only escaping for fresh air at night as the dark hid his infamy.

'So I have news!' she revealed. Benjamin perked up, surprised by his sister's sudden optimism. 'I have a job!'

'Oh that's great, Kid, what're you gonna be doing?'

'Working in a hotel. It's a bit of a step down from supervisor, but hopefully I'll be back to where I was in no time. It's a bigger hotel so hopefully there'll be more opportunities to progress.'

Benjamin stood up and hugged his sister, before retrieving two beers from the refrigerator. 'Let's celebrate then... to you!' They clinked their cans together and returned to their dinner.

'I was thinking maybe we could go out for a couple of drinks tonight? It's been ages since we've hit the town. I'm sick of being stuck inside in fear of being accused of something I'm not.'

Benjamin stared down at his dinner, his smile retracted. 'I'm not sure that's a great idea, Kid, maybe we should just have a few beers inside and rent a movie instead.'

'I don't understand how you spent all those years in Iraq, facing bombs, bullets and terrorists, but you can't face a few bitter words from the public!'

'There's a difference, Amelia. I'm trained to dodge bombs.'

'Let's go to The Village, people are always pretty nice around there. I know it's not your favourite place these days, but at least we can have a drink in a bar around friendly people.'

The Village remained an accepting place, regardless of background. The LGBT community of New York understood hostility all too well following years of persecution, ultimately leading to the Stonewall riots in 1969. Greenwich Village had since evolved into a vibrant and celebratory location, where everyone was welcome.

Benjamin considered Amelia's plan. He had a lot of bad memories from that area of the city from his teenage years, but his concerns fell beyond his troublesome past. He stroked his chin, contemplating his decision.

'OK, but I'm wearing my cadet uniform... that way people might give me a little respect and remember how much I've done for this country.'

*

They pulled up a pew in Bedlam Bar and drank mojitos. The cold bite of winter nibbled at their flesh. Amelia covered the wounds of winter skin with a violet ankle-length dress and a pashmina covered her sleeveless arms.

A skinny gentleman with silver hair approached Benjamin. His sexuality manifested in a red t-shirt with all the colours of the rainbow spread across the bottom and in bold letters the garment displayed a one-liner, *'I can't even think straight.'*

'Martin,' the man called. His eyes lusted for the veteran. Benjamin greeted the visitor with a nod of his head.

'Wanna hook up later?' the man asked, as subtle as Times Square at New Year. Amelia glared at the man, appalled by his forward approach. Benjamin rejected his offer, shaking his head and the disappointed flamer strutted off.

'Who was that? And why is he calling you Martin?' She slapped her brother's arm.

'He remembers me from my teenage days when I used to work the streets here. I used to use the name Martin in attempt to hide my identity.'

'And you used Dad's name?'

He shrugged.

Amelia turned towards the gentleman who advanced on her brother. He had now moved onto another table, buying drinks for a group of young men. The bitter taste of resentment towards the paedophile, who took advantage of Benjamin, filled her mouth.

'I'm surprised he still recognises me or even wants me now I'm an adult with one arm.' He laughed awkwardly but Amelia's silence suggested she found it far from funny.

'We've never really spoken about that period of your life.' Amelia said but Benjamin did not respond. 'I mean... it must have been awful. How did you do that every night?'

He shrugged his shoulders, reluctant to answer the questions he had avoided for years. Leading psychologists failed to obtain his darkest of secrets and he wasn't going to begin to divulge them now.

'I'm sorry, I didn't mean to sound so disgusted. I just struggle to understand how you did that every night, especially when you're not even gay.'

'Sometimes that made it easier...'

'What do you mean?'

'I would picture other people, but more importantly I'd focus on why I was doing it. I was doing it so we could have a better life. It was my job.' He hesitated from revealing that it had all been for her, refusing to allow her to bear the guilt of his actions. 'Do you understand?'

Amelia shook her head. 'I can't, I really can't. I just couldn't do it.'

'Well, look at it this way. You work in hotels. You know those little tasks that you hate doing every day, but you do them because it brings home the pay check?'

'Well sure, but at the end of the day, I still come home and feel proud of my achievements for the day because I made the guests happy. And my job doesn't go against morality.'

She despised plunging toilets when a customer complained of a blockage. It was degrading, but she accepted it was her job. Anyone who worked in the service industry enjoyed reading their names within a positive Trip Advisor review and Amelia was no stranger to this thrill. The same pleasure could not be obtained in Benjamin's line of work.

'But what if there's a customer who comes to your hotel with a confederate flag or comes across as a real pervert. You don't like serving the customer, but you do it anyway because it brings home the pay cheque.'

'Yeah but I don't have to sleep with them.' She threw up her arms and shrugged. 'Anyway, it doesn't matter now. I'm just glad you're not doing it anymore. Another drink?'

Amelia rushed off to the bar, escaping the awkward conversation, suddenly realising why they had never discussed his escort days before.

The alcohol lubricated their spirits, eradicating their fears of the outside world. The siblings received little fuss over their stint in the headlines and Benjamin's attire brought them a flock of *Thank You* messages from their fellow punters for his service to the country.

Two twenty-something guys approached and asked if they could join them. Amelia welcomed them to take a seat beside them. The boys did little for Benjamin's confidence; since his return home from the army, he spent little time partaking in physical activities, producing a protrusion to develop around his belly. Glen and his partner, Jake, worked hard on their physiques, showing off their muscles through their white tank tops. Amelia appeared anaemic next to the tanned couple, their skin coated in a seasonal pumpkin glaze.

Jake squinted at the siblings, assessing their familiarity. 'I know where I know you guys from, you've been on the news. Your father did that insurance scam!'

'Let's go.' Benjamin insisted, anticipating trouble.

'That was really rough on you guys. We believed you were innocent.' Glen said, holding up a hand onto Benjamin's arm.

Amelia grabbed Glen's hand. 'Thank you so much! You have no idea how much that means to me.' She wiped away a tear. 'My own fiancé didn't even believe me. He chucked me out after we were on the news.'

'No way?'

'Uh huh! I haven't seen him since. He hasn't called or emailed...' Her sorrow turned to resentment. 'He always complained that the news was corrupt, telling us one-sided stories rather than the whole picture. He called it entertainment, not news, but now... when it matters... he believes them over his future wife!'

'That really sucks!' Jake wrapped an arm around her. 'You don't deserve that. You give out your heart to this guy and he believes some news channel over you? Man, I'd be pissed.'

'I *was*!' Amelia yelled. 'He'd seen me torn up over my father. To suggest I'd been acting all those years is an insult to our entire relationship. He knew everything about me. I'd told him some of my deepest secrets and he's thrown it all right back in my face.'

'Well here's to the future.' Glen raised his glass and the others followed suit. 'Let's get drunk and forget that guy.'

The foursome carried on drinking into the late evening. They shared life stories and drunkenly made plans to meet for dinner, which neither party would follow through.

It was almost midnight when Benjamin returned from a short visit to the rest-room.

'I need to go, I feel nauseous.'

'Oh I'll come with you.' Amelia collected her phone and camera and placed them into her purse.

'No don't. Stay. You're having fun. You only said half an hour ago that you wanted to go out dancing! Go with these guys!' Benjamin turned to Jake and Glen. 'Will you boys look after my little sister?' They nodded their heads and lifted up their beers.

'Hey, I don't need looking after!' Amelia snapped, before breaking into a smile. 'But go on then, you've sold it to me. I'll go out!' She kissed her brother on the cheek and after shaking their new friends' hands, Benjamin left the bar.

'More drinks?' Amelia asked. The boys nodded their heads and cheered as she headed to the bar.

As she ordered their drinks, she witnessed the sleazy older gentleman, who approached her brother earlier in the evening, sneaking out of the bar. Deciding to give the pervert a piece of her mind, she looked over to Jake and Glen, ensuring they were distracted, and followed the man out. The couple were making out, giving her time to confront the paedophile.

She followed the man down Avenue C. He walked past several gay bars and turned right into a community park. The green space had gained infamy as a landmark to engage in cottaging.

Amelia ran to keep up with the pervert. Her intentions focused on saving a child from the humiliation her brother faced when he was a child. She turned into the park and witnessed him approaching a gentleman, perching on a bench.

That gentleman was her brother, Benjamin.

Chapter 18

Marty had lived through some painful Thanksgivings over the years since the day he left New York back in 2001, but this had to be one of the worst. He had lost the love of his life for good and he knew it.

Returning to Gary was a preposterous plan. The probability of bumping into Caitlin during their stay was high, but while they ran from the police, they required a quick solution to their problems. As Gordon helped him out during his previous escape, it seemed natural for him to return to this safe-haven.

This Thanksgiving, he had little to be thankful for. His wife and kids hated him, his fiancé loathed him and the entire country wanted his blood.

His room-mate, Gordon, prepared the Thanksgiving dinner, made up of an inedible microwave meal and a warm beer. Earlier in the morning, they watched the NFL game and witnessed the Indianapolis Colts kick the ass of the Green Bay Packers, which brought some joy for them to see their favourite team win. But now they rested next to the fire, grasping at straws for something to be thankful for, which led to a competition of '*Who has the worst life?*' to have the last cookie from the jar.

'I've lost my wife and my fiancé!' Marty started.

'Hey, at least you had a wife. I've been single for twenty years, never married or been close to a fiancé. But *you*… you lucky bastard, had two at the same time!'

'I miss her.'

'Which one?' Gordon asked. They both broke into laughter as the beer swiftly ran to their heads. 'If you want her, man, go after her!'

'You're right' Marty nodded his head. 'You're absolutely right.' He continued to swig from his beer.

'Well, what are you waiting for?'

'What? I should go now? It's Thanksgiving!'

'Absolutely! She'll be sitting at home, *alone*, being reminded by her family of what a loser she is without a man. The holidays are an emotional time for single people. Take advantage while you still can!"

'You're right! I'm gonna go and get her!' He grabbed the keys to Gordon's Skoda. 'Can I take your car?'

'Take it, but don't get caught, you've had far too many beers! But I doubt many cops will be out today, it's the holidays after all.'

Marty ran out of the shack that he called home, jumped into the car and drove off to get his girl.

*

Like most Illinois suburbs, Hoffman Estates became a ghost town at Thanksgiving. Locals travelled into the city to see the parade or left town to visit their families. Those who remained in the village stayed indoors, preparing their roast dinners.

Beverly Hahn pulled up in a taxi to a house which once belonged to her mother. Her mom died the year before and they struggled to sell the home since. The housing crisis had taken over the Chicago suburbs and this particular town had certainly taken a hit.

Beverly spent the night in a hotel in Downtown Indianapolis, before catching a train over to Chicago earlier in the morning. Chicago's transportation network continued throughout the bank holiday, allowing her to travel to the suburb from Union Station, before catching a cab to Aberdeen Street.

Stepping out of the car, she paid the driver and walked over to the house where she grew up. She held a lot of love for Aberdeen Street where she spent most of her childhood. It didn't matter how many years she spent in New York, this would always be home. The stone house at the end of the road was the original farm house, once inhabited by the farmers who ran the prairies before the housing estate was built on the land. Beverly dreamed of living in the farm house one day, but Marty's desire to move to New York caused her Illinois dream to go unfulfilled.

The house her mom inhabited was a two storey town house built in the nineteen-twenties. The blue wooden cladding had begun to rot and the grass had overgrown during her absence, but it still held the simple charm, which drew her adoration.

Towards the rear of the house, a small plant pot sat beside the garage. Beverly lifted the pot and collected a key hidden underneath it. Her mother always kept a key there. During Beverly's younger days, it was there so she could get in and out when she was at high school around the corner. During Marjorie's later years, it was used as an emergency in case she collapsed and needed somebody to enter the house quickly. Today, real estate agents used the key to bring potential buyers into the property.

Browsing around the kitchen, she saw little left of her mother's presence in the house anymore. Her dad supported her in ensuring Marjorie's belongings were delivered to a local charity store. Only an old dusty couch and a bed remained, which Beverly decided to keep there in case they were left with the choice of letting the place out to make money off the building.

Falling flat onto the couch, she turned over and grabbed a sandwich from her purse, which she had picked up from a gas station en-route over from the train station as the driver filled his tank. The cheese sandwich, which had no accompaniment, made up her Thanksgiving dinner. This had turned out to be the worst holiday since her husband disappeared ten years before.

The first Thanksgiving without Marty was a depressing one. The shock was as raw as a freshly cut wound as New York continued to pick up the pieces from Ground Zero. The Hahns had no turkey, instead, they stayed in and watched a movie with take-out pizza. But at least she had her children with her back then. Today she had nobody. Beverly had no television or radio. Searching for entertainment, she read the previous day's Chicago Tribune and ate her sandwich, chilled by the silence in the house.

A knock at the door disturbed her. Surprised, Beverly cautiously walked up to the door. Few visited the house on Thanksgiving; the estate agents were closed and the neighbours knew the house had remained empty for over a year.

Throwing the leftovers of her unsatisfying sandwich in the trash can, she brushed the crumbs off her hands and opened the door. The recognisable man behind the door caused her heart to skip a beat. Joyous that she had this friendly face back in her life, she jumped forwards and embraced him.

'Dad!'

*

In New York, Benjamin and Amelia sat around the dining table. They remained silent for the majority of the morning. The revelation that her brother continued to rent his body out to men sat uncomfortably with

Amelia. The man who approached Benjamin in the bar the previous night was not a pervert, which her brother had originally claimed. Benjamin met the older gentleman only days before on one of his late night escapades.

The previous day, he claimed his uniform acted as a protective bracket from the angry New Yorkers. The camouflage outfit was actually worn for a more sinister ploy. There were people who received a thrill from ex-servicemen and were willing to pay for the pleasure of being with one.

Believing he had left the game years before, the revelations had come as quite a shock to his sister. Neither of them had discussed the issue throughout the morning, but it hung over them like the Grim Reaper in a care home.

When she approached her brother in the park the previous night, he aggressively suggested she went home. He dragged her to the taxi and assured her that he would explain everything the next day. She begged him to return home with her, but he refused and abruptly told her to stay out of his business.

The time had arrived for them to discuss what had happened. They sat in front of the roast chicken which they had bought the previous day when they still had some optimism for Thanksgiving. They hadn't bothered with a turkey as it was too much meat for two people. The roast, which sat before them, was left untouched as neither of them felt hungry.

'What I can't understand is… why? We don't need the money. You have your pay out from the army to live on and I've got this job. We have no rent to pay and we've got Mom's account for expenses.'

'I don't have any money left from the army.' Benjamin hung his head in shame. 'Life's been tough since I was discharged. The memories of those months in Iraq really tortured me. I couldn't sleep and Dad's resurrection hasn't helped either. I've turned to smoking pot again. I've been buying marijuana in bulk for the last few weeks and there's barely anything left in my bank account.'

Benjamin stared at the chicken as he relived where his money had gone. He was riddled with regret, shame and disgust for his drug habit and how he was able to pay for it.

His drug habit failed to surprise Amelia. She heard her brother sneaking out of the apartment late in the evening and smelled the cannabis on his shirt when he returned hours later. Amelia assumed he had been on the roof terrace during his absence rather than returning to the sex trade.

'Even if that's the case, Benji, we have Mom's money! We have close to one hundred grand in that account. We're good for a while yet.'

'No, no we're not.'

'Surely your drug habit hasn't reached that level of expenditure? I know I'm not a user, but I'm sure marijuana isn't *that* expensive.' Amelia's heart skipped a beat.

'You see, what I didn't tell you is that we're being sued for one million dollars. They want the house, what's left of our savings and anything else they can take. We'll be bankrupt all over again.'

He slid the letter detailing their predicament across the table to her and she read over the contents. Even with her father's death looming over them a decade earlier, this had been by far the worst Thanksgiving they had ever faced.

*

Marty walked up to the house where his beloved grew up. He felt sick, worried by the reaction of its inhabitants. Marty caught a glimpse of her with her father inside talking.

Maybe I should have given her some time and space to think.

But he knew it was now or never to get this woman back. He knocked on the door and she answered.

'*Marty?*'

'Hi Caitlin. Happy Thanksgiving. Can we talk?'

She looked behind her to see her family, who were too busy clearing up the remains of their dinner to care about the visitor at the door. It was a friendly neighbourhood and they were used to the neighbours dropping in, whatever the season, lingering for a glass of her father's favourite Scotch. Hoping to avoid upsetting her father, she sneaked out and dragged Marty to the side of the house and sat on the bench.

The house was a three storey red-brick mansion. The courtyard held a large fountain, turned off for the winter months while the water froze. The Skoda borrowed from Gordon was scruffily left in front of the fountain, rather than the assigned car park at the back of the estate.

'What're you doing here?'

'I'm here to get you back! I love you, Caitlin.'

'You had a wife all this time and you didn't tell me! I don't want to see you again. You've broken my heart.'

'You wouldn't let me explain yesterday. Beverly is not my wife. We divorced many years ago, she ran off with another man. When I went on that trip to New York to visit my folks, we bumped into each other. I admit she took her hold on me all over again. I'm sorry she's always been able to do that. But as soon as I heard your voice, you brought me back to reality. I know what I want and it's *you*! I was weak! But you make me strong. Please take me back!'

'Why should I believe you? What stops you running off with her again?' Tears streamed from her eyes, which turned red as she rubbed them. Moisture ran down from her nose, freezing in the cold air.

'Because I want to marry you…for real this time….and soon.' He got down on one knee. The snow's cold moisture leaked into his jeans, chilling his kneecap.

'Caitlin Atkinson, will you be my wife?'

'Martin Reece... yes I will!' He stood up and kissed his fiancé. 'Come inside! We can tell the family!'

*

Francis Goldberg Jnr was a short chubby man with white hair, which he had grown to comb over, covering his bald patches. With his bowler hat and his cigar, he could have been mistaken for Winston Churchill. Since his retirement, he never dressed down unless he was on the golf course. Few saw him out of a suit.

While he could afford the most luxury of cars, he drove a Ford, an American brand. Buying American was a trait instilled in him from his own father, who worked in Henry Ford's factory in Detroit during the financial boom. Francis Senior remembered the prosperity the factory had brought to the area and since had never bought anything which hadn't been manufactured in his home country again.

In the doorway, Francis Jnr's daughter, Beverly, stood in shock, surprised by her father's return to a house where he hadn't lived for over forty years. He now owned the property as his ex-wife forgot to change her will after their divorce.

'Hello Sweetheart.' He lifted his arms out to invite her for a hug. She held him; it had only been a few weeks since she last saw him, but the embrace felt like they had reunited after many years.

'What're you doing here?'

'I could ask you the same question.' he replied.

'I needed somewhere to lie low for a few days. I didn't know where else to go.'

'Well, are you going to let me in?' he asked. She stepped out of the way to let her father through as he inspected the place. 'So where is he then?'

'In Indiana.' Beverly said. Francis raised an eyebrow and tilted his head. 'We broke up, it's a long story.' Francis sighed and sat down. Beverly closed the door and joined him on the couch.

'What happened to you, Sweetheart?' He grabbed Beverly's hand and stroked it.

'I don't know, Dad.' Beverly's eyes welled as she felt the disappointment from her parent. 'Everything happened so fast. Suddenly my dead husband was stood in front of me asking me to run away with him. I longed for that man every day for ten years.'

'It was quite a surprise when I saw you on the news. I was the talk of the town.'

She saw her father on the front of the Tribune when they first ran away from New York. Anticipating her father to be angry with her, Beverly found this gentleman before her to be surprisingly reserved. Updating him on her journey, Beverly detailed the miserable few weeks she had endured, including the shack her husband allowed her to sleep in and the secret other woman.

'So you still haven't told me why you're here. Shouldn't you be with Evelyn and her kids?'

'Well I usually speak to you at this time of year but you were gone. I wanted to be close to something that is part... or at least was *once* part of your life. Plus it gives me a little peace and quiet from Evelyn's family. I love her but her family are so loud, and you know me, I like a little quiet now and again. But then you came and messed that up.' Smiling, he placed his hand on her lap.

'Why didn't you let yourself in, who did you think was here?'

‘Well I forgot my key and the other one wasn’t under the plant pot. I thought I’d give it a shot that there might be someone here, even if it was squatters.’ he explained before changing the subject. ‘So you’re all alone on Thanksgiving, huh? I’m glad I came over. We can’t have you on your own.’

‘Well I didn’t mind. I was just glad to be away from that bastard, who I once called my husband.’

He wrapped his arm around her and kissed her forehead.

‘So I take it you haven’t had any Thanksgiving dinner?’ Francis asked.

She shook her head and pointed at the trash can to show the leftovers from the lunch she had tried to endure.

‘Well there’s a Jimmy John’s down the road if you fancy a sandwich?’

‘How festive.’ She laugh; the sandwich shop was comparable to a Subway take-out restaurant.

‘Well do you know anywhere better on Thanksgiving?’

She shook her head. The entire town shut down for the holidays and would remain closed until the madness of Black Friday the following morning.

They drove out into town and stopped by the gourmet sandwich deli, where they picked up two festive turkey and cranberry sandwiches and diet cokes.

‘Do you ever miss Mom?’

‘Errrr, well sometimes.’ It was a tough question to answer; he missed her as a person and a friend. But as a wife? He certainly didn’t. ‘I had a lot of happy times with your mother… and of course we had you. I miss a better time, but it was a different life. We were incompatible together and it was easier not to be in each other’s lives anymore.’

‘So you weren’t at her house today because you missed her?’ Francis stumbled for words. He considered telling her the truth but changed his mind; it was too soon. ‘It’s just I can’t believe you were there just because you missed *me*.’

‘OK, around this time of year, I miss your mom. We had the best of times at Thanksgiving. We had peaceful days in and now mine are filled with lots of people. I like to be reminded of the times we used to have. There you go. Are you happy now?'

Beverly smiled and rubbed her dad's arm. It brought her great joy to hear him speak kindly of her mother. Despite barely remembering them together, she spent years secretly desiring them to kiss and make up so she could have her parents together under one roof. That dream died the day her mother did.

'So it's your birthday soon, the big eight-o! How do you feel about that?'

'Don't remind me. I thought seventy-five was bad enough. It's another reminder of how little time left I have on this planet.' Francis cringed. 'Evelyn is planning a big party for me. I hope you'll be able to come. It's in a couple of weeks, down-town at the Waldorf Astoria.' Francis sighed. For somebody who disliked fuss, this was the last thing he needed.

'I'm not sure that'll be a great idea, Dad, what if someone sees me?'

Francis's eyes saddened as he considered his only daughter's absence from the charade that was going to be his birthday bash.

'Oh but you *have* to, even if it's in disguise. You're the only one who will make it bearable. You know I can't stand the limelight, maybe a few years ago it would've been something I could have endured but I'm too old for this now. If you were there, it would make it all worthwhile.'

'So you won't want one more person there to witness it all, will you? Come on, Dad, you know this isn't feasible.'

'But you *have* to!' he snapped, which followed by silence. Both of them remained surprised by his outburst. 'Sorry. It's just... it'll be my last birthday party, the least I should be able to have is my family around me.'

'What do you mean '*it'll be your last birthday party*?'' Francis was invincible; at least to his daughter. 'Of course it won't be, Dad. You've got lots of life in you yet. You'll make your ninetieth at least, and you know what Evelyn is like... she loves a party. She'll probably do the same next year, by which point, I might be able to show my face again in public! At least I hope I won't be still on the run by then... God help me if I am.'

‘I won’t be here next year.’ Francis calmly explained. He stared at his daughter, waiting for a reaction, but she refused to speak until he provided an explanation. ‘I’ve not told anybody this, not even Evelyn knows. I have cirrhosis of the liver. I have about ten months left to live.’ Beverly’s bottom lip trembled as she took in the shattering news. ‘I guess all that scotch had to have an impact one day, huh?’

‘How? I mean… when? I mean… what?’ Beverly had so many questions that she struggled to pick one.

‘I found out a few weeks ago. I wanted to get past my birthday first before I told anyone. I wanted to be around everyone for just one last time enjoying myself without people feeling sorry for me. The last thing I want is pity. I’d like to die quietly without being a victim.’

A tear stemmed down from Beverly’s eye. She grabbed her father’s hand and with the other she clutched onto her chest as she soaked in the reality of Francis’s fate.

‘So please come to my party and celebrate with me just one last time as I won’t be able to do it again.’

'How can I say *no* to a dying man?'

They finished lunch and drove back to the house. She embraced her father and struggled to let him go. She had few opportunities left with this man and she wanted each one to last as long as possible.

‘Promise me something, we’ll make sure every second counts up to my last breath. We have to spend time together. You can hide out here as long as you want. I’ll take the house off the market and you can be here, undisturbed for as long as you need.’

Beverly left her father’s car and stepped inside the house. The building felt cold and empty. She longed to talk about her discovery with someone other than her father, but she had no one. Despite having her father back in her life since her escape, she had never felt more alone.

Despite the pain he’d caused her, she couldn’t help but wonder how her husband’s Thanksgiving had gone. Two questions came to Beverly's mind: was Marty having an equally painful Thanksgiving, and had he thought about her?

*

Marty walked through the door of Caitlin's father's house. The hallway was grand with stairways lining both sides of the room. To his right, books covered the walls from ceiling to floor in a library and the left led to the dining hall.

An engraved brick at the entrance of the house stated the house was built in 1975, however the interior designer attempted to maintain a historic finish throughout the house as mahogany panels lined the walls and timber pillars stemmed up to the ceiling. Taxidermy and portraits of Caitlin's ancestors covered the landing and a buffalo-skin rug, shot by her father, was proudly presented at the entrance.

Caitlin's father, Joseph, stepped out of the dining room, lighting a cigar as he joined them. His weight had taken its' toll on his legs and he walked with a cane. Despite his wealth, his grey suit appeared worn and the buttons of his jacket looked fit to burst as his gut pushed against the tight-fitted garment. He hobbled over to his daughter's companion. Caitlin's face glowed with joy as she gripped onto her fiancé's arm. A white turtle-neck jumper and black jeans covered the figure, which she usually had on display.

'Who is this young man? I don't believe we've had the pleasure of meeting.' Joseph held his hand out to greet the man who his daughter clung onto.

'Daddy, this is Marty. He's just asked me to marry him.' She screeched with joy and jumped up and down.

'Is that so? Well how can he be your fiancé if he hasn't asked me for your hand yet?'

'Daddy, please! I love him!'

Marty cleared his throat trying to make his excuse to this traditional man. He placed his hand around Caitlin and squeezed her tightly and smiled.

'I'm sorry, Sir, I did want to ask you, but I wanted to ensure that she would say *yes*. I nearly lost her and I wanted to make sure that never happened again.'

'Well I suppose you had better come inside then.'

They made their way into the dining room. The table seemed to stretch across half the house. Marty counted that up to twenty people could fit around this grand table, but today just her mother and sister surrounded it. They wore identical clothing to Caitlin, but her mom had an orange leafed brooch clipped below her left shoulder.

Joseph introduced Marty to the family, but he had little time to speak to them as the women were ushered out of the room with his fiancé.

'Can't I stay with Marty?' she pleaded.

'You know the rules. Now go and help your mother clean up. Those dishes won't wash themselves.' She disappeared, leaving Marty alone with his future father-in-law.

'Sorry about that, Son,' Joseph said. 'We usually have help to clear all this away, but we decided to give them a day off this year as we don't have the family round.'

'I understand. This is a very nice house you have here, Sir.'

'It'll do. Are you a whiskey man?'

Marty shrugged his shoulders as he knew very little about the beverage. While Beverly's father was a keen Scotch drinker, he was very protective over it and refused to let anyone else touch a drop of his one-hundred-and-fifty dollar bottles he had imported from the highlands of Scotland.

'I'm easily persuaded.'

Joseph laughed and patted Marty on the back. They walked past the grand table and into a conservatory at the back of the house. While it was dark, Marty could see the vast amount of land which Joseph owned. Between two maroon leather upholstered chairs stood a small table with an ash tray and a deck of cards placed on top. To the side of the room, a cabinet filled with spirits and wines dating back to 1945 sat next to a rustic oak stool with a photograph of Joseph and his wife on their wedding day. Joseph filled two tumblers with whiskey and placed them on the coffee table and gestured to Marty to take a seat.

'So tell me about yourself, Martin.'

'Well Sir, I'm originally from New York. I've lived here in Gary for the last decade. I work down at a steel factory nearby, and I live on Jackson Street with a friend of mine.'

'And how do you suppose you will look after my daughter when you're in a minimum salary job?' Marty swallowed the lump in his throat as he waited to be thrown out of the grand abode. 'With that said, she isn't getting any younger and I want grandchildren. And she seems to really like you.' Marty sighed with relief.

To the side of the arm chair was a set of drawers. Joseph opened the top drawer and took out a cheque book.

'So here is what I'm going to do, I'm going to write you a cheque and you're going to give my daughter the best day of her life.' Grabbing a fountain pen, he began to write on the cheque. 'What's your second name, Martin?'

'Wouldn't you feel better writing it out to Caitlin? We've only just met?' Marty placed up his hand in protest.

'I couldn't trust her with a ham. No, you need to take this and ensure she has a wonderful day. Make sure my brother thinks this is the best god-damn wedding he's ever been to. I'm going to kick the ass of his daughter's wedding.'

The millionaire ripped off the cheque from the booklet and handed it over to Marty. The groom-to-be took the cheque. His eyes widened as he took in the figures on the paper in front of him. He had just been handed one hundred thousand dollars.

Chapter 19

The Law Office of Rocky McCartney PLLC was located on the Upper East Side of New York City. The firm had dealt with the Hahn family throughout the previous decade. It wasn't an easy task trying to register a missing person as dead. Through the many procedures required to sign over Marty's possessions, Amelia had become accustomed with this particular lawyer. Naturally she chose Mr McCartney now she was in trouble.

Black Friday was always a busy time and she had to push her way through the crowds of people, rushing to the shops to take advantage of the sales, before she finally made it to the law practice. As she approached the firm, she was taken-aback by the A1 banner across the entrance offering *'No-Win, No-Fee'* Injury Lawyer services. Rocky McCartney had always maintained a reputable practice but even he was forced to divulge into the compensation nation to survive the recession. Amelia took a seat while the receptionist phoned Rocky's office and moments later he appeared and greeted his client.

'Miss Hahn, I was awaiting your call, I'm just surprised it took so long!' Rocky escorted her into his office. Text books filled the office walls from ceiling to floor. Half of the room was dedicated to employment law alone. His multiple degrees were framed and displayed for all of his clients to see; there was no doubt over how hard Mr McCartney had worked to get to his position.

'Well I only found out yesterday how bad our problems were.' Amelia rooted through her bag for the document, which her brother had surprised her with the day before. 'It wasn't the greatest Thanksgiving gift.' She handed him the letter from the representatives of the 9/11 Victims Fund and the lawyer browsed over the contents.

'Wow. Well this is quite a claim.' He sat down at his desk and invited Amelia to sit before him. She slumped down on the maroon leather chair. The right arm was damaged by a cigar burn; an artefact from a time when people could smoke in offices.

'So do we have anything to worry about?' Amelia asked with anticipation. Rocky stroked his chin as he considered the legal implications of the claimant's case.

'Well it's fair to say they can't take anything away from you while your parents aren't here.' Rocky said. Amelia sighed with relief.

'All they have at the moment is a photograph of a man who looks like your father, although you haven't helped yourself by admitting that you saw him. You really should have contacted me to join you at the station.'

'But they can't take anything off me?' Amelia asked optimistically.

'Well no. This letter outlines they are suing your mom, not you, and while she's not around, and without any form of a court case to prove any guilt, they are unable to take any legal action against either of you.' Amelia laughed in relief. All the worrying had been a waste of time.

'But before you get carried away with excitement, it's not all good news. They can't take your home away from you, but they can freeze your family's assets. I will try my best to get around that. You need money to live, but I have to say, they have a good case to ensure that no money is spent before a court case. It's also likely that once they catch your mom, they will be able to take her to the cleaners when she's charged.'

'You seem quite convinced that they'll charge her. She didn't do anything wrong. She only found out the day before we did.'

'Yeah, but try telling that to a jury when she's on the run with the man whose supposedly been dead for the last decade. Even if your mom had no guilty part, she has no right to that money. Your father is alive and… well… I'm afraid they have a strong case. While I'll do everything I can, I'd recommend you appreciate every second you have left in that apartment.'

'So what you're saying is that I should hope my mom never comes home.'

'Exactly.'

*

Saint Paul's is a typically white American chapel, built in the early 1900s. It lies in the heart of Lancashire, a suburb on the lower-west side of Gary, providing a rural tranquillity for the wedding of Caitlin Rose and her fiancé, Marty. They arrived at the church for the Black Friday service to meet the minister who would marry them in just a few weeks' time.

'I've dreamt of getting married here since I was a little girl. I attended the Sunday school here with my sister. We came here for services when we were older.'

'I can't believe that in less than a month we'll be married! Although are you sure your dad is happy with this? He gave me the impression we're rushing into things.'

'He just wants a spring wedding, but he understands how excited we are. I told him the sooner we're married, the sooner he'd become a grand-poppy.'

Following the closure of the service, Reverend David Bishop joined them at the back of the church and knelt down before God. He silently prayed before rising up to sit beside them. David was of African descent with white hair, his clothes were of black silk and a white collar displayed his position within the church.

‘So you wish to marry in our house of prayer?’ David asked. The happy couple nodded in glee. ‘Well I’ve known Caitlin since she was a little girl and I know about her love of the Lord. But you, Martin, I know nothing of. Tell me about your faith.’

Marty hadn’t prepared for a religious quiz. A dribble of sweat poured from his forehead as he considered how to answer the reverend's question.

‘Well I was brought up in a God-fearing home, Sir. I was born a Methodist like you. I went to church in New York City and since my move here to Indiana a few years back, I’ve been attending St. Augustine's near my home.’

He passed the church every night on his return from the steel factory. He figured the Reverend would be too busy to ask for a reference from his current place of worship.

‘And you seem to be quite fond of our dear Caitlin?’ David placed his hand over the bride-to-be’s hand and smiled. ‘You’d better take good care of this girl as we deeply care about her.’

‘I love her, Sir… more than anything. I can’t believe I nearly lost her a few days ago. I want to be with her forever and I want that love to be recognised in the eyes of God.’

‘Then you have my blessing. I’ll marry you, but I hope you’ll come here more often. I’d like to get to know you between now and the wedding, and of course thereafter.’

'Of course we will, Sir. You have our word.' Marty stood up and shook the reverend's hand.

'I will of course need a deposit. Fifty dollars.' the reverend awkwardly asked. Marty delved into his pocket and retrieved his wallet. He licked his finger, counting out five ten dollar bills, and handed it to the religious leader. He tucked the money into his pocket and embraced the couple. 'You're going to have a beautiful day. Where are you having the reception?'

'Ah, well that's where we're going next. It's kind of a surprise.'

In Joseph's car, Marty drove the couple across the prairies and pulled into The Stanley Hotel. The white colonial-Georgian property had a long private drive and pristine gardens. A large pond filled the courtyard and fountains sprayed water out across the feature. Behind the hotel, a large hedged maze filled the gardens and a couple declared their vows beneath an arch in the distance.

They entered the hotel and were welcomed by Jessica, a young wedding planner who set up her own business straight after graduating from a local state college. The flame haired woman sported a white top and her company brand logo covered the breast pocket of her black suit jacket. She held a clip board in her hand, ready to take down the details of the couple's desires as she walked the couple through the hotel, describing the services on offer.

As they toured the property, Caitlin's smile never curved south, flabbergasted by the elegance of the venue.

'I never dreamed I would ever get married in a place like this.' she said in wonder as she squeezed her fiancés arm.

'Do you think you can accommodate us?' Marty enquired.

'It's a little short notice, but we've had a cancellation, so you're lucky.' The couple smiled with joy. 'But you'll have to pay the full amount up front if you want to secure it as it's so close to the big day.'

'Can we do it, Marty? Please, please can we get married here?'

'I need to visit the bank but I can get it over to you today, if that's OK?'

'That's fine, but I need it by five when I go home, otherwise no deal, OK?'

Marty nodded his head and assured Jessica that she would receive his money by the end of the day. The couple left the mansion, gleefully aware that in just a few weeks, they would be married.

*

John Barleycorn is a folk song by the Scottish poet, Robert Burns, which personifies the cereal crop, barley, used to create alcoholic beverages. An entrepreneur in Elk Grove Village, Illinois paid tribute to Burns's song by naming his bar with the same title. Barleycorns was converted from a speak-easy, which once inhabited punters illegally drinking during the 1920s prohibition. Today the saloon could pass off as a swanky cocktail bar, whilst still holding some of the original features that once allowed the locals to relax and secretly enjoy a tankard of prohibited moonshine.

Desperate for a drink after the terrible news she had received from her father, Beverly stepped into the bar. She pulled up a stool and propped herself up at the bar.

Frustrated with the itchy wig, she removed the disguise earlier at home and dyed her hair a dark black instead, hiding her red locks. Few would recognise her; she surprised herself when glancing in a mirror.

The bar staff brought her a bottle of wine before pouring the silky Merlot into the glass. She downed the first glass and refilled it, but took her time with the second intake. Hanging her head on the bar, she thought about how far she had come and wondered where she would be going next. The man who had promised her that everything would be alright could no longer make such promises as he sat at home dying.

'Well you look like you've had one hell of a day.' a gentleman passed comment as he stood next to her at the bar. He ordered a pint of *Sam Adams* and pulled up a stool. 'Not often you find a lady as pretty as you at a bar on her own. What's the occasion?'

'You wouldn't wanna know.' Beverly wasn't in the mood for small talk.

'You'd be surprised. In fact, if you tell me, I'll buy your next bottle.' Beverly turned to the gentleman to see if he was joking. He signalled to the barman to get the lone woman another bottle of Merlot. 'So come on then, tell me what's up?'

'Well first you have to tell me something. Why are you here drinking alone?'

'My wife on Thanksgiving decided to tell me that she wants a divorce.' he said. Beverly's head lowered and gave him a sympathetic head tilt. 'So come on then, what's grinding your gears?'

'My father told me on Thanksgiving that he's dying.' Her stomach turned as she relived the moment when her father revealed the news.

'OK, you win.'

'I should also tell you that I walked out on my husband just twelve hours before too.'

'Oh wow, double win. I should buy you two bottles.'

Beverly spat out her wine and laughed.

'I'm sorry!' She dabbed her mouth with a paper towel and blushed. 'It's been weeks since I've laughed.'

'Would you like to grab a booth?'

'Well I'm not usually the kind of woman to just grab booths with strangers, but I guess you've cheered me up. Why the hell not?'

The new-found friends walked over to a booth and began the war over who was having the worst Thanksgiving.

'So why did your marriage end?' Beverly bluntly asked. While she didn't necessarily find the man attractive, he had a certain charm, which made her wonder how anyone could divorce this fascinating man. 'I hope you don't mind me saying, you don't seem too upset about her leaving.'

'I was too committed to my work.' he explained. Beverly raised her head in empathy of the woman he left behind.

'Ah, I know what that's like. I was married to a director. The weeks spent at home while he travelled the world... I coped with it but I could understand other's struggling. It takes a patient woman to deal with that.'

'How about your marriage? Why did you leave your husband?' Beverly struggled to answer this question. There were so many reasons, but few that she could reveal to this stranger.

'There was another woman.' she said, explaining the easiest answer.

'Ouch. Men are bastards aren't they?'

'I don't know… you don't seem so bad.'

'So your father's illness… that's rough. I lost my mom last year to cancer.'

Beverly's hairs on her arms rose as she realised how much she had in common with this stranger.

'Mine too! I can't believe it. It nearly killed me losing her, I don't know how I'll cope a second time.'

'I'm not going to lie, it gets much worse.' the gentleman explained. Beverly sighed in disappointment.

'How did you cope?'

'I drank a lot, shouted at my wife, hit my kids and told them all how lucky they were to have me around. Ironic, huh? But then eventually I realised I was pushing away the people I had left and it woke me up. You can't live in the past. You have to just appreciate the now.'

Beverly thought of her own two children, she'd given up everything to live in the past. Chasing the past had destroyed her future.

'I should go.' She grabbed her bag and downed the rest of her wine, suddenly aware of how late it was.

'Oh OK, hey, did I at least cheer you up?'

'Oh, you sure did. Thank you.' She placed her hand on his shoulder and smiled.

'Listen, can we meet again? I've really enjoyed your company tonight.'

'Maybe, I'm not sure.' she said. He looked down in disappointment of her rejection. 'I'm just not too sure whether two people going through a divorce should really be spending too much time together.'

'Well I'm in here a lot if you ever want some company.' he said. She smiled and nodded, considering his offer. 'Misery loves company.'

'I'll bear that in mind. Hey, I never caught your name? I'm Beverly... Beverly Singer.'

He held his hand out once again, shook her hand and introduced himself. 'Lovely to meet you Beverly Singer….I'm Max Spielberg.'

*

Marty dropped off his fiancé and returned to the house, which he shared with Gordon. He entered the one storey house where he found his new father-in-law sat on the couch smoking a cigar.

'Joseph!' Marty called, surprised by his guest. Sat next to him was Gordon, shrugging his shoulders over the unexpected visitor. 'How can I help you, Sir?'

Gordon escaped to his bedroom to avoid the awkward exchange.

'Well I figured I would come and see where my future son-in-law is going to house my little girl.' Joseph looked around the room, judging the four walls around him. There was damp on one side of the wall and a rat trap on the floor next to the front door. This was no place for a millionaire's daughter. 'It don't look good, Martin.'

'Well I figured I would use some of that money you gave me towards a nice house when we're married.'

'You won't get much change from that hundred grand at Stanley.' Joseph raised an eyebrow. 'No, no. We must find you a nice house for you and my princess. I have a condo in Merryville, which I rent out, but I have no tenants at the moment. You marry my daughter, that house is yours.'

Marty broke out a laugh of joy. 'You can't be serious, Sir? That's very generous!'

'Call it my wedding present. I can't have my daughter living here with some man I never met.' He nodded his head towards Gordon's room. 'Anyway, that's all I came to say. I better leave you to your wedding plans.'

Joseph left and Gordon came out of his hide-out.

'Did you hear that?' Marty asked, a smile merging over his gobsmacked mouth.

'I sure did. You didn't mention this hundred grand he's already given you. When am I going to get my share?' Gordon asked. Marty gulped. 'I've kept my mouth shut while Beverly was around and when she left you, but I think it's about time I got my money. I've harboured a criminal for ten years and I don't put myself at risk for free.'

'Hey, calm down! I'll get it to you, OK?' Sweat dribbled from Marty's forehead and the colour drained from his face.

'When?'

'As soon as we're married. You heard the man, I've spent the money he gave me on a wedding, but as soon as we're married I get that house. Once my name is on the deeds, it's yours.'

'Where will you live?' Gordon asked, scrunching up his eyes in suspicion.

'We'll move out of the city, buy a dump and escape Indiana once and for all. Caitlin wants to be with me and she'll be with me wherever I go. But you have my word, that house is yours. I'm so grateful for you putting me up these last few years, I promise I *will* repay you.'

'Well you better…' Gordon warned, '…because you know I have that hand-gun.'

The hairs on the back of Marty's neck rose as he considered his landlord's threat. He was made aware of the gun when he first moved in. The device was locked away in his bedroom in a pass-code secured safety deposit box.

'I assure you, Marty Hahn, that I won't be afraid to use it should you ever deceive me.'

*

Across town, Caitlin browsed through wedding dresses, which a fashion designer had brought to her home. Alexander Laqois had designed clothes part-time while picking grapes at a vineyard in Southern France before he was offered an internship in Paris. He rose through the ranks and made his way to New York, where he opened his first store. Today he designed for The First Lady and Royal Weddings.

Joseph assured the designer that his daughter must have the best no matter how much it cost. He wanted everyone to see that even his most ugly of ducklings could be a swan for just one day. He loved that girl but he had been certain she was destined for a life of loneliness. In his eyes, she was no looker, nor was she smart, but she had a good heart and he was grateful that Marty could see that.

'You look magnifique, Mademoiselle.' Alexander announced with a European brogue. The designer had black gelled hair with a streak of white combed over to the side and a thin moustache rested above his top lip. While he was a fashion enthusiast, his own choice of clothing was a little to be desired. A black and white striped top, red pants and a beret on his head made him appear more like a mime artist than a designer. 'It has to be this one. Your relatives will just die when they see you looking *entourdissant.*'

The phone rang and her mother brought the handset to her. 'It's for you, dear.'

'Hello?' Caitlin answered.

'Hello Caitlin. It was lovely meeting you today.' It was Jessica, the wedding planner, whom they met earlier at The Stanley Hotel. 'I'm just sorry you decided not to use our services, but if you change your mind, please give me a call.'

'Excuse me?' Caitlin's heart raced; she was assured that her fiancé had booked the venue of her dreams. 'Marty drove over this afternoon to pay you, didn't he? We still want the venue!'

'Oh really?' Jessica sounded puzzled. 'Marty called me before explaining that you wouldn't want the venue. He said the wedding wasn't going ahead.' Caitlin dropped the phone in shock. What the hell was her fiancé up to?

Chapter 20

'The 9/11 Victims Fund has taken legal action to claim back the donation provided to the family of the man who faked his own death during the tragedy. Beverly Hahn received the million dollar fund back in August of this year, one month before her husband returned from the dead. However, the government have faced difficulty claiming back the donation as the couple are on the run and have yet to be found. Their two children are still living in the Manhattan apartment, which was purchased with the fund. The apartment has been valued at just below one million dollars.'

Amelia switched off the television, she'd heard enough about her family. She was simply grateful that she had somewhere to live until her parents returned home. Nobody could take that away from her. Yet.

Peering into her brother's bedroom, she found an empty bed, unslept in for another night. Clothes filled the floor, the curtains were permanently closed and it stank of his odour.

Hopefully he took home some floozy rather than pimping himself out.

Her stomach churned considering the latter. Aware of the wide variety of fetishes these grotesque men held, she remained surprised that a one armed veteran could be in such popular demand.

It was almost three and she had to get to work. She exited the apartment and travelled down the elevator as she began her journey to the hotel.

As the elevator doors opened, flashes of light blinded her view. Photographers fought their way through to the front to capture the inhabitant of the unwarranted accommodation. A glass door provided the only safeguard for Amelia who stood back against the wall, covering her face.

Mixing amongst the journalists were protesters, their placards demanding New York's money back. They banged the boards against the glass.

A security guard, disrupted from his afternoon nap, strolled in and gasped at the disturbance outside. He turned to a petrified Amelia and escorted her out of the fire exit towards the side of the building.

‘Are you sure you want to go out today, Mam? It looks a little dangerous.’

‘I need to go to work.’ Amelia insisted.

'Wait here.' The guard sneaked out of the fire escape and hailed a cab. He wolf-whistled at her, urging her to run towards the taxi. Amelia took one last look at the infuriated protesters outside of her apartment. With her safe space shattered, she ran and jumped into the back seat of the vehicle.

‘The Sleep Tight Hotel, right?’ the security guard asked. Amelia shook her head; she was heading there but she needed to make a stop on the way.

‘To the nearest Chase bank please.’

'There she is!' Amelia heard behind her. The protesters ran over to the taxi and smacked their placards against the window. She crawled into the brace position to hide her face. The driver slammed his foot down, causing the car to screech as it sped off.

The car pulled up to the bank and Amelia, now wearing sunglasses to hide her infamy, ran into the building. She was welcomed by a clerk.

'I need to withdraw as much money as possible from my account.' She handed her a passport and the details of her account. The cashier typed her details into the computer.

'One second, Mam.' She stepped away from her desk and re-appeared with a gentleman beside her. He introduced himself as Karl and explained that he was the bank manager before inviting her to join him in his cubicle. Inside the cubicle sat a desk and a chair on either side. On the desk sat a computer and photographs of his family.

‘How can I help you, Miss Hahn?’ Karl was of Asian descent, wore square glasses and a grey business suit. He took two paper cups and filled them with water from the cooler behind him and placed them on the desk for himself and his client.

'I need to take as much money as I can out of my account.' Amelia explained. The manager took her account details and typed them into the computer. He stroked his chin in thought before printing a document.

‘I’m sorry, Miss Hahn, but we’re unable to give you anything today. Legal action against your family means the bank is unable to withdraw any money from your account until all charges have been dropped.'

'I thought I had more time.' She threw her head down onto the table and sobbed. 'If only my brother had told me earlier we could have sorted this whole mishap. I need access to my money. I have nothing until pay-day!'

'I understand that, Miss Hahn, but the law's against you right now. There's nothing more I can do.'

Amelia left the bank, and for the first time, she hoped her brother had been out earning some money for them the night before, no matter how he earned it.

*

Marty had locked himself away in his room since the death threat from his room-mate. He was shaken by Gordon's passing message the previous evening, so much so that the banging of the door in the early morning caused him to hide under the covers.

Quivering, he listened out for Gordon, but besides the vigorous knocking, the house remained silent. Assuming his landlord had left the house for work, he stepped out of bed and looked out of his bedroom curtains to see who the persistent knocker was. It was Caitlin; her hair was unwashed and her face was a furious red. He rubbed his eyes, put on a dressing gown and opened the front door.

'Caitlin, what the hell is going on?' She wore a vest and pyjama pants.

'Why don't *you* tell me? Why have you cancelled our wedding?' Caitlin sobbed and punched his chest.

'Hunny, calm down. What's happened?'

She told him about the call from Jessica. Marty grabbed hold of his fiancé.

'Oh Hunny, you've got it all wrong. I haven't cancelled our wedding. I've just found us a better place to get married. It was supposed to be a surprise.' Caitlin stopped crying and looked up.

'You did?' She sounded more optimistic.

'Yeah I was just throwing you off yesterday. That place is a dump compared to where I'm going to take you on the big day.' Her eyes welled up and she began to cry again. 'What's up now?'

'I wanna get married at Stanley! I've dreamed of that place since I was a child. I have to get married there and it already has Daddy's approval. Please?'

Marty sighed. Caitlin was fifteen years his junior and could at times be so child-like. Her voice replicated his daughter's when she was young and wanted something from her easily seduced father. Amelia could get anything she wanted from him with that voice and so could Caitlin.

'But I've already paid for the other venue. I'll never get my money back now.' he explained but she continued to sob onto his arm. 'Hey, hey. I'll see what I can do. You just make sure you turn up on the day and I'll make sure you have the most memorable day of your life.'

*

A blizzard forced the city to become deserted. Snow fell heavily on the empty roads and the whistle of wind echoed between the skyscrapers. Lake Michigan froze and the only pedestrians brave enough to enter Chicago ran through the streets, carefully avoiding the falling icicles hanging from the tower blocks above.

It was a perfect opportunity for Beverly to meet her father; the locals were overly occupied in escaping the weather to notice a criminal on the run. She caught the Metra down-town from Palatine into the city and met him in The Italian Village restaurant on Monroe Street.

She walked into the restaurant and found her father sat propped up at a candle-lit table with a bottle of Chianti. He had lost a significant amount of weight and aged considerably than when he first announced that he was terminally ill. His skin was a faint yellow and just lifting the bottle to pour her a glass of wine was tasking. Francis was dying much quicker than he initially suggested and Beverly knew she would only have a few more evenings like this with her father before he met his unfortunate end.

'Are you supposed to be drinking?'

'Give me a break. What's the point of trying to be healthy now?' He laughed, but she refused to join him.

'I don't find it that funny. You seem to be dealing with this better than I am.'

'I'm sorry, it is a bit insensitive. I suppose I'm not too worried as it won't be me who'll be around missing everyone. I won't be the one grieving. I should've thought this would be hard on you, I saw what you went through with your mother last year.'

Beverly sat down and perused the menu although she had decided on her travels into the Windy City that she would have the spaghetti bolognaise. The pair caught up but their discussions naturally turned to his obvious declining health.

'Have you told Evelyn yet?'

'She thinks I've been on the sun beds, she's not a smart woman. I'll tell her once the party is over. You'll still be there, won't you?'

'Don't you dare think that I haven't had my concerns. I have. But you make it very difficult to say *no* to. If you were a kid, I'd take you down to Florida and let you swim with dolphins.'

'I don't suppose *Make a Wish* provide treats for eighty-year-old dying men. So what's new with you?'

'I'm seeing somebody. He's a wonderful man, he's called Max.' Her face glowed as she talked about him. She went to the same bar the following evening after their introduction. 'After our first meeting, I went home and woke up with a fresh perspective. Max makes me laugh, something Marty hasn't been able to do since he returned. It's been a long time since I laughed.'

'So you like this guy?'

'Oh yeah! I like him a lot. We've been on a few dates since we met. He's so easy going, I can just relax with him.'

'And have you told him about Marty?' His question leaned towards her infamy, rather than her infidelity.

'No, we're not quite there yet. But I will when we're comfortable. I'm just excited about building a new relationship at the moment. I've not felt this good in a long time.'

'So it's really over with Marty then?'

'That part of my life is far behind me. Marty hurt me and I can't go there again. He lied to me for ten years, Dad. How could he do that to me?'

'You should give the guy a break, he was going through a rough time. He thought he was doing his best by his family.'

'But he was seeing another woman! And he destroyed our family.'

'But that isn't fair. He never thought he'd come back. He had to move on otherwise it would destroy him.'

Beverly's fury towards her father's empathy turned to suspicion.

'What do you know?' Beverly asked, smelling a rat.

'I knew he faked his death.' Francis sighed.

'Excuse me?'

'He came to me about a year before nine-eleven and told me about your money problems. I have to say I was rather upset that you hadn't told me yourself.'

'You really don't have any room to talk. Don't blame this on me. Why didn't you just give him money? You have more than enough.'

'I tried, but you know what that proud son-of-a-bitch is like. He wouldn't take a cent.'

This did not surprise Beverly; she knew that would be the last resort for her arrogant husband.

'So I told him about some scam I read about in the news. Some British guy faked his own death and claimed the insurance money. I suggested he should do the same thing. I swear to God though, I honestly thought he was dead when the towers collapsed. I only found out when he called me a few weeks later to ask how you were.'

'And this makes things OK? I can't believe you did this! You've ruined mine and your grand-children's lives.' As she tried to piece together the series of events that her father had been involved with over the past decade, she was suddenly puzzled by one of his recent visits. 'On Thanksgiving, you came over to Mom's house. Why were you really there? Did you know I was living there?'

'Marty called me.' Francis explained. 'He said you guys had argued and you had stormed off. He was worried about you. I knew if you had come to Chicago that you would be there.'

Beverly stood up and grabbed her purse and coat. She couldn't face dinner with the man who told her husband to make the worst decision of his life.

'Do me a favour, Dad, and stay the hell out of my life.' Beverly stormed out of the restaurant, wondering whether she could trust anyone anymore

*

Joseph sat in his conservatory. He jabbed the end of his cigar into the ash tray and downed a glass of whiskey. The ailing millionaire stood up and looked at his reflection in the mirror; he may well be a lot older but he could still scrub up well. His housekeeper, Jolene, came in and attached a flower to his jacket.

'You must be pretty excited.' Jolene didn't usually speak to her employer unless he asked her a question, but this was far from a normal working day. Even the staff had dressed up for the wedding and Jolene had scrubbed up in a pink two-piece and matching fascinator.

'I'm a proud father today. I can't wait to see her.' Joseph straightened his tie and took out a hanky to dab his eye.

His daughter's voice echoed from the hallway and he hobbled over to meet her. Caitlin turned around and smiled at her father, who welled up as he saw his little girl. She looked like a princess dressed in her ivory attire. Caitlin's sister held the long train behind her. Along with her fellow bridesmaids, Lucy Atkinson wore a lilac satin dress with a white flower brooch upon her chest.

'That's my girl.' Joseph walked over and kissed his daughter's cheek. 'Is the car here?' He turned to Jolene, who nodded her head. 'Well then let's go and get you married.' In the courtyard was the silver Rolls Royce, used to escort the bride to the church. Pink ribbons covered the bonnet and a trail of flowers lined the trunk.

'I have to say, I did wonder whether this day would ever come.' Joseph said on the drive over.

'Me too. I've been dreaming of this day since I was a little girl, but I didn't think it would come. I know it's been a roller-coaster getting here, but I've finally met my prince.'

'I had my doubts about Marty when you brought him over on Thanksgiving, but I have to say, he's done a good job. He's chosen a great church and an elegant venue. I know the family will be very impressed.'

'I don't care about what the family think. I just want my Marty.'

'I know I don't say this often, Caitlin, but I'm so proud of you.'

They pulled up to St. Paul's. The car door opened, Joseph stepped out and lifted his hand out to his daughter, who lightly grabbed his fingers and exited the car. They walked over to the entrance where Marty's room-mate, Gordon, was stood in a charcoal suit and top hat. His skin was pale and he was shaking.

'Hey, the best man. Shouldn't you be inside?' Joseph sharply spoke, shifting his head in the direction of the church.

'We have a problem.' Gordon explained. 'He's not here.'

Caitlin gasped and fell backward. Her father caught her and pulled her aside, before turning to Jolene for support. Once he had his daughter out of the way, he returned to the best man and grabbed hold of him by his lilac cravat.

'Now listen here, you little punk. If he isn't here in the next ten minutes, I'll hold you personally responsible.'

A shaken Gordon slipped his hand into his pocket and retrieved an envelope.

'I don't think he's coming. I walked into his room this morning and found this on his bed.' He handed it to Joseph, who opened the package to find a note from Marty.

Dear Caitlin,

Please accept my deepest apologies, but I can't be there today. I do love you, but I love someone else more. You deserve so much more. Please apologise to your dad for me.

I'm sorry to do this to you on your special day. I hope you find a decent man someday.

Love

Marty

Joseph felt sick. He didn't know if he was angrier that his daughter had been embarrassingly ditched at the altar or that Marty had run off with his money.

Thank God I didn't give him the house before they married.

'He took all of his stuff. There's no trace of him in my house anymore. He owed me money.' Gordon explained.

'You and me both.' Joseph replied with gritted teeth. 'If you see him, you tell me immediately.' Joseph handed him his business card. He walked back to Caitlin. 'Come on, Hunny, let's get in the car.' She restrained as he tried to direct her to step back inside the executive vehicle.

'Where is he?' She sobbed, still unaware of the letter her father had hidden.

'I'll explain in the car, now let's just get the hell out of here.' Joseph instructed the driver to move quickly before the congregation, made up of friends and family, vacated the church to see a distraught bride. The Rolls-Royce zoomed off down the road, leaving the chapel behind them.

'Did he just panic? Maybe we can find him and bring him back? Most men get cold feet on the day, maybe we can change his mind.' Caitlin cried. 'Let's go to The Stanley Hotel, he might be there!'

Joseph was about to protest but figured this might not be such a bad idea. Marty had booked the hotel for the reception.

Maybe I can get some of my money back.

The chauffeur escorted them to the grand hotel. The building lost its charm as the bride's heart broke. The car pulled up at the entrance and Joseph ran into the hotel, insisting his daughter remained in the car.

At the reception desk, Jessica, the events planner, was stood propping up the flowers. To her right, Joseph could see a large conference hall filled with decorated tables, flowers and favours before every seat.

Shit, it's going to be hard to claim any of this back.

'Have you seen Martin Hahn?' Joseph banged his fist on the desk.

'Erm, no. Should I have?' a terrified Jessica replied.

'Well his wedding is here today, so I assume he would have been in touch.' Jessica shook her head and glanced at her diary.

'I'm sorry, we only have one wedding here today and that's for the Geller-Hannighan ceremony. Martin and Caitlin did come and look at the venue but they never made an official booking.'

Joseph slammed his hand on the desk again and screamed '*Damn it'*. Jessica flinched but Joseph waved his hand in sorrow.

‘I’m sorry, it’s just my daughter’s fiancé has screwed me out of a lot of money, I just don’t know how I’m going to tell her that he was never planning to marry her.’

*

It was three in the afternoon when Amelia finished her shift. She enjoyed working the early shifts as it allowed her to have the rest of the day to herself. During the previous weeks, she had taken a step back from customer service duties as she received threats from disgruntled guests. At first her manager stepped out and informed the guests that if they couldn’t accept the hotel’s employees, their custom was not wanted. Over time, however, it had become increasingly difficult and the manager had to intervene more and more to defend her employee. To save her integrity, she was placed in the housekeeping department, focusing on laundry to hide away from the prying public.

Now they had no access to their savings, Amelia had no choice but continue to work. Before, she worked to get out of the apartment and keep her mind busy. Before, work was a blissful distraction from the dark thoughts she encountered as her world crumbled around her. Now, it was a necessity to simply live.

She left the back-office and stepped into the elevator. As she was mechanically raised to the fourteenth storey, she stared down at the floor to avoid recognition by her fellow travellers. She left the lift and walked over to room 1425 and slid her electronic key-card into the lock. A click and a green light confirmed access and she pushed the door open.

'Hey Kid,' Benjamin greeted her, lounged on one of the two twin-size beds watching television. His sister smiled, closed the door and lay down on the bed parallel to his. On the television, he watched The Ellen Show.

Amelia had followed the same routine for over a week. Since she escaped the angry protesters outside her apartment, she hadn’t dared to return. Her manager offered them a room to stay in at the hotel, rent free, until they got back on their feet, while the security guard, who helped her dash from the furious New Yorkers, collected their belongings and delivered them to their new accommodation.

'Did you get my shaving cream?' Benjamin asked. She looked through her bag and lifted out several packets of shaving cream, along with toothpaste and sanitary towels, available complimentary from the housekeeping closet for guests.

'Yeah, but I don't know why you're bothering to shave. You never go out anywhere.' Amelia said. 'You know you need to go out sometime.'

'You don't have any room to talk. You only go downstairs for work and then come back up. Let's face it, we can't go outside. People are pissed and I'm not facing that mob.'

'I'm just grateful Sharon provided us a place to stay. We'd be pretty lost without her.'

The beds were three feet apart, acceptable for a night away, but as a living space for an unpredictable period, the siblings struggled to cope in the cosy accommodation. The en-suite bathroom provided the only private space away from the room and Amelia frequently lay away in a dry bath to escape her brother's irritations.

'I heard you screaming again last night.' Amelia said. 'I couldn't get back to sleep after it.'

'I'm sorry, I don't realise I'm doing it. The nightmares are still rough.'

'Have you considered seeing a counsellor? There's help for ex-servicemen.'

'I'm fine. I'll get over it. Can't you just ask for a second room?' Benjamin asked.

'Benji, it's New York. The hotel is always full to the rafters. We're lucky Sharon gave us this room, I'm not asking for another. We're just going to have to cope. Anyway, did you call the lawyer today?'

'Oh no.' Benjamin's eyes did not glance away from the screen as he talked. 'I'll do it tomorrow.'

'Benjamin, this has to stop.' Amelia raised her voice. She sounded just like their mother. 'I've asked you to do one thing and you haven't done it. We could be out of this mess if our lawyer knew about our situation. We need something to live on, Benjamin!'

Amelia would have called the solicitor herself but lethargy had overcome her too. She could barely face the simplest of tasks once she finished her shift. The short walk from the hotel lobby to her room was tiring enough.

'I'm sick of this. Come on, we're going out.' She threw his coat and shoes at him.

The siblings walked over to Central Park, where they enjoyed a relaxing meander around one of New York's few protected green spaces. It was nearly Christmas and the annual ice rink had propped up in the public grounds. They rented skates and spent over an hour gliding across the ice.

Amelia showed off her tricks to her brother by twirling on one skate, which Benjamin struggled to repeat with one arm. He could once compete with her, but today his balance was compromised. Confidence overtook her and she lost her balance, accidentally falling onto a passing skater. Benjamin laughed.

'Oh I'm sorry!' She giggled and grabbed the skater's arm. His buff physique allowed him to hold her up.

'Are you OK?' her saviour asked. Amelia looked up, recognising the voice.

'James!'

He held onto her, staring into her eyes. A moment of silent hesitation withheld them, contemplating their next moves. Amelia clung onto the warmth of his blue puffy winter coat, but lost her balance and fell back onto the ice. James dropped her and skated off.

'James, wait!'

But he had gone. She got herself up and turned around to find her brother stood there with his arm and stump at the ready to embrace her. Amelia had thought little of her ex-fiancé over the previous weeks as everything else had overtaken her life, but now they had reunited, if only for a second, it brought back the realisation of what she had lost. She broke into tears and held onto her brother.

They returned to the hotel and hid beneath their covers.

'You're right.' Amelia said. 'Staying in is much better.'

*

Snow hailed over the village of Arlington Heights, causing the trains in and out of the suburb to come to a complete halt. The famous racing track disappeared in the blizzard, preventing gamblers from enjoying a flutter on the horses.

Max Spielberg spent the morning helping his neighbours clear the car-park outside of the residential apartments. He wanted to show willing to his new neighbours since renting the apartment only a few days before. He hadn't expected to stay around as long as he had in the Chicago suburbs but it was certainly worth the investment.

His bills had built up, the hotels charging ninety dollars per night, and his girlfriend had become suspicious of him rejecting her requests to see his home. Before the move, he excused his aversion to her visit with a messy bachelor pad while he hid away in a motel just yards from her home.

Max had worked as a journalist for over a decade but had never been this involved in a case. Befriending and working for people who the journalist investigated was common in his field, but sleeping with them was frowned upon. Questioning his ethics, he struggled to stay away as his fascination towards Beverly Hahn grew, pushing the boundaries of moral journalism.

It was difficult to keep up the pretence but amongst all the struggles, Max reminded himself that Beverly was telling just as many lies. The dissolution of his marriage was one element he no longer had to lie about. His wife had enough of coming second to his work with the final straw landing after he abandoned her on the night he captured Marty Hahn, alive and well.

The length of time to carry on the charade was a predicament Max battled with. He had an inside scoop already but he wanted much more. He needed a confession. An explanation and details of her crimes in her own words would blow his story out of the water and establish him as a world-wide reporter. Book deals, investigative journalism and heaps of cash would follow and he could become one of the most respected writers in the world. He dreamed of winning the Pulitzer Award, one of the most prestigious prizes for journalists; the Oscars for newspapers.

The newspaper would usually fund the one-bedroom apartment he now resided in, but he wanted to keep his employer out of his activities. They would not only disapprove of his methods, they'd ensure he received little profit from his success, as to them, he was doing his job.

The residents abandoned the clear up of the car-park as the snow continued to fall, covering the areas they had just ploughed. Max returned in-doors and warmed himself up with a mug of hot chocolate. The ringing of his doorbell surprised him; he wasn't expecting guests.

Behind the door, a distraught Beverly sobbed. A white dusting covered her damp black hair, and black eye shadow ran down her cheeks. Her white shirt was transparent, her soaked jeans glued to her legs and her white pumps had disintegrated in the snow.

'Beverly, are you OK?'

'My life is in tatters!'

He brought her inside and provided her a towel to dry herself. He turned up the radiator and gave her the hot beverage, which he prepared for himself before she arrived. They cuddled up on the couch while she sketchily provided the details behind her tears.

'He's ruined my life!'

'Who has, Sweetie?'

'My father! I hate him, I just hate him. He's messed up everything.'

'What's he done?'

'Erm...' Beverly continued to sob, struggling to justify a reason for the fall out. 'I found out he's in touch with my ex-husband. He's been advising him. Why is he talking to him when he should be supporting me?'

'The worst part is he's made me feel terrible and yet it's him in the wrong.' Beverly continued. 'It's his eightieth birthday next week and he's asked me to be there. He's stressed that it's the last birthday I'll ever be able to attend with him and he needs me there.'

'Well you should go.' Max said. 'You can't *not* be there for your father. You don't want to regret this for the rest of your life, which you *will* if you don't go. Believe me. I lost my patience with my mom the last time I saw her and I can't stress enough how horrible that feeling is. It lives with you every time you think about them.'

Prior to their first meeting at Barleycorns, Max completed extensive research and discovered the details of her mother's death the previous year. He created a similar story for himself and Beverly was like putty in his hands. While it won over Beverly, in reality, his parents enjoyed retirement in sunny Florida.

'I don't know if I can.'

'Of course you can… and I'll come with you.'

'You will?' Beverly asked, taken aback by her boyfriend's offer. 'You haven't even met my family yet. Isn't it a bit soon?'

'I wanna be there for you.'

He placed his hope of a confession on ice. An insight into the family was far more enticing. He wanted to know how many were involved in her treachery.

'Thank you.' She kissed his cheek and smiled. 'Hey, let's go and get some dinner, there's a lovely little bistro in Lake Zurich I heard about.'

'That sound's great but I need a shower first.' Max stood up and walked over to his room, grabbed a towel and stepped into the shower in his en-suite. As he washed away the sweat from the physical labour of shifting snow, he laughed to himself.

She's so deluded.

The Bentley, the suburban mansion and the D&G watch were all on their way. He rubbed his hands considering the wealth Beverly would bring him while she would end up locked away.

Turning off the shower, he dried himself off and walked into the living room wearing nothing but a towel around his waist. Beverly had moved off the couch where he'd left her moments before.

'Beverly?' he called out. Max walked around the apartment but the fugitive was nowhere to be seen. 'Where are you?'

Her belongings had disappeared.

He sat down on the couch, his hair still dripping with water from the shower, pouring down onto his saggy chest and bulging belly. As he reached for his cell phone, he found his notepad on the coffee table. He placed it in his lap-top case the previous evening and hadn't taken it out since; somebody had placed it there. The notebook had newspaper cuttings from his previous articles on Marty, daily diary accounts of his encounters with Beverly and photographs of her captured on his smart phone.

Beverly had rumbled him.

Chapter 21

Amelia had lost the will to live. Stuck in her bedroom for days, she could only go out in disguise. She slouched on her twin-sized bed watching *Days of Our Lives,* although she struggled to keep up with the storyline as she lay depressed, reliving the last few weeks. Sick of looking at the same beige walls day-after-day, she needed to get out.

Where can I go? And how I can get there safely?

Benjamin sprawled out on the other bed. His eyes were closed and he nodded his head to a new Biffy Clyro song he'd downloaded. His music was so loud, Amelia could hear the ruffles of drums blasting out of his headphones.

Jealous of her brother's ability to block out the world, Amelia rolled onto her side and placed a pillow over her head to hide the sound and light which tortured her. She sobbed uncontrollably as she thought about James and the way he blanked her at the park.

If it wasn't for the vibrations rumbling through her bed, she would have missed her cell phone ringing. She sat up, rubbed her eyes and looked at the screen to see who had called.

630 – Illinois?

'Hello?'

'Hello Princess.'

'Granddad! How are you? It's been so long!'

They hadn't spoken since Marty returned.

'I'm good thanks, but I'm a little mad with you.'

'Oh God, not you too! Please don't tell me you don't believe we weren't involved either.'

'Hell no. You haven't wished me happy birthday! I'm eighty today!'

'My God, I'm sorry, Granddad!' Amelia clutched her chest, relieved, before tapping her head for forgetting the date. 'Things have been pretty tough here as you can imagine, I've had a lot on my mind.'

'Well I can understand that. So I haven't heard if you're coming tonight?'

'Coming where?'

'Didn't you get my invitation? I sent one in the post.'

'I'm sorry, Granddad, I haven't received anything.' She refused to visit the apartment since the protesters scared her away and the death threats put her off reading her mail. 'What's happening tonight?'

'I'm having a birthday party in Chicago. I would love if it you came.'

'I'm sorry, Poppy, I couldn't get on a flight today.'

'Drive then.' She could almost hear him shrugging behind the phone.

'It's a twelve hour drive!' she groaned.

'Well if you set off now you might just make it.'

It was nine in the morning. If they set off immediately they could get to Chicago in the evening. She looked at the four walls, which had become her prison for the past few weeks. As nice as The Sleep Tight Hotel rooms were, they had to get out.

'We're on our way.' Amelia hung up, wiped her eyes and threw a pillow at her brother, who lay in content, listening to his music. He sat up, dazzled by the assault, and looked towards his sibling. 'We're going to Chicago.'

With their bags packed and hire car ordered, they walked down to reception. Sharon stood behind the front desk on the phone, but hung up as soon as she witnessed the rare appearance of her illusive employee.

'I tried calling your room. James is here.' Amelia followed her boss to the bar where James was propped up on a stool. Hearing his former fiancé's voice, he put down his mug of coffee and turned around.

'Do you want me to stay?' Sharon asked.

'I'm good.'

Sharon nodded to Benjamin and exited the room with him, leaving the former lovers alone.

'What're you doing here?'

James had lost an unhealthy amount of weight and his sagging pale face now sported a beard.

'I can't do it anymore. I forgive you. I don't care what's happened, I love you. Please come home.'

Amelia hugged the man whom she absolutely adored and gripped him tight.

'Thank you, James. But I'm sorry. I can't come home.'

He pushed her back, confused by her rejection.

'You hurt me. You wouldn't believe me when I needed you to. And you clearly still don't, you're just accepting it. There's nothing to forgive me for, I've done nothing wrong and the fact that you don't get that just shows that we can't be together. I'm sorry.' She wiped a tear away from her eye, kissed his cheek and walked away.

'I can try.' He choked back the tears. She turned around and titled her head.

'It's not enough.'

And she left.

*

Francis stood in the conference room of the Waldorf Astoria Hotel, staring at his watch. His guest of honour hadn't turned up and he wondered whether she ever would.

His declining health became evident as he clutched onto his excruciating organs and his skin grew more yellow by the day. Evelyn made him promise to visit a doctor once his party was over.

'*Let me enjoy my birthday,'* he insisted.

His decision to avoid alcohol this evening led to questions from others, who were used to seeing the lush with a glass of his favourite whiskey in hand. The liquor, which was once so succulent to him, now brought him pain.

Golden 80 balloons floated around the room, hung from the chairs surrounding round tables and photographs from his youth filled the walls. The flashing lights from the DJ box blinded him and his favourite songs from the sixties boomed out of the speakers. Young children boogied on the dance floor with their mothers, while their fathers sipped from the open bar.

'You keep watching the door.' his step-son stepped in. 'You know, my mom put a lot of effort into tonight. The least you could do is enjoy it.'

'Why did you come, Steven?' Francis asked. 'You never liked me. You just never got over the fact that Evelyn left your father. That isn't my fault, but you've never let me forget it after all these years. Why would you bother coming to celebrate my birthday?'

'For my mother. Not for you.' Steven said. 'Who are you waiting for anyway?'

'They're here now.'

Through the door appeared Benjamin and Amelia. Benjamin dressed in his army uniform, Amelia borrowed a designer purple A-line dress from her colleague.

‘Granddad!’

'How are you kids? I'm so pleased to see you.'

'Exhausted, but it was all worth it to see that smile!' Amelia pulled at her grandfather's cheek.

The three of them pulled up a seat at a table and caught up on lost time. A waiter approached with a tray of champagne and handed a glass to each of Francis’s grandchildren.

'Why ain't you drinking?' Benjamin asked, pointing towards the glass of orange juice before his grandfather.

'Oh I'm trying to cut down. Alcohol has a lot of calories and I'm not too active these days.' Francis chuckled and patted his belly. 'Anyway, look at you, you really are my little soldier now.'

As Benjamin's cheeks turned red, another waiter approached them but had little to offer them on his empty tray.

‘Mr Goldberg. There is someone outside who wishes to see you. They say they’re related to you but they weren’t on the guest list.’

Francis nodded; he knew very well who his guest would be. He purposely left Beverly off the guest list in case somebody spotted her name and informed the press or the authorities.

A black and white marble floor spiralled round to the front desk, where guests were greeted with an abstract painting by Herbert Brandl. A crystal chandelier burst out from the high ceiling, designed by, the one and only, Coco Chanel.

With his grandchildren by his side, he walked around reception, looking for his surprise guest. Unaware of his surprise, Amelia and Benjamin stared at their fidgety grandfather searching every corner of the empty lobby. Frustrated, Francis walked out into the cobblestone courtyard and circled the fountain resting in the middle of the forecourt.

On his return, he found the waiter who informed him of the unexpected visitor. ‘I don’t understand. Where is my guest of honour?’

‘He’s over there, Sir.’

'He?'

The three of them glanced over at the shabby gentleman, hidden behind a Romanesque bust next to the check-in desk.

'Dad?'

*

Beverly was once again on the run. Her mother's home, which had provided a secure haven for her while she ran from the law, had now been compromised and the hope of hiding in one peaceful place had become unsustainable.

Betrayed by her lover, she felt used. Max had fooled her to achieve a headline story. She had read stories of undercover cops sleeping with their suspects to expose them, but this reporter had over-stepped the boundaries of moral and professional journalism. She felt nauseous as she considered sleeping with the man who planned to sell her to the public. Max had prostituted himself and she had submitted to his manipulation.

Upon finding Max's jottings, she escaped the apartment and made her way to her mother's house in Hoffman Estates where she hid inside for a few days, forming a plan. Collecting only her money, identity and a few clothes, she hired a cab and asked to be taken as far away as the driver would willingly go.

He took her to Normal, Illinois, a town as mundane as its name with endless rows of identical homes. It was the perfect *soccer-mom* town, depressing the mother who had anything but an ordinary life.

She put herself up in an In-keepers Lodge, a budget business hotel where she could sleep comfortably and undisturbed for the night. Busy business travellers were too occupied on their lap tops and Bluetooth headsets to notice a missing woman within their presence.

When morning broke, Beverly rented a car and drove south down Route 66 to St. Louis. Driving through Missouri, the temperature dropped, sparking an uncomfortable shiver to overtake her. Even for a Chicago girl, Beverly struggled to cope in the Mid-West winter.

Since losing her car to the bank ten years before, she had avoided driving in extreme weathers. It was an unnecessary and expensive mode of transportation in New York. The rental company in Chicago had provided insufficient tires for the journey she now embarked on and she struggled to keep control of the wheel.

Night loomed and she lost her way. Pot holes filled the road Beverly travelled along and the number of street lights decreased until she drove in complete darkness. The car skidded and she lost control of the wheel. She clung on in hope of regaining control. The vehicle dipped into a pot hole, skidded and flung off-road. Beverly screamed as the car rolled downhill, only stopping when it hit a large rock, crushing the roof of the car. Upside-down with an air-bag in her face, Beverly was left for dead.

Chapter 22

In room 359 of the Waldorf Astoria, Marty, Benjamin, Amelia and Francis sat in the living room of the hotel's premier suite. Francis invited his family to the room to allow them to talk privately away from his nosey step-family.

The suite was three times the size of the siblings' space in New York. The room had separate living and sleeping quarters, two bathrooms and a private elevator. A television hung above the fireplace and a dock for mp3 players allowed guests to play their own music on the surround-sound system.

Since entering the room, Benjamin bit his fist to prevent himself from punching his father, Amelia shook with rage, while Marty held his head in his hands.

'So where have you been?' Amelia began. 'And where's Mom?'

'I don't know where your mother is, I was hoping your grandfather could shed some light on that.' He looked up towards Francis.

'She's staying at Marjorie's house.'

'You know where she is?' Amelia glared at him. 'You've been in touch with her and you didn't tell us? We were going out of our minds.'

'I was hoping she would be here tonight. That was supposed to be the surprise. I didn't know *he* would be turning up.' Francis pointed at the unexpected visitor. 'I'm sorry I didn't tell you sooner.'

'But where have you been? Why isn't Mom with you?' Benjamin turned to Marty.

'We were in Indiana staying with a friend, we had a row and she left.'

'You were seeing another woman.' Francis interrupted. 'Where is this floozy of yours?'

'It was when we were apart. I hadn't expected to see Beverly again and I fell in love. That's all over though and I want Beverly back. Why isn't she here?'

'She didn't want to be seen, she worried she'd be caught.'

'Do you realise what you have left us with, Dad? Do you know we're two of the most hated people in New York? Osama Bin Laden isn't as detested as much as we are right now and yet we haven't done anything wrong.' Amelia scorned her father, poking her finger into his chest as she shouted. 'I've lost everything… my home, my job, my fiancé and my entire life because of *you!*'

'I'm so sorry. I was just trying to provide for you all. I didn't mean for you to get dragged into this.'

'Then you should have stayed away!' Francis shouted. 'None of this would have happened if you hadn't come back. You should have let them be.'

'I tried not to but I had to see her, I had to see Benjamin and Amelia too. It was agonising being away all that time, wondering how they were. Anyway, Francis, you're the last person who should be sitting on your high horse, this was all *your* idea.' Marty shouted. The grandchildren turned away from their father and glared at Francis. '*You* were the one who told me to fake my death.'

'You did what?' Benjamin stood up and approached his grandfather. 'This is all *your* fault? Can we trust anyone anymore? Come on Amelia, we're leaving. I can't stand to be around such deceitful people anymore. They're not family. Family wouldn't do this.'

Amelia grabbed her purse and followed her brother out of the room, but before they closed the door, she turned around.

'You better not stay around for long, Dad, because I'm not putting up with this bad press anymore. As soon as we get out of here, I'm calling the police and they'll be here in no time. I should have called them last time I saw you, it would've saved us a whole lot of bother.'

She slammed the door and left with her brother.

With little time to spare, Marty turned to his father-in-law for help.

'Is she still at Marjorie's house?'

'I don't know, I assume so. She fell out with me as soon as she found out I advised you to contemplate this stupid plan.'

Marty nodded his head, thanked Francis and left the hotel.

Exasperated, Francis opened the mini bar and grabbed a miniature bottle of scotch. He knew it would hurt to drink it, but the physical pain was nowhere near as sharp as the loss of his entire family.

He opened the bottle, poured the liquid into a glass and downed the poison.

*

Along a dark road in Missouri, Geraldine McMahon drove her truck, returning from a family dinner at her father's house. Her dad spent yet another evening expressing his disappointment in her for never bearing him a grandchild, nor had he had the pleasure of walking his daughter down the aisle. In his eyes, she was a failure.

The truth was Geraldine never wanted children, and while she desired marriage, the service she required meant she'd have to move to another state to be recognised, but she wasn't ready to share that side of her life with her bigoted father.

While her father was outspoken, her mother remained mute at the dining table, wondering who the people beside her were. Moisture dribbled down her lip and confusion welled within her eyes. Geraldine embraced these declining moments with her mother knowing she wouldn't have to make these dark journeys for much longer.

As she drove the truck along the vacant road, she spotted a large object in a ditch to the left of the side-walk. She squinted her eyes to assess what the object could be. As she drove closer, she realised it was a vehicle turned on its' side. The site of upturned cars in the snow was common in a state with brutal winters and this site came as no surprise to Geraldine. In most cases, the driver had managed to escape and found safety, but she always stopped, just in case.

The truck pulled up and she got out of her car, grabbed her tools and slid down the hill to the up-turned vehicle. With her spade from her truck, she dug around the snow and forced open the car door. Geraldine pulled out the woman from inside of the vehicle, who was unresponsive but had a pulse.

Pulling out her purse, Geraldine found details of the victim to inform the emergency services appropriately. She found a passport with the name *Beverly Singer* upon it. As she reached for her cell phone to call for an ambulance, she noticed a driving licence and retrieved it to see where this Beverly was from. Upon it, Beverly's last name differed from the name printed in her passport. This wasn't unusual, she may have married recently and forgotten to update her other ID.

However, the name Beverly Hahn had struck a chord with her. *How did she know this name?* She looked at the top left hand corner to see which state had distributed the identification: *New York.* As she read the Manhattan address, Geraldine remembered where she had heard this particular name; Beverly Hahn had been on CNN only recently.

Geraldine put the cell phone away and pulled Beverly away from the car. She was a broad lady and could lift a fair weight, especially a small skinny thing like Beverly. She lifted the breathing body over her shoulder and carried her back up the hill, placed her in the back of the truck and drove off into the night.

*

Snow avalanched off the roof of the blue wooden house on Aberdeen Street. Marty's fists penetrating the door unsettled the layer, urging it to tumble down, piling the white dust over his head and shoulders. It was light in weight and caused little harm, but a cold moisture dribbled down from his hair and leaked into his inner ear. He inserted his little finger and wriggled it, squeaking as he cleared the canal.

The lights were out and there appeared to be little activity inside the house where his wife grew up. If she was home, he needed to wake her up before the police arrived. As he banged and yelled, a neighbour walked outside, disturbed by the commotion.

'Can I help you with something?' the elderly gentleman asked. The old man dressed in just a dressing gown and slippers. A cold breeze exposed his genitals and Marty turned away to avoid eye contact with them.

'I'm looking for the lady who lives here.'

'You're about fourteen months too late, pal, she died last year.'

'Oh no, I'm looking for the younger lady who was here.'

'Oh, I see. Yeah there has been someone in and out, but she left yesterday with a bag of things. She looked like she was in an awful hurry.'

Marty sighed.

I'm too late.

'Thanks, did she say where she was going?' he asked.

‘Beats me, she never really spoke to the neighbours. This is a friendly community but she kept to herself.’ The gentleman said goodnight and went back inside.

Marty got back inside his car and slammed his head onto the steering wheel three times. A sharp pain radiated from his forehead; he placed his hand over it and felt heat rising from the bruise. He considered all the places Beverly could be.

He turned on the engine and Chuck Berry immediately came on the radio. As he arrived at the second verse of *Route 66*, Marty suddenly realised where Beverly might be. He had little time to consider her whereabouts as the sound of sirens roared behind him.

*

The drive back to New York was long and tiring. Exhaustion overtook Amelia as she battled the twelve hour journey. In the passenger seat, her brother, Benjamin, yawned. His missing arm conveniently prevented him from taking the wheel, leaving the pressure on his sister.

The pressure was heightened by the weather. The snow piled high and the wind forced the car off-centre. Amelia pulled hard on the steering wheel to keep the vehicle on track.

‘Do you think I’ve done the right thing?’ Amelia asked, regretting calling the police on her father.

‘Of course. If you hadn’t, I would’ve done it myself.’ Benjamin reassured her. ‘He’s put us through hell, at least this way people will understand that we’re not involved.’

'I agree, but I still feel bad. I'm so angry with him, but he did everything for us. He hasn't received any financial gain himself from the scam. His focus was on Mom and us.'

She clicked on the stereo to prevent her attention from drifting. The radio played the best of the nineties, but her sower mood prevented her from bopping her head to her favourite tunes.

‘I just don’t know what to do now. Our lives are a mess. I wonder whether Mom’s OK, maybe we should have gone and visited her?’

‘Let’s just go home, you have work tomorrow and I would prefer to be in New York, where everyone hates us, than in this brutally cold weather. How Mom lived here for all those years, I’ll never know.

Plus we have little money to stay in a hotel and I'll be damned if I take a cent off Granddad. He can go to hell for all I'm concerned.'

Amelia drove on, leaving Chicago and another family member behind.

*

The party had taken it out of Evelyn Goldberg. Her legs were tired from the hours of dancing and her throat was sore after nattering with old friends, many of whom she hadn't seen since her wedding to Francis.

The absence of her husband concerned her. He was last seen leaving with his grandchildren but had failed to return. She scowled, furious that his blood relatives had managed to soak up his attention once again, while her family went unnoticed.

His family had caused enough drama. She had to keep her head down for weeks down at the Rotary Club, while old friends and colleagues gossiped about her husband's infamy following his daughter's antics. Unlike Francis, she was ashamed of her association with the Hahn family.

Determined to find him, she left the events suite and located her electronic key-card in her purse. She took the elevator up to her room, which she had booked for the evening. As she opened the door, she was pleasantly surprised to find the lights on.

Oh good, he's here.

Walking into the living room, her relief turned to horror as she found her husband on the floor. Running over to him, she pounced onto his body and felt his pulse. He wasn't breathing. There were three empty miniature bottles of scotch on the coffee table and a crystal glass on its' side on the floor. The corner of the glass had broken off and a sticky liquid poured onto the laminate flooring. She grabbed onto his arm and cried.

Not now, why now?

*

The room was unfamiliar, but concussion caused her vision to blur. To her right was a bedside table, beautifully hand crafted. The bedding was flowery, the wallpaper had blue and white stripes and a beige carpet covered the floor. Wherever she was, she wasn't home, nor was she in the car where she last remembered being.

'*Where am I?*' Beverly pondered. She sat up but the pain in her back caused her to lie back down, she wasn't going anywhere soon. She pieced together the last memories before all went black. Her last location was in a car on her way to St. Louis.

'Hello?' she called out, but mere whimpers escaped her mouth. A tube ran out of her arm to a drip.

Am I in hospital? This is a nice hospital.

A door opened and in walked a broad stocky lady. The woman could have been almost pretty had she washed her short greasy hair and applied make-up. If it was a hospital, they have a relaxed attitude to uniform as this nurse sported a baggy sweat-suit.

'Hello Dear, how're you feeling today?' the stranger asked.

'Erm, where am I?'

'You're in Richmond Heights, Missouri. Around seven miles West of St. Louis.' the stranger explained. 'You were in a car accident last night and I brought you here.'

'Is this a hospital then?'

'I'm afraid not, you're in my home.'

'And you are?' Beverly quizzed.

'I'm Geraldine McMahon, lovely to meet you, Beverly.'

'I should really go to hospital.' Beverly had read enough Stephen King novels to be paranoid of this home-care operation. 'Please take me to a hospital.'

'Oh I couldn't do that, I'm afraid.' Geraldine explained. 'Because I know who you are, Mrs Hahn. It seems you're quite the wanted woman.'

Chapter 23

They heard the ringing before entering the room. Amelia returned to New York with her brother, exhausted from the twelve hour drive, and answered the phone on the bedside table.

'Hello?' Amelia answered. She spent several minutes in silence, listening to the caller, before thanking them and hanging up. The adrenalin woke her up from her drowsy state and the colour drained from her face. She turned to her brother and broke the news. 'Grandpa's dead.'

'Please don't tell me we have to drive back to Chicago, because twenty-four hours of driving is as much as I can handle.'

Benjamin dived into his bed, rolled over and closed his eyes.

It was ten o'clock in the morning; Amelia had not slept in over twenty-four hours and had driven for the majority of it. The shocking news of her grandfather's death prevented her from sleeping. Desperate for someone to talk to, she considered who she had left in New York for support.

The one person whom she would have once turned to had let her down, but there were few people left to help her in one of the most over-populated cities in the States. She didn't know whether he would still offer a friendly ear, but it was worth a shot. She picked up the phone.

'Hi James, can we talk?'

They met in a Starbucks on Canal Street. China Town offered a quiet sanctuary away from the public eye; despite the hustle and bustle of the oriental village, the locals paid little attention to the infamous tourist. The green corporate logo appeared distinct despite its neighbouring independent traders illuminating decorations flourishing their bay windows.

Following his visit to her hotel the previous day, Amelia hoped James would lend an empathetic ear, even if he wasn't inclined to believe what he heard.

'It sounds like you've had a rough couple of days. I should have been there for you.'

'Well you're here now, that's what matters.' She gripped onto his hand and smiled. 'How did you find out where I worked?'

'I spoke to Sandra.' James said. 'She shouldn't have told me really, but your boss asked for an employment reference from her. I was desperate to find you and you didn't seem to be at your mom's place, so I begged her to tell me where you were.'

'How is Sandra?' Amelia longed to speak to her old friend again.

'She's OK, but she's still really angry about everything.' James explained and Amelia bowed her head in disappointment. 'She's softening though. She asked about you when I got back yesterday from visiting you. She was glad to hear you were OK.'

'It was my dad who deceived everyone, nobody else.'

'Then why is your mom on the run?'

'I don't know. I wish I knew the answer. I guess she's just simply a woman in love. I don't know what I would do if *you…*' She paused before correcting herself. '… I mean, if I was in her position.'

'No, me neither I suppose.'

'I think it's quite obvious what you'd do because you already did it. You chucked me.'

She paused. It was awkwardly silent.

'I know what I'd do anyway, as I already did it too.' she continued. 'I let them escape. I was so angry, but I let them go. I wish I hadn't now, for their own sakes as much as mine. I'm the most hated woman in New York and the only thing I did wrong was let them run away. I think OJ Simpson would receive a warmer reception than I would in this city.'

'So it's not long until Christmas.' James tried to swiftly move on the conversation, shying away from the overbearing guilt of abandoning Amelia in her hour of need. 'What are you guys doing for it?'

Amelia grabbed her phone out of her clutch. She looked at the calendar application to check the date. 'It can't be close to Christmas, surely? Oh my, it's the 19th, I hadn't realised. Time's gone by so quickly, I hadn't even considered Christmas!'

'Haven't you seen all the decorations? How could you miss Macy's? It's like Santa exploded in there!'

'My head's been so distracted recently, I hadn't even noticed. Besides, it's been a long time since I went to Macy's. Even if I could afford to go there, I wouldn't risk being seen in somewhere so busy.'

'So then, I'll ask you again, what are you gonna do at Christmas?'

'I don't know, I'll probably be working.'

'You can't be working all day though?'

'No but I don't exactly have much family to celebrate with. It's only fair that my colleagues get the day off seeing they have someone to spend it with. This year will probably be spent with my brother in front of the television with a beer. That's if he's not working. The holidays are quite the money-maker apparently. Lots of lonely old men at Christmas.'

'What does he do?' James asked, curious to understand what he did now he'd left the army. He'd struggled to gain employment before he split up with Amelia.

'He's back on the game.' Neither of them said anything, but disgust spread across James's face.

'Well why don't you both come to my dad's?'

Amelia thought his suggestion over. It felt unusual to spend the holidays with her ex and his family, but it beat spending it alone.

'That sounds lovely, how is your dad?' She hadn't seen Ray since the morning he left her mom's apartment.

'He's fine. He was obviously a little surprised about your dad reappearing, but he thinks I'm mad to give you up over it.'

'That's nice to hear. I always got along with Ray. He's a nice guy. In a way it was just as hard losing your family as it was losing you.'

'I don't suppose you would come home?' James asked, moisture forming in his eyes.

Amelia considered his offer. While she missed him more than cats missed the nip, his inability to believe her side of the story still stung her.

'I'm sorry James, I can't. I want to, but I'm still hurt. The fact that you don't believe I wasn't involved shows the lack of trust in our relationship.' she said. James stared down at his coffee and swallowed the sadness which had lodged in his throat. 'I'd like it if we could be friends though.'

'I'd like that too.' James tried to force a smile. 'So when are you going back to Chicago?'

Amelia mused over that question. She was still exhausted from the last trip and could barely consider the drive back over to Chicago. Miles and miles of featureless terrain tortured her throughout the twelve hour journey.

'I don't know if I'm going to bother. My grandfather ruined our lives. None of this would've happened if it wasn't for him. If I went over there, it would only be to make sure he was definitely dead.'

'You're really not gonna go to his funeral? That's not the Amelia I know.'

'Well would you? After what he did?'

'Well, yeah,' James said. 'He might not have given the best advice to your dad, but he was thinking of you guys the whole damn time. He wanted what was best for you and your family and if that was the only outlet then he and your father swam out in a sea of desperation. But even without any of that... do you really not want to say goodbye? How could you live with yourself?'

Considering his argument, Amelia picked up the white mug before her. She blew gently on the top of the scalding latte, before cautiously taking a sip.

'I hate you sometimes. You're always right. I don't know if I can convince my brother to go. He's still pretty angry and he's a lot less forgiving than I am.'

'Then I will.' James said, grabbing her hand and rubbing it. 'I'll do whatever I can to support you.'

'Thanks.' she said, her smile glowing. 'It won't be until after Christmas now anyway I suppose.'

A sudden flash of light hit them. The couple looked out of the window to see a journalist with a camera taking photographs of them.

'Damn it, I thought we were safe in here. Drink up.' They downed their coffees and walked out of the coffee shop, pushing the journalist aside as his camera lens continued to flicker.

*

Her heart thumped, petrified of the strange woman before her. With her body broken and her arm locked to a drip, she had little chance to escape. She was now at the mercy of the stranger who had declared her knowledge of Beverly's real identity.

The narcotics did little to ease the hostage's mind. Did the stranger wish to hand her over to the police for a reward, or did she plan to extort the cash out of the runaway directly?

Beverly looked around the room for torture devices. It looked like a nice house, but even Annie Wilkes kept a clean home. She tried to stretch her neck to look out of the window, hoping to evaluate her situation. Was she in a suburb? A rural village? A sharp pain in her back restrained her from peering over the window ledge to see.

'Who are you?' The morphine slurred her speech. *Is this to numb the pain or stop me from escaping?*

'I'm Geraldine, Geraldine McMahon.' the lady said. 'I found your car in a ditch just near St. Louis. What were you doing out there with such shitty tires? You could have died.'

'I was…' but Beverly had no answers, apart from escaping the law, and in turn, her own family. The fear for her safety returned. 'I should really go to the hospital.'

'Do you really think that's a great idea? You're one of the most wanted women in America right now. They would hand you over to the police in a heartbeat.' Despite her rugged appearance, Geraldine had a warm smile, one which her grandmother welcomed her with whenever she visited.

'Why are you being so kind to me?' Beverly asked; it had been a while since she'd met the warmness of a stranger.

Geraldine pulled up a chair from the corner of the room and propped it up against the bed so she could sit beside the patient. The heavy scent of lavender filled the room.

'Well Dear, it's in my nature to be kind. You see, I'm a nurse.' Geraldine paused, before correcting herself. 'Well, at least I was. I haven't nursed for a long time now.'

'What happened?'

'I lost my job, sadly. I miss it every single day.'

Beverly sympathised with Geraldine. She imagined nursing to be a calling; something she'd never had the luxury of having. She went to Cornell to find herself and left with a husband and a baby.

'How come you can no longer nurse?'

'Errr... it's a long story. Do you want some water, Sweetie?'

Beverly would have probed further, but she was dehydrated. The morphine caused her throat to dry and she nodded in acceptance of her host's offer.

'Would you like to make a telephone call too, Hunny? Let someone know where you are?'

Beverly shook her head. She didn't know who she would call as she had no one left in her life anymore. Her children hated her, her husband and father had let her down, and her mother was dead. Who would she call?

'No thank you.'

'Can I ask a question?'

'Sure, go ahead. I can hardly deny you that after all you've done.'

'Did you know your husband was alive?'

'No. I found out a couple of nights before that photograph made the headlines.'

'Then why did you run away?'

'I don't know. Love? Or maybe I just wanted an adventure.'

'Pretty risky adventure.'

'When I left college, my friends went backpacking around the world, while I settled down, got married and had kids. My dad even offered to pay for me to go travelling, I thought he was trying to break Marty and I up so I resisted. Now look at me. I'm having a mid-life crisis. Running away like some college grad with no responsibilities.'

As she lay in bed, in pain, looking back on her life, in particularly the previous three months, she no longer desired that adventure. She wanted to make things right. There were things she needed to say, but she needed the right outlet.

'Well I'll let you get your rest.' Geraldine tucked Beverly in, grabbed the empty glass of water from the bedside cabinet and began to walk off. A hand clutched onto hers. She turned to Beverly, who squeezed onto her carer.

'Actually, please could I have that phone?'

The wheels of the trolley squeaked as it rolled into the room. A cordless telephone and a fresh glass of water sat on top of the carrier. A pink straw sprouted out of the glass.

Geraldine picked up the tumbler and fed her patient. The nurse then handed her the phone. Beverly dialled and on the third ring, the receiver answered.

'Hello?'

'Hi Max, it's Beverly.'

'Beverly, where are you? I was worried. You just disappeared. When are you coming home?'

'Spare me.' she said bluntly. She was in no mood to exchange pleasantries with yet another man who had deceived her. 'I need a favour. I'm willing to exchange the location of my husband if you grant it to me.'

'OK, that sounds good to me.' Max replied, intrigued by her offer. 'What's the deal?'

'You have to promise you won't track me down. After this call you leave me alone.'

'It's a deal.'

'And I need you to report a statement for me.'

'Let me get my Dictaphone.'

Geraldine left the room and for the next half hour, Beverly talked openly, something she'd been unable to do for a long time.

*

Christmas in New York was an exciting time. Florescent decorations filled the city and the Rockefeller Centre housed a one-hundred foot festive tree. The tradition of decorating the tree dated back to the great depression. Back then, the locals filled a smaller bush with tin cans to lift their spirits as they struggled to feed their families. Today, while on a much grander scale, it still brought as much joy to locals and visitors alike.

The tree managed to work its magic on the Hahn siblings, who despite facing the worst year of their lives, still managed to work up a smile as they passed the giant ornament. They approached the Rockefeller Centre on the walk over to James's father's house. Ray invited them over for a festive lunch.

Ray lived in a large apartment in the Upper-East side of New York. His apartment held a grand entrance, three bedrooms, a kitchen, a separate dining hall and a large living room. A roof top terrace provided inspiration for the impressionist who spent his days painting and his nights at exhibitions.

Like Beverly, Ray received a large pay out from the victims fund and could afford a luxury apartment following his wife's passing. A former train driver, he retired upon receiving the cheque and used his art as therapy to overcome the pain of losing his wife. He'd since gone on to sell his work and was now a renowned artist within the city.

Ray welcomed the Hahn siblings into his warm abode and walked them through to the dining room. A red cover, crackers and white dusting covered the table. An open fire roared and above it a gold antique clock ticked away on the mantelpiece. A snowy Central Park scene, painted by Ray, hung onto the sangria-red walls.

Conversation struggled to flow. This was the first time the Hahns and the Gates' had dined together since Marty's return. A lot had been said since and it was difficult to forgive.

Attempting to fill the awkward silences, Ray switched on the stereo. Wham and Slade made up the radio's play list, but a short news round-up paused the festive collection. The annual parade made the top headline, followed by an explosion in a Catholic church in Nigeria. The final news story caught their attention.

'The wife of a man who faked his own death in the 9/11 attacks on the twin towers has come forward to defend her family's actions. Beverly Hahn from Manhattan has explained that her husband, Martin, faked his death for insurance purposes as they were heavily in debt. Mrs Hahn insists neither her, nor her children, were aware or involved in his plan and her husband thought he was committing fraud against an insurance firm, rather than the 9/11 fund.'

The cutlery rattled onto the plates, dropped by Amelia and Benjamin. The sound of their mother's voice brought a shiver of surprise to them both.

'Please leave my children alone, they have done nothing wrong. They knew nothing of their father's plot and they do not deserve the persecution they are facing.'

'The Hahns whereabouts are still unknown, but it seems that neither plan to turn themselves in any time soon. Well that's all for today's news, we'll be back at six tonight but for now we will go back to the festive tunes. Have a wonderful Christmas and a Happy New Year wherever you are!'

The radio presenter finished her news feed before *Fairy Tale of New York* blasted through the speakers. The listeners in the Gates' kitchen were silenced by the headlines.

'Well that's good news.' James spoke first. 'She's stuck up for you both.'

'A little late don't you think?' Amelia said.

'And cowardly.' Benjamin added. 'Why didn't she come home and declare our innocence?'

'Will you two cut it out?' Ray snapped. 'All you two do is complain about your parents. At least you have your mother and father. James doesn't have such luxuries. He really did lose his mom in 9/11. I lost my wife. And believe me, if she came back tomorrow, I'd welcome her back with open arms. I'd embrace her and never let her go. You had the privilege of a second chance with your dad. I'm not surprised your mom ran away with him. We've lost everything and we will never get it back. Yeah, we have money and stability. But I'd give it all up to run away and spend time with Julie. I'd spend the rest of my days in prison if it meant I could spend just a few minutes with her. Have a little perspective, please?'

The room fell silent. Amelia and Benjamin turned to each other. Over the previous months they had been shouted at, spat at and drenched in scalding hot coffee, but no one had spoken to them like this. Benjamin stood up and grabbed his coat.

'I'm leaving, I don't need to sit around and listen to someone who doesn't know what the hell we're going through. How dare you sit there and lecture us. You know what? You're lucky you have wonderful memories of your wife. She didn't deceive you. I would rather my parents be dead than to have to live every day resenting them. Come on, Amelia, we're not sitting around listening to this.'

Benjamin grabbed her coat and handed it to her, but she didn't move. Instead, she looked down at her dinner, avoiding eye contact with her brother.

'Are you coming?'

'I'm sorry Benji, but he's right!' she said. Benjamin lowered his arm, which held her coat. 'For all those years, I wanted Dad back. Even with all those arguments we had to sit in and listen to every single night. I wanted it all back: the tension, the debt, the constant fear of being turfed out of our homes. We're pretty much in the same state now than we were then, except we were a family then. I want my daddy back, I'm sorry. The last time we spoke to Grandpa, we were horrible to him and now look, we can't even make up. I'm sorry Benji, but I'm inclined to agree with Ray. We are so lucky and yet we don't appreciate it. We have a mom and dad. So many people don't.'

Benjamin threw down her coat and leaned into her.

'You might be OK with the fact that Dad cleared off. You were a no-hoper. You were always going to amount to nothing. But me? I was an academic! I was supposed to be at Harvard! I should be a teacher now. But I've lost everything!' He lifted his stump into her face. 'I've lost limbs for that man. I've lost a career and I've lost my family.'

'I suggest you get out now before I throw you out!' James stood up and walked over to Benjamin. He broadened his shoulders and pointed towards the exit.

'Do you think you can take me on?' Benjamin squared up to James. The whiff of alcohol from his breath blew into James's nostrils, who turned away and squinted. Composing himself, he turned back to the drunk.

'What are you going to do? Stump me? You're a war hero! You should have some element of self-respect. You're an embarrassment to your regiment. Wasn't fighting in Iraq for your family? And here you are pushing them away. Just go.'

Benjamin lowered his fist and turned to his sister. 'Millie?'

'Just go, Benjamin. I don't want to see you right now.' Amelia turned away and sobbed. 'You've ruined yet another holiday. Thanks a bunch.'

Benjamin stormed out of the apartment, slamming the door behind him, while James consoled his ex. The three of them continued with their turkey dinners but Amelia ate very little, she had lost her appetite.

'I wish I could call my parents, but I don't know how. If the police can't find her, there's no chance of me being able to.' She cried hard into James's shoulder.

After dinner, the three of them retired to the lounge and watched *It's A Wonderful Life* on the television, a tradition that James's family held every year since he was a little boy. Amelia had never taken to the movie; two and a half hours of misery led her to wish

George Baily had jumped off the bridge to speed up the ending. She kept her negative reviews to herself as James reminisced of Christmas with his mother when he watched the film.

It came as no surprise to Amelia that Ray had fallen asleep half way through the movie. He had consumed a large dinner, a lot of wine and now he endured what she considered as one of the most boring movies she had ever witnessed. Worried they would wake him up from his peaceful nap, Amelia and James left the apartment to enjoy a quiet Christmas Day walk in Central Park. The bitter cold motivated James to place his arm around her.

‘Do you think your brother will be OK? I feel terrible about bringing up his injury. He's obviously sensitive about it, but I couldn't just stand there and listen to him insult you.'

'I'm sure he'll be fine, he needed a wake-up call in my opinion.'

'You know you're not a no-hoper, don't you. You haven't amounted to nothing.'

'You could have fooled me.' she pessimistically replied.

'You work really hard and you enjoy the work you do. Your achievements shouldn't be determined by how much money you earn or what society determines as success. You achieved your goals... and Benjamin? Well he's not a Harvard professor is he? He's the one who’s the failure, not you.'

‘I think that's what upsets him. He did hurt me though. When we were kids, he said that *‘If you judge a fish by its ability to climb a tree, then it’s destined to believe that it’s stupid.’* I guess we discovered today what he really believes.’

'I'm sure he didn’t mean what he said. He's just upset and angry that he didn't achieve what he wanted. He was supposed to be the strong one. I think you've overtaken him there.'

'You've got that right. He used to be my idol. So many kids look up to pop stars and actors, or God forbid, Jersey Shore stars. But not me. I looked up to Benji. He was my rock as a kid. He inspired me. He was so smart and brave, I wanted to be just like him. People say you shouldn't meet your heroes as they'll be a real let down. The same goes for when you're related to them.'

‘Do you think he’s still depressed from the war? Because they have help for people like him you know?’

'Oh yeah, he knows. The problem is he's also smoking pot daily. It alters his moods. One moment he's the happiest man in the world, the next he's wishing you were dead. I never know what to expect when I finish work and come back to our room.'

'I don't think being cooped up in a hotel room can do much for his sanity either.'

'No, you're right. I'm so mad. I finally thought this was going to be a nice Christmas. We had such a terrible Thanksgiving but I actually had some hope that this might be OK. How foolish was I? I'm sorry we ruined your dinner too. Please will you apologise to your dad for me?'

'There's no apology necessary, but I'll pass on the message. You're all stressed, and in a way, Benjamin was right. What the hell do we know about your situation?'

'As good as anyone because you *did* lose someone.' They fell silent, considering Julie Gates on the doomed flight.

'Well with everything we have learned today about forgiveness and losing people, don't you think you should go and speak to your brother?'

'You're absolutely right. Hey, thanks for making my Christmas somehow bearable.'

She embraced James and found she could not let go. His soft cheek slid gently past hers before their lips locked together. They kissed for several minutes, now oblivious to the cold and the honking of taxi horns, cheering on the smooching couple. Conscious of the time, they broke apart.

'God, I've missed you.'

'I've missed you too. But you should go. Sort things out with your brother.'

'I don't want to let you go. I've lost you once already.' She held onto the sleeves of his coat to prevent him from escaping.

'Honestly, go. I'm not going anywhere. We can meet up later or tomorrow.'

They departed, walking in opposite directions, but turned around every few minutes to catch a glimpse of their reunited partners. Christmas Day brought an eerie apocalyptic effect on Times Square, allowing Amelia to take a quiet tranquil stroll through the usually bustling honeypot.

The staff at the Sleep Tight Hotel gave Amelia a cold welcome, bitter of her time off when she had little family to celebrate with. Few had welcomed her with open arms when she joined the hotel, confused by their manager's decision to recruit the infamous daughter of the 9/11 fraudster. The hotel was quiet; while it had reached maximum occupancy, the guests spent little time in the property, instead they dined in New York's finest restaurants.

Avoiding her colleagues' glares, she hurried past the reception desk and slipped into the elevator. She arrived at her room and opened the door but felt an unusual aura inside. Her brother was not in his usual vegetative state on the bed, the television was off and the door to the bathroom was open with nobody inside. Amelia opened the drawers and found them to be empty, just like the closet, which once held their suitcases.

Benjamin had gone.

Chapter 24

'Just one more step!' Geraldine shouted. 'Come on, you can do it, Beverly!' The patient hovered, clutching onto the metal bars surrounding her, desperate to walk again, but the pain in her lower back prevented her.

'I can't.' Beverly cried. 'I just can't do it!'

'One more step! There's no such word as can't! Not in this house!'

With all her strength, Beverly moved her right foot forward and collapsed onto the chair in front of her, relieved that the ordeal was finally over for one day. The exercises would commence the following day, a routine they had worked on for several weeks.

'You sure are getting better, Sweetie' Geraldine reassured her patient, who had lost hope in her ability to regain her balance. 'You won't need the support bars soon.'

'I won't need to take advantage of your kind hospitality much longer either.'

'Oh you can stay as long as you need. Where are you going to go anyway?'

'I don't really know.' Beverly sighed. 'I came to Missouri on a whim, I had no real plans past a few nights in a budget hotel. I have to say, it is nice having somewhere to stay for a while. It's exhausting moving around all the time.

'Well stay here until you figure things out. Your man's been in the paper again today by the way.' Geraldine helped Beverly rest into a reclining chair in the living room, before running to the kitchen to grab the newspaper, which was sat on the cooker.

Over the previous weeks, Marty's story of deceit had been in the newspaper nearly every day, beginning with Beverly's story, which quickly followed by weeks of revelations after Max had contacted the people of Gary, Indiana, who had spent time with the criminal both before and after he returned to Manhattan.

Co-workers, friends and his landlord came forward, although Gordon later regretted his boasts after he was arrested for harbouring a criminal.

Few people mentioned Beverly as she hadn't engaged with the locals in Gary and kept out of Gordon's way during her stay at his home.

Max managed to source everything but Marty himself. Beverly assumed the journalist would have caught up with him by now. But all Max had managed to find was a time-line of events from the 11th September 2001 to the day Beverly left town.

Geraldine placed the day's newspaper on Beverly's lap. A lady in a white wedding dress covered the front page. It was Caitlin, stood outside the family home with her father by her side.

'He got married?' Beverly gasped. 'He's a bigamist.'

'Read on.' Geraldine said, tapping the headline: *DITCHED AT THE ALTAR!*

9-11 Fraudster, Martin Hahn, has taken another victim as he ditched his fiancé at the altar. Caitlin Atkinson of Gary, Indiana, was ready for her big day when her husband-to-be ran away with $100,000, which her father gave him to pay for the event. Hahn met Caitlin in 2009 when they worked together. Despite spending two years with the runaway, she was unaware of his double-life. There has been no sighting of Hahn since, or his estranged wife, Beverly, which is making the nation wonder whether they were both involved in the scam all along.

'How could they think I had anything to do with this?' Beverly yelled. 'I told Max my side of the story with the understanding that he would leave me alone. Now people are going to think I'm an even bigger bitch than they did in the first place. How could he do this to me?'

'He's a journalist, what did you expect?'

'But look what he's done. Not only do the public think I've ripped off the 9/11 fund, but now they believe I've stolen from a loving suburban family in Indiana! Freakin' fantastic.'

The Atkinson family were the perfect example of a good Christian family living the American Dream. Joseph Atkinson's father migrated from Ireland, living hand to mouth as he worked on the construction sites in Chicago. Joseph himself built up an empire from the motorcar industry. They were the type of family that the public loved to read about, who pulled at the heartstrings, and Marty's deceit on the humble bride would pull few favours from the American public.

Beverly threw the paper down on the table and sobbed.

'I can't believe Marty did this. For a man who claims he only wants to scam the corporate giants, he's doing a great job of hurting those around him. I just can't cope with this anymore. I feel for Caitlin, she's a nice girl. I met her. She doesn't deserve this. And the kids? God knows what they're going through in New York. How can Marty be this cruel? He's not the man I used to know.'

'He did it for you.' Geraldine said. 'He may have hurt people along the way but it's quite clear he's desperate. Desperate to make a nice life for you both. He's probably looking for you right now.'

'Well I'm not ready to see him…' Beverly paused. '…yet.'

'Ah, there's still something inside you that longs for that man then?

'I don't know why. I can't stay away from him. He was my first love, my only love.'

'The heart wants what it wants, Sweetie.'

'You've been so kind to me, thank you.'

'What do you want to do, Hunny?' Geraldine asked, hoping to keep her patient's mind at ease. 'Do you wanna play a game or try another walk?'

'Right now? Have you got any good movies?'

'Hell yeah, what haven't I got? What's your favourite?'

'*Meet Me In St. Louis.*' Beverly said. 'It doesn't matter how many times I watch that movie, I never tire of it.'

Geraldine ran to her storage closet and looked around her DVD collection. Within seconds she found her copy of Beverly's favourite movie and brought it over to her. 'It's one of my favourites too! I'm beginning to see why you came over here now.'

'I'd always dreamed of coming since I was a little girl. I can't believe I never came, especially as my parents only lived up the road in Chicago. Stupid really.'

'So you've never been to The Smith house Kensington Avenue?' Geraldine asked. Beverly shook her head. 'Well once you're back on your feet, you need to go. I'll let you into a secret, I moved to St. Louis because of this movie.'

They grinned at each other as they shared their embarrassing dreams to live like The Smith family. The pair sat back and watched the movie. A tear sprang to Beverly's eye as she remembered the last time she watched this classic; she was in the arms of her husband, making their own plans to visit this place together one day, but now she was here in St. Louis alone.

*

The Fourth Presbyterian Church of Chicago sat on the bustling Magnificent Mile. The church had an unsteady beginning as it opened on the 8th October 1871; the day the Great Chicago Fire hit the city and burnt the new-born ecclesiastical building down to the ground. Three years later, it re-opened and today is thought of as one of the most beautiful religious houses in the city. The water tower outside of the church was the only piece of architecture to survive the great fire.

Nearly one-hundred-and-forty years on, Amelia struggled to appreciate the elegance of the church as she stared at her grandpa's oak casket resting before the altar. The lid was open, displaying her grandfather's body to the congregation. Francis appeared peaceful, younger and oddly healthier than Amelia's last encounter with him.

To her right, her fiancé, James, held onto her hand. Ten years on from when they first got together, he was once again the rock of support, which he played all those years before. No one had been there for her like he had. Benjamin had come close, but his disappearance on Christmas Day prevented him from providing the support she now desperately required. She hadn't seen or heard from him since, despite numerous calls to his cell phone which went unanswered.

Benjamin's distance prevented her from providing the details of their grandfather's funeral, although she sent him a text in hope that it would reach him. His absence suggested it hadn't.

Another notable absentee was their mother. Her lack of attendance assured Amelia that Beverly was oblivious to Francis's fate. She would have made the funeral whether it led her to a conviction or not.

They sat several pews back from Francis's wife, Evelyn, and her family. It was quite clear that Evelyn put herself and her children above Amelia in the hierarchy as she took pride of place in the front pews.

There was no invitation to the wake after the ceremony, nor were they invited to make a speech at the service. Rather than becoming bitter, Amelia remained grateful that she'd been informed of her grandfather's death at all.

The organ chimed, instructing the congregation to rise up and sing. They sang in harmony *'There is a Green Hill Far Away',* a popular hymn at funerals due to the lyrics focusing on the last days of Jesus Christ before his demise. Francis shared the name of its composer, Cecel Francis Alexander, but Amelia found an even bigger connection in the lyrics.

'He died that we might be forgiven. He died to make us good.'

The press had eased off her since her grandfather's death, leaving her to get on with her day without being followed by the paparazzi. Her colleagues tried to engage with her more, offering to cover her shifts while she attended the funeral. Francis's death had brought her and James back together and had provided some perspective to Amelia, who could now see beyond her father's crimes and see that he had done all he could to provide for their family. *He died that we might be forgiven. He died to make us good.*

The hymn finished and Evelyn stepped up to the pulpit. She talked longingly about the fifteen years they spent together. She described Francis as a father and grandfather figure to her own offspring, but neither Amelia, nor any of the Hahns, received a mention. In the eyes of the congregation, Amelia and her family did not exist. However, she cared little for Evelyn's approval; she came to say her own goodbyes.

The service ended and the congregation dispersed. Amelia walked up to the coffin and placed her hand on her grandfather's cold wrist. She wept and whispered '*I'm sorry, I love you'*. James held her as she broke down and her tears poured onto his rented suit.

The casket lid closed and was lifted out of the church. A private service at a local crematorium had been planned for immediate family, which Amelia was not assumed to be a part of. Outside, the congregation gathered to talk about the service and the man whose life they joined to celebrate. Evelyn spotted Amelia and strutted over to her.

'If it's money you've come for, there isn't any. Not for you anyway.' Amelia's step-grandmother bitterly explained.

Evelyn had aged considerably. She covered her wrinkled face with a black veil and her white roots poured through the sides of her fascinator. She wore a black jacket with a fur surrounding her neck. A long skirt wrapped around her thin waist and black netted tights warmed her legs.

'I came to say goodbye to my grandfather, nothing else.'

'Good, you caused quite enough drama in his last months. Your family were always troublemakers. Do you know how much embarrassment your parents caused him with their little scam? It was probably them who made him ill. Your family killed my husband.'

Amelia walked away. It would have been easy to explain to Evelyn of Francis's part in Marty's plans, but she decided to remain the bigger person. Evelyn followed in pursuit.

'I hadn't finished.' She rooted through her purse and grabbed a set of keys. 'He left you these. They're technically your mother's, but seeing she's not bothered to turn up today, you might as well take them. They are the keys to your grandmother's house. He wrote it into his will before he died. I made it quite clear that I didn't want that old witch's property. Couldn't sell the damn place anyway… scruffy little suburban shack. Who in their right mind would want it?'

Evelyn threw the keys at Amelia, who caught them. The keys still had the New York key-ring, which she bought her grandmother when she was a little girl to remind her of the family while they lived hundreds of miles away.

'That woman is dead. Have some respect.' James intervened.

'Leave it, James. I can't be bothered to argue. Thanks for the keys.' As they walked away, Evelyn's eldest son elbowed his mom in the arm and nodded his head. She grunted, glaring at him, but he raised his eyebrows in disapproval.

'There's one more thing too.' Evelyn shouted after her step-granddaughter as she pulled out another item from her purse. 'He wrote this for you, it was in the hotel room when I found him.'

Reluctantly, she handed her an envelope, which had *Amelia & Benjamin* hand-written on the front. Amelia recognised her grandfather's handwriting. She took the letter, thanked the bitter woman before her and left, blowing a kiss to the hearse, which held her grandfather's casket.

Across the road stood the Hancock tower, once the tallest building outside of New York, before the Sears Tower (today known as the Willis Tower) took over in the 1970s. At the top of the tower, a bar and restaurant allowed tourists to enjoy a meal or a cocktail while enjoying the views of Lake Michigan.

James and Amelia walked across to the tower, named after the prominent patriot of the American Revolution, and took the elevator up to the ninety-fifth floor to The Signature Room. They exited the elevator and reserved a seat by the window, which faced North-West towards the house they had just been given.

'We could just stay out here.' James said. 'We have nothing in New York. We have a house here and it can't be that difficult to bag a couple of jobs in a hotel. The great thing is that no one will know us. We can start again, you and me.'

'It would be nice. I've always fancied the suburban life. I could be a proper *Soccer Mom.* Have a perfect nuclear family. Drive a giant Hyundai and go to PTA meetings. Make iced-tea for the kids when they bring their friends home. So unlike my mom. She hated that Sarah Palin image of life. It's probably why she's so far away now on the run.'

'We could have that.'

'Maybe. I'm not too sure though. I still don't know where Benji is and I need to go back to New York to find him.' Amelia explained. James's disappointment resided on his face. 'Besides, Chicago hasn't half got a history of dodgy politicians. It isn't called *'The Windy City'* because of its' weather.'

'Hasn't the entire country?' James shrugged. 'So are you going to open that letter?'

They were so consumed by their White Russian cocktails and their dreams of a life in Illinois, they forgot all about Francis's last words to his grandchildren. She opened the envelope and read the contents.

Dear Amelia and Benjamin,

I can't apologise enough for my actions over the past ten years. My advice to your father was despicable and I sadly see that now I have witnessed the devastation I have brought to your lives. I regret it immensely. I want you to know that I love you both and I would have never recommended your father had taken such drastic actions had I known what pain and suffering it would have brought to you. Please forgive your mother, she was simply in love. I assure you she didn't know of his whereabouts, and like you, had assumed he had evaporated within the buildings that devastated so many lives that day. Looking at his actions since, I believe your father (in some way) did die in the towers that day. He's not the man he once was, but he is still your father and loves you dearly. Like me, he only wanted the very best for you both.

I hope you can forgive me.

All my love,

Grandpa

Folding the letter in half, she replaced it into the envelope and returned it to her purse.

'He knew.' Amelia said. 'He knew he was going to die that night. This is his goodbye.'

Holding up the envelope to hide her face, she sobbed. James grabbed her hand as she grieved. The guilt of her last words to her dying grandfather lingered. Fellow punters stared at her and mumbled, concerned by her tears.

Few would believe she'd just left a funeral; she'd worn a bright yellow dress, an opportunity to bring some light to the service for a man who lived a colourful life.

'Can we go home?' she asked.

'Sure, I'll see when the next Amtrak out of here is.' He retrieved his cell phone out of his pocket to look for scheduled train times for the cross-country transportation network.

'I think you might only need the Metra for where we're going.' She held out the keys and James smiled. They walked down to Union Station and boarded the shuttle train to Hoffman Estates.

*

Beverly was left alone in the house while her carer visited her mother. Geradline's mom had taken a turn for the worse as the Alzheimer's disease rotted her memories. Elizabeth McMahon couldn't be trusted to be left alone at home as she burnt herself on the kettle and left the stove on when she left the house. She became an increasing strain on her husband, therefore the family decided to put her in a care home, where she could have access to round-the-clock assistance and ensured safety.

The move into a nursing home was a blessing to Geraldine, who could ensure her mother's wellbeing and dodge her father by avoiding his typical visiting hours.

In Geraldine's absence, Beverly amused herself by watching her favourite soap opera, *Days of our Lives.* During her months on the run without a television, she had missed the show, but she could now catch up on the antics of her favourite characters, whose lives were somehow more disorientated than her own.

A knock at the door disrupted her alone time. Few visitors had called by since her arrival, so the knocking came as somewhat of a shock. Geraldine appeared to have few friends and the neighbours kept to themselves.

She hobbled over to the door. Behind the spyhole, an older lady gingerly waited. A net wrapped around the woman's grey matted hair and a pinafore decorated with birds of prey covered a pink blouse and blue chords. She held onto something. Beverly carefully lifted herself up onto her tiptoes to peer down into the spyhole to capture the object, which the lady held. It was a red cast-iron casserole dish. Content that she had seen enough, she lowered herself but the pain caused her to fall forward and she banged her head on the door. The thud exposed her presence and the stranger waved into the spyhole.

Damn it.

Beverly hadn't showered and wore a yellow onesie, a joke gift from her daughter the previous Christmas. She felt her greasy hair and sniffed the odour of sweat radiating from the garment, which covered her decaying body. She wasn't prepared for guests.

'Hello?' Beverly gingerly greeted the visitor.

‘Oh hello, Dear, I don’t believe we’ve met, I’m Pamela. I was wondering if Geraldine was in?’

‘I’m afraid not, she’s gone out to see her mom. Can I give her a message?’

‘Oh well, I was just a bit concerned. She’s had the curtains closed for a few days, I wondered if she wasn’t well. I brought her a casserole to make her feel better.’

‘It’s me who’s not well. Geraldine has kindly been looking after me.’

‘That’s very nice of her, well hey, why don’t you have the casserole? Or Geraldine can have some time off cooking and you two can enjoy it together?’

‘Thank you very much, would you like to come in for a coffee?’

Doubt came over the lady's face, who appeared too uncomfortable to accept the invitation. Pamela appeared as nervous as an Angolan crossing a minefield.

‘OK, thank you.’ Pamela hesitantly accepted the offer and stepped into the house. She placed the casserole on the kitchen work-top and returned to the living room, where Beverly had reclined on the couch.

‘You didn’t tell me your name, Dear?’

‘Oh I’m sorry, I’m Beverly.’ Her question comforted Beverly; Pamela knew little of her past.

‘How do you know Geraldine?’

‘We’re just friends. I had an accident and she took me in, she’s been very kind.’

‘So you didn’t know her before the accident?’ Pamela quizzed with an accusing tone.

‘Errr… well no. Not really. She pulled me out of a wreck and here we are.’

‘How has she been treating you?’

‘Oh, she’s been wonderful. She’s been helping me get back on my feet.’

‘Why are you not in a hospital?’ Pamela scratched her head.

‘I don’t have insurance.’ Beverly confidently answered, assured her excuse was a valid one. ‘Is everything OK? Why are you so concerned by Geraldine’s care?’

Pamela stared towards the patient and opened her mouth, but nothing came out. Her jaw quivered. She looked up towards the ceiling, closed her eyes and took a deep breath before re-joining eye contact with Beverly.

'I have to admit to you the real reason I'm here. You see I'm not really a friend of Geraldine's.'

Beverly's stomach churned.

'You see, I'd suspected that she was nursing again. She isn't supposed to be. Did she tell you she was struck off the register?'

'She had mentioned it, but she hadn't told me why.' Beverly gulped. 'Am I in danger?'

'I don't know. I was concerned over what she was up to in here and I saw a few days ago that somebody else was inside the house when she was out. I live just over the road and can see directly into the window. I waited until she went out again before I visited. I was worried about you.'

'Why the hell should you be concerned about me?' Beverly didn't know whether to be angry or scared. 'Geraldine has been nothing but kind to me.'

'I'm glad to hear that, Dear, but I'm apprehensive about the level of care you are receiving from her. You see, Geraldine was struck off because she caused great harm to her patients when she worked in care homes. She was imprisoned for murder after several patients died in strange circumstances. People who were perfectly healthy but needed extra help with mobility were brought into her care and died within weeks.'

'I think you had better leave, this is slander.' Despite the pain it brought to her back, Beverly stood up and pointed towards the exit to indicate where her unwelcome guest could return to. Pamela sat and stared at Beverly, who held her back in agony.

Reaching into her purse, drooped around her neck, Pamela pulled out a newspaper cutting and handed it over to the wounded woman before her.

'What is this?' Beverly asked as she grabbed the paper.

'Read it.'

Beverly unfolded the paper. The cutting had grown creases and the ink had smudged with age. Geraldine's mug shot filled the page. Above her photograph, the title read *'CARER KILLER JAILED!'*

A nurse at a top private care home has been jailed for the deaths of four elderly patients who were residing in her care. Geraldine McMahon, 53, has been found guilty of manslaughter and will spend a minimum of fifteen years behind bars. Her lawyer made no statement when leaving court but her accusers hailed it as a fantastic result. The families of those who died in the hands of McMahon became concerned when their relatives died suddenly despite seeming healthy during previous weeks. The nurse, who had been caring for over thirty years, was described as being insensitive upon revealing the tragic news of the deceased to their devastated love ones. The families were heard cheering as the judge read out the guilty verdict. While some are disgraced that the carer received such a light sentence for the many lives she ended, they are relieved her infamy and revoked nursing registration will mean she will be unable to cause harm to patients again.

Beverly soaked in the details. Everything Pamela had informed her of was true. She sat back down and considered her own fate.

'Do you see why I was eager to come and ensure you were OK?'

'I can't believe it. It all makes sense now. She seemed so kind but she was taking advantage of me. She knew I had nowhere to go and that I couldn't go to the hospital without...' Beverly paused before she could reveal her reservations about going into hospital. '...without being charged as I didn't have insurance. She seemed so natural, so kind.'

'There's nothing kind about that woman. She's evil. She took you in so she could relive her enjoyment of inflicting death upon another human being. She gets a kick out of it.'

'She avoided questions around her career and why she left a job that she's clearly fit for.' Beverly placed her finger over her lip, puzzled by Geraldine's ability to manipulate, before considering another person whom she cared for. 'Oh my God, her mom!'

'God help her. It wouldn't surprise me if you've been off your feet longer than you needed to be. You would have been walking within days in hospital. She's probably causing more damage than good.'

‘What should I do?’ Beverly panicked, petrified of her rehabilitation being sabotaged any further.

‘You can come home with me. We'll get you somewhere safe.’

‘I can’t.’ Beverly said. The fear of the police catching up with her failed to live up to the fear of a life in prison.

'You have to!' Pamela yelled, horrified by Beverly's reluctance to leave a house which could soon become her tomb.

‘Why isn’t she still in jail? It doesn't make sense. If she's so dangerous, why is she here? Why is she a free woman?'

Before Pamela could answer her questions, a car pulled up at the front of the house. It was Geraldine’s.

‘I have to go. I’ll come back for you!’ Pamela ran out of the back door and escaped down the path towards the side of the house. She hid until it was safe for her to return to her own condo across the road. As Beverly closed the back door, Geraldine walked in the front carrying shopping bags.

‘Hello Dear, how’re you doing?’ Geraldine walked into the living room. She placed the bags down on the couch and looked up at her panicked patient. ‘Well look at you all up and about!’

‘I’m feeling much better, thank you so much for your help. I was considering maybe getting myself out of your hair soon.’ Beverly nervously lied as she hobbled back to the living room, attempting to hide the pain away from the potential killer.

‘What’s that over there?’ Geraldine pointed at the casserole pot on the side-bench in the kitchen. Beverly looked in the direction of where Geraldine’s finger pointed and saw the present, which Pamela had left behind.

‘Oh that.’ Beverly searched for an excuse. ‘I made it for you as a thank you.’ She nervously giggled.

‘You left the house then? You could barely walk this morning and now you’re going out unaided. I'm amazed.’

'Well you're obviously an amazing nurse!'

‘And then you came back and got back into your pyjamas?’ Beverly looked down at her onesie; she didn’t look like somebody who had recently left to go shopping. She had more pride than to go out in her pyjamas and her carer knew this.

‘Comfier,’ Beverly shrugged her shoulders and faked a laugh.

‘Well thank you, that’s very kind of you. Although I did have a casserole pot myself, you didn’t need to buy one.’ Beverly exhaled in relief as she managed to lie through Geraldine’s interrogation. The nurse walked back into the living room. ‘I do have one question though…’

‘Oh yeah, what’s that?’ Beverly walked into the living room.

‘What the hell is this?’ Off the couch, Geraldine picked up the newspaper cutting, which Pamela had brought across, outlining her murderous crimes.

Chapter 25

The house differed from her last visit, but it had been over four years since she last stepped into this nostalgic abode. It was emptier; any evidence of her grandmother had disappeared. Aberdeen Drive remained unchanged, but the house Amelia now owned had aged, left to rot since her grandparent's passing fourteen months before.

Beverly kept the grandchildren away from Majorie's decline in her final years. On Amelia's last visit, a Christmas tree filled the lounge and flowers decorated the skirting of the front lawn. Now the blue tinted cladding had faded and the flowers had wilted.

Despite the building's decay, it still felt like home to Amelia, who spent many summer vacations swinging from the trees in the yard while her parents worked back in New York. Her dreams returned to the very building she now held the keys for.

James pulled the *FOR SALE* sign out of the ground, poking out of the front lawn. The advertisement was redundant now they were prepared to move to the suburban haven. A porch rested on the front of the building and a rocking chair sat to the right of the door. Upon arrival, an infant Amelia ran up to Marjorie, who knitted scarves in the rocking chair as she awaited her family's arrival. Now the chair rocked alone as the wind brushed against it, leaving a ghostly aura of Marjorie's past.

Amelia rooted through her purse and found the keys, which her formidable step-grandmother reluctantly provided at the funeral, and unlocked the door, but as she opened it, a rustling inside startled her. Afraid of what inhabited her grandmother's house, she shut the door again.

'What's up?' James asked.

'Somebody's in there!' she whispered.

'Who could be in there? You have the key.'

'Maybe they broke in? I don't know but somebody's in there.' Amelia pulled away from the door, unsure of what action to take. Frustrated, James grabbed the keys off his girlfriend, brushed past her and opened the door. He quietly entered, keeping his back to the wall and tip-toed through the house. It didn't look like a crime scene.

A rattling echoed from the second floor of the two storey house. He whispered to his fiancé to stay where she was, before sneaking up the stairs. The oak flooring creaked as he tiptoed across, wincing with every sound. The landing provided little light and his view became distorted as he edged deeper into the dark corridor.

James placed his ear against each door, listening to the activity inside, but each bedroom remained silent, besides the final door. A rustling echoed from the master bedroom. Swinging the door open, James jumped inside.

'Got ya!' he yelled.

'James?' the man called out. 'What are *you* doing here?'

'Amelia!' James shouted towards the front of the house. 'You should come up here.'

The clapping of her heals across the house indicated her adherence to his call. Amelia walked around the corner and peeked into the master bedroom.

'Benjamin?'

*

'Are you going to tell me what's going on?' Geraldine stood in her living room, glaring at the woman whom she had nursed for several weeks.

She placed her right hand over her hip, while her left held onto the newspaper cutting, which outlined her crimes. The mug shot and the guilty verdict, highlighted in bold capitals, managed to shine on the musty paper, which had grown yellow after years of exposure to glaring sunlight.

'I'm so sorry. Your neighbour, Pamela, came over and she was saying these things... I asked her to leave.'

Geraldine's eyebrows arched as she soaked in Beverly's eventful morning. She said little to ease the patient's worried mind.

'I promise you, I didn't believe her!' Beverly said, unnerved by her carer's silence.

'I wish I could believe you. You're just like her, you're just like everyone else... judging me and believing the lies that were spread about me.'

Geraldine slammed herself down on the couch and her large heavy frame caused a thud. Air exhaled from the brown leather couch under the pressure of her weight. Beverly eyed up both doors, judging which was closer to escape, but the excruciating pain in her back prevented her from fleeing.

'I'm not! I'm not like everyone else. I promise. It's just… well why are the newspapers saying this?' Beverly pointed to the paper, which Geraldine had thrown onto the floor in anger. The paper provided damning evidence of her guilty part in the elderly patients' deaths.

'Have you not asked yourself why I'm not in jail? If I was given a minimum fifteen year sentence and that was written only five years ago, then why am I sat here?'

Beverly picked up the screwed up newspaper and gazed upon the date in the top left hand corner of the newspaper. *1st March 2007.* She was right. Geraldine would have still been serving her sentence had the details been correct.

'I hadn't seen the date but I did wonder why you weren't in prison.' Beverly sat next to her carer and placed a hand on her knee. 'So tell me what happened.'

'I used to love being a nurse. I enjoyed it so much. I loved bringing that little bit of happiness to people who had nothing left. Even when they died, it brought me fulfilment that I was able to make their final moments of this life that little bit more comfortable.'

Beverly gulped, wondering whether Geraldine's story would lead to a confession. She thought back to a British doctor who enjoyed delivering a peaceful end to his perfectly healthy patients' lives.

'But then the cut backs occurred. The owners of the home became more concerned with their return on investment, rather than the people they looked after. The recession had begun and everyone was feeling the pinch. The owners made cut backs so severe that it was down to just me running the entire home and I couldn't look after people twenty-four hours a day, not properly anyway.'

'You didn't...' Beverly paused.

'I didn't what?'

'...try to make the workload more bearable yourself by reducing the number of patients?'

'My God, no!' Geraldine gasped.

'Then how did you cope?'

'I didn't. I was rude to the families who visited and raged when the owners came in trying to make more cut-backs. I was always kind to the patients though. I would've given my life to ensure they were OK.' Geraldine sniffled as she reminisced, before continuing her story. 'But then patients began to die. It was always suddenly, never the weakest of the pack. I knew why of course... they caught bugs because I hadn't been given time to disinfect everything the way I used to.'

'But surely there must have been post-mortems, they must have realised you couldn't have harmed them purposely.' Beverly reasoned. 'No court in America could surely allow an innocent person to be imprisoned without sufficient evidence?'

'Of course there were post-mortems, but I was set up. The management were petrified of being sued, so they made me look like the bad guy before the police could even begin their investigation. I was on the front of the morning newspapers before the police had even shown up at my door.'

'But you had your day in court.' Beverly's own stint in the press had made her question the validity of the stories she read. She now reserved her judgement for the outcome of a trial, decided rightfully in the hands of the American justice system.

'Yes I did, but... oh Hunny... I can tell you haven't been in trouble with the law before now. That's why I like you. In America, we say you're innocent until proven otherwise, but that's simply not true. People can say what they like about you in this country and the onus is on *you* to prove otherwise. Seven lots of lawyers, including the millionaire owners of the care home, against my state funded budget defence made it a tough fight for me. They paid doctors huge sums of money to say on oath that the evidence all pointed towards my guilt. I had no hope.'

'So how did you get out of jail?'

'Two years ago, an appeal was granted. The doctor who gave evidence in my trial was charged with taking bribes from pharmaceutical companies. He was wrongly diagnosing patients so he could feed them drugs that they didn't need. The evidence in my trial was compromised, so I was released.'

'I'm sorry, Geraldine.' Beverly hung her head. 'If you want me to go, you only have to say the word and I'll pack my bags.'

'Don't be silly. You wouldn't be the first person to be bought in by the press. The difference with you is that you believe me now you've given me the chance to explain. She hasn't.' Geraldine nodded her head towards the house across the street.

'Why didn't you tell me about this earlier? I asked you about your job, you could have told me? I could have told that woman where to go if I knew the truth.'

'Because for once it was nice that somebody didn't know who I was. You must know what that feels like. Everywhere you go, everyone knows you're the evil witch who has been plastered all over the papers for crimes that ain't necessarily true. You came along so worried about your own fate that you were oblivious as to who I was. It was nice. It's also why I took pity on you. I miss nursing so much, but I also know what you're going through.'

'Thank you.' Beverly grabbed Geraldine's hand and squeezed it tight. 'We won't speak any more about it, but I do have one last question.'

'More questions? What more do I have to do to prove my innocence?'

'What was prison like?' Beverly asked, considering her own future. 'I have to know. There's a chance I might end up there. I have to know if it's still worth running away because I'm exhausted.'

Beverly rubbed her eyes; her time on the run had shattered her. An uncomfortable Geraldine wriggled, unsure of how to answer her friend's question having experienced a similar fate.

'I don't wish to scare you… but it's an awful, vile place.' Geraldine explained. 'If I were you, Beverly, I'd keep on running.'

*

The drawn curtains cut out any action in the parallel house. An iron basket, lined with coco, hung above the doorway, swinging the multi-coloured begonias against the white cladding of the two-storey condo.

It had been an hour since Pamela bravely entered the house, which she now stared intensely at, praying for the safety of the disabled woman inside. She considered calling the police, but she had little evidence to support her fears.

She selfishly considered the dish, which she left at the house, confident that she wouldn't see the pricey pot again. Her concerns soon reverted back to Beverly, anxious the pot could have exposed her interference.

The blue front door opened and out stepped Geraldine. She carried the red cooking pot towards Pamela's house. The old lady's heart pumped hard. Geraldine's face roared with thunder. This wasn't the first time that Pamela had interfered, but it would certainly be the last.

A knock on the door confirmed her arrival. Pamela remained silent, reluctant to open the door. Staring at the phone, she considered calling the police as the visitor's fists pounded harder, vibrating the wooden house. She took a deep breath and opened the door.

'Hi Geraldine.'

'Hi Pamela.' Geraldine answered with a broad smile. 'I just wanted to say thank you so much for this wonderful casserole. Beverly and I really enjoyed it. It was so thoughtful of you.'

'No problem, Geraldine.' Pamela forced a smile and exhaled. Her voice shook as she spoke. 'I can't stop and chat, I'm a bit busy.'

'I won't keep you.' Geraldine excused herself. Pamela smiled, nodded and began to close the door, but Geraldine put her hand in the way to prevent it from closing. 'But I will give you one warning. If you try and turn any of my friends against me again, you interfering old bitch, you can join the long line of biddies who are now lying in a cemetery because of me.'

Pamela slammed the door shut in fright, almost catching the hand of the intrusive visitor. She collapsed onto the floor, curling up behind the door. She placed her hands around her legs and sobbed into her knees and cuddled the pot.

*

Geraldine whistled a heavenly tune as she stepped away from Pamela's house. The scent of a rose distracted her and she took a moment to inhale the blissful aroma of Pamela's garden. She reached into the pocket of her baggy jeans and lifted out a small pair of sheers. She carefully cut the tip of the flower, placed the petals into her pocket and walked away.

The shadow of a familiar face caught the corner of her eye. She turned around and found Beverly hidden in the alley between Pamela and her neighbour's houses. They smirked and broke into laughter.

'Oh that was fun.' Beverly cheered.

'The biggest fear is *fear* itself. It's so much fun to use that against the morons who believe what they read in the papers.' They walked back to the house together, linking arms.

'Hey, you're walking has improved. No more hobbling!'

'I know! I can't believe it. I think it's time for me to go.'

'I'll really miss you. We've really bonded over the last few weeks. I don't know what I'll do without you in the house.'

'I'm really going to miss you too, Geraldine.' Beverly said. 'You've brought me back to life!'

'You're welcome to stay as long as you want.'

'Thanks, but I can't stay much longer now I've been seen by the neighbours. It won't be long before people realise who I am. I can't allow you to get into trouble.'

'So what will you do?'

'I'm going to take your advice....' Beverly said. A tear ran down her face as she considered saying goodbye. '... I'm going to keep on running.'

*

'What the hell are you doing here?' Amelia screamed at her brother. Benjamin stood before her, surprised by his sister's return.

'I've been worried sick for weeks wondering where you were or if you were even alive! You were the only family I had left and you ditched me. Thank God I had James, otherwise I would've had nobody.' She hammered her fists into his chest. 'What are you doing here?'

'I had nowhere to go. I knew there was a key behind the back door, so I let myself in. I knew nobody was using this place and I figured I had some time before the lawyers would kick me out.'

Benjamin followed his mother's footsteps in his grand plan to run away from the madness of Manhattan. They discovered at their granddad's birthday party that she had resided in the suburban retreat when she escaped the clutches of their estranged father, but now she was on the run again, far away from the house where she grew up.

He wore his uniform, which appeared worn and unwashed, and a thick black winter coat over his shirt. A cold breeze blew through the house. James fiddled with the thermostat but he failed to warm the house.

'How could you not call me? I thought…' Amelia sobbed trying to catch her words.

He walked over and held her.

Behind Amelia, James glared towards Benjamin. They hadn't spoken since he stormed out of his father's house on Christmas Day.

'Are you OK?' Benjamin asked, unnerved by James's glares.

'I'm a lot less forgiving than her.'

Letting go of his sister, Benjamin walked over to James and held out his hand towards him. 'James, I'm sorry for everything I said at Christmas. I was angry.'

James stared at Benjamin's hand. Amelia elbowed her hesitant boyfriend. She had her *puppy-eyes.* Those eyes which James could never say *'no'* to. After a moment of contemplation, he took the man's hand and gripped onto it tightly. They stared into each other's eyes with a small sneer.

'Let's get one thing straight, Ben. I don't like you. But we have to get on for your sister's sake.'

Benjamin nodded his head. They turned to Amelia, who bounced up and down on her feet and wrapped an arm around each of them.

'You boys used to get on so well before we broke up. I know you'll be good friends again in no time.

'Mmm,' James grumbled.

'Anyway, we have to get along because we all have to live together.'

'What?' the boys asked in harmony.

Amelia reached into her bag and lifted out her keys, dangling them on the end of her finger.

'Grandpa left us the house.' Amelia said. 'Well, he left it to Mom, but as she's nowhere to be seen, we can stay here until she gets back. There'll be a load of legal stuff to deal with, which we'll have to complete until Mom shows herself, but we've got every right to stay here until that day comes.'

‘And *he’s* staying here?’ James asked. 'After everything he's done? He betrayed you. This was supposed to be our new home to begin a new life together. Everything we ever wanted is right here but it won't be if he's here. Two's company. Three's a damn crowd.'

‘James, he’s my brother. I can’t kick him out. Where will he go?’

‘Back to New York is where he can go. He has a perfectly usable apartment there.’

‘Back to the apartment which could be taken away from us at any time? Back to an apartment which has a group of protesters outside ready to lynch on him? Back to a city that utterly hates us? I can’t do that to my brother, James.’

‘Yeah, James, this is as much *my* home as it is Amelia’s.' Benjamin stepped in, broadening his shoulders as he approached James. 'I’ve got every right to be here. What right have you got? None. So I suggest you shut the hell up before I shut you up.’

‘Don’t you threaten me! Do you hear this?’ James turned to Amelia in protest. ‘This man let you down.’

‘As did you, James.’ Amelia said. Silence filled the room as James soaked in the reality of his recent behaviour. ‘You let me down. You didn’t believe me and you ran away. You left me without a home and I still forgave you. Why don’t you have a little compassion for my brother, like I had for you?’

She was right. He had no right to question Benjamin’s commitment to Amelia when he himself had abandoned her in her hour of need.

‘I’m sorry, Benjamin, I’m just a little angry. I just saw how upset she was when you took off.’

‘And I consoled her when you threw her out.’ The boys nodded at each other and shook hands again.

‘I’m also sorry to you, Amelia. I was just excited about starting our lives together, privately.’

'What are you going to do about your apartment in New York?' Benjamin asked. 'Don't you have rent control on that thing?'

'Yeah, it’s controlled.' James confirmed. If he gave up his apartment, he would struggle to find a similar apartment at the same monthly rate should he need to return to New York.

'Maybe you should hold onto it for now... you know... just in case things don't work out here.'

'I'm pretty happy here thanks, Benjamin.' James bit onto his bottom lip.

'Now come on, let's go to the living room, we can't stay cooped up in this bedroom all day. As much as I love this house, it is rather poky.'

The house was built on prairie land by her great-grandfather. The space surrounding the property was vast, but limited resources at the time meant he had to settle for a smaller house with a larger garden, appearing miniscule compared to the mansion next door. The house had since been passed down the family. When their grandmother met Francis, the wealthy stockbroker, she insisted they remain in the heirloom, rather than the multi-million dollar apartment he kept downtown, until their divorce. The sudden consideration of her grandfather, reminded Amelia of Benjamin's absence at his funeral.

'Where were you today? Did you know it was Grandpa's funeral?'

'I received your messages. I couldn't face it though. I'm still so angry that our lives have been turned upside-down because of some ridiculous advice he gave to Dad a decade ago.'

'He may have given stupid advice, but Dad didn't have to take it.' Amelia raised her voice. 'How could Francis possibly have any inkling as to how our lives would be like today? He assumed the money would pay off our debts, provide Mom a chance to pay off the mortgage and allow you to go to university.'

Her justification remained unsavoury to Benjamin, who remained silent with his head hung. She realised she was fighting a one-way battle so she changed the subject.

'So what have you been doing in Chicago and what are you doing for money?'

'Well believe it or not, rent is cheap when you're squatting in someone else's house.' He shrugged his shoulders.

'But what about the bills? They aren't included.'

'No, but you'll soon see the electricity doesn't switch on, and if you want a shower, you're in for a shock as it's pretty cold.'

'Great, so we have our work cut out for us.' Amelia sighed. 'I can't believe you've been living in this house, wrapped up in your coat, without heating or hot water. Was life in New York really that bad that?'

'It was pretty bad, Sis, we were sharing a tiny twin room, petrified of the outside world. I needed out.'

'But what about food? Please don't tell me you've been eating those vegetables.' She looked out towards what was once her grandmother's cabbage patch and perused the rotten vegetables, which had been neglected since her death.

'Well…' he paused. 'Boys Town is only down the road and Elk Grove hosts quite a popular gay bar too...'

'Oh no.' Amelia gagged. 'How can you resort to this? You're not even gay. You're an academic and a war hero. You shouldn't be a gigolo.'

'Well you better think fast about what you're going to do for money, it's really not cheap to live here.'

Amelia turned to her boyfriend, realising her brother was right. They needed to find work, and soon.

Over the following weeks, the three of them restored the house. They had the electricity and heating returned, and dug out the rotting vegetables in the garden.

During a clear-out in the attic, they found old photographs, which their grandfather had mistakenly left behind. Included in the bundle were love letters between Francis and their grandmother.

'I wish Francis had seen these.' she groaned. 'It would've been nice for him to know that she kept onto them, that she still loved him despite everything.'

'I bet he knew. Those feelings can't completely go away.'

Amelia called her manager, Sharon, in New York and managed to arrange a transfer to a hotel in the near-by suburb of Schaumburg. The district was a hub of corporate offices for some of the largest companies in the world. Due to the vast numbers of business tourists flying into the area, hotels had popped up all over the town, offering an abundance of opportunities for Amelia and James. While she struggled to cope with her brother's choice of lifestyle, Amelia accepted the money Benjamin brought in.

James and Benjamin avoided each other where they could and remained in their own bedrooms when Amelia was out. While they had remained civil with each other for the most part, they clashed over trivial events. Benjamin spent over an hour in the shower, while James waited outside of the bathroom, eager to get ready for work.

'Why are you even up at this time?' James yelled, banging on the door. *'You don't even need to go to work until later!'*

A despairing Amelia suggested they all spend an evening together. She supplied beer to ease the warring room-mates, but her efforts backfired as the alcohol heated their frustration towards each other and she stood between them to avoid a punch-up.

A ringing from her purse distracted her from the civil war unfolding in her living room. She picked up the phone and gasped as she read the contents of the text message on her cell.

'Will you two shut up?' she yelled at the boys. They turned to Amelia, who was as white as a ghost. 'I've received a message you both need to read.' She handed them the device and Benjamin read the text.

Miss You Pumpkin x.

'Who is that?' James asked, suspicious of the sender who missed his girlfriend.

'It's our mom.'

Chapter 26

Detective Grisham landed in Chicago. He flew out from Newark Airport to O'Hare to meet with the children of Beverly and Marty Hahn. The trip was far from kosher, but the NYPD were eager to close the case and bring two of the most deceitful fraudsters in America to justice. Grisham had to catch them for his colleagues.

The detective was off work on annual leave back on that fateful day in 2001, but when he witnessed the twin towers on fire on the news, he quickly left his New Jersey home and drove across to Manhattan to help rescue the thousands of Americans trapped inside the building. The New York Fire Department had the tower covered, therefore, as a policeman, his job was to ensure that those who were outside of the towers were taken to a safe place. Neither he, nor his workmates, could have foreseen that the towers he protected would collapse.

Stood by his side on that day was Lieutenant Jefferson. Like Grisham, Jefferson had also gone into work voluntarily that morning to help his colleagues defend the city. Grisham was also a Lieutenant at the time; the terrorist attacks led him to take up a career in solving crimes, rather than fighting them. The two policemen passed their probation together and became two of the most respected members of the NYPD. They were also great friends; Jefferson often invited Grisham over to his home for dinner with his wife and two ten-year-old twin boys. They trained together, won awards together and protected each other in some sticky situations.

Together they stood, side-by-side, in front of the towers, stopping have-a-go heroes from entering. Husbands and fathers pushed through to help save those they loved inside. Behind them, they heard a creaking. Jefferson turned around and looked up. Debris fell from the skies and the ground rumbled.

'Run!' Jefferson shouted. Selflessly, he urged Grisham to escape, while he himself stayed back to protect others. Despite Grisham's protests, Jefferson remained adamant that he took those who could get away to safety.

The building collapsed to the ground faster than a losing turn of Jenga. A dust storm followed, taking the lives of all in its path. Grisham ran for his life; a challenge as his lungs filled with dust.

A laundrette sat to the right of Greenwich Street; running for cover, Grisham hid inside behind a washing machine. Glass shattered as debris blasted through the windows as the storm passed.

And then there was silence.

A grey cloud of dust filled the laundrette. Holding his jacket over his mouth, Grisham slowly walked back out into the street. The formerly clear sky of a sunny September morning had descended into a black cloudy winter. For just a few seconds, there was complete silence. No panic, no sirens. Just silence. The world had ended and this policeman walked alone in the derelict city.

Pandemonium returned. Grisham ran back to the scene of the crime. On the ground, where he stood only minutes before, was a member of the NYPD force. The face was black with dirt, making it difficult to distinguish who out of their department had fallen. Grisham wiped away the dust from the dead cop's badge and recognised the four digit identification number, which belonged to Jefferson.

That day changed him. His determination to protect the city had grown more than ever. These fraudsters took advantage of the event, which killed his colleague, and that really bothered him. As someone who had been affected by 9/11 personally, he shouldn't have been on the case. Detectives shouldn't bring their personal issues into work, but when the case came up, he jumped at the chance to investigate it.

Grisham would never have the chance to bring down Osama Bin Laden, nor would he take down the terrorists who remained a threat in the city; a specialised force in the CIA looked after that. However he did have this case. Now he had the chance to make it up to his colleague, to ensure that those who took advantage of that tragic day were punished.

On his last encounter with Amelia and Benjamin, they covered up for their parents' deceit and allowed them to escape. Today they actively approached him to provide him information of their mother's whereabouts. After weeks of no sightings, this news of potentially vital information was welcomed by the detective and his managers back home.

Amelia opened the door to find the detective on the doorstep, before welcoming him into their home. The dark haired detective carried a takeaway coffee cup and cream clung to his moustache. He wore a white checked shirt and blue tie; only his badge clipped to his belt gave away his status in the force.

He shook hands with Benjamin. The former trooper smiled at the cop; despite the interrogation, they had really bonded on their last encounter at the police station. While James and the detective had not met, Grisham recognised him from the papers.

After the introductions and the small talk had been exhausted, Amelia brought the cop some fresh coffee and brought their attention to the impending discussion of their mother.

'So I hear you received a text message.' Grisham broke the ice. Amelia grabbed her cell phone, located the text message in question and handed the device to the policeman. Grisham read the contents. There was no contact name attached to the number. 'Do you recognise the number?'

'No, it's not my Mom's, but she left her cell at her apartment in New York before she left anyway.'

'I see. How do you know it's her?'

'She always calls me '*Pumpkin'*.'

'Is there no one else it could be? An old boyfriend maybe?' He looked towards James to gage his reaction.

'No, it can't be. James is the only boyfriend I've ever had. You read the papers.'

The detective nodded his head. Few had avoided the stories of the celebrity couple after their initial engagement. They were seen as a subject of hope for the city.

'I hate to break this to you, but this might not be your mom.' A mild groaning echoed from the siblings. 'You see, in situations like this, there are often people who like to play games and upset those involved. We get the same thing when someone has been murdered and it becomes a public case. People come forward pretending to be psychics or write letters and cards from missing people.'

'That's sick! But I'm sure it's her.' Amelia insisted. 'Not many people knew that she called me *Pumpkin*. I know it's a stereotypical nickname but I'm sure this is her.'

'OK, we'll follow this up. But I don't want you to get your hopes up. Even if we track where it's come from, it's a possibility that your mom has moved on again or bought a new phone. We may never find her.'

'We have to try. We have to end this madness.' Benjamin insisted. Grisham nodded.

'Indeed we do.'

*

Bags lined the hallway, filled with garments which Geraldine had bought for her patient. The clothes were not to Beverly's taste, but she had little else and a change of style might hide her infamy as she travelled across America.

Beverly looked around her room. The interior looked tired and needed a lick of paint, but Geraldine had provided a warm, comfortable home for her over the past weeks and they had become good friends. Their last evening together was spent watching Beverly's favourite movie, *Meet Me In Saint Louis,* in celebration of her final night in the city, or at least the nearby suburb of Richmond Heights.

'So where are you going to go?'

'I don't know yet. I think I'm going to head west and see where I end up. Marty has family in California, I might stay with them but I'm just going to take each day as it comes. But I can't rely on your hospitality anymore. I can't risk you getting into any trouble.'

Geraldine protested against Beverly's departure for days but she had made up her mind. It was a sad end to a beautiful friendship.

'Well you can't go away without going down-town,' Geraldine insisted. 'Would you like me to come with you and give you the tour?'

'Oh no, that's very kind to offer, but you've really done enough for me. Besides, you need to go and visit your mom.'

'Very well then, I guess this is goodbye.' Geraldine held out her arms and embraced Beverly. They held onto each other for some time, both holding back the tears and battled the reality of when they'd be able to meet again.

'Thank you so much for everything you've done for me. You have no idea how much it's meant.'

'Not a problem.' Geraldine said. 'You are welcome here any time. Don't be a stranger.'

Outside, a horn beeped. Beverly's taxi had arrived. They untangled themselves, pulled back, gripped hands and smiled.

'You've saved me as much as I saved you.' Geraldine stroked the cheek of her friend. Beverly smiled and nodded. She collected her bags and walked out to the taxi. The driver stepped out of the car, collected her belongings and placed them in the trunk, before opening the passenger door to allow Beverly to get inside.

'Where to, Mam?' the driver asked.

'Kensington Avenue please, St. Louis.' The car revved its engine and drove off down the street. Beverly waved at her companion, who stood on her porch waving back, until she was out of site.

*

Grisham resided in a nearby hotel in Barrington, Illinois. The length of his trip remained unknown, but he had the authority to stay in the suburb until he caught the fraudsters.

The detective had sent the details of the text message to his department, who worked with the phone networks. Like he had warned, they managed expectations around the reality of finding Beverly from a text alone.

It had been an interesting twenty-five years in the force. Only five more years and he could retire. Grisham loved his job but it made him very bitter. It was a tough job holding back as he was deceived by some of the most notorious criminals in America.

Only once had he allowed his emotions to take over. The detective beat up a suspected paedophile, who abused and killed his own two children. As a father himself, who hadn't seen his own children since they were young, it infuriated Grisham. He would do anything to see his children again, but this man murdered his.

The truth was Grisham had lost a lot more than just Jefferson on that fateful day in 2001. Shortly after his colleague's death, he drank heavily. He couldn't see good in people anymore, nor could he see hope in America. He questioned the point of his own job when he couldn't even defend his colleagues and citizens against terrorists.

The drinking took its toll and he became aggressive at home. His frustrated wife left home, taking the children with her. He hadn't seen them since. Now he was clean and didn't even drink a sip of champagne at the annual policeman's ball, but his children were still nowhere to be seen. He had tracked down some of the most inconspicuous underground gangsters in America, yet he couldn't find his family for love, nor money.

The loss of his own family was another factor in his desperation to find Marty. Grisham would give up everything to see his kids again, yet this guy abandoned his for a million dollars. The advantage Marty took of the charity which he benefited from brought a bitter taste to Grisham's mouth.

Evidence proved Marty was in the twin towers that day. He must have seen people die. How could he have witnessed all those horrific scenes yet still be encouraged to exploit it?

Grisham was in too deep with the case. He struggled to hold up his professionalism and feared his response when he finally caught up with Hahn. His colleagues may have turned a blind eye to the detective's aggression once, but they wouldn't a second time.

Grisham sat in his hotel room watching American Idol. The television had poor reception but he'd managed to pick up just this one channel. Bored with the sound of his own thoughts, the show brought a blissful distraction, despite his distaste for those who sought a fast way to the top.

A phone call disrupted the announcement of the contest winner. The call was from the telephone network regarding the other people he had grown a distaste for in recent months.

'Hi Detective Grisham, we have an update regarding the cell phone which sent the text message to Amelia Hahn.'

'Go on.' Grisham never allowed for small talk, it wasted valuable time.

'We still don't know whether it was a prank, but we've located where the text message was sent from.'

'And where was that?' Grisham's heart pounded as he searched for a pen and paper.

'A suburb in Missouri called Richmond Heights, near Saint Louis.'

*

Geraldine took off the bed sheets from the spare room and placed them in the washing machine. The house seemed eerily quiet now her companion had left and the silence dampened her mood.

She hoped her friend had managed to get far away, although she worried the further she travelled, there was a greater chance of her being seen. At least while she was in her house, she could protect her from the outside world. She'd also have kept onto her friend and have avoided the sense of loss she now endured.

Geraldine had felt loss before; for ten years, she was in love with her best friend. Deborah Pollard was married when they met, but her abusive husband made it an unhappy marriage. Fed up, she ran away and stayed with Geraldine. Soon after swearing off men, they formed a relationship together. However, their relationship was cut short as Deborah discovered she had cervical cancer. At first they celebrated as they caught it early, but it soon spread to her liver and groin. Within weeks, Deborah passed away.

That loss, which Geraldine felt fourteen years before, had now returned. While Beverly was alive and well, and was far from a lover, her platonic affection brought the company Geraldine craved; a friendship she struggled to source naturally since her infamous downfall in the care-home.

She watered the plants in the guest room. They were neglected during Beverly's stay. As the water trickled from the watering-can onto the window-sill greenery, Geraldine looked out at the street. The neighbours gossiped at their gates and the village postman raised his cap to all he passed

Across the road, the curtains twitched. A figure behind the window glanced at the scene, which Geraldine herself had been looking at. She was not proud of scaring Pamela, but Geraldine was tired of the lies spreading around the town. Pamela looked up and locked eyes with Geraldine, before closing her curtains once again.

A vehicle pulled up to her house. She had few guests so the visitors came as a surprise. For just a moment, her heart skipped a beat, considering Beverly had changed her mind, but before she could blink, two gentlemen stepped out of the car and scanned the area, before walking up to her door.

'Hello? Can I help you?' Geraldine answered as she opened the door. The two men held out their badges which had the Metropolitan

Police of St. Louis logo displayed upon them. The gentleman to her right also held out a sheet of paper with her address upon it.

'Geraldine McMahon, I have a warrant to search your home. I believe you may be harbouring a criminal.' The detectives brushed past her and began to search around the house. Geraldine closed the door and followed them.

'Who have I supposed to have hidden?' Geraldine asked.

'Beverly Hahn.' the detective said bluntly as he opened the drawers in the living room.

'And she is?'

'Don't you watch the news?' the second detective quizzed. Everyone knew who Beverly Hahn was, surely? She had made every newspaper headline for months. 'She fraudulently claimed money from the 9/11 fund when her husband faked his death.'

'Oh, no I don't watch the news. I once *was* the news so I take little notice of what's on that box. It's all fiction, you know? The news. It's made up of lies.'

'Yeah, I heard about your previous convictions.' The detective raised his eyebrow.

'I was also cleared of everything.'

'Mmmm, so I hear.'

He walked upstairs and browsed around the bedrooms.

'Who lives here?'

'Just me.'

'So you've had guests then?' the detective asked. Geraldine's eyes widened.

'What do you mean?'

'You've clearly had someone staying here.' He pointed towards the stripped bedding.

'Oh, yes sorry. My cousin came to stay for a few days.'

'And her name is?'

'Mary.'

'Please can you provide us a contact for this *Mary*. We'll need to speak to her.' He looked out of the window towards the street of gossiping neighbours. 'Your local residents seem quite chatty, did they meet your cousin, or any other guests you may have had?'

Geraldine moved the detective away from the window and glared down at Pamela's house, wondering how the policemen discovered that Beverly had inhabited her residence.

'What proof do you have that this *Beverly* has ever been here?'

'The night Beverly Hahn came to Missouri, she was driving a Jeep, let out by a Chicago based leasing company. That car has just been discovered under a pile of snow just a twenty-five mile drive away from your house. The snow has melted away since, but there was nobody inside. When we looked back at the CCTV from the night which the car went missing, we traced your car driving down the same road soon after Beverly Hahn drove her vehicle off-road.'

'Well hundreds of cars must have driven down that road that night. I hope you'll be ransacking their homes too?'

'Well no, we came to yours first because we had other information which made us suspect you too.'

'Oh yeah, and what is that?' Geraldine's bottom lip trembled.

'A text message sent to the daughter of Beverly Hahn…' the detective paused. '…from your cell phone number.'

*

Beverly got out of the car on Kensington Avenue, asking specifically to be dropped off at house number 5135. She asked the taxi driver to wait around until she returned, before walking up to the pink Victorian mansion, which played the central location of her favourite movie.

She gasped in delight as it was exactly how she imagined it. She had dreamed of visiting this place since she was a little girl. It reminded her of her father who had first introduced her to the Smith family from *Meet Me in St. Louis.*

The house was constructed for the purposes of the movie by MGM at the time of filming. The stately home had since become a residential property, and while the area had degraded since, it maintained the magical charm which was affluent in the famous film.

As she looked up at the grand house, she felt someone creep up behind her. The shadow of the figure's reflection towered over her and darkened the entrance to the elegant home.

'Hello Sweetheart.' a recongisable voice spoke. Surprised, she turned around and looked at the man who made her stomach flip every time she saw him.

'Marty.'

*

Geraldine read the text message, which proved the fraudulent fugitive, Beverly Hahn, had resided in her home. *When had Beverly managed to get her phone? She must have gone into my bag.*

Beverly took advantage of her trusting nature and put the woman who cared for her at great risk with the police, before running off so she could avoid the consequences. How could she do this when she knew Geraldine had been in trouble with the law before?

'So Ms McMahon, are you going to tell us where Beverly Hahn is?' The detective raised his eyebrow and presented a smug smile, confident that he had this suspect rattled.

'I've been caring for somebody called Beverly, but I didn't know she was a wanted criminal.' Geraldine lied. She gulped and the detective registered her guilt.

'So why did you lie about who came to stay here? You said it was your cousin who came to stay. Why would you lie about your guest if you thought this Beverly was an innocent woman?'

'I'm... I....' She stumbled for words as she tried to scramble out of the hole she had dug.

'I know about your past, Geraldine. I know what you've been accused of. I imagine a reputation like that could do you some serious harm in court if we charged you for harbouring a criminal.' the detective calmly explained. 'But here's what I'll do for you. You tell me where she is now and we'll forget you allowed this woman to stay here.'

'I honestly don't know where she's heading to. She mentioned California.'

'You must be able to give us more details than that. Did she mention anything, or did you over-hear her speaking to anyone on the phone about where she intends to visit?'

'I really don't know.' Geraldine assured the detective.

'I'm throwing you a life line, Ms McMahon. I advise you take it because we will make things very difficult for you if you do not give us something pretty quickly.'

The detective leaned in closely to the suspect causing their noses to touch. She tried to pull back, but the detective grabbed her arms and pulled her in. Her face grew pale and sweat dribbled down from her scalp.

Conflicted, Geraldine couldn't decide between standing by her friend and ensuring a future of freedom. Could she really betray someone she cared about? But on the other hand, she felt angry. She had been taken advantage of and put at serious risk after Beverly decided to use her phone to text her daughter.

The detective lost his patience with her and lifted out his handcuffs. 'Geraldine McMahon, I'm arresting you on suspicion of harbouring a criminal. You do not need to say anything…'

'Wait!' she yelled. The detective shut up. 'Have you seen *Meet Me In Saint Louis?'*

*

The snow sparkled in the sunlight, slowly dying away as it set. The overcast brought a sharp breeze, nibbling on the arms and legs of the reunited couple.

Marty's presence came as a bigger surprise than his resurrection the previous September. His overgrown hair and unwashed clothes displayed the battle he had endured to remain alive in the Mid-West winter since his escape from Indiana, after ditching his fiancé at the altar with a hundred thousand dollars in hand.

There were so many questions to answer but Beverly was dumbfounded by this familiar face. Since she left Chicago, she had been surrounded by strangers and right now she was in awe of this familiar man, who knew her better than anybody.

'I've missed you.' She grabbed him, gripping her hands around his waist, whilst rubbing her cheek against his chest, breathing in the familiar scent of *Old Spice*. He was the one person she needed during the lonely Thanksgiving and Christmas holidays, which she spent away from her family. He was the one she desired when she found out that her father was terminally ill. It was he whom she wanted caring for her by her bedside when she was injured in the car accident. She now held him tight and could not bear to let go.

'How did you know I was here?'

'Hunny, we've watched that movie a million times and every time you dreamed of coming here. It was the only place I thought there was a chance you would visit so I pulled up in my car here every day and waited, just hoping you would eventually come.'

He escaped Chicago on the night his children called the police at Francis's birthday party. On the radio the song *Route 66* sang out the lyrics.

Well it winds from Chicago to LA
More than 2000 miles all the way
Get your kicks on Route 66
Well it goes from St Louis, down to Missouri
Oklahoma City looks oh so pretty

He knew where his wife's heart would take her had she seen the signs for the famous route as she escaped Chicago. He spent his days waiting in the snow for the arrival of his wife and his nights in a cheap motel down the road from the movie location.

With a six figure bank balance under the name of Martin Singer, Marty had the means to travel in style, but he had their future to consider and wasted little of the funds, which would allow them to purchase a property once they found a permanent landing spot.

The plan took weeks to deliver. Following the acceptance of Joseph Atkinson's cheque, he put the funds in the account named under *Martin Reece*. The original name kept him in work during his ten year absence, but his return to Indiana required him to set up a separate identity in case his former one became compromised.

As soon as the cheque cleared, he spent weeks subtly taking out moderate sums of cash under his old name and manually walking into his new bank, registered under *Singer,* to make the deposit. Bank transfers of large amounts could have sparked interest with the IRS, causing unwanted attention for the runaway.

Now he stood before his wife, who tried to adjust to his story of how he found her before the police did.

‘You know me too well.’ She hummed in content as she rubbed her head against his chest. For just a moment, her problems were far away, she was safe once again without a care in the world. Sadness fell upon her as she realised the true reality of the situation she was in.

‘I can’t be on my own anymore. I’m so angry with you. I’m so mad. You’ve hurt me more than anyone ever could. You’ve hurt our children and you’ve hurt that poor red-neck in Indiana. But I know that everything you have done has been to ensure that we have better lives.’

'I wish we could go back ten years, Marty.’ she continued. ‘Even with all the financial insecurity, I would take that life back any day over this. Now we've got more money in our pockets than ever before, but it's all worth nothing. We can't buy ourselves out of this situation.'

Marty pulled his wife away from him, wiped the tears away from her cheeks with his thumbs and held her head in his large hands. He held her cheekbones like a proud bowler holding his prize ball for the first time.

'But we have each other, Beverly. It doesn't matter how little money we have or how much trouble we're in, if we have each other, we can't go wrong. That's why we can't get caught as we'll be separated. You're the key to our success, Bev, and even though I don't deserve you, I beg you to give me another chance.'

They perched on the red brick wall outside a neighbouring house across the street and stared on at the building, which had captured their imaginations throughout their marriage. The pink cladding appeared rougher than their memories and much of the street had been left to decay since Hollywood moved out. The couple caught up on their ventures since they departed in Indiana, including the doomed wedding to Caitlin.

‘I feel terrible about everything I've done for the past ten years. I’m sorry I ruined everything. We’re in this together now though. There is no going back for either of us as they'll put us in jail if we do. If we’re going to keep running, surely we should be running together?’

'I've dreamed of this reunion over and over again since we split up. I thought about making you suffer for the way you've treated our family. I'd planned every word I would say to you... they weren't very nice. Would have been bleeped out if I was on TV. But now you're here... I think if it had been another time... another place... it would have been different. But you're here in front of the house we've been watching throughout our entire marriage. If that doesn't mean something, I don't know what does, and the fact that you knew where I'd come just shows how much you know me. You're really determined and I can't turn my head away from that. If you can fight for our marriage, so can I.'

He wrapped an arm around her and she lay her head on his shoulder. They stared onwards in silence, enjoying the quiet ambiance of the famous street. Petals of snow floated down, soughing as they drifted past them, gently patting the ground.

'We always dreamed of coming here on Route 66 when we retired, do you remember?' she reminisced.

'I think we talked about doing it sooner than that. It was going to be when we were out of our financial crisis.'

'Oh yeah, and you wanted to stop in Vegas and renew our vows. So tacky.' she laughed.

'I still do.' He grabbed her hand, but her numb skin failed to feel his touch. 'I still will if you'd let me show you how dedicated to you I am. Open and honest. No more lies and no more hidden secrets. Let's get married as the new Mr and Mrs Singer.'

She snorted with laughter.

'Miss Beverly Goldberg, will you marry me?'

'Yes.' she replied. 'Yes I will!'

In the distance, a faint sound of sirens echoed through the blizzard. Marty looked up and squinted his eyes, focusing on the long stretch of Kensington Avenue, disappearing in the snow storm. A flashing red light flickered as the sirens grew louder.

'We better go and do it fast then.'

They jumped into a metallic blue Ford Focus, Marty had hired, and sped off out of St. Louis and onto Las Vegas.

Chapter 27

The snow melted fast in Chicago and the suburban village of Hoffman Estates began to flood. The garden of Amelia and Benjamin's new home was swamped. The tips of the soaked grass poked out of the shallow lake in their garden.

Public transport had been compromised, preventing Benjamin from heading down-town to visit the glamour of Boys Town for work. He downloaded online applications onto his phone to connect him to potential customers in the local area, but his sister banned him from bringing his work home with him. They were in enough trouble without their house becoming a brothel.

The tension had risen as the three of them spent increasingly long periods together in the small abode. Despite their fall-out at Christmas, Amelia was sure the boys would soon develop a friendship again over time, but her hopes went unfulfilled.

Benjamin's temper rose, bitter of the world for the tough hand he had been given. The arguments with his family allowed him to drown out the voices in his head and the screams from the Iraqi cinema.

A lonely Amelia spent more and more time on her own in an increasingly quiet house. She watched television alone in the living room while the two boys spent their lives in their bedrooms, watching their televisions or listening to their MP3 players to avoid confrontation with each other.

Meal times brought them together, but they sat in silence, gobbling up the dinner she'd prepared, before disappearing to their rooms as soon as their plates were scraped without as much as a thank you. Her relationship with both of them had worn, failing as a mediator between the warring future in-laws.

'He needs to see a doctor or a counsellor.' James said.

'He's fine.' she replied. 'We've been through a lot, how can a counsellor solve our problems?'

Once again she attempted to bring the boys together to play Monopoly, but the competitive game tore apart the closest of families, and did little to bring together this warring one. James accused Benjamin of cheating when he opted to be the banker which erupted in a row. They returned to their rooms, leaving Amelia alone once again.

The cheers of supporters echoed from the television in her bedroom as her boyfriend watched major league soccer. He supported LA Galaxy and the evening's game took him away from their quality time together.

'It's an important game.' he argued. 'David Beckham is back from Milan, so I can't miss it.'

'Well can't we go down to Champs and watch it together?'

'You don't even like soccer. You'll start questioning me about the off-side rule again and I can't be bothered to explain it again. It's just easier if I watch it here alone.'

She hoped Benjamin would make an appearance so they could go out, but the silence from his room suggested he was asleep or listening to his MP3 player.

A knock on the door broke the silence. She ran to the door, eager for company. Behind it, Detective Grisham waited. His visit came as no surprise; he had stopped by their house almost daily since they informed him of the text message from their mother. Until now, he had few developments but assured her that his team were working around the clock to bring their parents home.

'Detective, come in.' Amelia stood back as he walked past. He sat down without an invitation to and turned his radio off. 'We haven't heard any more off Mom since your last visit.'

'Well that's not a surprise.' the detective explained. 'A police force in Missouri have caught and arrested her.'

'Was it…' Amelia paused. '… the text message?'

The detective nodded and Amelia lowered her head. Families were supposed to stick together.

'She's been hiding in a house near St Louis with a lady called Geraldine McMahon, do you know her?'

'No, she's never mentioned her and we don't know anyone down there.'

'She sent the text message from Ms McMahon's phone and ran off. This lady she stayed with told us where she was heading and we caught her in Downtown St. Louis. Her identity hasn't been officially confirmed but she is a close match. We haven't caught your father yet. Mrs Hahn was with a gentleman at the time, who ran off upon our arrival.'

'I see, thank you. What happens now?' Amelia asked.

'You need to come and identify the suspect at the station and confirm she *is* indeed your mother. At the moment she is insisting that she isn't, so we need you to come and confirm that she is who we believe she is.'

'That's fine. Will I need to go to St. Louis?' Amelia sighed, considering more travel.

'No.' The detective shook his head. 'We're bringing her to Chicago as we speak. She should be here in a couple of hours. We'll need you to come down to the precinct and you can identify her behind mirrored glass, so you won't need to worry about betraying your family, do you understand?' Grisham said. Amelia nodded her head. 'In which case I'll go, we should be ready for you later this afternoon around four, so whenever you're ready…'

The detective let himself out and James walked out of his bedroom.

'Hey, I heard the door, is everything OK?'

Amelia turned to her boyfriend with tears in her eyes, holding the phone with the text message upon it.

'They've found her.' James raised his head but remained silent. He walked over and placed his arms around his fiancé. 'I have to go and confirm it's her this afternoon. Will you come with me?'

'Of course.' James kissed her forehead. Benjamin's door rattled and he walked out. 'Hey, Benjamin. They've arrested your mom.' Benjamin stood in his cartoon covered pyjama bottoms but his torso remained bare. He silently mouthed an *'oh'* and walked over to the pair, rubbing his sister's back in support.

'Well I suppose that's that. Hopefully they'll soon find Dad and that will be them out of our lives for good. The sooner, the better.'

He let go of his sister and walked over to the bathroom, a small crack in his cheeks formed. The door closed and a cheerful tune echoed from the bathroom where he whistled.

'Don't tell him we're going to identify her, I don't want him upsetting anyone.' She pushed her boyfriend away and wiped her eyes. A ringing from her phone distracted her and she ran to answer it.

'Hello?' she said. A mumbling echoed from the device, but James struggled to hear it. He moved himself away from her to give her space. 'Oh OK, give me one second.' She lifted her index finger up towards James and returned to her room, shutting the door behind her.

As one door closed, another opened. Benjamin hobbled out of the bathroom, naked, with only a red bathrobe around his waist. His skin remained dry as he rushed towards his bedroom to collect his shower-gel. The previous day they'd argued about James's use of Benjamin's toiletries, leading to him hiding them away in his room away from his loose hands.

'Hey, you know you could be a little more sensitive around your sister. She's really upset about your mom.'

Benjamin simply shrugged. His bare torso displayed the stump, which still appeared sore as it healed at the tip. The amputation was usually hidden away under a sweat-shirt, but this rare exposure reaffirmed his suffering, which his house-mates could usually block out as they focused on their own problems.

'Dude, stay out of our affairs, OK? You're not family yet.' Benjamin gave his sister's boyfriend little time to retaliate as he rushed back into the bathroom and slammed the door behind him.

The bedroom door reopened and Amelia returned to the living room, her cheeks red raw from the salty tears irritating her skin.

'Who called?'

'Oh… it was Evelyn. She was complaining because the police had been to see her about Mom, saying how it embarrassing it was. She also said we have to sort out legal proceedings soon.' She rushed to grab her bag and coat. 'Anyway I'm going to Woodfield Mall. If I'm gonna have to identify my criminal mom, I wanna be dressed appropriately.'

'Do you want me to come with you?' James asked. She shook her head and grabbed her purse.

'No I want some time on my own, thanks.' She quickly ran out the door, leaving a confused James suspicious of her distant behaviour.

*

The red brick building displayed little evidence of its inhabitants. Only the black and white striped cars outside provided any sign that this was a law enforcement office. It sat between the bright lights of an international food chain and the hotel, which Grisham resided in during his weeks in Illinois, attempting to bring Marty and Beverly Hahn to justice.

James and Amelia arrived by taxi to prepare for the identification of the woman caught earlier in the day in St. Louis. Detective Grisham welcomed them to the station and made them both a coffee as they waited for the officers to align several suspects into a light room with white walls. A waving hand signalled the officers were ready for the couple to enter the identification room.

The couple walked down a darkened corridor. Luminous arrows guided their way to the centre of the room. To their left, a glass pane provided the view of the suspects. Ten women lined up in order of the number they held in their hands. The women dressed identically in orange rags and their haircuts and figures were similar. They stared towards the girl who was now ready to identify the criminal amongst them. A mirrored wall prevented them from seeing the girl who had the power to end their freedom.

'OK, so as you can see, Miss Hahn, the suspects are numbered from one to ten. You have to tell me which number your mother, Beverly Hahn, is. If your mother is not here, you simply tell us that it is none of the suspects. Do you understand?'

Amelia nodded her head. She walked up and down the room, spending a few seconds in front of each suspect to determine whether the person before her was her mother until she got to the last suspect.

'Are you ready to tell us your answer, Miss Hahn?' the detective asked. She spent an extra few seconds glaring at a particular figure more than she had on the other members in the line-up.

'Yes I am, Detective.' Amelia paused. Grisham and James waited in anticipation. 'It's number three.'

James flinched, turning his head from his girlfriend to suspect number three. He spent a few seconds staring at her intensely, before returning to his girlfriend, who fixated on the person she had just named as her mother.

'Are you sure, Miss Hahn?'

'Yeah, I'm absolutely sure of it. It's number three.'

'OK, Miss Hahn, that's all we need.' The detective walked the couple out of the darkened room. 'Listen, this is highly unorthodox, but would you like to see her? I'm sure you girls must have a lot you want to talk about.'

'Oh no!' Amelia barked. 'No, I don't want her to know I'm responsible for her being here.'

The detective nodded and opened the door allowing her to leave. James followed on, remaining silent over her choice.

*

The shadows of trees towered over the road, casting them into almost complete darkness. The gleam of an elk's eyes, reflecting from the headlights, sparked a rush of adrenalin as the animal ran across the carriageway, narrowly missing the hood of the vehicle.

Little was said along Golf Road. The olive skinned taxi driver had attempted conversation, but his broken English caused the interchange to become challenging. His poor communication allowed James to approach his girlfriend regarding a troubling matter.

'So.... .' he stuttered. 'So that wasn't your mom....'

'No, it wasn't.' Amelia spoke bluntly as she stared out of the window. Her eyes were vacant, deep in thought as she plotted her next steps. Her behaviour had been unusual for the majority of the day, accepting dubious calls and hurrying off to the mall alone.

'Who called you today?'

'My mom.' she spoke softly. James rested his shoulders, relieved by her ability to open up to him.

'Where is she? What did she say?'

'She's with my father. They're on their way to Vegas to get married.'

'Why did you lie to Detective Grisham?' James asked. 'I don't understand. Before you were keen to shop them in. Why didn't you just tell them where they are?'

'Because I couldn't do it. Not again.' Amelia explained. 'My mom told me when I was a teenager that my dad wanted to take her to Vegas and marry her once their money issues were over. Now they can do that and I don't want to be the one to take that away from them, no matter how many lies have run through this family over the years. My dad lied to protect our family, now I'm returning his favour.'

'I see. What are you going to say when they find out that the woman you claimed was your mom turns out not to be, because they will find out, you know? One way or another.'

'Well it's bought us some time.' she said. 'There was something else my mom asked of me on the phone.'

'Oh yeah, what was that? Does she want us to kill some people and harvest their organs too? Because I think that might be a step too far.'

'She wants us to go to Vegas for the ceremony.'

'And you want to go?' James asked, petrified by what the answer might be.

'Yeah. It's up to you if you want to join me. But if I go alone, I'm afraid it's over for us...'

*

The lights were on but little action occurred inside. Despite the thin walls, little noise radiated from the building. The drawn curtains prevented the detective from witnessing any movement within.

Grisham stared intensely at the Hahn household, suspicious of their motives. He failed to mention that nine out of the ten people in the identity parade were actors. It was standard procedure to ensure the witness coming in had the correct person. The individual Amelia had chosen was one of the actors he paid to stand in line.

Upon choosing a stand-in from the line-up, the police would usually drop the charges upon the suspect. In most cases the witness was a victim of crime and had no previous association with the suspect; choosing the wrong person was common and understandable. But to fail to identify her own mother was a cause for concern and Grisham now had enough evidence to bring criminal charges upon Amelia for aiding her family's escape.

The offer of a meeting between the witness and her mother was highly unorthodox, and had this been a standard identity parade, he would never have offered the introduction. Instead, his offer gave him the opportunity to see her reaction and how she would deal with coming face-to-face with the actress she had identified as her mother.

The detective struggled to understand Amelia's motives. A few days before, she appeared keen to help them with their enquiries, but something had distracted her and caused her to slow down their search. If she had chosen the suspect he arrested earlier in the day, the search for Beverly would have halted, providing more time for her to get far away from the Mid-West.

The suspect arrested earlier in the day would remain in custody. The Barrington police force would have to follow up on her reasons for running from the police. She could be innocent; some people acted oddly when chased by the police. He had seen completely innocent citizens panic when they had little to hide.

But for now, Grisham's concerns were focused on Amelia. She was the key to finding Beverly and Marty. He would find them and he didn't care how far he had to travel to bring them to justice.

Chapter 28

Route 66 has many names. It is commonly known as the Will Rogers Highway, Main Street of America and The Mother Road. Despite the numerous titles Americans have for the cross-country highway, one peculiar element of the most famous road in America is that it doesn't actually exist. The road, which was developed in 1926 to provide a connection between Chicago and California, was removed from the highway system in 1985 in replacement of a new interstate highway system. Despite it no longer being in existence in name, the original road is still popular with American and international drivers alike, who continue to make the historic journey, which the migrants made in the 1930s Dust Bowl.

Songs and movies have been inspired by the remarkable journey which Marty and Beverly embarked on. They spent days driving through the dusty desert. Their companionship made it a durable drive, one which would be torturous alone.

The landscapes changed in drifts. Along the dusty highway, they passed sky rise statues, museums and attractions, which nearby residents had built to entice tourists to their small towns. Dozens of gas stations and cafés claimed to have been visited by Elvis Presley. How many could truly claim entitlement to serving the singer remained unknown, but it made the journey all the more interesting either way.

As they headed closer towards the desert, the snow decreased and the heat rose to a sweltering level. The desert in front of them blurred as the heat haze of conflicting temperatures caused interfering patterns to the eye.

'I wonder how my dad is.' Beverly broke the silence.

'He seemed OK to me when I saw him in Chicago. Of course he wasn't very happy to see me.'

'He's dying.'

'I know.' Marty said.

'I left things with him in a terrible state. I said some horrible things. I shouldn't have left it how it was. I should have fixed it before I left, especially as I know he doesn't have much time left.'

'Hey, he did lie to you. Don't beat yourself up too much. You had every right to be angry. You still do.'

'But I've had time to reflect since. I know he was just trying to help out. As were you. I forgive him, like I forgive you. Whether I'll ever get the opportunity to tell him that, I don't know.'

'You could always call him.'

'Are you joking? He'll be on tight surveillance. I'm sure the police know we've been in touch now. His phone will be tapped and they'll monitor his every move. No, we better just leave him alone.'

'You could have invited him to the wedding. He could have found an excuse to leave Chicago.'

'I don't think he'll have the strength to travel. He wouldn't be able to cope with the heat.'

'I'm so sorry, Hunny.' He took one arm off the steering wheel and placed it around his wife, before giving her a gentle squeeze. 'I'm so sorry I came back, Beverly. I should have stayed away. Well no, in fact I shouldn't have gone away in the first place. Maybe it would have been better had I actually died that day. That way you guys could all be rich and wouldn't be in trouble with me.'

'That's not fair. No. We would still have our problems. And we wouldn't have you. No matter what torture we have to go through, I have you in my life. That means more to me than any amount of money.' Beverly smiled at her husband and he returned it.

'I've not come across as a very nice person. I've done a lot wrong. I've lied to you guys, I've broken people's hearts and I've stolen a lot of money. I sometimes look at myself in the mirror and wonder what the hell I've become.'

'Desperate.' Beverly said. 'You were desperate and you'll do anything to ensure your family survive. It's like stealing a loaf of bread from the store to feed your family.'

'I wish the law saw it the same way.' The conversation paused as they considered the reality of their situation and returned to staring out of the window.

The office blocks declined and their surroundings grew dustier. Nevada was close and they would soon arrive in Las Vegas. Unbeknownst to her husband, Beverly would soon be reunited with her daughter.

*

One hundred miles behind, James and Amelia drove along the desert in a Cadillac, which they leased earlier in Chicago. The vehicle provided the perfect ambiance to make the historic journey they now embarked on.

James had battled over his decision to join her. They rowed, cried and he stormed out of the house twice before finally returning, accepting that he needed her in his life.

They left the house in the early hours of the morning while Benjamin was sleeping. The less he knew the better; he'd only hinder their plans. Instead, they left a note explaining they'd gone on vacation to escape their troubles.

The red Cadillac was an older model and the air-con had broken. The heat became unbearable and Amelia removed increasing amounts of clothing along the journey to cool. She sniffed her bra and gagged as she took in the aroma of her own scent.

'So, what if we're seen? Or what if the police realise we're lying about your mom?' James asked.

'I thought you said you were going to be supportive?'

'I am, but we need to think about the reality too. We need to consider what we're going to say. Right now we're breaking the law and we could be put in jail. We would be separated. Do you want that?'

'No, of course not. But I have to see my mom one last time.' She began to sob. 'The last time I saw my grandfather, I was awful to him. I will not allow another relationship to go down the drain while I still have a chance. The day I thought my father died, I text him that morning before the attacks happened. I sent him the most awful message. I had one opportunity to make it up to him when he returned last year. But I didn't. I told him where to get off. Then he came to Chicago to Grandpa's birthday and I told him to get out of my life again. There are only going to be a small number of chances left with both of them before I lose them completely.'

'Hey,' James took one hand off the steering wheel and rubbed her back. 'I understand. I felt that way every night after I threw you out. When I saw you at Central Park, I was devastated. When I thought I'd lost you forever, it crushed me. I couldn't lose you again and this is why I'm protesting so much. The police could take you away from me. However, if this is what you really want to do, then I'll stand by you one-hundred per-cent.'

‘What would you do if it was *your* mom?’ Amelia asked. He considered Julie Gates on that United 93 flight heading towards Washington and the years he spent without her.

‘I would do exactly what you’re doing right now.’ He squeezed her shoulder and they drove on into the tumble-weaved desert, unaware that Detective Grisham was driving his unmarked police car just five hundred yards behind them.

*

Las Vegas is culturally known as *The Entertainment Capital of the World.* It’s filled with casino hotels complete with multiple theatre complexes, theme parks, museums and shopping malls across each hotel resort. Also known as *Sin City,* it is a place which has managed to legally side pass prostitution laws and is one of the few places in America where you can smoke indoors and drink outdoors.

It was the perfect environment for a soldier on a break from the brutality of Iraq to relax and let off steam. This was the case for Private Charles Henningway, a member of the US Army, who had returned from a stint in the Middle East.

Henningway had endured a tough few months; he had seen his colleague die and played witness to a dear friend lose an arm in the same attack. Support, counselling and time off had been offered to him, but like many soldiers who only wished to serve their country, he wanted to get back into the game and destroy those who ended his friends’ lives.

While his disabled colleague remained very much alive, the army was his life and his disability compromised his career in the forces. They'd had little contact since they brought home the body of their fallen soldier, Private Ross.

Since that day, Henningway had read up on his former colleague. It had become apparent that his father, whose death had forced his friend to join up to the military, had fraudulently faked his death for financial gain in the most horrific terrorist attack America had ever seen.

The regiment expressed their distaste for their former trooper's involvement, convinced he had prior knowledge before his father returned. However, Henningway knew better. They were friends. They had bonded. They knew their reasons for signing up. They were even together in the movie theatre when the explosion happened. There was no room for formalities when their friendship was as strong as theirs. Rather than responding to their regimented titles, his colleague called him *Charlie* and he called his former trooper *Benjamin.*

Benjamin had shared with Charlie his story, revealing his disappointment of leaving a life of academia behind to fight the terrorists who murdered his father. Had Marty come home that day, Benjamin would now be a professor at an Ivy League colleague.

Instead he joined the army on the same day as Charlie, trained together and stood side by side at their Passing-Out Parade as they were formally sworn in. They met each other's families and Charlie was introduced to the woman who was now considered one of the most infamous felons in the USA.

As part of what Charlie and his fellow troopers jokingly called '*recess'*, they were put up in The Bellagio Hotel, one of the grandest properties along the strip. Inside they had access to a full bar, a private swimming pool and casinos.

They witnessed horrific scenes out in Iraq, and for many of the troops, this was their therapy. The Grand Canyon and a showbiz residency wasn't on their agenda, nor would they bother to visit the world-famous fountains, which aligned the front of their hotel for the nightly show. The aim of the trip was to consume as much alcohol and drugs, sleep with as many women and to blow as much money as possible.

The respect, received from their fellow citizens for their service, prevented establishments from banning the unruly soldiers. Their antics were no secret; the hotel would have to write off the rooms for a week after they departed so they could have the carpets professionally cleaned.

Charlie was hung-over. After the heavy session the previous evening, the dehydrated soldier desperately needed water. Waking up in his suite, he found several of his colleagues passed out with girls lying naked next to them. Smashed bottles and traces of cocaine scattered across the floor. His memory from the previous evening was hazy, but the chaos surrounding his bed suggested it was a good night.

The reception shop sold bottled water at a premium price; he could've bought it cheaper off a street-tradesman but a hangover was murder in the desert and his throat was as dry as timber. Convenience won.

As he walked past the reception desk, he noticed a familiar face. A lady, around five-foot-four, slim with pale skin, checked into the hotel. The colour of her hair had changed since their last meeting but he could see her natural tint shining through her roots.

He struggled to place her identity at first. His hangover messed with his memory. She could've been a celebrity; it was The Bellagio after all.

Giving up on his personal game of *Guess Who,* he made his way to the store. He treated himself to a two litre bottle and downed the ice-cold drink as soon as he handed the money to the shop keeper. His thirst mirrored an African child having access to a well after a four mile walk. Water splashed all over his chin and shirt, but he didn't care; hydration was finally here.

On his return to the elevator, he noticed the same lady again. He squinted trying to place her. *Who was she with?*

The man beside her looked familiar too, but they hadn't met. *He's been on the news. They both had.* He'd met the lady at the Passing-Out Ceremony; it was a few years before. He was eighteen back then. She'd aged; they both had.

From this moment, he was no longer on *recess*. He had to return to the man he was in Iraq: the professional soldier who stood by and protected his fellow man. He was no longer Charlie, but Private Hemmingway. He ran to the pay phones, which sat opposite the reception desk, and dialled. On the third ring, the receiver answered.

'Hello? I have somebody you may want.'

Chapter 29

Beverly and Marty looked out of their bedroom window taking in the view of the Glitter Gulch that made up the strip of Las Vegas. A collage of empty desert and corporate giants lay before them.

The glare of the sun, reflecting off the pool, blinded the couple who were soon to be married. The glass pane was too hot to touch. They had come a long way from the snowy Midwest. The feeling returned to their fingers and their legs no longer bled from winter's brutal impact on their skin. Now they could moisten their bodies with sun lotion and allow the heat to heal the scars that the minus temperatures had inflicted upon them.

'I can't believe we're getting married tomorrow.' Beverly said giddily. 'It's ridiculous to be this excited but I am! It's like I'm twenty-one all over again.'

'It's crazy isn't it? I'm like a young man, I actually feel younger.' Marty giggled with excitement, threw his wife on the bed and jumped on top of her, before kissing her. The king size bed provided the luxury experience they longed for since their escape from New York. Macro photography lined the plum coated walls, a recessed wardrobe slept parallel to the large bed and an entertainment station sat upon an illuminated dressing table.

'I'm so glad we eloped. It's going to be wonderful just being the two of us this time. I feel so naughty like Britney Spears or something. I hope our marriage lasts a little longer than hers though. But I'm so excited that it'll be just us, alone, making our vows.'

'Well we won't be completely alone.' Beverly said.

'Of course not, we'll have a reverend and witnesses, but you know, we'll be alone in that no one will know who the hell we are.'

Beverly pushed her husband away from her and sat up. She held her head in her hands.

'Are you ok, Hunny?'

'I called Amelia.'

'You did *what*?' Marty barked.

'I'm sorry! I had to call her. I missed her so much. And she's coming to Las Vegas. Our children are coming to see us get married.' Any hope of him becoming as excited as she was for the arrival of her daughter died.

‘Do you understand that it was *our children* who called the cops on me last time I saw them? We need to get out of here fast before the police arrive.’

‘Please wait, honestly I’ve spoken to her, she’s coming over to see us get married.’

‘No she isn’t! She’ll be sitting at home with the police tapping her phone waiting for you to call, while there are probably cops surrounding this whole joint knowing we’re inside.’ Marty grabbed his case and repacked his bags. ‘I can’t believe you could be so stupid... and you lied to me!’

‘Hey, don’t you pull that one on me. Your lies over the years outweigh any lie I could ever tell Martin Hahn!’ Beverly stood up and pointed her index finger in his face. ‘I want my children here. I love them and I want them at our wedding. I want them here if it’s the last thing we ever do. If you can’t accept that then just go, but I’ll be waiting right here for the arrival of our kids.’

‘Well you’ll be waiting alone. Good luck when the police arrive.’ Marty grabbed his suitcase and stormed towards the door. He opened it to find two familiar faces before him. James and Amelia were stood with their arms out stretched, smiling.

‘Surprise!’ Amelia cheered. Marty poked his head out of the door, browsing the corridors to ensure they were empty. ‘So are you going to welcome us in or not?’

Marty, satisfied that they were alone, whisked them into the large suite.

‘Are you two OK?’ Amelia asked, shooting a suspicious glare to her father.

‘We’ve just had a bit of an argument, I thought…’ Marty paused.

‘He thought you were going to call the cops on him.’ Beverly said.

'You didn't know we were coming?' James asked.

'No he wouldn't have come if he knew. He thought you would have stitched him up by now.'

‘Well we did in Chicago, so that’s understandable.’ Amelia laughed. ‘Sorry about that. We’re alone now, I promise.’

‘You must be James.’ Marty held out his hand towards his daughter’s boyfriend. While he had seen this young gentleman’s face as he hid in the bushes in New York, they'd never met. James cautiously shook his future father-in-law's hand. 'Don't worry, it's always a nerve racking experience meeting the in-laws. I won't threaten to break your legs. You've looked after Amelia a lot better than I have over the last few years.'

'It's a pleasure to meet you, Mr Hahn.'

'Please call me Marty... it's not that I don't like formalities, but the Hahn name will get me in trouble these days.'

'Where's Benjamin?' Beverly asked, registering his absence.

'He's not here. He's still really angry. I couldn't risk telling him where we were going.'

'I understand. It's a shame, I really gave up a lot when I ran away, didn't I? I deserve the resentment, I'm just lucky I didn't lose both my children. I've gained an extra one too.' She nodded her head towards James and smiled. 'I'm glad to hear you two are back together.'

'It's been a roller-coaster.' James said.

'How's your grandfather?' Beverly turned back to her daughter.

'Oh… I thought you knew. Grandpa died. We've been staying in Chicago at Grandma's house. We've been there since the funeral.'

'Oh God...' Beverly collapsed onto her bed and cried. Her face grew pale and she shook vigorously as the grief took over. Her tears poured into the white linen, which lined the bed.

'I thought I had more time. I should have called. I should have put my pride aside for once and just made up with him. I knew he was dying and I let him go to the grave believing he had ruined everything. I know what it's like now Benjamin despises me. It's the worst feeling in the world and I did that to my own father.'

'He left us a note asking us to forgive you. He loved you so much, Mom.' Amelia said. She subtly shook her fists to the side of her as she realised she had left the last letter Francis wrote at home in Chicago. 'He wrote it at his birthday party. He died later that night.'

'I was supposed to be at the party.'

'I know. He invited us to see you.'

'I planned to be there but things went wrong. I got caught.'

Beverly kept back the details of who caught her. She hadn't told Marty about Max, who'd duped her into a relationship. She'd kept him at bay by selling him her husband's location in Indiana and hadn't seen him since.

'Look, Grandpa knew the stress you were under, after all it was he who put you under it with the stupid advice he gave to Dad. He loved you, he loved all of us, and if it helps, Benji and I didn't leave on the best of terms with him either.'

Amelia, bent down on her knees and held onto her mother's arm. Marty knelt on her other side, resting his head against her back, rubbing her shoulder as she cried.

Beverly poured her heart out for over an hour. They sat in silence as they contemplated the fate that Francis Goldberg had faced in his final hours. His whole family had divided and few spoke to him.

'I know you're upset, Hunny, but we have a wedding to plan.' Marty said. 'Do you girls want to go and find dresses while James and I suit up?'

James, Beverly and Amelia looked at each other in disbelief.

'Are you kidding? Now is *not* the time, Dad!' Amelia shook her head and shot her father a furious stare. Beverly rubbed her daughter's back and smiled.

'Your father is right, Amelia. Come on, let's go and get ready for this wedding and have a good time. Dad would hate me to be sat here crying over him. We're in Vegas for God's sake. And you know what? I was upset before you guys came because Dad wouldn't be there tomorrow. I now know that he will be there now… in spirit.'

They smiled, embraced and walked their separate ways as they planned the ceremony, which they'd dreamed of for over a decade.

They walked downstairs and separated at reception. Marty and James headed to the MGM Grand to enjoy pre-wedding beers and find a suit, while the girls visited The Venetian for cocktails and gather their garments for the following day.

As they walked their separate ways, unbeknownst to them, they passed an equally oblivious Detective Grisham checking in at reception.

*

Flight 737 to Las Vegas prepared to depart from Midway Airport. On the flight was a young man who had flown many times, but commercial planes always made him uncomfortable. After witnessing the planes fly into those buildings on that fateful day ten years before, he knew how risky these flights could be. Today terrorists could detonate a bomb on a plane without even boarding the flight.

When the young Benjamin Hahn boarded the JB-52E Stratofortress in the Middle East, he had the security that the jet was built with enough armour to withstand a missile and enough ammunition to take out any enemy. Now sitting on a Boeing American Airlines plane, he felt vulnerable but he had one final mission to complete.

Charlie had blown the cover of his family's antics. He called Benjamin after bumping into them at The Bellagio Hotel on the Las Vegas strip. While he couldn't be sure if it was really them, Benjamin felt sure enough to go and investigate, determined to make his parents pay for their deceit.

*

The orange haze of the sun, drowning in the horizon, settled over the desert. A warm breeze drifted through the French windows. A bottle of Champagne's finest sat beside a vase, filled with rich red roses. Thorns scattered across the white linen covered table, the corners gently flapping within the light air current, simmering across the balcony.

Amelia walked out and found James in a black tuxedo, a white shirt and a black bow tie, holding out a crystal glass filled with sparkling wine.

'Wow, don't you look smart.' she said, holding her arms over her own attire: a dowdy white tube-top and a multi-coloured sarong wrapped around her waist.

Collecting the flute from his hand, she clinked the glass against his and sipped the wine. She placed a hand over her stretched cheeks, struggling to reduce the glowing smile, which felt so unnatural after months of turbulence.

James collected a stem from the vase and placed it in his mouth, catching his tongue on a thorn. He winced and spat out the copper taste of blood,

'Damn, I was hoping to be romantic.' They broke into laughter.

'What's all this in aid of?'

'So I was talking to your dad today…'

'Well I would hope so, otherwise it would have made a very quiet and uncomfortable afternoon alone for you guys.'

'He asked about our situation. I explained that we were once engaged but we broke up and now we're back together.' James explained. 'He didn't seem too happy to hear I was sleeping with his daughter without a ring on her finger.'

'Well I don't think my dad really has a leg to stand on when it comes to throwing his parental authority around seeing he wasn't in my life for over ten years.'

'No but he's right, you should have a ring on your finger. And we have to face the reality that tomorrow could be the last opportunity we get to spend any time with your parents. They could get arrested and put in prison for years, or they could be on the run. There may never be an opportunity for your dad to walk you down the aisle or your mom to help you put on your dress.'

'So what are you saying?' Amelia apprehensively asked.

'Let's get married tomorrow with your mom and dad.'

Amelia screeched with joy as James retrieved a ring from his pocket; the same ring he provided her months before. She'd returned it to him upon their departure but now it was back in its rightful place.

'I have two more for the morning. If you don't like them, we can take them back. They're just for the ceremony. But what do you say? Shall we do it?'

Amelia considered his proposal, hovering to build suspense.

'Yes!' Amelia screamed, hopping between feet, tapping the soles on the floor in celebration. She wiped a tear away from her eye. 'I'm overwhelmed. My dreams have come true! I never ever thought I'd see my dad at my wedding, but now I can. Thank you, James.'

*

Unbeknownst to Amelia, one more member of the family would be joining them in the morning. Charlie Henningway eagerly waited at boarder control for the special guest. Getting off the plane at McCarran International Airport was Benjamin Hahn, ready to bring the family who deserted him to justice.

Chapter 30

A champagne breakfast was consumed by the Hahns and their soon-to-be new relative, James. They avoided the traditions of hiding away from each other before the ceremony, they'd endured enough bad luck and some superstitious tradition wasn't going to ruin their big day.

They made their way down to the lobby where two limousines awaited to take them to The Little White Chapel on Las Vegas Boulevard, where their short but sweet ceremony would take place.

Their attire caught the attention of their fellow guests, giving away their plans for the day. The spectators wolf whistled as they passed, capturing the two couples' big day on their smart phones and digital cameras.

Beverly waved the white veil over her face, avoiding the flashes; with social media, their location could have been revealed in seconds if anyone managed to recognise the infamous family. Similarly, Marty lifted his top-hat, providing a courteous greeting to those who passed on their well-wishes, whilst hiding his identity with the brim.

They walked out of the lobby and down some stone steps out of the hotel. Two white stretched limousines sat waiting for the wedding party. They separated by gender with plans to reunite at the chapel where they would enjoy a collaborated ceremony.

The boys hurried into their car and rushed off down the boulevard, providing them time to wait at the front of the chapel for their brides, while Amelia helped her mom with her puffy white train, which ran along behind her as she stepped into the second vehicle. As Amelia placed her leg into the car, she heard a familiar voice behind her.

'Amelia!' She turned around to find Benjamin stood on the entrance steps. To the right of him stood another man, whom she recognised from the ceremony where her brother was signed off as a competent member of the US Army.

The bride placed her head in the car and asked the driver to wait, before closing the door to hide her mother from her unruly son.

'What are you doing here?' she asked, pulling the lilac lace cover over her shoulders. She shiftily glanced around the entrance, establishing if the authorities had joined her brother.

'I could ask you the same question. Are you all in this together?'

His fists tightened and he shook. Moisture poured down his head, a mixture of heat and anger sweating from his skull. The hotel's concierge spotted the commotion and stepped forward to intervene, but Amelia shook her head, relieving him of his duties.

'Benjamin, it's not like that. Come and sit down.' She grabbed his hand and walked him towards a bench, which rested outside of the hotel entrance. 'You need to calm down. I'm here today because I'm fed up of arguing and being angry. I couldn't tell you because you're not there yet. But I am. We've lost a grandfather who died after leaving us on a sour note. I don't want that again for any of us.'

'And what's this? You're getting married now? Don't I get to see my little sister get married?' Benjamin held out his palm towards her dress. She was overdressed for any other occasion.

'I want you there more than anything, Benji, but I need you to forgive Mom and Dad and just be there for us all today. We love you and want you to be with us. We wouldn't have secrets if you weren't so angry all the time. You need to calm down, get yourself sorted and be there for us. Look at the hostility you give to James and yet he's been my rock. I can't do this anymore. You need to meet us half way.'

'I've got a lot to be angry about.' Benjamin said.

'Yes you do, but you need to sort it out. Otherwise all that work you did in the army to help save other people's lives has been for nothing if you can't even enjoy your own. We can't take back the past but we can sure as hell make the future a better one. You might not be able to help save the lives of civilians in the Middle East anymore, but you can save our lives, and believe me… we need saving.'

She placed her arm around her brother as he cried. The tears brought the release he'd longed for since his return from the army. For months, his emotions had poured out through his temper, which exploded at the slightest nudge.

'I'll get help.' Benjamin said. Amelia smiled, squeezing his hand. 'You better go and get married, I'm keeping you.'

'Please come.' Amelia pleaded. 'You can't come all this way and not be there.'

'I don't have a suit.' Benjamin had little time to pack a bag and now wore a Black Sabbath t-shirt and jeans.

'I don't care about what you wear. I just want you to be there.' She turned towards his companion. 'Do you want to bring him as your date? Otherwise you might look a little lonely.'

Stood by the limousine, Charlie patiently waited. Pedestrians attempted to glimpse into the blacked-out windows to witness who required the security of the US Army as the soldier guarded the door in his uniform. He threw the last of his cigarette on the floor and stamped his foot on the burning butt.

'OK, but don't you dare tell him it's a date. *Don't Ask Don't Tell* might be over in the US Army, but it doesn't mean he's anymore comfortable with that.'

Amelia winked at him and ran over to the limousine. Opening the door, she gave a *thumbs up* to her mom.

'Room for two more?'

'I think they can probably squeeze in somewhere.' Beverly laughed; the stretched vehicle could have fit Charlie's whole regiment. The boys climbed into the limousine and drove off to the Little White Chapel.

*

The chapel district of Las Vegas Boulevard by day is filled with drug dealers, addicts and prostitutes. The decaying hub holds an eerie silence as those who recover from the night before linger around bus stops, passed out from the poison which fills their blood.

By sunset, the district bustles with weddings for couples of all backgrounds. Some of the richest people in the world have married in the dingiest of chapels, from Bette Midler to Britney Spears. A range of services are available, from religious elegance to fast-food-style drive-through services with Elvis impersonating registrars.

The Hahn clan chose a quaint little church known as The Little White Chapel, at the very end of a cluster of churches before the Boulevard hit the glamour of Freemont Street.

Inside the chapel, James and Marty eagerly waited for their future wives, concerned by the hold-up. The brides were seconds behind them when they departed the hotel, but were now nowhere to be seen. The grooms hung around for twenty-minutes, restlessly waiting for their fiancés to appear.

The registrar aired his concerns. The church was fully booked for the remainder of the day and the backlog of couples waited outside, frustrated by the hold-up. If the ladies failed to arrive soon, the wedding would have to be postponed to another day.

The doors opened and in walked the brides. Beverly wore a white gown with a long train behind her. Her daughter, Amelia, wore a satin pansy purple dress. Their lack of preparation since James's late-evening proposal prevented her from hiring a white wedding gown, much to the young bride's disappointment.

Behind the two brides was Benjamin dressed in his army uniform, which he borrowed from his former colleague, Charlie, who sneaked to the back of the chapel to find a seat. In the distant pews, he could hide the Black Sabbath t-shirt and jeans, which he'd swapped with the former soldier in the limousine ride over.

The grooms double-took a glance at the formerly hostile soldier, who only a hours before had threatened to shop the runaways in. Now Benjamin stood proudly with his mother and sister by his side, ready to give away the girls to their husbands-to-be.

Benjamin took the arms of the two most important women in his life and walked them both down the red-carpeted aisle. Beverly gripped onto his sleeve, which hung below his stump. As the brides reached the front of the chapel, the reverend began the service.

'We are joined here today to see a mother and daughter marry the two men in their lives. They have travelled all the way from New York to get married in our little chapel here in Nevada. Now as we're running out of time, I assume you are ready with your rings and vows.'

James nodded and rooted through his jacket pocket for the rings. He grabbed the bands and placed the first one on his fiancé's finger.

'Amelia, we've known each other for over ten years. It was a tragedy that brought us together, but today we stand in celebration. I would never ever wish for the things that happened ten years ago to happen to anyone, but if it had to happen, I'm glad I was united with you. You have got me through so much pain and I can't imagine my life without you. I will stand by you for as long as we're alive.'

Amelia, dabbed her eye with her wrist, covered with a lace glove. She grabbed the second band and placed it on James's finger before beginning her own written vows.

'James, what can I say? You've been so much of a rock through the many tragedies and complications that my family has faced. The last few months have been an utter wreck, but somehow it was all bearable with you by my side. I know whatever we face, we'll get through it, as long as we're together.'

Amelia and James kissed. They lingered, but a cough from the impatient registrar broke them up. She pulled back to allow her parents to begin their vows.

'Marty, there have been times when I have utterly hated you.'

The small audience of strangers sat behind them gasped.

'You've made some stupid decisions. But every decision you've made has been for our family. Every act you have made, no matter how crazy and risky, your intentions were always focused on making our lives better. I judge people by their intentions, rather than the results of their actions, and I know how much you love me and our children. Therefore I marry you today so I can guide you and ensure that from now on we make the decisions together, so our lives will have the best of intentions and the best of results.' Beverly placed the band on her husband's finger before he took over to complete the last of the vows.

'Beverly, all I can say is… I've seen my life with you and I've seen my life without you. I never want to be without you again.'

Marty placed the ring on his wife's finger and kissed her. The audience behind them cheered and the two couples left the chapel. They returned to just one of the limousines with Charlie and Benjamin beside them. They opened a bottle of champagne, chilled in an ice bucket inside the vehicle, as the driver took them through Freemont Street. From the stretched car, they sat back in awe of the lights, which danced to music on the ceiling of the ninety-foot barrel-vault-canopy, before returning to The Bellagio hotel.

Inside their accommodation, they gambled in casinos and downed more champagne. Their heads grew fuzzy. Worn out, they sat down at the bar with a small tipple of port each and snacked on crisps and nuts.

'Some wedding breakfast this is.' Beverly quipped.

'What are you going to do now?' James asked his new brother-in-law.

'To be honest, I'm probably going to find an apartment. It's about time you guys got a proper home to yourselves as a married couple. Plus you'll be having kids soon and well… let's just say… I'll make a better uncle because I won't be around all the time imprinting my attitude on your children.'

'Woah kids?' James held up his hands in defence. 'That's a bit soon! Maybe one day but not quite yet, we need some money coming in first. Besides, half the house is yours and we can't afford to buy you out.'

'Call it my wedding present. I don't feel comfortable claiming ownership to a house simply because it belonged to a dead relative of mine. No, you take it and start your life. It's about time I started to make something of mine.'

'What will you do?' Amelia asked. 'Please tell me you'll consider giving up the escort business.'

'Maybe I'll join the hospitality business, although it's likely to be something you need two arms for with all that silver service.' Benjamin sighed, lifting his stump.

'Why don't you go to college?' Marty said. 'You didn't go because of me. Well I'm telling you to go now. It's what you're good at and what you should be doing. You could easily get a grant at Cornell with our family history there.'

'Dad, I think our family legacy there has been destroyed by your little stint in the news. Besides, I don't want to go to Cornell. I wanted to move out to Boston and go to Harvard, but it's sixty grand a year there and there's no way I'll get a grant. I can get a grant for a community college with the army but there's no way I'm going to one of those.'

'Hey!' Amelia protested. 'James and I both attended community colleges and we've been just fine.'

'Did you graduate?' Benjamin quizzed with a raised eyebrow.

'Well no. But hey, at least we started. It's more than you ever did.'

Feeling left out, Charlie scanned the room for a distraction and spotted his colleagues at the bar. He lifted out of his chair to join them, allowing the newly married couples to enjoy their night together alone.

'The guys are over there, why don't you come and see everyone, Benjamin? They'd love to see you.'

'Erm, no thanks.' Benjamin lifted up his stump. 'I don't think I quite meet up to their expectations these days.'

'Don't be ridiculous, they'd love to see you. They talk about you all the time and they miss you.'

Benjamin looked over at the guys, who waved him over. He obliged and joined his former comrades. As he walked over to the bar, they stood up and applauded in honour of their former trooper and the sacrifices he made for his fellow men.

The two newly married couples were now alone. They sat back and relaxed with more complimentary drinks. They laughed like they didn't have a care in the world, but their joy soon evaporated as an unwanted visitor approached them.

'Well, well, well. What have we here?' The four of them looked up at the unexpected guest. Beverly and Marty glared at the stranger, baffled by his approach. They had never been acquainted with the man but they could hear a New York accent.

'Amelia, I'm surprised at you. I thought better of you.'

The young bride hung her head in shame, embarrassed by the disorientating trail she had allowed the detective to follow.

'Mom, Dad, this is Detective Grisham. He's been looking for you guys.' She avoided revealing her own support in his investigation.

'Indeed I have and now I'm going to arrest you all. What a pleasure this will be.'

Chapter 31

The ringing of winning fruit machines drowned out the pianist, softly performing in the corner. The taps of chips and the rattle of dice blended with the groans of bystanders, witnessing the losses of the millionaires who travelled far to gamble away their fortunes. The thick fog of smoke rising from cigars hovered over the guests of The Bellagio like a rain cloud, ready to break.

Uniformed troops lined the bar for the second consecutive night, drowning away their hangovers by exploiting the hair of the dog theory. They'd spent months sober on tour, but they were certainly making up for it.

Within the crowd of soldiers, Charlie and former trooper, Benjamin, celebrated their return to America. Charlie ordered another round for his fellow comrades, but as he turned around, he witnessed commotion at the Hahns' table. A gentleman towered over the four newly-weds, his left hand covering the holster attached to the left of his belt. Their visitor pulled out a brown leather wallet and threw it onto the table, exposing the metal buckle representing his law enforcement status.

Charlie elbowed his buddy, Benjamin, who turned around to find a pale startled soldier, his pupils expanded as he witnessed the action unfolding before him.

'Are you OK?' he asked and grabbed his bottle of beer. Charlie nodded his head towards the table before them and Benjamin followed his eye-line towards the cop who interrogated their parents.

'That's Detective Grisham.' Benjamin said. 'He's been hunting down my parents. He must have followed Amelia over.'

The criminals stood up and held out their arms. A pair of handcuffs attached to the belt loops on the detective's beige trousers. He unhooked the cuffs and prepared to place them around the wrists of his suspects.

'I need help, Charlie. I've just got my parents back. I know they've done wrong but I can't lose them again.'

Charlie looked to his troops beside him; there were enough men to ensure they could pull together a plan. They needed something fast without bringing attention to their brigade.

Charlie ran over to the rest-rooms, located to the side of the bar. He looked around to ensure nobody could see him. Their attention drew to the pianist who played ballads to entertain the crowd surrounding his instrument.

With one quick punch, Charlie smashed the glass of the fire alarm. The noise deafened the crowd, who made their way out of the fire escape. Only then did Charlie begin to advise his troops.

*

The panicked crowds poured out of the entrance of The Bellagio, failing to remain calm as the alcohol destroyed any rational cells. The guests, dressed in their suits and evening dresses, gathered outside in the car park, holding onto their drinks, which they sneaked out of the establishment.

The four newly-weds, blinded by the bright lights of the strip, staggered out of the hotel, handcuffed to each other as the armed detective hovered behind them, holding his handgun to Marty's back.

'Don't even think about running.' Grisham said.

Four uniformed servicemen approached the detective, who held a tight grip on his suspects. The army officers surrounded the four bewildered criminals and placed a hand on each of their shoulders, assuring they refrained from escaping.

'Excuse me, Sir, but at times like this we can't allow you to have your gun on show. This could be a terrorist scene for all we know, so I need you to put your gun away and make your way to the fire safety point across the street.' Private Johnson said.

Grisham in turn took out his NYPD badge, displaying his identity for the soldiers to see. Johnson inspected the badge and handed it back to the detective.

'Thank you Detective Grisham, in which case can we do the honours of ensuring these four delinquents are taken in with us and delivered to the nearest police station on your behalf?'

'I'd quite like to do it myself, if you don't mind.'

'If *you* don't mind, Sir, we're really concerned about the safety of the guests and I can ensure these four are looked after.'

'Is this a terrorist attack?' the detective quizzed. Little had been communicated regarding the reasons behind the alarm, but there were few indicators to suggest the pandemonium was a result of a terrorist attack.

'I don't know at this time, Sir, but I need you to trust me and hand over these villains so that I can ensure they are handled responsibly. You can be assured that they'll be looked after and taken to the nearest station for you immediately.'

The detective continued to protest but Johnson interrupted him.

'The way I see it right now, you're on your own with no back-up trying to arrest four people with a handgun and people are already panicked out here. You don't even work in this state. What you gonna do if one of them tries to run away? I suggest you allow us to take over here.'

The detective relinquished control and handed the Hahns and James over to the four army officers.

'We'll be down at the precinct on Freemont Street.' The officers rushed the four criminals around the back and into a transit van, parked in the hotel car park.

The fugitives sat uncomfortably in the dark on the floor of the van. Their legs sprawled out across the floor and the grooves of the metal floor numbed the cheeks of their backsides. They panted, recovering from the adrenalin. The future appeared bleak for the two couples who had just exchanged their vows.

A bright light stung their eyes, the rays beaming from the square bulb on the ceiling. As their eyes adjusted, they witnessed the two army officers who were now responsible for their arrest. It was Charlie and Benjamin.

'Alright guys? Ready to get the hell out of here?'

With their arms now free, the four escapees gasped with relief. They cheered and high-fived each, before hugging their rescuers. Charlie started the engine and drove out of the car park, heading west out of Sin City.

*

Hundreds of red lights illuminated Las Vegas Boulevard, shining from the rear-ends of the static vehicles. Inside, the impatient drivers groaned, eager to leave the sparkle of Las Vegas.

Trapped in traffic, Detective Grisham chewed on a cocktail stick, frustrated by the Army's intervention on his arrest of the Hahn family. He was so close to becoming New York's hero by bringing the fraudsters to justice alone. His idol status remaining as motionless as the traffic piled up beside the casinos.

When did the US Army have authority over us? They're supposed to protect and support in these situations, not take over.

He had to back down to their demands. Nobody wanted to see anyone arguing with cadets, even if he was a cop. He didn't have a uniform. Even if he had, cops didn't gain the same respect as the army; they didn't have a day dedicated to them and their work didn't make headline news unless they'd managed to shoot some black kid in the Bronx.

As he drove down the strip, he turned a blind eye to the prostitutes lining the streets, luring passers-by into their lair; they were the responsibility of the Las Vegas Metropolitan Police, not that they'd care. The beep of a horn caught the attention of a whore, leaning against the side of a roadside motel. The sole of her foot rested on the wall behind her, bending her knee forward towards the traffic. The smoke from her cigarette blew into her afro and the gold metallic polyester bra and panties barely covered her olive skin. A tattoo of a skull and crossbones covered her upper-arm. She dropped the cigarette and placed her foot over the end, twisting it from side-to-side to extinguish the fiery tip, before entering the car.

After half an hour, Grisham had barely managed to get past Ceasers Palace, a mere few metres down from where he set off. Frustrated by the delay, he lifted out the red detachable dash-light, packed away in a holdall underneath the passenger seat. He wound down the window and placed the flashing bulb on the roof. Ringing the siren, the detective pulled out of the queue and sped off down the boulevard.

Within minutes he reached the crossroads of Freemont Street. The vintage old-town was more rustic than its modern counterpart. A waving neon cowboy welcomed visitors into the district of 99cent steaks and all-you-can-eat diners. He took a right onto Freemont Street and focused his eyes on both sides of the road, looking out for the station described by the army officer.

A drive down to the end of the street provided no sightings of a police station. Confused, he turned around and drove back to the other end in case he missed the precinct, but the return journey was as unsuccessful. The detective pulled over to the El Cortez Hotel and a concierge walked over to his aid.

'I'm sorry, Sir, I've never heard of a police station on this street.' the concierge explained. A bewildered Grisham thanked the concierge and drove on. He pulled out his radio and tuned into the Nevada district police force frequency.

'Detective Grisham, NYPD, to Las Vegas Metropolitan Police. Over.'

'Grisham, we hear you over here. How can we be of service? Over.'

'I was at The Bellagio earlier tonight. I want an update on four criminals I arrested over there. Four members of the US Army on duty took them to a police station. I would like a location on that station. Over.'

'We'll check that up, Detective.' The radio fell silent and crackled as the detective waited in suspense for several minutes.

'Detective Grisham? Over.' the officer called in.

'This is him. Do you have an update? Over.'

'We're just a bit confused; there were no army officers on duty this evening in that area. Over.'

*

Driving down Highway 115, Charlie took the villains to Laughlin, Nevada, south of Las Vegas. The city, filled with parks, hotels and casinos, twinned with the entertainment capital of Las Vegas, but struggled to pull in the same crowd as Sin City.

The ride over proved uncomfortable to those on the floor of the van. The vehicle usually carried the troops' luggage and provided a rocky ride for the inhabitants without seat belts to protect them.

Charlie pulled up at a car rental garage, the same chain whereby Amelia had arranged a rental-car in Chicago to drive over to Vegas two days earlier. She walked in and handed them the keys to collect the car which they were forced to abandon in Vegas. The runaway requested another vehicle for the next step of her journey

As she provided the details of her driving licence, James entered the garage and whispered into his girlfriend's ear. She looked up at her husband, bewildered by his request. They mumbled, mouthing an argument towards each other.

The salesman walked away to give them some space. He was used to their debates; the guys wanted their sports cars while their wives wanted something a little more practical. Nothing surprised this salesman.

The couple before him finished their mumblings; their decisions now made. Amelia held out her hand to grab the attention of the salesman.

'Excuse me, sorry.' Amelia called. 'Please could we make that *two* cars.'

*

The bright lights of the casinos had all but gone. The landscape grew rockier as the buildings disappeared. Morning was near but a dusting of stars continued to twinkle across the clear purple sky.

Below, two four-by-fours broke the silence of the desert as they rumbled across the barren land. Benjamin, Amelia and James travelled in one vehicle, while Marty and Beverly hovered behind. The road before them disappeared as they approached the Grand Canyon.

The popular tourist attraction was as quiet as a cemetery while America slept. Rainfall from the previous day had delivered a green tinge to the red dusting and the angry spines of cacti appeared as sharp as a razor.

Benjamin and James slept throughout the overnight journey, while Amelia drove the vehicle, using the stereo to keep herself awake. Behind, Marty and Beverly discussed their future plans.

'I can't do it anymore, Marty.' an exhausted Beverly explained. 'I can't run anymore. This is supposed to be our fresh start as a newly married couple and look at what we're doing to ourselves. Look at what we're doing to the children. We need to end this now.' A tear sprang down from her vacant eye as she stared out of the window.

'What do you suggest we do?'

'It looks like a long way down there.' Beverly raised her head to glimpse into the deep canyon.

*

The cars pulled up across the way from what is famously known as Eagle Point due to the wing-shaped rock formation within the cliff. The noses of the cars faced the canyon and out of the doors stepped all five members of the Hahn clan.

Benjamin, James and Amelia slipped out of one car, while Marty and Beverly stepped out of the other. They rested on the hood of the black Hyundai four-by-four, which Marty had driven over from Nevada.

The temperature dropped and a gust of air forced them towards the steep drop. Together they huddled for warmth and support, while watching the sun rise. They gasped, witnessing the canyon's metamorphosis as the sun climbed into the sky.

'What are we going to do?' Benjamin asked.

'Well, I think it's time we went our separate ways.' Marty explained. 'You guys have been in enough trouble. You need to go home.'

'Where will you go?' Amelia asked. 'You can't keep running and I can't lose you again.'

'We'll be fine. You need to go. Go and live your lives. We've had ours, we're exhausted.' Beverly embraced her daughter.

Marty lifted his wallet out of his jacket pocket and handed his son a piece of paper. Opening up the folded document, Benjamin saw that his father had written out a cheque under the name of Martin Singer to him for the sum of sixty-thousand dollars.

'What is this?' Benjamin asked.

'I've let you down for all these years. Your sister's managed to sort her life out. She has a home, a husband and a job. It's you I worry about. You wrote off all your dreams for me and now it's time you got them back. It won't pay for all of your college fees but it'll at least help you along the way. Put it in your account fast and get yourself on that History course at Harvard.'

Benjamin nodded and took the cheque. He embraced his father. 'I love you, Dad.' Three words that Marty never believed he would hear again from his son.

The children spent several minutes embracing their parents, before Beverly let go and grabbed her son-in-law.

'Promise me you'll look after our little girl.'

'I can assure you that while she's with me, she'll always be safe.'

They walked back to their cars. Amelia took the wheel of their Ford. James sat on her left side, while Benjamin rested his feet up in the back. The car reversed away from the canyon and back onto the road which surrounded the ravine.

They remained static as they witnessed their parents' rental car roll forward towards the canyon. The Hyundai rolled off the cliff and fell six-thousand feet. Their hearts pounded as they heard the crunch of the vehicle hitting the bottom. The faint sound of a stereo echoed out of the chasm.

'And I think to myself... what a wonderful world.'

Chapter 32

It had been six months since Amelia and James returned to Chicago. The first few weeks had been far from easy; they were arrested upon entry to the Barrington police station, where they handed themselves in and were charged for harbouring criminals. They were later released on bail.

When asked where they last saw Marty and Beverly Hahn, they explained that they were last seen at the Grand Canyon, where they said their goodbyes and went their separate ways.

Amelia refused to take her brother with them to the station. The police had no evidence that Benjamin had any part in their escape plans. On their last encounter with the war hero, Benjamin had actively helped locate the fraudsters. Detective Grisham remained convinced the veteran held enough resentment towards his mom and dad that he had no desires to help them.

Seven nights later, Detective Grisham turned up at their door and explained that their parents' rental car had been found at the bottom of the Grand Canyon. Several items of clothing, which they'd been spotted wearing earlier in the day, had also been discovered further down the river at the bottom of the valley.

The police explained that their bodies had not been discovered yet and it would be unlikely they ever would be. Their bodies had likely been dragged along the river and into a cave, left to rot away beneath the canyon.

While the hostility towards the remaining Hahns had died down, there were still those who fought against the pay-out, which they received in September 2011. While they couldn't sell the apartment without their mother's consent, they gave up their place in New York to allow Sharon, Amelia's former manager, to stay in the luxury apartment. Sharon hadn't received a pay out after her husband, Billy, died in the towers as there was little evidence placing him in the buildings. Selflessly, Sharon provided Amelia a job and a home when her luck was down as the rest of America resented the innocent siblings. Amelia now returned the favour to her former boss by providing her a luxurious place to live.

The Hahns assured the Victims Fund providers that should they ever receive full ownership of the apartment in New York, they would donate it back to the government, but until that day came, they would do whatever they could to return the privileges, which they received from the pay-out.

Their day in court arrived. The eyes of the world were on the recorded sentencing of Amelia and her husband, James. They announced their guilt; too much evidence piled against them for them to claim otherwise. The newspapers expected their sentences to be long, anticipating the judge to make an example of them. However, the judge was convinced that neither Amelia, nor James, had initially known about her father's whereabouts, and like everyone else in the city, were convinced he had died in 2001 in those towers before he reappeared in 2011.

The judge understood that when Amelia's mother called that day to her cell phone, Amelia had a moment of madness and would do anything to see her parent again. A mother-daughter bond never dies and he empathised with that. For these reasons, they both received a twelve month suspended sentence and were allowed to return to their home in Chicago.

Amelia had since returned to work and climbed her way up the ranks to Front Office Manager and hoped to progress onto an Operations Manager role as soon as a vacancy opened. James finished his qualification at a local community college. He transferred the course over to Harper College in Illinois and was now a qualified plumber. However, their careers would soon have to be put on hold as the life in Amelia's womb kicked harder every day.

As they sat in their grandmother's home, looking through the baby-shower brochures, a ringing sound echoed from the electronic tablet, which rested on the glass coffee table. James picked up the device and showed his wife the ID of the Skype caller. It looked a little different from the last time she had dialled in. Instead of stating Iraq, the ID today read '*Benjamin Hahn – Massachusetts.*' James clicked to answer the call.

'Hi Buddy! How are you? When are you gonna come and see us over here?' James said.

'When are you coming to see me, more importantly? You can come and sleep on the floor of my student digs.'

The veteran applied for a grant at Harvard when he returned to New York. As soon as the scholarship was confirmed, he got in touch with Joseph, the father of the woman whom Marty planned to marry before he left her at the altar, stealing one hundred thousand dollars from the family. Benjamin returned sixty grand of the amount, which Marty had given him to help him towards his studies, to its rightful owner. At first, he was tempted to keep the funds as living costs were high at Harvard, but he wanted to begin his new life at university conscious free.

Or at least mostly free…

'So where do you imagine they are these days?' Benjamin asked. Amelia sat in wonder. Her father was extremely resourceful and wherever they were, he would ensure a safe-haven for their mother.

'South America? Or Canada? I really don't know!'

She couldn't believe they'd got away with it, especially given their father's past. They sat and watched their parents push the car off into the canyon, strip off their coats and shoes, before throwing them down the hole behind the car.

Once their car was in a position to assume the worst, Marty and Beverly squeezed into the back of Amelia's rental car and drove off. They got to Reno, where they dropped Marty and Beverly off, said their final goodbyes and never spoke to their parents again.

Amelia was understandably upset that she hadn't been able to speak to her parents since or tell them about their first grandchild, but it wasn't forever. One day when the world had forgotten all about her infamous parents, she could slowly regain that contact, which she had temporarily lost. In the meantime, she kept an online family blog, just in case anyone wanted to keep up to date with their news without having to get in touch.

While ashamed of her lies, she felt relieved that her parents left for the right reasons. They had barely any money to their names anymore and were running away, not for the cash, but for a life together as husband and wife. Neither Benjamin, Amelia, nor James could take that away from the runaway love birds.

The following September, Amelia and James met with Benjamin in New York. Amelia had funded her father's name to be professionally removed from the memorial and paid for three thousand tulips to surround the names of those who really did pass on that horrific day.

On the anniversary, as the President read out the names of those who died, she wept for every person who had been inflicted with pain either directly or indirectly on that fateful day. She cried for Sharon's husband, Billy; for James's mother, Julie; and Detective Grisham's former colleague, Lieutenant Jefferson. She cried for the soldiers who died fighting for the country because of that event, like Private Ross.

The soon-to-be mother placed the last tulip on the name before her, which was James's mom. She gripped onto her husband as they paid their respects to the mother-in-law, which Amelia had missed out on. Behind her, her former manager, Sandra, rubbed her shoulder. The manager of the Lincoln Hotel had clocked her former colleague in the distance and moved over to stand with them as they mourned the losses of the country together. The small squeeze on her arm reassured Amelia that there was no more animosity between them.

As the lights beamed into the sky in memory of the buildings which once stood before them, she looked back to that day eleven years before. Back then she thought of her father scrambling for survival. Today she saw her father on a beach with a cocktail in one hand, with her mother's hand in the other.

As The President walked up to the plinth, Amelia realised that she had some claim to grieve on that day. It wasn't an entitlement she necessarily wanted, but she hated the dirty feeling of guilt, which she was riddled with every time she thought back to the tragedy.

She had lost a home, a family, and as she looked to her brother and his missing limb, she realised that he had put himself at risk every day to fight back against the terrorists who tried to kill the spirit of New York.

As she glanced around her at the fellow grievers who surrounded her, to her husband, her brother and her friends, she saw the tremendous spirit that had never been lost in New York. America had not let the terrorists win as the public of New York stood together in unity and awaited The President's speech.

'On that clear September morning, as America watched the towers fall, and the Pentagon burn, and the wreckage smouldering in a Pennsylvania field, we were filled with questions. Where had the attacks come from, and how would America respond? Would they

fundamentally weaken the country we love? Would they change who we are?

The last decade has been a difficult one, but together, we have answered those questions and come back stronger as a nation. Today, a new tower rises above the New York skyline. And our country is stronger, safer and more respected in the world.

Instead of turning on each other, we've resisted the temptation to give in to mistrust and suspicion. We are the United States of America. Our freedom and diversity make us unique, and they will always be central to who we are as a nation.

Instead of changing who we are, the attacks have brought out the best in the American people. And finally, instead of turning inward with grief, we've honoured the memory of those we lost by giving back to our communities, serving those in need, and reaffirming the values at the heart of who we are as a people. We are one American family. And we look out for each other – not just on the difficult days, but every day.

Eleven years later, that's the legacy of 9/11 – the ability to say with confidence that no adversary and no act of terrorism can change who we are. We are Americans, and we will protect and preserve this country we love. On this solemn anniversary, let's remember those we lost, let us reaffirm the values they stood for, and let us keep moving forward as one nation and one people.'

(Barack Obama, September 11th 2012)

Epilogue

Along the grapevines of Cafayate, hundreds of Argentinian farmers picked the fruit of the country's future wines. The farmers were joined by immigrants who fled the dangers of their home countries to start a fresh in the safety of an Argentinian settlement. They were also joined by students who worked to fund their travels across South America.

Amongst the workers were two Americans who had escaped the clutches of US law. They had driven over six thousand miles from the dusty city of Reno. They said very little to their fellow farmers and didn't need to as their work was manual and required little communication between colleagues, while those they worked alongside spoke very little English.

It was unbeknownst to everyone within the field that this couple were once two of the most wanted individuals in America, who cheated the government out of one million dollars. Their co-workers wouldn't have asked about the Americans' situation, even if they could speak English, as they all had their own stories, whether they had escaped the clutches of the law, the drug gangs or the immigration office. Everyone was in this village to work, keep their heads down and have a fresh start.

An engine caused the workers heads to rise. A coach appeared in the distance and a group of fresh agricultural assistants arrived to work. It was prime season and more interns had arrived routinely every day over the past month.

On that bus was a gentleman who had made a similar journey as the Caucasian couple who roamed the fields, as he too was an American. He sat next to a man of Indian heritage, who had chattered all the way along the lengthy journey over to the winery. The American humoured him and listened to the Asian man's stories of his life as a doctor back in his home country. The gentleman had come over to the continent to earn money, which he could send back to his family in New Delhi.

As they pulled up to the winery, the Indian noticed how little his new-found friend had spoken along the thirteen hour journey.

'You didn't tell me what you did in America.' The man was innocent enough to believe that those from the USA had also come across to this Southern American state for a better life.

'Oh, I was a journalist.' he explained.

'Ah, investigative journalism. What a wonderful industry. Something to get your teeth stuck into.' he replied in wonder. 'We didn't trade names, it would be nice to know somebody around here, otherwise it can get quite lonely. I'm Asif Khan.'

'It was lovely to meet you, Mr Khan, I'm Max Spielberg.' he took Asif's hand and shook it.

'Two people of different backgrounds shaking hands. What a wonderful gesture of peace.'

Max stepped off the bus and smiled. *How naive he is, it's not peace that brings me here.* He looked out at the field where he would soon plough. He took out his cell phone and took several photographs with the camera application.

'I hope you find what you are looking for in Argentina, Mr Spielberg.' Asif said.

'I'm sure I will.' Max smiled and zoomed in with his cell phone camera towards the American couple, who ploughed ignorantly away just one hundred yards away.

'I'm sure I will...'

The End

Note from the Author

I remember that fateful day back in September 2001 like it was yesterday. I was just thirteen years old and in school in Preston, Lancashire. I remember our history teacher being asked to go outside where he was told the news. When he returned, he simply told us that when we went home that night we would see something in the news which would change the world forever.

On the bus route home, people were gossiping and talking about it but I couldn't really understand what had happened. When I got off the bus with my friend, his mother walked out of his house to tell us that World War III was beginning.

I rushed home to watch the news and before me I saw those buildings collapse. I'd never seen anything like it before.

In 2005, I went to New York for the first time. I visited the site where the World Trade Centre once stood, I paid my respects and I was reduced to tears. I hadn't been impacted in any personal way with the events, I didn't know anyone involved, but somehow, I was devastated by what had occurred in that empty space.

The original draft of this book never featured a terrorist attack. It was never supposed to fall under the category of 9/11 fiction. However, the reaction of the public to the Hahns' story meant that an event which really pulled at the public's heartstrings was required to really allow the reader to believe their struggle with the injustice of Marty's actions.

After I chose the twin towers to be part of the story, my biggest fear was for the work to not be approached sensitively and I hope I've managed to maintain a balance of developing a thrilling novel, whilst avoiding offending anyone who may have been affected by that day.

I dedicate this book to all those affected by the events of that day, all the fire fighters and police who saved lives, all those who died and the loved ones they left behind. My history teacher was right; the world did change that day. To the People of New York City, this book is for you.

David Hatton

With Thanks

I would like to say thank you to the following people:

- Mum and Dad - who always believed in me
- My partner, also called David, who was ignored for months whilst I finished this book… and your continuous jibes that I'd never finish it spurred me on
- Chris Davis -who helped me edit my work
- Joanne Moss – who always encouraged my thirst to write fiction
- Kerry Wilkinson (Author of the Jessica Daniels series: *Locked In, Think of the Children, Vigilante*) who encouraged me to take the leap! Your work is fantastic and if I manage to share a glimmer of your success, I'd count myself very lucky

Coming Soon…

The Exhumation

by David Hatton

In 1876, a plot to steal President Lincoln's body in exchange for ransom was foiled. Over 130 years later, the body has been snatched once again. Detective Darnell Jackson is on the case to find the former President's body but soon discovers it was stolen for more than just money. As Jackson becomes more emotionally involved in the case, he discovers the secrets that America has hidden away from their citizens for too long. Should Detective Jackson reveal the darkest secrets of their former president?

Coming soon….

The Medium

By David Hatton

When Michael Walker is approached by a psychic medium, claiming to know the whereabouts of his missing wife, he faces the difficulty of choosing between his belief in science and the desire to find his wife. Is the psychic really what she claims to be?

For up to date information on new releases, visit:

The website: **www.david-hatton.com**

Email David at: **davidhattonbooks@gmail.com**

Follow on Twitter: **@davidhattonbooks**
Follow on Facebook: **fb.com/dhattonbooks**

About the Author

David Hatton was born in in Preston Lancashire. He moved out to Chicago in 2008 where he spent a year living his own American Dream. When he's not writing, he's recruiting for a large retail firm. Today he lives in Greater Manchester with his partner, David.

33319937R00169

Printed in Great Britain
by Amazon